CW00863702

Fragile Hope

Fragile Hope

Justice Keepers Saga Book IX

R.S. Penney

Copyright (C) 2020 R.S. Penney
Layout design and Copyright (C) 2020 by Next Chapter
Published 2020 by Beyond Time – A Next Chapter Imprint
Cover art by Cover Mint
Edited by Gregg Chambers, Jourdan Vian
This book is a work of fiction. Names, characters, places, and incidents
are the product of the author's imagination or are used fictitiously.
Any resemblance to actual events, locales, or persons, living or dead,
is purely coincidental.
All rights reserved. No part of this book may be reproduced or transmitted in any form or by any means, electronic or mechanical, including photocopying, recording, or by any information storage and
retrieval system, without the author's permission.
@Rich_Penney
keeperssaga@gmail.com
https://www.facebook.com/keeperssaga
If you enjoy the Justice Keepers Saga and would like to get your hands
on exclusive, patrons-only content, you'll find it here.
https://www.patreon.com/richpenney

Prologue

Admiral Telixa Ethran peered through a large window that looked out on a field of stars against the eternal darkness of space. A darkness that was broken only by a cloud of blue gas that made an almost diagonal line from corner to corner. The Ra'toh Nebula was less than a lightyear away, and yet it loomed like a demon. The nearest Class-2 SlipGate was located there, which meant they could be surrounded by Leyrian ships in a matter of moments.

Telixa stood in a busy corridor with a black-tiled floor, her posture stiff, her hands clasped behind her back. People rushed past her, going this way and that, but she paid no mind to their hushed voices or muffled footsteps. Her thoughts were elsewhere.

"Admiral."

Lifting her chin, Telixa felt her expression harden. She narrowed her eyes. "What can I do for you, Lieutenant?" With exquisite precision, she turned on her heel to face the young woman who had spoken.

Lieutenant Saera Ladon was short and petite with a pale complexion and red hair that she wore tucked under her gray officer's cap. The woman kept her gaze fixed on the floor tiles. "They're ready for you, ma'am."

It was a short walk through a crowded hallway to reach the meeting room. Officers in gray uniforms saluted as she passed, and she favoured them with a glance or a nod, but she could not have named them. Not even one. So distracted was she that she would not have recognized her oldest childhood friend even if Lina Jhalia stood right in front of her.

A set of double doors opened into a room that was dominated by a large table in the shape of a crescent moon. The men and women who sat along the outer perimeter of that table all wore epaulettes that marked them as members of the Admiralty.

"Telixa," Roan Divol said, rising from his chair. He was tall and well-muscled, but ten years behind a desk had gifted him with a bit of a paunch. His dark hair was marked by wings of gray over each ear. "Thank you for coming so quickly."

"Would any of you have delayed when summoned by the Admiralty Board?" Her curtness could be off-putting – Telixa knew that – but she was not the sort of person to engage in idle pleasantries.

Standing at attention with gloved hands balled into fists, Telixa nodded once. "Let's get to it then, shall we?" That made a few of them stiffen. Good. "When we learned about the Class-2 SlipGates, I recommended a policy of reconnaissance and observation."

Telixa dropped into the nearest chair, crossing one leg over the other and running her gaze over the lot of them. "I now believe that the time has come for a more proactive approach."

Admiral Toran Jaal, a dark-skinned man with a ring of thin, gray hair, drummed his fingers on the table. "Are you suggesting war?"

"I'm suggesting that we consider planetary security."

At Telixa's command, the space station's central computer displayed a holographic representation of her battle with the Leyrians. Small fighters swarmed around her battlecruiser like angry hornets, each one spitting green or orange plasma. Shields flickered as they were struck.

"Until recently, our only contact with the Leyrians was in the form of long-range communications through the SlipGate Network. Based on their attitudes and their endless pleas for a cultural exchange, we assumed them to be a planet of pacifists with very little in the way of military technology. Easily conquered and no threat to anyone."

Several of the admirals frowned at that; a few of them exchanged furtive glances. She knew some of them well. Others, however, were not much more than strangers. Dral Sovon would almost certainly favour an aggressive posture. Military might was a source of pride for the Ragnosian people; Dral was the sort who would not suffer a rival.

On the other hand, Rob Ixalon was all but guaranteed to advise caution. She could already hear his objections. *A costly war with a reasonable chance of defeat should not be entered lightly.*

Telixa stood up, facing them all with her hands folded behind herself, pursing her lips as she chose her next words. "We were wrong," she said at last. "Leyrian technology is comparable to our own. Even superior in some cases."

Admiral Jaal leaned back with his hands on the chair arms, appraising her. Was she supposed to wilt under his scrutiny? Any inclination to do so had been squelched a very long time ago. One did not learn the ways of command without developing a thick skin. "You will forgive me if I am hesitant to agree," he said. "A lost battle, while unfortunate, is more indicative of a poor commander than it is of an unbeatable enemy."

Perhaps that was supposed to rile her.

Crossing her arms, Telixa backed away until she was leaning against the wall. She shook her head slowly. "How little you understand the danger." It was a biting comment but no worse than what Jaal had offered. "Computer, display footage from Cell Thirteen."

The hologram rippled, fading away, and then a new one appeared in its place. This one showed Jack Hunter holding one of her security officers in an armlock and throwing the man face-first into a wall.

Several of the Admirals sat up straight as they watched another one of her officers step into the frame only to receive a kick to the belly from Hunter. The traitorous Novol Raan. Telixa would see him executed sooner or later. She took betrayal very personally.

"What are you implying?" That came from Admiral Jessi Vataro, a tall woman with dark eyes that were just a little too big, giving her a somewhat child-like appearance. "If the countermeasures that Slade provided are insufficient…"

Countermeasures.

They referred to creatures that had once been living, breathing and *thinking* human beings as "countermeasures." Military officers did love their euphemisms. Perhaps it was the only way to ease the distasteful nature of what their jobs entailed.

Telixa stepped forward, held the other woman's gaze for a moment, and then let the ghost of a smile play across her lips. "These Justice Keepers disabled an entire deck of my ship," she said. "They attacked critical systems, outmaneuvered security teams, battle drones and even Slade's pet. They are experts in the field of infiltration, and we have no way of measuring their number. If that doesn't frighten you, you are a fool."

"Then what do you propose?" Roan Divol inquired.

"Computer," Telixa said. "File Ethran 7B."

A massive hologram of Leyria filled the space between the two prongs of the table. It was a lush world of green continents and blue oceans. Thin, white clouds drifted over mountain ranges, grassy lowlands, forests and cities.

A purple moon swung around the planet in a slightly elliptical orbit, turning slowly on its axis. "Our target should not be Leyria itself," Telixa began. "But rather its primary moon: Laras."

The moon grew larger and larger, pushing Leyria out of the way until it filled the space that its mother planet had occupied just a moment earlier. Through the thin, purple atmosphere, she could see craters and jagged rock formations on the surface. There were brief flashes, like lightning in storm clouds, but she knew them for what they really were.

"Laras is home to a strange species," Telixa went on. "Organic cells permeate the atmosphere and communicate by electrical currents. Individually, they are… Well, they're nothing but cells. But together, they form a collective intelligence unlike anything that we have encountered before.

"The Leyrians have dubbed them 'Nassai,' and it is these Nassai that give the Justice Keepers their incredible power."

Everyone looked nervous; they knew where she was going with this. Telixa forced herself to press on anyway. "Eliminating these Nassai is our primary objective. Sustained gamma-ray bursts should be enough to render the moon lifeless."

Jessi Vataro shot out of her chair, her cheeks colouring as she watched the spinning moon. "You're talking about genocide!" she spat. "These Nassai are no threat to us."

"But their masters are."

"I will not take part in the extinction of an entire species."

Telixa ignored her, opting instead to turn away from the others, and walked over to the door. She paused there, glancing back over her shoulder. "The Leyrians will make an adequate workforce, once they are properly civilized."

"I see," Admiral Jaal put in. "And you believe this to be a necessary step to ensure planetary security?"

With a quick about-face, Telixa rounded on them and strode back to the table. "I do indeed," she said. "So, the question is: Do we have the stomach to do what is necessary? There's no way to covertly place ships in the Leyrian System. They'll detect our approach before we get within a dozen lightyears of their world."

The hologram rippled as she walked through it, and then Telixa bent over with her hands on the table, staring Admiral Jaal right in the face. He recoiled as if he thought she might bite his nose off. "Which means any attempt to enter Leyrian Space would be an open declaration of war."

The Queensboro Bridge stretched over the East River, its metal framework catching the light of a sinking that was just starting to dip behind the skyscrapers of Manhattan. A few boats were out on the river, but they were too far off to see him.

In cargo pants and a denim jacket, Nate stood with his arms crossed, his brown hair cut short. "So," he said. "You got my money?"

The man who cowered against the metal railing that overlooked the river refused to make eye-contact. And Nate really couldn't blame him. Robbie was a skinny dude with pale skin, short dark hair and a mole on his cheek. "Half of it."

"Half?"

"Okay, *almost* half."

Tossing his head back, Nate felt creases lining his brow. "Gotta say, Robbie," he began. "Things aren't lookin' good for you."

Robbie flinched as if someone had waved a knife in his face and pressed his body even harder against the railing. The sound of his heavy breathing was so loud it should have drawn a crowd of people.

Except there were no people.

The strange creature that had bonded with him had given Nate eyes in the back of his head. He could sense the buildings behind him, trees along the sidewalk and even the odd person walking by. No one was close enough to pay him much attention.

He stepped forward, grabbing Robbie's shirt, pulling the man close so they were almost nose to nose. His lips parted to show clenched teeth. "I hooked you up with some damn good stuff."

Robbie turned his face away, a tear leaking from the corner of his eye. He was shivering; he knew perfectly well what Nate could do. "So," Nate continued. "I'm giving you two weeks to pay me or-"

He shut up right quick when he sensed a silhouette coming up behind him. As the figure got closer, he could tell that it was a small woman with long hair. Now, what did this bitch want? Nate would gut her right here and now if he hadn't spent the last nine months trying to stay off the Keepers' radar. He knew what his powers were, and he knew what those god damn aliens would do if they got their hands on him.

"Is this what passes for a suitable host these days?"

Releasing Robbie, Nate whirled around to find the woman standing just behind a bench that faced the river. She was short and slender and kind of hot in a white sundress with thin straps.

She had a round face, olive skin and long dark hair that fell to her shoulder-blades. "Harassing street vermin," she said. "Can you think of no better use of your power?"

"Who the hell are you?"

She stepped forward with a sexy smile that made him want to cut that dress off her body and actually reached up to lay a hand on his cheek. Instinct told Nate that he should have pulled away, but he allowed it.

Closing his eyes, Nate breathed deeply as he savored the warm touch of her hand on his skin. "All right," he muttered. "You got guts, lady. I'll give you that. Now tell me what you want."

"Concentrate," she said. "Focus on the sensations you get from your symbiont. Do not think. Just feel..."

There was something about her...Something strange. The creature Nate had Bonded was reacting to her in some way.

No…No, it was reacting to another of its kind. This lady had one too! Was she a Justice Keeper?

"Who are you?"

He opened his eyes to find her smiling up at him, and to his shock, she stood up on her toes to give him a peck on the cheek. "I'm called Valeth," she said. "And I'm pleased to see that the rumors are true. You inherited Flagg's symbiont."

"Who?"

"All will be explained to you in time."

Valeth snapped her fingers.

Some Asian dude who had been leaning against a streetlight on the sidewalk heard the noise and came stomping up behind her. He reached up to lower his sunglasses so he could peek over the rims. "Forget what you have seen here."

Nate looked about in confusion.

Only then did he remember Robbie, and when he turned around, the dumb-ass was slumped against the railing with a dull glaze in his eyes and drool leaking from the corner of his mouth.

"Forget," the Asian guy said. "And never trouble Nathaniel again."

Just like that, Robbie shuffled off with his hands in the pockets of his sweater and his head bowed. Nate had never seen anything like it. He'd heard rumors about telepaths and the strange things they could do, but they were supposed to live on Leyria or Antaur or one of the other worlds that he couldn't pronounce. They weren't supposed to be living here on Earth.

Baring his teeth, Nate turned his gaze on the strange woman. "That guy owes me a lot of money," he whispered. "You should have told him to pay me before you sent him away."

Valeth smiled up at him, and for a moment, he thought she meant to pay Robbie's debt in a way that would almost make up for the lost cash. Then she chuckled and turned away from him. "The time has come for you to embrace a grander view of the universe."

"What the hell is that supposed to mean?"

"Come with me. Together, we will discover your true potential."

The soft patter of rain on her living-room window was soothing. Almost soothing enough to put her to sleep, but every time she started to drift, stress pulled her right back to full consciousness. Her Nassai was beginning to worry.

Curled up on the couch in a tightly-belted maroon robe, Larani pressed her cheek into the pillow and tried to rest. For once, she had allowed herself to go home early. She had planned on curling up with a good book, but the fatigue made her want to just sit and do nothing.

She rolled onto her back, scrubbed a hand over her face and pushed her hair out of her eyes. "Yes, I know," she whispered for the symbiont. "I should get some sleep."

It wasn't easy.

The pile of things that demanded her attention just seemed to keep growing. Now there were rumors of people with Keeper abilities hijacking ships on the Fringe. Slade's people, no doubt. She had ordered two of her best teams to investigate, but so far, they had found no answers.

Agent Hunter's recent encounter with the Ragnosians left her with a sick feeling in the pit of her stomach. The Sub-Council on Planetary Security was still trying to decide just how much of that story should be released to the general public. Things were already tense enough without inflaming the xenophobes who would use news of Ragnosian ships on this side of the galaxy as justification for their vitriol.

Speaking of xenophobia, Dusep's popularity was rising. The latest poll numbers all said that he had a strong chance of winning over a quarter of the electorate. Just ten short years ago, a man who displayed such open hostility to foreigners would *never* have found mainstream acceptance. There was little chance of him defeating Sarona Vason, but little chance was not no chance.

She kept thinking that she ought to be doing something to stop that man's rise to power, but politics was not her province. The Justice Keepers protected the innocent; they did not set public policy. Jack kept insisting that he had an idea, but he was dragging his feet in doing whatever it was he intended to do. So far, Larani had decided not to push him. After his ordeal last month, he needed rest.

On the coffee table, her multi-tool beeped.

"Answer call," Larani mumbled. "Audio only."

It surprised her when the Prime Council's voice came through the speaker. Sarona Vason had a curt way of speaking that made you want to sit up and pay attention. "Larani, I hope I'm not disturbing you."

A yawn stretched Larani's mouth, a yawn that she covered with the palm of one hand. Her eyes dropped shut despite her best efforts. "Not at all," she said. "What can I do for you, Prime Council?"

"Turn on the video," Sarona barked. "I want to see you."

Standing up with a sigh, Larani tied her belt even tighter and then nodded. "Allow video call," she said. "Holographic display."

The ghostly figure of an older woman in gray pants and a smart jacket appeared above her coffee table. Sarona Vason had a stern but kindly face of dark skin. Her short, curly hair had gone white a very long time ago. "My apologies," she said when she saw Larani. "I didn't mean to disturb you."

"No disturbance. What can I do for you?"

"My office just received an interesting message from the Antaurans," Sarona began. "It seems they want to talk peace."

Standing before the other woman with her arms folded, Larani shook her head. "We have made countless attempts to bring them to the negotiating table," she said. "And they have ignored every one. What changed?"

The Prime Council shut her eyes and let out a slow breath. "I wish I could say," she replied at last. "Their message was rather short and to the point. They have extended an invitation to a summit that they hope will result in a formal alliance between Leyria and Antaur."

"To what end?"

"I don't know," Sarona replied. "But it wouldn't surprise me if the Ragnosians have been encroaching on their territory as well."

Hunching up her shoulders as a shiver ran down her spine, Larani nodded. "Better the devil that you know…"

"I beg your pardon?"

"An Earth saying," Larani clarified. "Whatever animosity they may feel for us, the Antaurans know that we will leave them alone. The Ragnosians, on the other hand, have made numerous aggressive actions."

The Prime Council turned and began pacing a line, though the hologram remained fixed in place. "Yes, that was my assessment as well," she said. "And there is one other thing. The Antaurans have invited Earth."

"Earth?"

"I received confirmation from the United Nations Security Council this morning. As you've no doubt surmised, we'll be sending a delegation of Keepers to accompany the Diplomatic Corps. I want Lenai and Hunter to be part of that delegation."

Larani sat down on the couch with fingertips covering her mouth, her eyebrows slowly rising. "That could be a problem," she said. "The boy has a head for politics, but he's unpredictable and disdainful of rules he doesn't like."

"A typical Keeper then."

"Lenai, on the other hand, is one of the most talented investigators I've ever seen." Sarona's withering glare made it clear that she wasn't interested in Larani's objections, but Larani pressed on anyway. "But she's blunt. One glimpse of the way Antaurans treat the disabled as second-class citizens, and she will almost certainly say something to upset the talks. It may be wiser to send more seasoned officers."

Sarona whirled around to face the camera with her fists on her hips, and before the woman uttered one word, Larani knew the argument was over. "Those two represent one of our greatest accomplishments," she said. "The first Earther to Bond a Nassai and the woman who brought him into the fold. They're a symbol, one that we very much need if these talks are to have any chance of success."

"I suppose I can't argue with that."

"Good," Sarona said. "Then have them prepped. They'll be leaving in a few days."

Part 1

Chapter 1

A light drizzle splashed against the cafe window, blurring Harry's view of the street outside. There were people hurrying along with umbrellas and the odd automated car that zipped past, but it was mostly quiet.

Harry sat back with a cup of tea in one hand, steam wafting up to carry the scent of peppermint to his nose. "This is nice," he said. "You know, we don't do this often enough. When was the last time you and I got caught up?"

Jack sat across from him with hands folded behind his head, smiling lazily. "Oh, probably right before your daughter's birthday party," he answered. "We don't really hang out enough."

Except for the two of them, the cafe was empty: just a couple dozen round tables spread without a single patron in sight. One of those cylindrical maintenance bots rolled past to polish the floor, but other than that, they were alone. Harry paid the damn thing no mind. He was less bothered by robots when they weren't in *his* house.

"So, how are things?"

Jack cast a glance out the window, seemingly distracted by something he saw out on the street. "Well, now that she's all moved in," he began, "Anna's in full nesting mode. I think she said something about needing more closet space."

"And you're-"

"Loving every minute of it."

"Oh, really?"

Covering his mouth with his fist, Jack shut his eyes and cleared his throat. "But you see," he said. "Obligatory standards of masculinity require that I make a pretense of mild exasperation. Please sign the form as witness to my having done my due diligence."

"Signed and witnessed."

Harry cradled his cup in both hands, inhaling the sweet aroma. Cautiously, he lifted it and slurped as he took a sip. The tea was still a bit too hot for his liking, but better that than too cold.

When he looked up, Jack was watching him with that squint-eyed stare every cop learned after enough time on the Force. "Come to think of it," he said. "I'm surprised you haven't given me the Dad Talk."

"The Dad Talk?"

"You know: 'It's too soon. You've only been dating for a few months. Rock music attained perfection in 1967. Have you heard of Jethro Tull?' "

Of course, Jack's mind would go there. Sometimes Harry wondered why he hadn't gone insane now that most of his friends were barely more than half his age. Moving to Leyria had been... an educational experience. It bothered him that the others saw him as a bit of a stick in the mud. Did kids these days still use the phrase 'stick in the mud?' After all this time, Jack still didn't understand him. Not completely.

Harry was smiling into his lap, shaking his head slowly. "Kid, I thought you knew me better than that," he said. "You and Anna have been in love for five damn years. So, you're finally doing something about it? My response is, 'It's about damn time.' "

Besides, Harry Carlson was in no position to lecture anyone about their relationship choices. Not when he and Sora were sneaking around like a couple of teenagers. A pang of guilt flared up when he thought about the implications of dating his daughter's teacher, but the sneaking only made it more exciting.

Jack studied him again, the cop-stare returning with renewed intensity. So, this was how it felt to be on the wrong side of an interrogation table. Huh… "Yeah, I'm not buying it," Jack said. "What's going on, Harry?"

"Nothing."

"Uh huh…"

Harry was blushing now, and he felt the slight tingle of sweat on his brow. "I'm just glad that you and Anna are happy." Damn it! There was no way in hell Jack wouldn't see right through that pathetic response.

The kid leaned back with his arms folded, smiling like a father who had just heard about his son's first crush. "Do you have a girlfriend, Harry?"

"No."

"What's her name?"

"Shut up!"

Much to Harry's annoyance, Jack folded up in his seat and trembled with laughter. "Okay then," he wheezed. "Well, you just tell Shut Up that I'll be eager to meet her just as soon as she's ready."

Harry groaned. Why did they always do this to him? First with Jena and now with Sora. Everybody seemed to find a perverse amount of entertainment in his reluctance to openly acknowledge a relationship. Well, maybe Harry would feel differently if he didn't keep getting into relationships that required a certain amount of discretion.

Oh, Jena had been more than willing to acknowledge their connection. In fact, she had struggled to understand why Harry had such a hard time doing so. Well, if you were going to engage in an office romance – a bad idea at the best of times – the very last thing you should do was let your colleagues in on the secret. No one wanted to be the subject of water-cooler gossip.

And now, he was dating Sora. Say what you will about office romances, but at least there had been no conflict of interest in his relationship with Jena. Harry could not say the same about dating his daughter's teacher.

Only then did he notice that Jack was looking out the window again. Hell, the poor kid seemed downright perplexed. Something was eating away at him.

Slouching in his chair with a hand over his chest, Harry pursed his lips as he looked up at the ceiling. "Okay, now it's my turn," he said. "Spill it, Kid. What's on your mind?"

The corner of Jack's mouth twitched, but he never turned his gaze away from the window. Hard little droplets of rain pounded the glass. "What makes you think there's something on my mind?"

"I've seen that look before."

Jack crossed his arms, hunching over the table and barking a laugh. He shook his head. "There's no look, Harry." Of course, he was lying. You didn't spend fifteen years interrogating criminals without developing a sense for these things.

Harry lifted his cup in one hand, sipping his tea. All the while, he let his own cop-stare linger on Jack. "Now, who's paddling up Bullshit River?" he said at last. "Trust me, kid; I know that look."

"And what look is that?"

"The look of every detective who wants to pull his hair out because he just can't see how the clues fit together." Harry waited a moment, and then added, "The look of a good officer who just saw a scumbag walk on a technicality."

When Jack finally looked up, he blinked several times and then sighed. "Okay," he said. "You're right. There is something on my mind, but I don't think you can help."

"Try me."

"Nah," Jack said. "Let's just go."

Harry's first instinct was to protest, but he was old and – in this case – wise enough to know that when someone didn't want to talk, you couldn't force the issue. So, he just nodded and finished his tea.

Once they were out on the street, the rain seemed to pick up a little, falling hard on Harry's big black umbrella. It was a spoke-street, one that ran all the way to the SlipGate terminal at the centre of town, but it was still pretty quiet. Foot traffic was at a minimum due to the lousy weather, and Leyrians seldom used cars.

At one point, a bus came rolling past, heading toward the downtown core. Harry saw lights in the windows of distant skyscrapers despite the fact that there was still plenty of daylight. Autumn in Denabria always brought rain, and with it, an almost perpetual gloom. It almost made him miss Ottawa's many snowstorms.

Jack walked along with his hands inside the pockets of his denim jacket, his face a granite mask of consternation. "So, are you going to tell me her name?" The total lack of enthusiasm told Harry that his friend really wasn't looking for an answer. He just wanted to take his mind off his troubles.

Before Harry could think up an excuse to change the subject, he caught sight of two young women in hooded windbreakers coming up the sidewalk. Well, it was really their conversation that snagged his attention.

"That's him," one said, pointing.

Harry's mouth dropped open. He winced, then slapped a palm against his forehead. "No, no, no." It was a pitiful prayer, one that he knew would go unanswered. "Please, not this again!"

At his side, Jack paused and cast a glance over his shoulder, frowning in confusion. "You've seen these two before?"

"Just wait. You'll understand."

Like a moth to a flame, one of the young ladies came rushing forward with a smile on her face. "Mr. Carlson," she said, offering him both hands. "I hope it's not too much trouble, but my cousin just applied to Arethelia University, and it would mean so much to her if she had your blessing."

"I'm not a religious icon," Harry broke in.

The girl blinked as if he had just said that the sky was red and the sun green. "But I thought…" she mumbled. "Those videos on the Link…"

"You were mistaken," he said roughly. "Go back to worshiping your Companion or whatever it is you did before I came along."

"But-"

Harry pushed past her and ignored the dirty look that he got from her friend. Damn it, he was *not* a messianic figure, and he had no intention of becoming one. He could just imagine what his grandfather, a devout Catholic, would think of that. Strangely, Melissa seemed okay with it even though she was the only one in their family who had any real faith. "God has a plan for everyone," she insisted whenever he brought it up. Harry was an agnostic who leaned toward atheism. He believed in facts, in observable reality. He was not about to encourage other people down the path of superstition. Jack actually had to run to keep up. "Pretty harsh," he said.

Harry rounded on him, standing with the umbrella in one hand and scowling. "I am not a religious icon," he repeated for what felt like the hundredth time. "The sooner they learn that, the happier we'll all be."

Biting his lower lip, Jack nodded slowly in understanding. "I get it," he said. "But how did Harry Carlson, Messiah for hire, become a thing anyway?"

"Melissa didn't tell you about my fight with Isara?"

"She Coles-Notesed it for me," Jack answered. "But I was still on that Ragnosian ship at the time. I know the bullet points."

Tilting his head back, Harry exhaled and then narrowed his eyes. "People saw me using the N'Jal," he explained. "A human using Overseer technology. Apparently, there's some prophecy about a man who can turn the gods' weapons against them."

Jack's wry grin actually set Harry's teeth on edge, and it only got worse when the kid laughed and shook his head. "So, they think it's you," he said. "Well, Harry, there are worse jobs than personal Lord and Saviour."

"Shut up!"

"Will you bless my shuttle the next time I go out?"

"You know, I have the N'Jal with me." Thinking of the Overseer device made Harry aware of it singing in his mind. The song was a companion now; he could tune it out with very little effort. But the N'Jal offered far more than raw power. Being able to determine the chemical composition of the air with a thought, being able to sense another person's mood by measuring subtle physiological responses…The N'Jal offered *perspective,* and a part of him longed for that. "Any time you want an ass-whooping, just let me know."

"Hmm," Jack said. "It seems you're a vengeful god."

"Oh, shut up!"

The first thing Jack saw when he walked through his front door was Anna sitting on the couch in pajama pants and a little blue tank-top. Her hair was down – a rarity for her – and she seemed to be ready for a very early bedtime.

The instant she heard him come in, she looked up and smiled that special smile of hers. "Hey, you," she said. "How was your day?"

Chewing his lip, Jack felt his eyebrows rise. "Not bad." He stepped into the apartment and shut the door behind him. "Harry wants us to know that he really hates his new job as messiah to the Leyrians."

Anna was sitting with her hands on her knees, smiling into her lap. "So, you got to listen to his fun new rant?" She barked a laugh. "The last time I was over there, Melissa was having way too much fun teasing him."

Jack approached her.

The instant he was within range, Anna got off the couch, stood up on her toes and kissed him on the lips. It was a soft kiss, tender and sweet, but it soothed away some of his frustration. Well...Okay...*Most* of his frustration.

Instinct kicked in, and he slipped his arms around her, holding her close and letting her rest her head on his chest. "What's all this for?" he asked.

She looked up at him with her lips pressed together, concern shining bright in those big blue eyes. Concern for what? He was about to ask when Anna hugged him tight and said, "I want pajama cuddles. Just you and me and a big warm blanket."

"Sounds wonderful."

A few minutes later, Jack returned to the living room in gray shorts and a big blue t-shirt, pausing with one hand on the wall to admire his girlfriend. There were moments when he marveled at how a guy like him could end up with a woman like her.

Anna was stretched out on the couch with the blankets pulled up to her shoulders, her head turned so that she had one cheek pressed into the pillow. For half a second, Jack thought she was asleep. Then she startled him by saying, "Are you gonna come join me?"

He didn't need any more prompting.

It felt so good to get under the covers with her. Pretty soon, he was lying on his side with his arm around Anna's tummy, sighing as she pressed her back against him. All safe and snuggled up. The warmth of her body seemed to drive away autumn's chill.

Jack nuzzled the back of her neck. "You're amazing," he whispered in her ear. "This is just what I needed."

She rolled over to face him, wrapping an arm around him, and he knew right away that she was worried. More to the point, Jack knew that he was the cause of her anxiety. "Something's been eating away at you," she said. "I was hoping you'd tell me what it is."

Jack shut his eyes tight, trembling as he drew in a breath. "Oh, you don't want to talk about that, do you?" It was more of a plea than a question. "I'll be fine by tomorrow. I promise."

By the time he finished speaking, Anna was lying on her back with her arms folded, staring angrily at the ceiling. "You've been stressed out for weeks," she said. "You think I don't notice, but I do. Out with it."

He propped himself up on an elbow, resting his cheek on the knuckles of one fist. "You really wanna talk about this?"

"I do."

Jack sat up and ran a hand over his face, pushing dark bangs off his forehead. "It's about what happened on that Ragnosian ship," he began. "On the day that you and Cassi came to rescue me."

"Go on," she urged.

"My fight with Arin…"

"What about it?"

"I lost."

With a heavy sigh, Anna sat up and shook her head. "Sweetie, is this some kind of Earth masculinity thing?" she asked. "Because I'm pretty sure we talked about this in the medical bay. Everyone loses sometimes."

"No, it's not that," Jack assured her. "I just keep…I keep thinking about Ben. About how I couldn't save him. And then there was Arin…I beat him once before and I was sure I could do it again. But I was wrong. I just keep screwing up. Maybe I don't have what it takes to be a Justice Keeper."

Gently, Anna laid a hand on his cheek and turned his face toward her. She touched her nose to his. "My poor Jack," she said. "You are the strongest person I know, and not because you can Bend space-time."

"Then why?"

"On the day I met you," she said. "You put yourself in harm's way to help a perfect stranger. And then you did it again for

Summer. That cop Hutchinson had a gun pointed at your chest, remember? He gave you a choice: give him the symbiont and he would let you go."

All of those memories came rushing back. Suddenly, Jack was right there in his big sister's living room. Hutchinson was standing over a passed out Harry, choking up on his pistol, snarling like a dog that wanted to sink its teeth into something.

He remembered all of it: the terror, the sense of helplessness and the growing fire in his belly that refused to let him back down even when he knew he couldn't win. And then he remembered meeting Summer. Those memories brought warm emotions, and not all of them were his. Summer loved him; he knew that.

Anna pressed her lips to his cheek. "You decided that you would not sacrifice an innocent creature to save your own life," she whispered. "Even though you knew it was futile. Hutchinson would kill you and take the symbiont anyway. It didn't matter. Right is right regardless of its futility. *That's* what makes you an amazing Keeper."

"Well…When you put it like that." There were times when Jack forgot his greatest hits. It wasn't as though he had lost those memories, but it had been so long since he had thought about those events.

His selective amnesia on the topic of how he became a Justice Keeper seemed to annoy Summer. And really, could you blame her? Forgetting the events that led to their Bonding had to be an insult. He offered Summer a silent apology, but that just intensified her irritation. Jack gave up trying to understand what he had done to provoke his Nassai. She could tell him the next time they talked. "But," he said. "I'm the only one in our little group who keeps piling up defeat after defeat."

"Oh, really?"

He knew he was in trouble when Anna got off the couch and stood over him with her hands on her hips. "Six months ago," she said, "Isara got out of her cell and ran into me on her way out of the building. We fought; she overpowered me and went on to kill several people before Melissa took her down."

"Yes, but-"

"Two months later," Anna continued, speaking right over him. "We tracked Leo to that castle. I fought him, and I had him subdued, but he triggered a hypersonic pulse and escaped. The oldest trick in the book.

"Harry took on Cara Sinthel and got shot," she added without pause. "Melissa and Rajel both fought Isara when she attacked Justice Keeper HQ, and she tossed them both around like a cat toying with a pair of field mice. We've all had our setbacks. That's what happens when you go up against powerful enemies."

"Okay, I take your point."

"Good."

Anna hopped into his lap, slipping an arm around his back and snuggling up close with her head on his chest. "Because you're wonderful and brave and clever," she added. "And I love you with all my heart."

Jack squeezed her tight.

They spent the rest of the night in each other's arms, cuddling, laughing, sharing the details of what they had done that day. After a light dinner, they curled up together under the blankets and put on a movie. Some Leyrian sci-fi flick about time travel. Jack always found it interesting how Leyrian fiction – especially anything that might be considered sci-fi or fantasy – often found ways to work the Overseers into the plot. And more often than not, they got the details wrong. But the movie wasn't the highlight of his evening. It was feeling Anna doze off in his arms that made his night complete.

The arch-shaped window in the library should have been admitting warm sunlight into the room, but water flowed over the glass in sheets so that all you could see through it was a vague gray haze.

It was so odd to see a library without books. There were no stacks, no shelves. No physical books of any kind. Leyrians kept all of their books electronically, accessing them through tablets or customized e-readers. There were repositories where hard copies were stored, but they were designed mainly as a way of safeguarding knowledge in the event of some planet-wide catastrophe.

Instead, this library was filled with small tables, spaced out to give students plenty of room for quiet study. Harry found his daughter at one near the window with a tablet propped up and connected to a keyboard made of nanobots. Clearly, she was using it as a laptop. And she was stressed. He could see that.

Maybe the container of hot soup he had brought would help. He smiled inwardly. So, he had finally reached the point where his kid was up all night studying for exams. That was some kind of milestone, wasn't it?

Melissa looked up and blinked at him. "Dad, hey." Squeezing her eyes shut, she stiffened. "Are you *really* here or is this some hallucination of my sleep-deprived brain?"

"I brought you some dinner." Harry set the container of hoy chicken soup down next to her. "I think maybe you're working too hard."

"End of term," Melissa grumbled. "Can't be helped."

He sat down across from her, resting his hands on the chair arms and watching her for a very long while. "You don't have to push yourself *quite* this hard," he said. "You've already got a symbiont. They're going to make you a Justice Keeper no matter what."

Melissa bent over with her elbows on the table, covering her face with both hands. Her groan made Harry flinch. "True," she agreed. "But that's no excuse for slacking off."

"I've taught you too well."

"Yes, you have."

Clamping his jaw shut, Harry nodded once in approval. "Well, then," he said, rising from his seat. "I'll leave you to it. But don't work too hard. We don't need another Aiden situation on our hands."

Melissa threw her head back, staring blankly upward with glazed eyes. "Oh, don't remind me." So, she'd had no luck on that front. When Harry first met that boy, he had liked him. But now he was beginning to wish that his daughter would just cut ties. There were days when he wanted to ask what exactly was going on between her and Aiden, but pushing a teenager – even one who was technically an adult – could result in them shutting you out.

He turned to go, slipping away with his head down and his coat pulled tight against his body. "Dad," Melissa called out behind him.

When he looked back, she was sitting up straight with a bright smile. You would never have known that she had been strung out just a few minutes earlier. "Thanks," she murmured.

Harry nodded.

He moved quietly through the library to a set of double doors that led to the lobby. Once through them, Harry found himself face to face with the hologram of an old woman who wore her white hair pulled back in a clip. "Thank you for visiting the library," she said. "Did you find everything you needed?"

"Yes, thank you."

She vanished when he answered, allowing Harry to carry on to the front entrance where raindrops pelted the window pane. The heavy glass doors required some effort to push open, but he grunted and shoved, and then he was out in the drizzle.

The university was a small collection of white and gray brick buildings with a line of windows on every floor. Skywalks on the second level connected each one to its neighbours so that students could easily traverse the campus in the event of inclement weather. That being the case, there were few people out on the street.

Harry followed a concrete path around the library to a road lined with skeletal trees that dripped water from every branch. The small, igloo-shaped houses on either side of the street were naked without foliage to conceal them. He saw lights in several windows.

The gray sky was beginning to darken. Evening came early at this time of year; he would need to get home to make sure that Claire had something to eat. Though, of course, she could order Michael to prepare her dinner.

Harry walked under his umbrella, humming softly to himself as his shoes squished in the puddles. A part of him wanted to call Sora and see if she was free this evening, but it was probably best to have a quiet night on his own.

Hair stood up on the back of his neck.

Cop instincts made him listen for the sound of footsteps behind him, and there were several. He counted at least four people – maybe more – all moving rather noisily. It was probably nothing to worry about. Just some kids walking home from class. Still, he didn't like having people behind him.

He turned.

There were six in total, four young men and two young women, all about Melissa's age. And they were a perfect rainbow of hues. One boy had a strong chin, a pale face and short, blonde hair. Next to him, another young man with dark-brown skin and curly hair glared daggers at Harry.

One of the girls was short and petite with tanned skin and long honey-coloured hair. The other was strikingly pale with blue hair cut boyishly short. The diversity in their little wouldn't have mattered much to Harry – this *was* Leyria, after all – except that they were all dressed alike, each one in a formal high-collared shirt under a dark sweater. "You're right," Blue-Hair said. "That *is* him."

Clenching his teeth with a hiss, Harry shook his head. "Whatever you're thinking," he said, stepping forward. "Put it out of your minds right now. I'm not a religious figure, and I have no intention of becoming one."

"No, you're not," the blonde boy agreed.

"Who says we want you to be one?" Blue-Hair added.

Harry blinked, then took a moment to recover his wits and smother the anxiety that made his heart beat a little faster. "Well, then. So long as we agree." He turned to go but caught motion in the corner of his eye.

It was one of the young men, a short, olive-skinned fellow with closely-cropped dark hair and a thin mustache. "You're what's wrong with this planet." His voice was ice cold. "Foreigners. You move in, spreading your ideas."

"I thought Leyrians had evolved beyond talk like that."

The long-haired girl practically sneered at him as she came forward to stand beside her friend. "It's hard to evolve," she spat, "when savages like you keep trying to drag us back into the Stone Age."

Harry shut his eyes, his head sinking with the weight of his dismay, and rubbed his brow with the back of one hand. "I get it," he said. "This is Leyria. Prejudice, bigotry, it's all ancient history to you kids."

Lifting his chin, Harry let his gaze linger on the young woman. "But it's not ancient history for me," he went on. "For me, it was cold, hard reality since the day I was born. I have seen first-hand what prejudice can drive people to do."

They were hanging on his every word, watching him with guarded expressions. But he could see that he had piqued their curiosity. "It's a poison of the mind," Harry went on. "You let it in – even just a little – and it will twist you into-"

He cut off when the blue-haired girl pushed her way through the others and faced him with a snarl that belonged on a rabid dog. "You see what he's doing?" she snapped. "He says he doesn't want to be worshiped, and yet here he is. Trying to lead us out of our ignorant ways."

"That's not what-"

The young man with blonde hair was the next to approach Harry, and though his cheeks were flushed, he managed to effect an outward calm. "You don't belong here," he said. "This is our world, not yours."

"I beg to differ," Harry countered. "This city is my home."

"Not for long."

Mr. Blond strode forward without a moment's hesitation as if he were absolutely certain that his companions would back him up. The others waited only a second before falling in behind him.

Panic welled up inside Harry, but it vanished in an instant. The N'Jal was singing in the back of his mind. All he had to do was reach into his pocket and take its power. These young idiots were no threat to him.

But he didn't take the N'Jal.

Instead, he flung open his trench coat and drew the small pistol that he wore on his hip. A good thing that he had obtained a concealed-carry permit just last month. If he was going to be working with the Justice Keepers, then there was always a chance that one of Slade's lackeys might decide to attack him on a routine trip to the park. And the next time one of them tried it, he would be ready.

Harry pointed the gun at Mr. Blond's leg. The kid was in such a rage that he just kept coming anyway. "Crowd Control!" Harry yelled. All three LEDs on the barrel turned green.

Mr. Blonde tried to rush him.

Harry fired.

A bullet struck the young man's left shin, then bounced off and fell to the ground. Mr. Blond yelped, hopping on one foot and clapping a hand over the wound. "Damn it!" He tumbled over, landing on his side, stretched out on the rain-slick sidewalk.

The others converged on Harry.

He swung the pistol in a wide arc, pointing it directly at Blue-Hair. She froze, then backed away from him with her hands up. Once again, Harry adjusted his aim, this time pointing the gun at Mustache.

That guy took two more steps and froze.

"Go home," Harry said.

The five of them were slinking away, moving cautiously as if they thought that the sight of them running away might provoke Harry to start shooting. Mr. Blond was still on the ground.

He was sitting now, clutching his wounded leg and hissing from the sting. The kid would have a nasty welt but nothing more. Good cops learned how to defuse a situation with minimal force. Harry had not forgotten his training.

"Come on," Harry said. "Let me have a look at your leg."

"Stay away from me!"

"Fine!" Harry growled. "But a word of advice. Maybe you want to rethink who you spend your time with. This group will get you into trouble."

Chapter 2

Pressing her lips together, Anna felt her eyebrows rise. "So, we're going to Antaur," she said. "Because the people who have considered us bitter enemies for over a century suddenly want to talk peace"

She wore a simple pair of beige pants and a white top with a round neck, her hair done up in a bun with sticks through it. And she sat in what had to be the most uncomfortable chair, right in front of Larani's desk.

On her right, Jack was hunched over with an elbow on his knee, fingertips covering his mouth. "They must be spooked," he mumbled. "You think maybe the Ragnosians are violating *their* borders too?"

"It's a reasonable guess," Larani replied.

The head of the Justice Keepers stood with her back to the pair of them, staring out her office window at a gray afternoon that was miraculously free of rain. The days were getting colder. That thick ceiling of clouds seemed to choke the sunlight before it could provide any warmth. "The Prime Council believes that the two of you will be a symbol of the cooperation between our two worlds. Though I'm inclined to think that more seasoned officers would be better suited to this assignment, I can't argue with her logic."

"Will we be participating in the talks?"

"I think it's best to leave that to actual diplomats."

Tilting her head back, Anna squinted as she considered the implications. "So, we're there just to be symbols," she said. "Show up, look pretty, smile for the guests and don't spill anything on the furniture."

Sighing, Larani turned away from the window.

She practically fell into her big, cushioned chair, grunting on impact and wheeling it closer to the desk. "Operative Lenai," she began in patient tones. "I realize that this is not the sort of assignment you would prefer. You like to be the centre of attention."

"I resent that," Anna protested.

When she glanced to her right, she found her boyfriend watching her with a raised eyebrow that spoke volumes. Well…Okay. Maybe she *did* steal every scene. She couldn't help it! She just had a lot of thoughts and wanted to voice them. But she could be mousy if she had to. *If* she had to.

Anna sank into her chair with arms folded, exhaling roughly. "Okay," she muttered. "I take your point. I'll behave myself."

"Excellent," Larani said. "Now, on to other issues."

The glass door swung open, and Anna saw Harry's silhouette striding into the room behind her. He moved at a brisk pace, grumbling under his breath. "You have a problem," he said. "A big one."

Larani was out of her chair in an instant, standing with her hands clasped behind herself. She frowned, then nodded once to Harry. "Mr. Carlson," she said. "I'm glad you stopped by. You'll be going to Antaur with these two for the peace talks."

Harry's jaw dropped, and he blinked at her. "But I'm not a diplomat." He shook his head so fast he must have made himself dizzy. "Why in God's name would you send me to Antaur?"

"You were a liaison between us and Earth's law-enforcement agencies."

"Yes, but-"

"Your presence will be a symbol of cooperation." In the last year and a half, Anna had come to recognize Larani's many stares. This one said that refusing to back down on this point was a good way to find yourself doing a *lot* of boring paperwork. Not that she had any real authority over Harry, but with Larani, that didn't seem to matter. The woman had a talent for making other people buckle down and do whatever it was she thought they ought to be doing.

"I have daughters," Harry protested. "I can't just go gallivanting around the galaxy."

"And if you wish to ensure their safety," Larani cut in, "then you will do everything in your power to make these talks succeed."

Jack was swiveling around in his chair, grinning on the point of outright laughter. "Oh, come on, Harry," he said. "It'll be fun! We'll ride on a big spaceship, do some sightseeing and listen to the Antaurans lecture us on our genetic inferiority."

"Lectures that you will endure without comment, Agent Hunter." Larani's tone was dangerous. She gave them both a lot of leeway – Anna still felt ashamed of the way that she had snarled at the other woman when Jack was a prisoner of the Ragnosians – but this was one of those times when she wanted them on their best behaviour.

It wasn't hard to see why. The fate of the galaxy could depend on this.

Harry puckered his lips and blew out a breath. "Well, then," he said, approaching the desk. "Since that's settled, let's move on to a new topic. You had better do something about your fascist problem."

"You mean Dusep?" Anna inquired.

"No, I mean the college kids who attacked me in broad daylight yesterday," Harry growled. "They're getting bolder."

Anna was out of her chair in an instant, walking over to Harry and laying a hand on his arm. "Are you all right?" she asked him.

"Yeah, I'm fine." Harry's voice was gruff. "But if we've reached the point where these kids are openly attacking immigrants…"

Larani was bent over with her hands braced upon the surface of the desk, her head hanging. "It means the situation is deteriorating," she said. "Dusep's rhetoric, no doubt. A pity. Were you not otherwise engaged, Anna, I would have assigned this investigation to your team."

"You think this is task force business?" Anna wasn't sure she agreed. It was hard to see how Slade and his pals could be the driving force behind this incident. True, Isara had provided weapons to the Sons of Savard, but the Sons had been planning a coordinated attack on the city's infrastructure. Anna had come to suspect that the attack had served its purpose, stoking fear in the hearts of Leyrian citizens, making them more sympathetic to harsher security measures and authoritarian policies.

Transforming a bunch of college kids into bigoted little wankers would hardly have the same effect. Not everything was the result of some conspiracy, and there were plenty of mundane explanations for how some dumb kids got radicalized.

Turning away from Harry, Anna brushed a lock of hair off her cheek and marched back to her chair. "I don't know, Larani," she said. "I'm having a hard time seeing Slade's fingerprints on this."

"I wouldn't put anything past that man."

"Fair enough, but I still don't think it was him."

Jack was slouching with his arms crossed, frowning as he nodded his agreement. "I don't either," he said. "These kids aren't terrorists. This is a job for local cops, not Justice Keepers."

With agonizing slowness, Larani eased herself back into the chair and gripped the armrests. She almost seemed to deflate. "Perhaps you're right," she said. "But it's clear to me that we need to be more proactive in rooting out this scourge."

"Well," Jack said, "That 'plan' I've been working on is ready."

Anna's head whipped around. What plan was that? Whatever he was up to, he was keeping it pretty damn close to the chest.

It kind of bothered her that he'd been working on some kind of anti-fascist initiative without even telling her. Not that he didn't have a right to keep some things to himself, but…

"And what do you have for us, Agent Hunter?"

The smile on Jack's face was downright devilish. "42 Labec Avenue," he replied. "Tonight at 13:00. Be there, and you'll see."

Jack saw a big, red boxing glove coming at him.

He leaned back, frowning as it passed over his nose, then snapped himself upright. Before he could so much as blink, the other glove was coming his way.

Jack ducked.

He threw a quick jab into Novol's stomach, causing the man to grunt as he backed up. Normally, he didn't retaliate – Novol had this silly game where he kept insisting that he could hit Jack eventually – but he wanted a break. That one punch drove his opponent all the way to the edge of the ring.

Sweat drenching his face, Jack shut his eyes. "Good." He rubbed his forehead with the back of a gloved fist. "So, you've been here for about a month now. How do you like Leyria?"

Novol was leaning against the ropes with his arms spread wide, head lolling as he tried to catch his breath. "It's amazing," he wheezed. "It would be perfect if I could just find a way to hit you."

Grinning with a bit of forced laughter, Jack looked down at the floor. He shook his head. "I keep telling you that I have enhanced reflexes," he said. "Why is it so important for you to land a punch?"

"Military training," Novol answered. "They used to drill it into us. Think, analyze, find a weakness and exploit it."

Jack removed his gloves. Should it bother him that Novol was thinking of him in those terms? As a puzzle to be solved? A challenge to overcome? After all this time, he was starting to hope that Novol had come to see him as a friend.

Summer was equally saddened by the man's response. Jack could tell that she was coming to like Novol.

He dropped to one knee at the edge of the ring, picked up a towel and dried off his face. "I get it," he said. "But you have managed to hit me on more than one occasion. So, maybe you could stop stressing about it?"

Novol's mouth twisted, but he nodded slowly in response. "You're right," he said, getting off the ropes with a grunt. "I guess it just bugs me to think that... Well, it feels like you have an unfair advantage."

"I do."

Jack decided that it was time to change the subject. Knowing that his abilities irked the other man left him feeling a little uneasy. Not because he didn't trust Novol. The guy had been nothing but helpful from the moment he set foot on this planet; Novol seemed to think that since he had already betrayed his own people, he may as well commit to the Leyrian cause. Except Leyria didn't really *have* a cause.

Novol's discomfort with the Justice Keepers' enhanced physical abilities made Jack feel uneasy because it said something about the way Novol saw himself. About the way he had been trained to measure his own worth against others rather than recognizing his own intrinsic value. "Are you settling in okay?" Jack asked. "Is there anything we can do to help with that?"

Turning his face up to the ceiling, Novol frowned as he thought it over. "You've all done so much for me already," he mumbled. "I keep wondering when the bill is going to come due."

"No bill."

"So you keep saying."

Jack felt a smile blossom as he remembered some of his first experiences with the Leyrians, in the early days of his training as a Justice Keeper. He remembered going to the food dispensers on Station Twelve and feeling a little uncomfortable when they didn't demand some kind of payment. Almost like he was stealing. "It was the same for a lot of Earthers who came here."

The sound of heels clicking on floor tiles told him that their little sparring session was over, and he didn't have to look to know who it was. Hell, he didn't even need spatial awareness for that.

Keli Armana strode toward the ring in a long-sleeved white dress, her face grim as she studied them. "Agent Hunter," she said. "If you're done with him, Novol and I should begin his language lesson."

Forcing a smile, Jack nodded to the woman. "You can take him if you want." He got up, spun to face her and gripped the top rope in both hands as he leaned over it. "But I thought maybe he could use a day off."

Keli stared up at him with lips pursed, as still as a statue. "We have a set schedule," she said at last. "In another few weeks, he will no longer need my aid. I suggest that you plan your social outings then."

Jack saluted.

Keli glowered at him.

Accepting his fate, Novol stood up and climbed over the ropes. He jumped down to the floor outside the ring and strode across the room with a smile. "That's all right, Jack," he said. "Ms. Armana has been a wonderful teacher."

"Come along," Keli said.

When they were gone, Jack was alone in the gymnasium, lost in his own thoughts. Memories of Ben still flashed through his mind. Pain and guilt as well. He hadn't lied to Anna last night – her words *did* make him feel better – but there was still a part of him that couldn't help but blame himself. It was the Jack Hunter way.

The soft sound of footsteps drew him out of his reverie, and he looked to find Rajel Aydrius marching toward the ring in gray sweatpants and a matching tank-top. The man wasn't wearing his sunglasses, which was unusual. "Agent Hunter," he said.

"Rajel..."

With a surge of Bent Gravity, Rajel jumped and sailed effortlessly over the ropes, landing inside the ring. "Are the rumours true?" he asked. "Are we sending a delegation to a peace summit on Antaur?"

Jack turned his back on the other man, pacing to the opposite side of the ring. He paused there, wiping damp hair off his brow. "Word travels fast, I see," he said. "It's true. We'll be leaving in a few days."

"You'll be going with this delegation?"

Jack felt his eyebrows climbing. "I will indeed." He spun around to face the other man. "And I'm sensing some apprehension. Is there a reason you don't want me stomping around your hometown?"

Rajel came forward with his head down, sighing softly. "I can't help but wonder if it's a good idea." Of all the answers he could have offered, that was not one Jack would have expected. Who *didn't* think peace was a good idea? "Why would the Leyrians even attend these talks?"

"Just a thought," Jack said. "But I'm guessing the sharp decline in fatalities will be a major selling point."

"At what cost?"

"There's a cost?" Jack spluttered. "You're gonna have to help me out with this one, Rajel. I'm having a hard time seeing the half-empty."

To his surprise, Rajel brought his fists up in a fighting stance and began bouncing on the balls of his feet. "All right," he said. "You want to understand what the problem is? Spar with me."

"I don't think so," Jack said. "I've had enough sparring for one day."

"I wasn't giving you an option."

"Rajel-"

That was all he could get out before the other man closed the distance between them in one quick sprint. Rajel jumped, twirled in midair, kicked out behind himself and slammed a boot into Jack's chest.

The pain drowned out Jack's awareness of almost everything else. He was barely cognizant of falling against the ropes and using them to spring back to his feet. His body was already healing, but Rajel was coming at him again.

Jack threw himself forward, somersaulting across the gymmat, moving past Rajel before the man could attack him. He came up in a crouch, then quickly stood and put a little more distance between them.

When he turned around, Rajel was striding toward him with the kind of unrelenting focus you might expect from a *ziarogat.* What the hell was going on here? "I don't want to fight you," Jack protested. "Stop!"

Rajel kicked at his belly.

Jack bent forward, slapping both hands down on the other man's leg. His opponent spun for an arcing hook-kick.

By instinct, Jack snapped upright and leaned back just in time to see the sole of a black boot pass within inches of his nose. Rajel came around to face him, drew back his arm and threw a hard punch.

Twisting his body, Jack turned his shoulder toward the other man and caught Rajel's wrist. He kicked the back of Rajel's knee.

That knocked the guy down onto his back, but Rajel was quick. He rolled aside and got up on his knees. A moment later, he was rising to stand at full height. "You will never make peace with my people."

Rajel jumped and kicked high.

Ducking low, Jack felt the man's foot pass over his head. He waited for the *thump* of Rajel landing right in front of him, then popped up and exploited the brief second that he had gained.

Jack punched the man's face with one fist then the other, a pair of blows that landed with a vicious *snap, snap.* The impact made Rajel waver, spreading his arms wide to keep his balance.

Jack spun and back-kicked, driving a foot into the other man's chest. Propelled by that powerful hit, Rajel went sprawling backwards until he slammed into the ropes, then dropped to his knees.

Wiping his mouth with the back of one hand, Jack squeezed his eyes shut. "What's the matter with you?" he panted. "You trying to challenge Anna for the title of most hot-headed Keeper in the building?"

Rajel was on his feet again, bent double and shaking his head. "I'm trying to make a point," he rasped. "My people would never believe that a man like me could challenge a man like you."

"So?"

When Rajel straightened, his face was flushed and there was sweat glistening on his brow. "So," he replied, "how can your people – people who claim to believe in equality – even consider an alliance with people like that?"

"I'm not Leyri-"

In a heartbeat, Rajel was charging across the ring like an enraged bull. Anxiety hit Jack hard. This was quickly transforming from a simple training exercise to outright conflict, and he wanted no part of it. Not that he had a choice in the matter. In seconds, Rajel was leading with a fierce left-hook.

Jack ducked, evading the hit. He threw a pair of jabs into Rajel's stomach, then rose to upper-cut his foe across the chin. That made Rajel's head snap back. The guy stumbled but quickly recovered.

He fell backward, slamming his hands down on the gym mat, bringing both feet up to strike the underside of Jack's chin. Darkness clouded Jack's vision, and he nearly lost his balance.

He saw Rajel as a blurry figure that flipped upright and came forward to press his attack. The man jumped and kicked hard, pounding Jack's chest with a big, black boot. A flash of pain made it hard to think. Jack felt the ropes flex when he hit them.

Rajel was still coming, almost as though he had forgotten that they weren't really enemies. The guy was pissed – that much was obvious – but Jack had absolutely no idea what he had done to earn this treatment.

Rajel threw a mean right cross.

Bending his knees, Jack reached up with his right hand to seize the man's wrist. He lifted Rajel's fist above his head and did a little twirl under it, coming up to trap the other man in an arm-lock. He flung Rajel into the ropes.

The guy bounced off.

Jack punched the side of his head.

Rajel fell over, landing stretched out on the gym mat, groaning from the pain and the dizziness he must have felt. "Damn it…" He rolled onto his belly. "Okay, points for that hit."

"You're gonna wanna stay down," Jack spat.

Of course, the other man ignored him. Rajel rolled onto his back, curled his legs up against his chest and sprang off the floor. He landed with a grunt and then launched into another attack.

Grinding his teeth audibly, Jack scrunched up his face and trembled. "All right," he said. "You want a fight? Fine!"

He offered a back-hand strike.

Lightning quick, Rajel turned his body. He clamped one hand onto Jack's wrist and the other onto Jack's elbow. Trapped as he was, it was easy for Rajel to twist Jack's arm and force him down onto his knees.

Pain shot through Jack's body, but he didn't try to get free. He could sense that the other man was not trying to press his advantage, and he was hoping that this would all be over soon. "Is there any doubt in your mind," Rajel began, "any doubt at all that I can do this just as well as you can?"

Red-faced, Jack looked up to squint at him. "I never said you couldn't," he growled. "If this was all just to prove-"

Snarling like a hungry wolf, Rajel shook his head. "No, *you* didn't," he agreed. "But my people did. Over and over and over, they told me that I was worth less than a sighted man. And you think it stops with a physical disability?"

He released Jack and turned away, pacing across the ring and grabbing the top rope with both hands. "They have tests of genetic purity," he went on. "Tests to measure one's proximity to the bloodlines that developed telepathic abilities."

"So I've heard."

"And you want an alliance with these people."

Closing his eyes, Jack felt a bead of sweat sliding down his forehead. "I don't know, Rajel." He got back up on his feet with some difficulty. "What do you suggest? You think we should just let the fighting continue?"

Rajel leaned forward until it looked like he might tumble over the rope. "Of course not," he answered. "But if we ally ourselves with them, we legitimize what they do. And they might demand that Leyria adopt their practices."

It was a good point. Jack hadn't given much thought to what the Antaurans might require as the price of peace. He had just assumed that it would be an agreement to stop shooting each other. "I'm sorry," he said. "You're right."

"Not entirely," Rajel mumbled. "This treaty does have to happen. It's just…"

Exhausted, Jack shuffled over to join the other man and leaned against the ropes beside him. "Maybe you should go talk to Larani," he suggested. "Ask to be a part of the delegation. I think these talks might benefit from your input."

"Maybe."

He left Rajel to think on that.

Chapter 3

The warp bubble slid to a stop in a room with floor-to-ceiling windows on either side of the Gate. Keli could see the lush green grass outside as a rippling smear of green and the sky as a blurry field of blue. She could also make out the distorted image of the man who stood behind the control console.

The bubble popped.

Keli stood before the triangular SlipGate in her sleeveless white dress, effecting an air of regality. "Dr. Siroc," she said, stepping forward. "I didn't expect you to come down to meet me."

The good doctor wore a high-collared white shirt and a pair of glasses. His pale face was marked by rosy cheeks and wrinkles across his forehead, and his white hair was getting a little thin on top. "You always come to visit him, Ms. Armana," he said. "You're the only one who does. I wanted to say thank you."

Keeping her face smooth, Keli nodded to the man. "How is he doing?" she asked. "Better than last week, I hope."

The doctor hung his head, bracing his hands upon the console and sighing. "There is still some resentment," he said. "And too much hostility. Adren has good days and bad days, I'm afraid."

She nodded.

The door behind the console led to a walkway under a gabled roof supported by thick wooden pillars. Once outside, she felt an intense muggy heat and heard the chirping of birds in the nearby trees. This rehabilitation centre was located in Leyria's tropical zone, just a few hundred kilometers south of the Equator. Plenty of sunshine and nice weather to help the inmates heal their damaged minds. After the life she had lived – years of being trapped in a cramped, little box – Keli could appreciate the logic behind this prison. And it was a prison, no matter what they called it. Treat a person like an animal and they became an animal.

The doctor walked with his clasped behind himself, his eyes focused dead ahead. "I'm afraid that he's been having a difficult week," he said. "He's asked for you several times now."

Shutting her eyes, Keli took a deep, calming breath. "You could have called me," she murmured. "I would have come."

It surprised her to realize that she meant it.

At the other end of the covered walkway, they came to a large building with a huge domed roof that acted as a massive solar panel. Doctor Siroc opened the door for her and let her step into a long hallway with doors at even intervals. A small cylindrical robot was polishing the floor.

Keli folded her arms as she walked beside the man, grimacing as she contemplated Adren's state of mind. "Have there been any specific triggers?" she asked. "Anything that I should avoid?"

"His moods are quite volatile," Dr. Siroc replied. "Some days, he seems to be quite cooperative. Others…Well, on more than one occasion, he has reminded me that I am just a maggot that he will squash as soon as he gets that collar off."

The slaver's collar was the only thing impeding Adren's telepathic ability, the only thing that made imprisoning him viable. Keli was not at all surprised to hear about such outbursts. On Antaur, telepaths were viewed as being one step below divinity. Such a life tended to foster arrogance. Even Keli herself had some of that, she was coming to realize. Oh, she had not been treated as divine. No, she had been treated like a caged beast. A very dangerous beast that could kill its jailers for a moment's inattention. And that too fostered a kind of arrogance.

The hallways in the residential sector were wider with large metal doors leading into each cell. Most of the other inmates would be in the common area at this time of day, but it did not surprise her to learn that Adren did not get along with them.

The door to his cell slid open with a whooshing sound.

Inside, she found a small living area with a bed, a wooden table, chairs and a work station. The back wall was a massive window of ballistic glass that looked out on a small yard surrounded by a towering concrete wall.

Keli found Adren outside, crouched down on one knee as he used a watering can on a garden of roses. Out here, she could see that there were actually three walls surrounding this little yard, each thirty-feet high and utterly smooth. Impossible to climb. She knew that even if a prisoner somehow managed it, force-fields would snap into place to form a ceiling, trapping them inside.

"I know it's you," Adren said without looking. "I can still sense the flavour of you, Keli. The unique sensation of your presence."

Keli planted fists on her hips and waited for a long moment before answering. She shook her head slowly. "I should certainly hope so," she said. "I would hate to think that your talents had atrophied."

"Impossible."

The man inhaled as he got to his feet, then turned to face her with a smile on his face. "I was hoping that you had come," he said. "It's been so long since I have had the pleasure of civilized company."

Dr. Siroc was waiting inside the cell. He usually liked to give Adren and Keli some small amount of privacy. But she had no doubt that he was listening. In fact, she could all but taste his apprehension. It radiated off him in waves. It wasn't that the man thought her untrustworthy – she had brushed his mind enough times to know that – but he definitely did not trust Adren.

"I heard you called for me," Keli said.

"I did."

"Why?"

Adren's grin widened. He let his head drop and then shrugged his shoulders. "I want you to touch my mind again."

Pressing her lips into a thin line, Keli steeled her nerves. "I will do nothing of the sort," she said. "I have no inclination to experience what you saw in those woods again. If you have something to tell me, you may speak it aloud."

"And so you restrict me to this primitive form of communication."

"You have forfeited the right to your talent."

It startled her when Adren laughed. He backed away from her, leaning against the wall with his arms crossed. "Gods be good, Keli," he said. "They've made you into one of them."

"One of who?"

"The normals," he said. "Those who would restrain us because they know that we are one step above them on the evolutionary ladder."

Evolution did not *have* a ladder. Natural selection didn't work that way. In the last twelve months, Keli had availed herself of the opportunity to study subjects like biology and physics. Lessons that had been denied to her in her cell. Evolution had no direction. Organisms mutated, and those mutations that proved beneficial were passed on. But the notion of an evolutionary ladder – of an *intended* finished product as the end result of natural selection – bolstered the myth that telepaths were indeed superior.

"What do you want, Adren?"

"I told you," he said. "I wish to commune with you."

She turned her back on him, pacing back to the door that led into his cell, and froze when she heard him curse. Gods above, she should just leave and let the doctors try to treat him. "Why do you wish to touch my mind?" she found herself saying.

"We are alike," he answered. "To the best of my knowledge, you are the only other telepath on this planet. I long for contact."

"I think not," Keli said. "Good day-"

"They are coming."

When she turned around, Adren was standing there with a lopsided grin that made her shudder. "They will blaze across the galaxy like a wave of fire," he whispered. "All will be consumed in the tempest."

Keli felt sweat on her forehead, but she forced herself to remain calm. "What are you talking about?" She strode toward him, her heels clicking on the cobblestone path. "Who is coming?"

"You know who," Adren said softly. "You saw them. On Abraxis." His sudden fit of giggles made her jump back. "Very soon now, Keli! Very soon!"

Anna marched through the door to Gabi's office and found the other woman sitting on a couch with a SmartGlass tablet in hand, frowning as she read through the contents of some documents. Gabi wore simple gray pants and a blue, short-sleeved shirt. Her black hair was up in a long ponytail that fell past her shoulder blades. "Hello there, Anna," she mumbled absently. "How have you been?"

A light rain hit the window behind Gabi's desk, fat droplets leaving trails of water on the glass. Outside, the afternoon was gray. Autumn had entered that dreary phase that preceded the onset of winter.

Pursing her lips, Anna looked up at the ceiling. Her eyebrows tried to climb into her hairline. "How've I been?" she mumbled. "Oh, not bad…Except I'm going to be part of a diplomatic envoy."

"So I've heard."

"And I could use your advice."

Saying as much was not easy. Anna knew damn well that she had a penchant for bluntly stating her opinions, and well, okay, maybe that wasn't the best way to go about building a relationship with a hostile foreign power. Fair enough. But the idea of shutting up and playing nice for the sake of appearances just irritated her. Seth's calming presence in the back of her mind made this a little easier. She could tell that Seth loved her, but he also seemed to find this whole thing amusing. Which was even more aggravating.

Gabi sat with one finger over her lips, seemingly lost in thought. "My advice…" she murmured. "I hadn't expected that."

Anna took a chair across from her, hunching over with her hands on her knees. She shook her head. "All I want you to do is teach me how to blend in with a bunch of snobby diplomats. Can you do that?"

When she looked up, Gabi was watching her intently. Bleakness take her, why was this so hard? "I'm afraid not," Gabi said. "This isn't the kind of skill that you can learn in a few days."

Closing her eyes, Anna took a deep breath and then nodded. "So, in other words," she began, "it's time to fall back on my father's all-purpose contingency plan. 'Keep your mouth shut, and everything will be fine.'"

"No."

"No?"

Gabi stood up with a sigh and paced across the room, standing before Anna with her hands on her hips. "Unrelenting silence does not make a good impression," she said. "But I think you're stressing out over nothing."

With two fingers, she tilted Anna's face up until they gazed into one another's eyes. Was this the part where they kissed? It seemed like kissage would be a natural outgrowth of this situation. Of course, she felt a sharp pang of guilt for wanting to since that would be cheating on Jack. "Sometimes," Gabi said, "the best way to earn another person's respect is to speak your mind without reservation. You underestimate how many people respect you for doing exactly that."

"I'm not so sure about that," Anna muttered. The long list of outbursts that she later regretted came rushing into her mind like a tidal wave. Telling off Larani when the other woman asked her to face the possibility that Jack might be dead. Or lashing out at Jack when she was angry with herself. Punching Keli after the other woman killed one of the Antauran telepaths. Okay: that one was justified.

But the fact remained that Leana Delnara Lenai had a talent for pissing people off, and they seldom sang her praises afterward. "Sorry," she added at last. "I didn't mean to disturb you."

Gabi stepped past her, and she saw the other woman's misty silhouette in her mind, standing before a screen of SmartGlass on the wall. "Oh, it's fine," Gabi said. "I was just working on something for Larani."

"And what's that?"

"Come look at this."

Anna stood up and turned around to face the screen with her arms folded. "Okay," she said. "You've got me intrigued. Why exactly are you calling up data on social media accounts?"

The screen displayed a bar graph that tracked the number of accounts that had been banned from TellTale, one of Leyria's largest social media platforms, since the middle of last year. From left to right, the bars were growing increasingly larger.

"The platform uses algorithms that have been designed to target hate speech," Gabi explained. "Vitriol directed against immigrants or Non-Leyrians. Not so long ago, people knew better than to say such things aloud. TellTale uses a three-strike system. Users are given a written warning after their first offense. A second offense results in a three-month suspension, and after that, their accounts are permanently deactivated."

"And there have been more and more repeat offenders..."

"Yes."

Anna frowned as she studied the display, then stepped forward. "Which means that hate speech is becoming normalized," she whispered. "Dusep?"

Gabi leaned her shoulder against the wall next to the screen, her face twisting with barely restrained anger. "Almost certainly," she replied. "Politicians with fascist leanings have a tendency to bring out the worst in people."

"So, what are we going to do about it?"

"That, I do not know."

Anna didn't know either. All her life, she had taken pride in the fact that her world had outgrown skin-colour prejudice or gender-based discrimination. Leyria was a bastion of equality and tolerance: that was what every child was taught. She was beginning to see that she had been misinformed.

What was it that Reverend Carlea used to say? Evil is most powerful when you stop believing in it. Well, she believed it now. She definitely believed it now.

Melissa knocked on the door with her fist and, of course, received no answer. She waited several minutes before calling out, "Aiden! It's me! I know you're in there!"

She stood in the hallway outside his apartment in white pants and a tight black t-shirt, her long hair pulled up with a clip. Her face was tight with anxiety as she raised her fist to knock again.

Before she could, the door swung inward, and Aiden poked his nose through the crack. He looked strung out, with dark circles under his eyes. "What do you want?" he said. "Today's not a good day."

Backing away from the door with arms crossed, Melissa glowered for all she was worth. "What do I want?" she demanded. "Is that any way to talk to your girlfriend?"

He shut the door.

"Fine!" Melissa bellowed. "Then I guess we're done!"

Her heart was pounding; her chest felt like it was being squeezed by a giant's fist. How *dare* he treat her this way? She had dealt with her fair share of entitled dudes, but this was a whole new level.

Just before she stormed off, the door opened again, and Aiden stepped out into the hallway. Oh boy, was he ever strung out! He was barefoot, dressed in a pair of old shorts and an oversized t-shirt that looked like it hadn't seen the inside of a washing machine in over a month. "I'm sorry."

Melissa shut her eyes, a single tear gliding over her cheek. She sniffled. "I'm sorry too," she said. "I don't know how to help you."

Of all things, he stepped forward and took her in his arms, holding her close. She wasn't sure how she felt about that. There was anger and pain and… A part of her wanted to break up with him, and another part of her wanted to cry her eyes out at the thought of losing him. And yet another part wanted to hold him until everything was better.

Aiden kissed her forehead, then pulled back and breathed in slowly as if savouring the scent of her perfume. "I feel like I don't deserve you," he whispered. "After I failed…"

"That's stupid!" Melissa growled, making no effort to lower her voice. "You think I care about that? My father isn't a Justice Keeper, but I respect him more than anyone else in my life, including Anna. Including Larani."

It surprised her to realize that she meant it. She and Harry had butted heads many, many times over the last few years, but even though she wasn't a little girl anymore, he was still her hero.

Aiden went back into the apartment.

Melissa followed him in and was pleased to see that his kitchen was actually quite neat and tidy. What she could see of the living room from here indicated much the same. She had half expected the place to be a pigsty, but it seemed Aiden could take care of his home better than he could take care of himself.

"I think," she said, "that you should consider seeing a therapist."

Aiden froze in mid-step, then rounded on her with such intensity she almost jumped back. His face wasn't angry, however; it was pale with shock and fright. "You really think it's come to that?"

"Aiden, you're not handling this well." That was an understatement. She didn't want to say this out loud, but she was coming to see why the Nassai had rejected him. "You do not have to be a Justice Keeper to have a meaningful life."

"So you say."

"And is there some reason you don't believe me?"

He hopped up onto the kitchen counter with both hands gripping the edge, his eyes downcast as he struggled to find the word. "It was all I wanted all my life," he said. "And now it will never happen."

Melissa seated herself in one of the chairs at his small table, folding her hands in her lap and watching him for a very long moment. "Yes, I know," she replied softly. "But maybe we should ask *why* you wanted it so badly."

"I wanted to be a hero."

"And maybe that's the problem."

"What do you mean?"

She took a moment to compose herself before answering. This would require a certain amount of delicacy. "Aiden…" she began. "There is nothing wrong with wanting to make a difference in other people's lives, but if your primary motivation is status and recognition, well-"

"No!"

His feet thudded on the floor when he jumped off the counter, and Melissa almost flinched despite the fact that she was several times stronger than him. She didn't like that Aiden was starting to display a temper. Had that always been there? A few months ago, he had seemed as gentle as a lamb.

"All right," she said. "Then why is it so important for you to be a Justice Keeper?"

His face reddened, and he averted his gaze. "I told you," he said. "I wanted to be a hero. It doesn't matter now because I will never be one."

"You don't have to be a-"

"Yes, yes, yes, I've heard it all before." He waved a dismissive hand at her before turning his back and pacing to the other side of the kitchen. He braced one hand against the pantry door. "I don't have to be a Keeper to be a hero."

Cautiously, Melissa stood up and chose her words with the utmost care. "I can't do this anymore." Getting that first bit out had seemed impossible, but now that it *was* out, the rest followed like water through a cracked dam. She could feel Ilia's sympathy. Thank heaven for that. "I don't want to abandon you when you need me the most, but you push me away. You take your frustrations out on me. Did you ever really *feel* anything for me, Aiden? Or was I just…convenient?"

He stiffened more and more with every syllable, but he refused to turn around and look at her. "Of course I felt something." His voice was husky, strained. "What kind of question is that?"

"The kind of question you ask when someone treats you like garbage."

"I-"

With a shuddering breath, Melissa turned her face away from him. Tears welled up and threatened to spill freely if she didn't maintain tight control of her emotions. "Speak to a therapist, Aiden," she said. "Ask your family for support. But this relationship does not work. And I'm ending it."

She was out the door before he could protest.

Chapter 4

When Anna made it to the address Jack had given her, she found a cafe with nearly two dozen round tables spread out in front of a stage with a red curtain. As soon as she walked through the door, she saw at least half a dozen people she didn't recognize. So, Jack was going to perform? Perform what, exactly?

Clasping hands together behind her back, Anna strode into the room with her face turned up to the ceiling. "Well, this should be interesting." It irked her that Jack hadn't told her his plan, but she chose a small table and waited patiently.

A few minutes later, Melissa came plodding into the room with her head down, her eyes fixed on the floor. Bleakness, the poor girl was obviously distraught. She didn't even see Anna as she passed.

"Melissa."

The young woman froze in place, then turned around, scrubbing the back of her hand across her brow. "Sorry," she muttered. "It's been a long day."

Melissa seated herself next to Anna, hunched over with her arms folded across her belly. She seemed to deflate as she exhaled. Well, that pretty much confirmed it. It wasn't so long ago that Anna was in her late teens, and there was only one thing that evoked that kind of response.

"What did he do?" Anna asked.

"We broke up."

Wrapping her arm around the girl's shoulders, Anna pulled Melissa close and let her sob. It came out as a little squeak, barely audible to anyone more than five feet away, but painful nonetheless.

"Oh, sweetie," Anna whispered. "I'm so sorry. Come by when...whatever this is...is finished, and we'll talk. Okay?"

"Yeah."

She let Melissa go, and the young woman composed herself with remarkable speed, using a napkin to dab away her tears and putting on the kind of brave face that every girl learned the first time someone broke her heart.

Anna sank into her chair with arms folded, cocking her head to one side as she watched the stage. "Now," she said. "What do you think this is all about?"

"Jack didn't tell you?"

Pressing her lips together, Anna felt creases lining her brow. She shook her head. "No, he did not." It bugged her to realize just how much she hated not knowing. Damn it! She had always been so chill with her other boyfriends. "I think he deserves a swift kick in the butt. How 'bout you?"

Melissa's smile was so bright and beautiful, you would never suspect that she had been crying just a few moments earlier. "I don't know," she said. "Maybe it's a surprise."

"Like what?"

"Maybe he'll serenade you."

"Then I'd *definitely* have to kick his ass."

They were interrupted by the arrival of Larani, who marched up to their table with that stern expression that had become her resting face. She took a seat without invitation. Not that she needed one, but it was clear her mind was elsewhere. This was just business to her, and she wanted it over with.

Harry showed up right on her heels, looking positively flustered for reasons Anna couldn't even begin to fathom. He gave them all a curt nod of acknowledgment, pausing to let his gaze linger on his daughter.

Melissa was pretty calm now; for all Anna could tell, there was no sign that she had been upset, but Harry could tell. Somehow.

Harry opened his mouth to speak, but before he could get one word out, the curtain rose to reveal a woman in a sleeveless black dress on the stage. She was gorgeous with tanned skin and long brown hair that framed a round face. "All right," she said into the microphone. "Let's get this evening started. My name is Deadra, but you can call me Dee. I'll be your host tonight. Our first act-"

There was plenty of activity backstage – a man reviewed his material on the small screen on his multi-tool; a woman paced back and forth, whispering to herself, no doubt rehearsing her act – but they all did it quietly.

Leaning against the wall with his arms crossed, Jack frowned as he watched them. "Not long now," he whispered to himself. Normally, this would be the part of the evening where he chastised himself for thinking that he could pull off something so gutsy, but he resisted that inclination.

He had thrown on a simple pair of dark jeans and a black, collared t-shirt, and his hair was in its usual state of disarray, bangs crisscrossing over his forehead. Classic Jack Hunter. Perfect for what he had planned.

"All right," Dee said into the mic. "Our next act comes all the way from Earth. In fact, he was the first Earther to join the Justice Keepers."

Several people clapped for that.

Jack winced.

He was proud of the work he did as a Keeper, but sometimes he thought that being the first Earther to join that prestigious club earned him a bit too much praise. He was no better than any other Keeper. Summer grew annoyed with his self-deprecation. Well, let her. Sometimes, it helped.

Dee flung her hand out toward him and favoured him with a smile that could light up a windowless holding cell in the basement of the Pentagon. "I give you Jack Hunter!"

He marched across the stage to more applause.

The glare of the spotlight hit Jack hard as he took the microphone and looked out on a sea of round tables with candles burning in glass jars. Maybe he should have been nervous – weren't people nervous when they did stuff like this? – but he actually felt kind of energized. Anna was there at a table in the second row, waving to him. Harry, Melissa and Larani as well. Nothing like performing in front of your boss for that added boost of confidence.

"Thank you," Jack said, pacing a line in front of them. "Thank you. As some of you know, I'm from Earth." Someone in the back shouted, "Woo!"

Biting his lip as he ran his gaze over the lot of them, Jack let his eyebrows climb. "Ah," he said. "I see some of you have visited."

Soft laughter.

Well, it was a start.

"No, it's good," Jack went on. "I've been here about eight months. I knew it was gonna be a bit of a transition. I was like, 'Okay, Jack, it's a different culture. You're gonna have to make some adjustments.' Wasn't quite prepared for some of the conversations. You wanna know the question I get asked most?"

He waited just long enough to let them wonder.

Planting one fist on his hip, Jack squinted at him and bobbed his head as he spoke. " 'What's with that?' " he asked in a high, shrill voice. "Like suddenly I'm an expert on all the weird, fucked up shit seven billion humans spent ten thousand years perfecting."

More laughter.

"No, it's true. 'Really? You're from Earth? And your coffee is served in disposable cups that later end up in your oceans? *Fascinating.*' Sometimes, there's no preamble. They find out I'm from Earth, and out comes some weird little knickknack they fabricated for kitsch value. I had one guy shove a fidget spinner in my face. 'EXPLAIN!!!'"

He faced them with a gaping mouth, shaking his head. "I don't fuckin' know!" he shouted. "Dude, I'm still deprogramming myself from twenty-three years of news media designed to keep me in a constant state of anxiety. Could you give me five minutes to get over the trauma? Thanks."

Jack raised one finger on his free hand and waited for silence. "You guys wanna understand Earth?" Several people cheered in response. "You wanna understand Earth? Let me make it simple for you: we're a planet full of evil geniuses."

That earned him a round of applause.

"It's true!" he said. "It's true! When it comes to natural selection, cunning beats brute force every time. You guys have particle beams and warp drives and energy shields. We have syndicated reruns of Duck Dynasty five days a week." Several people chuckled, some looked confused. "Yeah, yeah, don't pretend you don't know what I'm talking about. When you met us five years ago, you gobbled up every last piece of our media – and…my condolences – but don't tell me you haven't heard of Phil Robertson. You see, the goal is to make the planet look as unappealing as possible. That way you fuckers won't invade!"

He was winning them over; he could tell. Time to wrap this up and put a bow on it. In that brief second when he waited for the laughter to die down, he caught sight of Anna smiling at him, and it warmed his heart. Any last trace of self-doubt vanished.

"We have a television channel," Jack said, "that over the course of its four-decade run, has featured the following programming." He ticked off his fingers one by one. "A show about toddlers being forced to compete in misogynistic beauty contests while their mothers get into cat-fights. A show about the dysfunctional family of a wealthy woman who owes her fortune to her father's tenure as a crime boss. And a show about science-denying blowhards with poor hygiene who built an empire on whistles that emit the perfect duck call. And do you know what they call this channel? Do you know what they call this channel?" He waited five seconds. "They call it the Learning Channel."

One guy actually folded up in his seat and slapped his leg as he wheezed. His wife was shaking as she smiled into her glass of wine. Yup, he had done it. Hard as it was to believe, Jack actually felt proud of himself.

"And then you got people like Dusep," Jack added.

Instantly everyone went silent.

Jack paced across the stage with the mic in one hand, grinning as he let out a peal of bitter laughter. "You know, some people say I should be offended," he went on. "Guy's always talking about how much he hates foreigners, how much he can't stand anyone who wasn't born on this planet. Really, I take it as a compliment."

He paused for just a few seconds to let them stew in their confusion. "Dusep," he said at last, "is trying to turn *you* into *us*."

The applause he got from that was like the pattering of a heavy rainfall on the roof. Some people actually shouted, "Woo!" and one older woman stood up and clapped for all she was worth.

Of course, the joke had pissed off a few of them. There was one guy in the back who just kept sneering and shaking his head. Jack knew the type. Guys like him always thought comedy was great fun so long as they could punch down at someone else. "No," Jack said over them. "No, no, please! Go right ahead! Be more like us! Just between you and me, Earth's a little tired of being the butt of every joke. It'll be nice to let somebody else take that honour."

He let them chew on that.

When the laughter died down, Jack shook his head with a rueful chuckle. "That's it for me, folks. Thanks so much for having me. And remember." He thrust one fist into the air. "Bash the fash!"

People were cheering and hooting and hollering as he walked off stage.

Twenty minutes later, during the intermission, Jack emerged from backstage to find all of his friends still sitting at their little table. They all stood up when they saw him and started clapping. Even Larani was smiling.

Anna looked positively radiant, like she was seeing him for the very first time. She rushed over, stood up on her toes and kissed his cheek. "You were incredible."

Blushing hard, Jack closed his eyes and chuckled. "It wasn't that good," he said. "I imagine that a professional comic would find all kinds of little errors. That sort of thing that any amateur would-"

Grabbing a fistful of his shirt, Anna yanked him down until he was practically bent over. Then she kissed him on the mouth. A fierce kiss. A passionate kiss that… Okay, they were pretty much making out in the middle of this little comedy club. Jack heard people clapping and cheering him on, which only intensified his chagrin.

When Anna finally pulled away, she blinked once and then grinned. "Learn to take a compliment, sweetie," she said, patting his cheek.

She stepped aside to let Harry say his piece, but the other man just stood with his hands in his coat pockets and nodded once. Melissa came next, throwing her arms around Jack, patting his back. "That was great."

"Thank you."

Finally, there was Larani.

She waited by the table with the formal posture that she often adopted whenever she had to speak in front of politicians, but she wore a sly little smile. "Well done, Agent Hunter," she said. "A fitting way to speak the truth."

"Thank you, ma'am. I-"

"Jack!"

He whirled around to find Dee striding toward him with a tablet in one hand. Her face lit up at whatever she saw on the screen. "We livestreamed your act," she said. "And take a look at this."

She gave Jack the tablet, and when he checked the video's stats, he nearly gasped. His set had ended less than half an hour ago, but in that time he had gained more than ten thousand views. "But..." he stammered. "I'm just some nobody they've never heard of."

He passed the tablet to Anna.

Dee looked up at him with a raised eyebrow that called him an idiot. "*You* are the first Justice Keeper from Earth," she replied. "And you had something important to say. Seems people are interested in that."

Jack fell into an empty chair, doubling up with his hands on his knees. "I don't get it," he said, shaking his head. "No one wants to hear what I have to say; that's why I don't bother with social media."

Behind him, Larani stood with her arms folded, and though her image in his mind's eye was blurry, Jack could tell that she was glowering at the back of his head. "I believe you will have to revise that inclination, Agent Hunter."

He twisted in his seat.

Larani still wore that stern expression, but after a moment, her mouth cracked into a smile, and Jack was certain that she was taking some perverse pleasure in seeing him so flustered. "I told you to find a way to counter the spread of fascism," she said. "It seems you have a platform now. Use it wisely,"

Summer thought this whole thing was hilarious.

Sometime later, as the evening was drawing to a close, Anna sat with Jack's arm around her shoulders, her head resting comfortably on his chest. She sighed. "Why didn't you tell me?" she asked. "About the show."

There was a glint in Jack's eye as he smiled at her. "Well, in case I sucked," he said. "I didn't want to build up your expectations only to let you down."

"You're silly."

"No, I'm not."

Anna sat up, and strands of hair fell over her face. She brushed them away with one hand. "I suppose now is as good a time as any to tell you," she mumbled. "But you're not gonna like it."

His smile never wavered, almost as if he trusted her completely. It broke her heart because she was going to have to tell him that she was not worthy of it. "What's wrong?" he asked in a gentle voice.

"It's about Gabi," Anna began. "This afternoon, in her office... she was giving me some advice, and there was a moment when we looked into each other's eyes. For just a second, I wanted to kiss her! I didn't do it! I swear! But I wanted to..."

"Oh, is that all?"

Of all the reactions he could have given, that was not one she would have expected. Was he not mad or threatened? Not even a little bit? Did that mean that she didn't mean as much to him as he did to her? Seth kept trying to calm her down, but she was nervous. All those thoughts kept tumbling through her head, but the only word that Anna could force through her lips was, "Huh?"

Taking her by the shoulders, Jack pulled her close and kissed her forehead. "Anna, I'm not gonna blame you for a physiological reaction," he said. "And I'm glad you talked to me first, but next time, just kiss her."

Blinking in confusion, Anna pulled away from him. "What?" she stammered. "You wouldn't be jealous…or upset?"

A blush put some pink in his cheeks, and he lowered his eyes to stare into his lap. "I'm crazy about you," he murmured. "But I've been meaning to tell you for a while now, if you find yourself wanting to have sex with someone – man or woman – go for it."

"You're saying you want me to sleep with other people."

Gently, Jack took her hands in his and gave them a squeeze. "I'm saying that you're a smart, empowered woman who makes no apologies for going after what she wants, and that turns me on *so* much."

This was not going as Anna had expected. It wasn't that she wanted Jack to be mad at her, but she would never in a million years have thought that he would tell her to just throw caution to the wind and make out with his ex-girlfriend. Did that mean *he* wanted to sleep with other people? Just picturing it was like a knife in the chest.

Anna sat there with a gaping mouth, then shook her head slowly. "I'm…I'm not sure what to make of all this." Her voice was a breathy whisper. "Jack, when I think about you having sex with other women, it tears me up inside."

"Well, then I won't ever do it."

"But wouldn't that be unfair?"

"Not necessarily," Jack murmured. "It's not something that I want for myself. Other women just don't excite me the way you do." He ran his fingers through her hair, and by instinct, Anna leaned into his touch. "I won't lie. I think I'd be pretty insecure if you were hooking up with someone new every other night. But once in a blue moon? Yeah, I'm all right with that."

"Okay, but…Me and Gabi?"

Jack narrowed his eyes as he thought about it and then nodded as if the implications were only just becoming clear to him.

"Yeah, it might be a little weird given that she's my ex," he said. "But hey! We could compare notes!"

Anna punched his shoulder.

Leaning in close, Jack touched his nose to hers. He smoothed a lock of hair off her cheek, tucking it behind her ear. "Anna…" The way he said her name with such reverence – like it was something precious to be cherished – made her heart flutter. "If you want to be monogamous, I'd be perfectly happy with that too."

Anna let herself fall into his arms, burying her nose in the side of his neck. "I love you," she whispered as he lightly ran his hand over her back. "And I think I would like us to be monogamous. For now, at least."

"Okay." He squeezed her tight. "I love you too."

This little bar in the slums of Rekanath was dimly lit and very quiet. The bartender, an older fellow with a big belly and thinning gray hair, stood silently behind the counter and watched his three customers with a sour expression. He never moved unless someone ordered a drink.

Corovin suspected that there were other things that might spur him to action. A guy like that usually had a gun under the counter. But he had no desire to test that theory. No, it was best to just sit quietly.

It was a dreary little place with booths along one wall, lit only by dim lamps that hung from the ceiling. A young man with a dark complexion and stubble on his jawline sat at one of the many tables spread out across the dusty floor, staring hopelessly into his drink. Corovin pondered his story. What had brought him to a pit like this? Probably lost his job with little chance of finding another any time soon.

Sitting at a booth with a drink in one hand, Corovin watched the way light refracted through the whiskey in his glass. Sometimes, that was his way of forgetting.

A tall and lean man with a pale face marked by sharp cheek-bones, Corovin wore his red hair cut short and his neatly-trimmed beard cut even shorter. He grunted as he tilted the glass this way and that. If his contact didn't arrive soon, boredom would drive him to leave this shit-hole of a bar.

As if his thoughts had summoned her, a short woman in a brown hood approached his booth and sat down across from him without invitation. "Corovin Dagmath," she said in a breathy whisper. It wasn't a question. She knew exactly who he was.

"And who are you?"

As if he needed to ask. There was only one person who demanded that he meet her in these backwater taverns. It had been at least two years since he had accepted a contract from this woman, but he couldn't say he wasn't pleased that she had called again.

She removed her hood to reveal a stern but pretty face framed by a bob of brown hair. Telixa Ethran gave him a stare that probably sent her officers scurrying. However, it had never done much to motivate him.

A grin split Corovin's face, and he chuckled softly before taking a swig of his drink. "Admiral," he said. "To what do I owe the pleasure?"

She leaned over the table, her lips twitching in a sneer of contempt. "I have work for you." Once again, she whispered. As if anyone in this room cared about her secrets.

"What kind of work?"

"Not here!"

Corovin felt his eyebrows shoot up. "You were the one who insisted that we meet here." He slouched down, stretching his legs further under the table. "And now you want to go elsewhere to discuss our business."

Telixa never moved a muscle, but her eyes flicked their corners so she could watch the bartender without giving the appearance of doing so. "This mission will require the utmost secrecy," she muttered. "I could hardly meet you in my office."

"So, you come to Rekanath," Corovin said, making no effort whatsoever to lower his voice. "I thought your kind never came down from those floating islands."

She stood up and gave him one last withering glare before turning to go. "I can see that you're not interested in my business."

"Sit down, Admiral," Corovin said softly. "If we must play your little game, then by all means, let's play."

She cast a glance toward the solitary man who never raised his eyes from his mug of beer. Then she resumed her seat across from him. "I need you to do a job," she said. "The only job you're good for."

Corovin stretched out with fingers laced over the back of his head, smiling lazily. At last, they were getting somewhere. "Who do you want dead?" he asked. "I do hope it will be a challenge this time."

"Oh, I think so," Telixa murmured. "You'll be going to the other side of the galaxy. To a world called Antaur."

"Really?" Corovin purred. "I must say my interest is piqued."

"Come with me then," Telixa whispered. "And we will discuss the details."

Chapter 5

The ground was still wet, but thankfully, the ever-present ceiling of clouds was no longer unleashing a cold, stinging rain. Puddles dotted a concrete path that ran through a field of brown grass and snaked its way between the university's science and engineering buildings.

Melissa walked along that path with her hands in the pockets of her thick, brown coat, her eyes fixed on the ground under her feet. With heavy, lethargic steps, she passed beneath the skywalk that connected the two buildings.

She rounded a corner and followed a path that ran in front of the science building, toward the student center. It would be a quick walk, but she was glad for that. She was so tired. She wasn't sleeping well. Two nights ago, after the comedy show, she had stayed up way past her bedtime, talking to Anna. And then, last night, she had done it again. She just did not want to be alone, and thankfully, Anna was willing to accommodate her.

Unfortunately, she wouldn't be able to rely on the other woman for support for at least a few weeks. The delegation was leaving for Antaur later this afternoon; Jack and Anna would be gone, and for some reason, Harry was going as well. And taking Claire! Claire got to go gallivanting across the galaxy, while Melissa was stuck in the house all alone. And she really didn't want to be alone.

Ending her relationship with Aiden, even though she knew it was the right thing to do, still hurt. It was as if a little lump of sadness had taken up residence in her chest, right where her heart should be. Ilia was sympathetic; she could feel the Nassai's love and compassion, and she took a surprising amount of comfort in that.

She only had one more exam left to write and then a term-paper to turn in, and then she would…Well, if all went according to plan, she would advance to field training and become a Justice Keeper within the next six months.

Not long ago, she would have expected Aiden to make that journey with her. But fate, it seemed, had other plans. Anna had agreed that she had made the right decision in ending the relationship; that didn't make it any easier.

The student centre was a white-bricked building with stone steps that led up to the side entrance and two wheelchair ramps slanting down on either side. She seldom went in through the main entrance anymore. Not since she and Jack had fought Isara right in front of it.

Melissa shivered when she remembered that day. The touch of Brinton's blades on her skin, the pride she had felt in subduing him. It was the first time that she had faced an enhanced opponent, after all. But that pride had turned into humiliation when Isara tossed her around like a rag-doll not five minutes later.

When she neared the foot of the stairs, she saw about half a dozen students standing on the top step. Normally, that wouldn't even evoke a second thought from her, but these kids were all dressed alike, all in dark pants, sweaters and high-collared shirts.

One of them, a young woman who stood at the centre of the group, was short with a notably pale complexion and short blue hair. When she recognized Melissa, her face split in a cruel grin. "Getting a snack, are we?"

"I don't see how that's any of your business," Melissa said. "Now, let me pass."

She started up the stairs.

None of those kids moved; in fact, they seemed to have formed a line to block her passage. When Melissa scanned the group of them, she felt uneasy. They were a perfect cross-section of Leyrian society – both men and women, some light, some dark – but the clean-cut formal attire stood out to her. Melissa remembered what she had learned about fascist movements on Earth, and that was one of the major signifiers.

With a sigh, Melissa rested one hand on the railing, her head hanging in frustration. "I see you're going to make an issue of this," she muttered. "Look, you can't block other students from entering the-"

"You're a disgrace to the Justice Keepers."

The blue-haired woman was sneering at her…No, not just sneering; her teeth were bared almost to the point of a snarl. "That's right, we know you are," she said. "And your kind should never have been allowed to bond a symbiont."

"My kind?"

"Terrans."

Shutting her eyes, Melissa turned her face up to the cloudy sky. It took a moment to calm herself, but she did it. "It's ironic," she said. "A girl that no Nassai would ever Bond lecturing me on who should or shouldn't be a Justice Keeper. Let me pass."

Ms. Blue-Hair folded her arms and stared Melissa down for a few seconds. Finally, she shook her head. "You're the Justice Keeper," she said. "Make me."

Which, of course, would be exactly what the woman wanted. No doubt one or more of these kids was recording this exchange on a multi-tool. Abusing her powers on camera would be exactly the kind of proof these kids needed to show that Earthers did not belong among the Justice Keepers.

Melissa simply turned around and walked away, ignoring the muffled laughter she heard just behind her. Looks like she would be going through the main entrance after all. It made her blood boil. All her life, she had dealt with casual racism from teachers, from other kids, from goddamn cops who thought she and her friends might have stolen something from a corner store simply because they were hanging out in front of it. She was the only non-white girl in that group, but that didn't make a difference. They never had a problem when Melissa wasn't there.

Leyria was supposed to be a reprieve from all that, and now, here she was, dealing with the same old crap, only now it was hatred of Earthers. It made her want to tear apart sheet metal with her teeth.

As she went around to the front side of the building, she found a field of concrete with two rows of black lampposts and some benches. There was no sign of the damage that Isara had caused – bots cleared that up within a week of the incident – but there were more kids blocking the entrance. Kids who wore their sweaters and high-collared shirts almost like a uniform. As if they were openly declaring their political views. That made her very uneasy.

A grimace contorted her features as she shook her head. "Brilliant. Just brilliant." She strode forward at a brisk pace. "Multitool active! Record audio and video and save to my public folder."

The tool chirped in response.

Melissa approached the group with her head held high, projecting an outward calm that would make her father proud. "Excuse me, please," she said as if she did not know that they were up to.

The group parted to reveal a skinny young man with olive skin and thick, brown hair standing right in front of the door. Clearly the ringleader. He smiled menacingly and said, "No. This building is for Leyrian students only."

"Is that so?"

"Yeah. It is."

"Well, it looks like you got me," Melissa replied. "Only, I wonder if you've read the university's codes of conduct. Discrimination against other students for any reason – including planet of origin – is punishable by expulsion."

The ringleader's smile vanished in a heartbeat, and he stood there with his mouth hanging open. He recovered quickly, stepping forward. "You think you're clever, huh?" he hissed. "Well, go ahead and report us. You've got no proof."

Melissa lifted her left fist so that her knuckles were just half an inch away from his nose, giving him a good view of the multi-tool on her wrist. "Smile for the camera," she said. "This is your closeup."

The man tried to seize her arm.

"I wouldn't!" she cautioned. "Assaulting an officer of the law is grounds for a lot more than expulsion."

The colour drained out of his face as he backed away from her. "Let her through," he said at last. "Come on. Let's get out of here."

They dispersed fairly quickly.

With a sigh, Melissa went through the door and made her way to the cafeteria. She had every intention of forwarding the video to the dean anyway. The man ought to know what was going on on his campus. But one thing was clear to her now. These fashy kids were organized, and that suggested they weren't acting alone. An underground fascist movement in the planet's Capitol city was exactly the sort of thing that the Keepers should be investigating.

The window in the starboard side of this star-ship bound for Antaur looked out on an endless, empty void. Nothing but blackness as far as the eye could see. Oh, there were stars out there, but at FTL speeds, you would never see them.

In tan pants, a white shirt and a long brown coat, Harry stood with his hands in his pockets, gazing out upon the empty night. He sighed softly. So, here he was, roped into yet another adventure.

Claire ran up to join him.

Despite the ship's comfortable climate, she wore green jeans and a windbreaker as she braced her hands on the window-frame and leaned forward, nearly touching her nose to the pane. "This is so cool!"

Harry closed his eyes, breathing slowly through his nose. "You didn't think so when you were on the ship that brought us to Leyria."

Claire spun around and leaned against the slanted window-frame, staring sullenly across the narrow hallway. "That was because I was sad about having to leave my home and my friends."

"I'm sorry about that."

"It's all right."

Harry drew her in close with an arm around her shoulders, and they started up the corridor together. "Listen," he said. "I wasn't going to leave you at home, not with your sister running around at all hours. But this could be a dangerous mission for me."

The look on Claire's face became deadly serious. Kids understood a lot more than you gave them credit for. And she wasn't really a kid anymore. What exactly did you call an eleven-year-old? "What do you want me to do?"

"Well, I'm told the Antaurans have given us a suite at one of their finest hotels," he said. "You'll be spending a lot of time there. I'm sorry. I don't think there will be all that many kids about."

Claire frowned as she thought about that, then nodded slowly. "Well, maybe I could go exploring."

"I don't think I want you wandering around a city where you don't know the language." Harry dropped to one knee so that he could look his daughter in the eye. "And between you and me, I'm still not sure we can trust the Antaurans. Do *not* repeat that."

"Do you really think it will be dangerous?"

"It could be," Harry admitted. "On the other hand, you'll be surrounded by security teams from three different planets, in a building that was specifically designed to protect heads of state. It's hard to imagine a safer place than that. And, if this goes well, you'll be witnessing history in the making."

Claire threw her arms around his neck and kissed him on the cheek. "Well, I guess I'm not scared then," she whispered.

Harry stood, grunting at the slight ache in his back. Damn it, he really was getting too old for this. "Why don't you head back to our quarters?" he said. "I'll join you in an hour, and we can check out the ship's Kids Zones."

She scampered off down the hallway.

For a little while, Harry just wandered, getting the lay of the land, so to speak. The ship had been at warp for barely two hours, and it was a five-day journey to Antaur. He was going to be spending a lot of time on this ship; he wanted to know where everything was. It made him feel safer.

This was the first moment he had gotten to himself since boarding. As soon as the Leyrian delegation was on board, they were invited to a luncheon in which dignitaries from Earth gave long, ponderous speeches about what a momentous occasion this was. Their Leyrian counterparts did the exact same thing not five minutes later. Harry noted that Anna's father was actually quite the orator. But the whole thing had been agonizingly boring. It got so bad that, at one point, he was actually wishing for Jack to crack some ill-timed joke.

The ship looked pretty uniform in most places: hallways with white bulkheads and windows along those corridors that passed near the outer walls. There was a huge garden in the middle with fields of lush grass and coniferous trees that stretched toward a domed roof. He only took a brief glance in there.

On the lower decks, there was a nightclub, but he wouldn't be caught dead in there. There was also a pool and something like an arcade where kids could play games. This was a passenger ship, designed for comfort. Ordinarily, he might have been wary about taking a ship like this into the territory of a potential enemy, but they had an escort of twelve Leyrian Phoenix-Class cruisers.

On one of the upper decks, he found a wide, open doorway that led to a restaurant, a restaurant set upon a large balcony that hugged the wall of the domed garden. Serving bots maneuvered carefully between large, round tables with white, linen tablecloths and a vase of fresh flowers in the middle.

Harry approached the railing, folding his arms as he leaned over it and taking in the sight of the massive garden. "I'll say this for you Leyrians," he muttered. "You know how to travel in style."

Cobblestone walkways lined the perimeter of the grassy field, and there were several crisscrossing through the middle of it, with bubbling fountains wherever two or more paths intersected. Some of those walkways ran through beds of flowers – roses and lilies and some plants that Harry was sure had never been cultivated on Earth – or past large, towering trees.

"Harry Carlson!"

He knew that voice.

With slow, deliberate movements, Harry stood up straight and then shut his eyes as he barked a laugh. "Well, I'll be damned," he said, turning around. "I never thought that I would run into *you* of all people on this ship."

Aamani Patel sat at one of the round tables in a black pantsuit, and as usual, her long, dark hair was pulled up in a clip. "It's good to see you as well," she said. "I'd heard that you moved to Leyria."

Grinning happily, Harry shook his head. "Director Aamani Patel," he said, striding toward her and offering his hand. "How are you?"

Her handshake was just as firm as he remembered, but it surprised him when she returned his smile with one of her own. "Actually, it's Ambassador Aamani Patel now," she said. "I'm part of the Earth delegation."

"Get out of here!"

"It's true."

Harry sat down across from her, studying her for a moment and then nodding once in approval. "It suits you," he said at last. "You know that Anna and Jack are here, right?"

"Yes, I saw them at the luncheon," Aamani replied. "I meant to find them and say hello, but there was so much commotion when the damn thing ended. Everyone wanting to get back to their quarters."

"Can you blame them?"

Bracing her hands on the table's surface, Aamani leaned forward as if she expected him to whisper some dirty, little secret. "Tell me honestly," she said. "How do you like it on Leyria?"

"Can't complain."

"Are the rumors true?"

"Rumors?"

They were interrupted by the arrival of a serving bot. Well, more of a motorized drink cart that rolled up to their table and used a metal arm to grab the stem of a wine glass and set it down in front of Aamani. A moment later, it was heading to the next table on its list.

Aamani took the glass and lifted it, inhaling the aroma before she took a sip. "We have reports of a growing fascist sentiment," she said. "And that one of the candidates for Prime Council is only throwing gasoline on the fire."

Harry's momentary silence gave away more than he would have liked. He could see it in the way Aamani looked at him.

Anything he said at this point would only confirm her worst fears. So, he may as well be honest. "It's true," he said. "A pack of college kids attacked me the other day."

"Really?"

"Mmmhmm."

Aamani glanced this way and that as if making sure that there was nobody else in earshot. Then she raised her hand to the side of her mouth and whispered, "Did you use that Overseer device to subdue them?"

"No!" he said forcefully. Mention of the N'Jal only reminded him that it was in his pocket right now. He could hear it singing in his mind once again, and he pushed the song away with some effort. "I wouldn't do that."

"I wouldn't blame you if you did."

Harry sat back with his arms crossed, glowering at her. "You don't use that kind of power against kids." His irritation spiked despite his attempts to force it down. "I hit one of them with non-lethal ammunition, and even *that* might have been too much."

"I wouldn't be so sure," Aamani murmured into her wine glass. "Fascist tendencies, even in the young, are exceedingly dangerous. They might have killed you if something got their blood hot enough."

They wouldn't have done that, would they?

Though he wanted to tell himself that they were just stupid kids who put too much stock in a loudmouth demagogue, he knew from experience that Aamani was right. He had seen it. Anger that was rooted in bigotry had a way of bypassing the higher brain functions and bringing out the worst in people.

"I should probably go," Harry said. "I promised to spend the afternoon with my daughter. But maybe we could have dinner sometime."

"I'd like that."

The sheet of SmartGlass on Larani's office wall displayed a news anchor who sat behind a desk with a stern expression. Behind him, clouds loomed over a backdrop of Denabria. "This latest scathing criticism from Earth's first Justice Keeper," he said, "has Councilor Dusep's supporters up in arms."

The feed cut to a woman with long, brown hair who stood on the front lawn of her house. "I mean who is this guy," she said. "He's been here for what? Less than a year? He doesn't know what's best for our planet."

Sitting on her couch with hands clasped in her lap, Larani frowned as she watched the broadcast. "Well done, Agent Hunter," she murmured to herself. "Well done indeed."

A knock at the door made her look up.

"Come in."

A moment later, Melissa Carlson stepped into her office. The girl had a wary expression, and Larani got the distinct impression that she wasn't going to like this conversation. "My father told me that you raised concerns about a growing fascist movement after he was attacked."

Craning her neck to study the girl, Larani chose her words with care. "I did," she said, nodding once. "We concluded that it would be best to let local police investigate the matter."

Melissa stiffened at that, glancing out the window behind Larani's desk. "Well, I'm here to ask you to revise that decision," she said. "I read my father's report. At least one of the students who attacked my father tried to block my way into the student centre this morning."

"You want me to investigate campus bullying?"

"No," Melissa said coldly. "They were trying to goad me into violently forcing my way past them. I'm quite convinced that at least one of them was recording the event. And you needn't worry. I didn't fall for their trap."

Larani stood up with a heavy sigh and then clapped a hand onto the young woman's shoulder. "I'm glad to hear it," she said. "But I suspect that's not the end of the story."

"I acknowledge the possibility that this might just be a bunch of local kids stirring up trouble," Melissa began. She took a moment to visibly calm herself. "But the amount of planning that went into their scheme – learning my schedule, gathering enough people to block multiple entrances – suggests organization. On my world, after the disastrous resurgence of white supremacy in the 2010s, groups like this were rightly identified as potential terrorists."

Clasping her chin in one hand, Larani tapped her lips with her index finger. Her brow furrowed as she thought it over. "And you believe that we should do the same," she said. "I'm inclined to agree with you, Cadet."

"I want to be part of the investigation."

Larani froze.

Melissa stood before her with her fists on her hips and an expression that said she would stare down a stampede of bulls. "You've let me go on more dangerous missions," she insisted. "I can handle this."

Dropping back onto the couch, Larani crossed one leg over the other and looked up to hold the young woman's gaze. "I'm sure you can," she said. "But I wonder if you had considered how your face makes you a poor choice for this assignment."

"My face?"

"You gained a fair bit of notoriety after you defeated Isara six months ago," Larani explained. "Your face is easily recognizable. How do you think those students knew to target you?"

A blush put some colour in the girl's cheeks. "I didn't think about that." A moment later, her backbone returned. "But there has to be *something* we can do! Some way to disguise me."

Larani grunted.

The Companion save her from young Keepers with too much enthusiasm and not enough caution. Of course, the smart thing to do was to explain that this was not a movie and that her agents didn't go around donning wigs and adopting aliases. But perhaps she was changing after having spent so much time with Lenai, Hunter and the rest of their little group. She had come to realize that, properly directed, passion could be a Keeper's greatest asset.

"I will speak with Ms. Valtez," Larani said. "She has a background in intelligence. If there is some way that we can include you without compromising your safety or the mission's success, we will do so."

Chapter 6

The scent of pine needles was strong in this part of the domed garden, and every now and then, Jack caught the sound of a maintenance bot trimming the grass. None of that registered with him, however; his mind was focused on the chessboard on the small stone table between him and Anna. After having lost one game, he really wanted to win this rematch.

Jack sat forward with his elbow on his knee, his fingertips covering his mouth. His eyes narrowed as he studied the board. "Pawn to A3," he said. That ought to buy him a little time to think.

The scowl that twisted Anna's face told him it was the wrong move before she even shook her head. "No, no, don't do that," she said. "Look here, see? My queen on E8 has a direct open file all the way to E4."

"Yeah…"

"So, if I put my other bishop on E4, it forks your queen on C2 and your rook on H1. You can't take it with your queen because my queen guards it. Which means, best case scenario, you lose a rook and I gain a lot more mobility."

Gaping at her, Jack blinked once. "Wow…" He lifted his queen and put her on the C4 square instead. There was nothing to threaten her there. "How did you get so good at this when *I'm* the one who taught you this game?"

Anna sat back with her arms folded and smiled as if he had just said something that made her day. "I practiced," she said. "You're still thinking in terms of using a single piece to attack or defend certain squares. You have to learn to coordinate your pieces."

"So, I see."

"Just practice. You'll get it."

They were cut off by the arrival of Anna's father. Still handsome at the age of fifty-two, Beran Lenai was a compact man with red hair that was turning gray and a goatee that had more than a few flecks of silver. "So, here you are," he said, resting his hand on Anna's shoulder.

She looked up at him with a nervous expression, and Jack could tell that she was treating this conversation as if it were another game of chess, trying to guess what her father might say next. "You weren't even going to stop by to say hello? Beran asked.

"I thought you would be busy prepping for the summit," Anna said. "I didn't want to disturb you."

Her father smiled and chuckled softly under his breath. "Nonsense," he said. "In fact, I was hoping that the two of you would join me for dinner tonight. I haven't had a chance to get to know Jack."

Well, that was an intriguing prospect.

Anna went pale and shot a glance in his direction, no doubt hoping that he would save her by coming up with some excuse. Not that Jack had any intention of doing any such thing. Sooner or later, he was going to have to spend some time with Anna's family – besides the quick pleasantries they had exchanged at Alia's wedding – so there was no point in trying to put it off.

That said, he wouldn't accept the invitation on Anna's behalf. That wasn't his place. No, for once, Jack Hunter just kept his mouth shut.

Anna looked up at her father with that nervous expression she often got when she knew she had to do something she didn't want to do. "Sure," she said. "We'd be happy to join you for dinner."

A few hours later, Anna walked into the restaurant on the upper level of the domed garden. The massive lights that nourished the plants – each one perfectly tuned to mimic the frequencies of Leyria's sun – had dimmed, creating the appearance of twilight.

Her mouth tightened as she surveyed her surroundings. "Are you sure this is a good idea?" She spun around to face Jack. "He's probably going to find some excuse to judge you… or me."

Jack stood in the doorway, smiling down at himself. "It'll be fine, An." He stepped forward, took her by the shoulders and kissed her on the forehead. "Come on. I think he's getting a little antsy."

Anna wanted to scoff at the idea of her father being the one to get antsy but she put that desire aside. She was going to have to be on her best behaviour tonight – soft-spoken and demure and all the things that she hated being – so it was probably a good idea to get into character now.

The restaurant looked kind of ritzy for her taste: large, round tables with pristine white table clothes and bouquets of flowers in the centre of each one. She caught sight of a few serving bots maneuvering deftly between them. At this hour, nearly every table was occupied by at least two people.

Some were in Leyrian fashions, others were clearly from Earth. A few glanced in her direction and whispered, "That's Anna Lenai." Great. Just what she needed. A little *more* attention.

Her father sat alone at a table near the edge of the balcony and looked up when he heard their approach. His face lit up with a grin. "There you are!" he exclaimed. "I was beginning to fear you weren't coming. Sit, sit."

Anna sat down across from him, folding her hands in her lap and pasting a big, fake smile on her face. "Dad," she said with a curt nod. "Thanks for inviting us."

The instant Jack's butt landed in the seat next to her, a holographic waiter appeared. This one was tall and slim, and dressed in a black vest over his high-collared white shirt. "Good evening sirs, madame," he said. "Are you ready to order?"

With a wave of her hand, Anna summoned a holographic menu that floated above the table in front of her. She scrolled through the pages with a flick of her wrist. So much looked good.

"I'll have the black bean burger," Jack said. "Curly fries on the side."

"Excellent."

"Pasta *Jianara* with broccoli," Anna muttered.

Jack patted her knee gently as if to remind her to not be sullen. May the Companion save her, this was not going to be an easy night. Even Seth seemed to be a little irritated by her tone. Fine! She would be good.

Across the table, Beran scrutinized the two of them for a very long moment. "That's right, I'd heard," he said. "You became a vegetarian after your stay on Earth."

"Well, if you'd seen what they do to their animals..."

"Yes, it's most disturbing."

Anna lifted her glass of water, shut her eyes and took a long drink. "How's work, Dad?" she asked. "I imagine you must be spending a great deal of time on Earth."

"More than I would like if I'm honest," he answered. "No offense, Jack. Yours is a lovely world, but I do wish I could come home more often. See my girls. From what Alia tells me, I might be a grandfather soon."

Gaping at him, Anna felt her eyes widen. She shook her head. "Alia never told *me* she was trying to get pregnant." It was more of a mumble than a declaration, but she went with it. "I didn't…I didn't know."

Beran gave her that exasperated stare she had seen every time she stayed out a little too late. "Well, can you blame her?" he asked. "You two never talk."

Anna felt a sudden warmth in her face. Her head sank. "No," she murmured. "No, I guess I can't."

Under the table, Jack took her hand and gave it a gentle squeeze. That took the edge off some of her anxiety. There were days when Anna wondered how she ever got through life before he'd come along.

"And you, Jack?" Beran asked. "How do you like our world?"

"Oh, it's beautiful."

"Really? You don't miss Earth?"

Jack replied to that with a casual shrug of his shoulders. "I miss my family and the friends I haven't seen in a while," he said. "But the truth is I never really felt at home on Earth anyway."

They talked for maybe ten more minutes before the food came, and by the time it arrived, Anna was feeling famished. Her meal was delicious: pasta in a cream sauce with big chunks of broccoli. While she ate, she pondered what Jack had said. He had never felt at home on Earth.

Beran was sitting back and lifting his glass of red wine, studying it before he took a drink. "You must both feel very honoured," he said. "To be here I mean. I never dreamed that I would be part of the delegation that made peace with Antaur."

"It's a pretty big event," Jack agreed.

"Yes," Beran said. "And so I trust, Leana, that you will be able to keep your temper in check."

Anna stiffened as she drew in a deep breath. There it was: the criticism that she had been expecting from the moment she had agreed, against her better judgment, to sit down and share a meal with her father. She didn't mind being the black sheep of the family, but maybe – if that was how they saw her – they could just leave her be and stop expecting her to attend family gatherings.

A thousand possible responses came to mind – most of them biting – but, of course, saying them out loud would only prove her father's point. Funny how that worked. Anna was searching for a diplomatic reply when Jack squeezed her hand again.

Glancing over his shoulder, he favoured her with the most beautiful smile she had ever seen. "Actually," he said softly. "It's been my experience that Anna never gets angry without a good reason. I discovered a long time ago that if she's upset about something, I should stop and hear her out. Because she's probably right."

Once again, she was blushing, but whatever embarrassment she might have felt was nothing compared to the relief Jack's words brought her. To not be seen as just the angry child who didn't know when to keep her opinions to herself…

Closing her eyes, Anna rested her head against Jack's shoulder. "Well," she said. "I do sometimes go overboard."

When she looked up, her father was wide-eyed with astonishment. "You two really are perfect for each other," he stammered. "I'm glad you found one another."

"So am I," Jack said.

After dinner, they walked hand in hand through the garden. Tall rose bushes were in full bloom on either side of the cobblestone path they followed, and somewhere nearby, a fountain was bubbling. Its sound did little to soothe Anna's exasperation. Even with Jack's support, her father's words still got under her skin. Parents had that effect on their children, she supposed.

Looking up toward the distant ceiling, Anna blinked a few times. "So, that was an interesting experience." she muttered. "I didn't mean to put you in a position where you had to stick up for me."

Jack was smiling at her, and there was a glint in his eye. "Oh, it's my pleasure," he said. "Besides, you've been there for me plenty of times when my dad decided to offer his opinions. Is it still getting to you?"

Releasing his hand, Anna strode forward.

She crossed her arms as she walked along the narrow pathway, sighing at the thought of what her father had said. "Knowing my dad, he's probably talking to the other diplomats right now," she grumbled. "Fretting about what his daughter might say to ruin the peace talks."

In her mind's eye, Jack's silhouette was standing with hands in his back pockets. "I'm sure it's not that bad," he offered. Which only served to annoy her. He really didn't know her father.

Anna spun around to stand in front of him, craned her neck and held his gaze. "Oh no?" she asked. "And how many times did Harry and Aamani lecture me on moderating my tone?"

"A few."

"I'm pretty sure you got in on it, too."

Jack backed away from her with his hands raised defensively, his eyes fixed on the ground beneath his feet. "Hey, that was five years ago," he said. "Isn't there some kind of statute of limitations on these things?"

Pacing toward him with hands folded behind her back, Anna pursed her lips as she looked up to study him. "My point," she began, "is that if you guys were concerned about my temper, just imagine how my diplomat father must feel."

Instead of answering, Jack took her by the hand and led her through the corridor between the rose bushes. Once they were out, the path curved slightly to the left, toward the fountain she had heard earlier.

Poplar trees formed a half-circle around it, and beyond them, stone steps led down to the bank of a narrow stream. Night was falling on the garden but small lamps around the fountain provided just enough light to make it romantic.

Jack seemed to notice as well.

He moseyed up to one of the trees, brushing his fingers across the trunk as he took in the sight. "I used to dream about flying on spaceships," he mumbled. "But I never quite imagined anything like this."

"That's one of the things I love about being your girlfriend."

He turned around as she approached, standing there with a look of confusion on his face. He was probably trying to figure out what she was getting at. "Everything is new to you," Anna explained. "Even after all these years. And I love being the one to show you my world."

"Aww."

To her surprise, Jack took her hands and pulled her close. Before she knew it, she was wrapped up in a hug. "Hot-tempered, outspoken and rebellious," he said. "Seems I'm dating a bit of a bad girl."

"You are."

"That being the case," Jack went on, "Want to risk a diplomatic incident by having sex behind those bushes over there?"

Just the thought of it sent a little jolt of excitement through her. She mulled it over and concluded that they could probably get away with it. The garden was almost empty, and they were in a secluded little corner of it.

Anna nuzzled his chest, sighing softly, and Jack held her a little tighter. "Oh, you know I do," she panted. "But I promised I wouldn't do anything to jeopardize the talks. Maybe on the return trip?"

"Okay," Jack said softly. "But I'm feeling romantic. How 'bout we make this a date night?"

"I would love that." Gently, Anna pulled out of his embrace and then looked up at him. "But if we're going to make this a date night, then let's do it right. Wait here. I'll be back in ten minutes."

"Huh? Where are you going?"

"Just wait here."

"Oh, okay."

At first, Jack didn't know why Anna had chosen to interrupt their date, but he did as she asked and waited patiently by the apple trees. The artificial sunlight was all but gone now, and lamps around the fountain created a warm glow.

Jack leaned against a tree trunk with his hands in his pockets, chewing on his lip as he stared off into the distance. "At least the scenery is nice," he muttered. "If you're going to get stood up, this is definitely the place to do it."

"Heh-hem."

He gasped when he saw Anna standing on the cobblestone path in a neon-blue sundress with thin straps and a skirt that flared. She had a white flower in her hair and beads on the thin strands that framed her face.

Blushing hard, Jack closed his eyes and bowed his head to her. "Wow." He really should have been able to come up with something better than that, but for once in his life, he was speechless. "You didn't have to do that."

Anna glided forward until she was right in front of him, then looked up at him with intensity in her deep, blue eyes. "It's date night," she said. "I wanted to look nice for you, *and* that reaction made it worth it."

"Yeah, but now I feel underdressed."

Tilting her head to one side, Anna raised an eyebrow as she studied him. "You look very dashing." Of course, Jack didn't really agree, but he wouldn't argue the point. "And what was that you were saying about getting stood up?"

"Merely the incoherent ravings of a foolish man."

"Well, that's good to know," she teased. "I would hate to think that you had so little faith in me."

They walked arm in arm along a cobblestone path that traced the perimeter of the garden, passing small groves of deciduous trees and beds of colourful flowers. Jack could see why the ship designers would create this little self-contained ecosystem. True, it wasn't quite as refreshing as actually being outside, but it was close.

For a little while, they walked in silence, and Jack found himself surprised by how comfortable he was with that. There were plenty of things he could have talked about – their duties for the remainder of this mission or what they might find on Antaur. He had always been a little curious about Keli's home planet – but right then, he was content to just enjoy Anna's company. And Summer? Summer was practically humming in the back of his mind.

Their wanderings eventually took them to a game room where Anna beat Jack at two more games of chess. She had wanted to go easy on him, but Jack had insisted that she play to her full potential. Which, she had to admit, was preferable. Not that she cared all that much about winning, but she would never have been comfortable in a situation where she had to hold back to soothe a man's pride. Once or twice, maybe – if she really loved him – but as general practice? Definitely not.

After that, she taught Jack to play *Jhin Talan*, a Leyrian card game that he picked up very quickly. He seemed to have a knack for cards. They spent at least two hours in that room. It was nearing her bed-time when she dragged him down to the night club on Deck Four. She knew that wasn't exactly Jack's scene, but she didn't want the night to end just yet.

This place wasn't like some of the places she had been to on Earth. No fog machine, no colorful floodlights shining down on a crowd of people who just kind of haphazardly flailed against one another. On the contrary, this little bar was quite well lit.

A brass railing up on the second level overlooked a faux-wood dance floor where about a hundred people performed *threnadiar*. Anna was pretty sure that Jack wouldn't be up for that, and she didn't know if she could teach him even if he wanted to try. The closest Earth equivalent would be swing-dancing.

So, she just watched the live band on the raised duroplastic stage. They were pretty good. Sometimes bands booked gigs on starships in an attempt to get their work noticed. Leyria may have abandoned the use of money centuries ago, but artists still went to great lengths to get some recognition for their work.

She sighed.

Jack stood behind her with his arms wrapped around her tummy, smooching her on the cheek. "I'm getting the vibe that you wanna go down there." He had to raise his voice to be heard over the music.

Anna turned around, smiling as she stood up on her toes to brush his lips with hers. "We don't have to," she said. "I know that dancing's not really your thing. So I'm happy to just spend time with-"

He cut her off by taking her hand and leading her toward the stairs that went down to the first level. Was this really happening? "Where are we going?" she asked, unsure of what to expect.

"Down there!"

"But you don't like dancing."

With a gentle caress, Jack brushed a lock of hair off her cheek and then leaned in to kiss her nose. "But you do," he replied. "And there's nothing that I like more than making you happy. So, why don't we just start off slow, and you can teach me the basics?"

She did just that, taking him by the hand and leading him to the edge of the dance floor. She could tell that Jack was nervous – and she would be lying if she said that his movements weren't a little stiff at first – but he picked it up fast enough, which shouldn't have surprised her. Jack had reached a proficiency with hand-to-hand combat that rivaled her own. If he could do that, he could dance the threna-diar. By the end of the night, she was smiling every time she twirled under Jack's outstretched hand, laughing every time she fell backward into his arms. He always caught her.

Anna didn't want their date to end, but midnight came and passed sooner than she would have liked. And they *did* have actual work to do on this ship. Tomorrow, they had to attend a briefing on the security arrangements for the Leyrian delegation. The Keepers were mostly here as an honour guard, but the fun part of being in an honour guard was that you had to, you know, *guard* things. So, she reluctantly agreed that it was time to turn in.

The tiny bedroom in the quarters they shared had a carpeted floor and curved walls of gleaming duroplastic.

Anna walked backwards through the door, pulling Jack by his hands. "Come on," she said. Once they were both inside, she let her weight fall against him and sighed as Jack held her tight.

"Are you tired?" he asked.

"Very."

"Want me to rub your back? Help you fall asleep?"

Stepping out of his embrace, Anna clasped her hands together behind her back and smiled sheepishly at the floor under her feet. "Not just yet," she said. "There's one more thing I want to make my night complete."

"Oh? What's that?"

She didn't answer. Her boyfriend could be downright adorable when he needed a moment to comprehend that yes, she really *was* that into him. It took him a second, but when he figured it out, he grinned that mischievous grin of his and kissed the side of her neck.

The window in their bedroom offered a wonderful view of the garden, and now that morning was dawning, the massive lamps had come on to create the illusion of sunlight. Some of that filtered through the glass pane and woke Jack from a peaceful sleep.

91

The first thing he noticed as consciousness dripped into his mind was the soft skin of Anna's back against his body, the warmth of her tummy beneath his fingers. She was still sound asleep. Jack could tell.

He touched his nose to the back of her neck and gently nuzzled her. The scent of her hair…like strawberries. A stray thought entered his drowsy mind. He really hoped she kept using that new shampoo.

Jack kissed her shoulder.

Anna sighed, stretching in his arms as she woke up. "Morning." She twisted around to face him. Her smile made his heart melt. "I love you."

"I love you too," Jack whispered. "Did you sleep well?"

Anna giggled, laying a hand on his cheek, her fingers tracing the stubble along his jawline. "Like a baby," she murmured. "I always sleep well when we make love. Do we have anything planned today?"

Rolling onto his back, Jack blinked as he tried to recall their schedule. He was just about to ask his multi-tool when it all came back to him. "Actually, yeah," he said. "We have that briefing in two hours."

"Nope."

"Nope?"

Anna snuggled up beside him with an arm around his belly, her soft cheek on his chest. "Nope, I'm not going to any meetings," she insisted. "Just gonna stay right here with you and cuddle."

Jack couldn't help the devilish grin that her declaration inspired. He shook his head slowly. "Director Varno won't like that," he said. "We might get a reprimand."

"It'll be worth it."

"Tell ya what," Jack whispered. "Why don't we go to the meeting, take notes, then come right back here and spend the rest of the day together?"

In less than half a second, she was on top of him, braced on extended arms with a hand on either side of his head. Anna made a face that said she was highly skeptical of his suggestion. "Does this plan involve me putting on clothes?"

"Ideally, yes."

"Then no deal."

Jack cupped her face with both hands and then rose up to kiss her lips. "But if you don't put on clothes," he said, "I won't get to peel them off you one piece at a time, going extra slow just to drive you crazy-"

He couldn't finish that sentence because Anna was suddenly kissing him again, and this time, there was heat in it. She pulled away, gasping, thin strands of hair falling over her face. "Damn you and your infuriating levels of self-control."

"So, we have a deal?"

"Yeah, we have a deal." Anna let herself fall into his embrace, sighing softly as she nuzzled the side of his neck. Without even thinking, Jack slipped his arms around her and trailed his fingertips over her back. "But we have two hours to kill, and I just had an idea."

"Yeah?"

"You know how the vibe showers make every inch of your skin tingle?"

"Yeah."

Anna jerked her head toward the bathroom.

"Oh, hell!" Jack said. "Let's do this!"

Chapter 7

Melissa studied herself in the locker-room mirror.

The person who stared back at her was a complete stranger, a tall and reed-slender young woman in a black vest over a sleeveless gray t-shirt. There was a mole on her left cheek now. Her hair was cut boyishly short and it stood straight up, black at the root and silver at the tips.

Closing her eyes, Melissa leaned forward, bracing her hands on either side of the sink. "Such is the price of a career in law enforcement," she muttered. "You want to go undercover, you have to look the part."

In the mirror, she saw Gabi standing behind her with the tips of two fingers over her mouth. "Not bad," the other woman said. "It will fool anyone who doesn't look too close, but there is a risk."

Turning around, Melissa leaned against the counter with arms folded, shaking her head. "There's always a risk," she said, "But I want to do this. If we can figure out how these fashy kids are organizing…"

Gabi nodded.

The change-room door swung open, and Cassiara Seyrus came marching into the room. Though she was probably in her late twenties, she looked to be about Melissa's age, and the bright pink hair only added to the effect. "I gotta hand it to you, Ms. Valtez," Cassi said. "Your friends at LIS do good work."

"Well, they do specialize in intelligence."

Melissa hopped onto the counter, resting her hands on her knees and staring into her lap. "So, what's our next step?" she inquired. "Do I make contact with the kids who accosted me at school?"

"Your next step is to change that posture."

"Excuse me?"

Gabrina Valtez strode forward, her high heels clicking on the tiles. She looked so imposing in her black skirt and maroon top, and the way that she frowned as she looked Melissa up and down was unnerving. "Look at the way you're sitting," she said. "Melissa Carlson is soft-spoken and somewhat demure. Don't be Melissa Carlson. Sit up straight, eyes forward. Make me believe that you're thinking about punching me."

Melissa did as she was told, and... No, no. She realized that if she was going to pull this off, she would have to change the way she thought, not just the way she behaved. A good actor became their character. "Don't tell me how to sit!" she snapped.

"Melissa, you will have to learn-"

In a heartbeat, Melissa was standing up and towering over the other woman. "I'll sit however I wanna sit!" She shoved Gabi hard enough to make her retreat a few steps. "You got a problem with that, then we can settle this right now."

For a moment, Gabi just stared at her with shock on her face; then a smile replaced wide-eyed disbelief, and she laughed. "Very good," she said. "Keep practicing that until it becomes second nature."

Cassi leaned against the wall with a hand over her stomach, smiling as she watched the scene play out. "Not bad, kid," she said. "But if you're going to go undercover, you'll have to figure out a backstory."

"I'm an angry college kid pissed off about all those alien freeloaders coming in," Melissa suggested. "Maybe I'm from someplace nearby. Like Pelor? I think I can fake a Denabrian accent."

Cassi grunted.

It pleased Melissa when Gabi did the same. "That could work," she said. "I'll have to make contact with some people at LIS. We'll need to devise a strategy for approaching the group."

"And," Cassi added. "All of this hinges on Larani's approval."

A frown tightened Melisa's mouth – Larani seemed to be convinced that there was no way she could blend in – but she chose to let her true personality reassert itself. There were times to be forceful, and there were times to be patient.

This was the latter.

Keli sat alone on a small couch that faced a window in the port side of the starship that carried them to Antaur. Outside, she saw nothing but blackness, and she wouldn't see anything more until they dropped out of warp. Such a depressing view, but it suited her mood right then.

In a beige, sleeveless dress, she sat with one leg crossed over the other, her arms spread over the back of the sofa. This ship was teeming with life. So much of it! So many emotions in such a confined space. It was almost too much.

Keli shut her eyes, breathing deeply. Calming her own emotions required a little effort in light of the pressure on her mind, but it was a skill she had learned early in her captivity. A telepath had to master her own mind first.

She felt the presence of another approaching.

Two others, actually.

It was no surprise when Rajel emerged from a hallway, stepping into the small lounge area near this window. He crossed his arms and leaned his shoulder against the door-frame, frowning thoughtfully.

"Can I do something for you, Operative Aydrius?"

"I was wondering how you were holding up."

"Your concern is touching," Keli said. "I suppose you expect me to tell you that I'm overwhelmed by the thought of going home after all these years, but the truth is that my memories of Antaur are dim."

With a sigh, Rajel came forward, pacing a line behind the back of her couch. "Well, I remember that place all too well." He stopped as he neared the wall, turned on his heel and stomped off in the opposite direction.

Keli sat back against the cushions, turned her face up to the ceiling and blinked. "I assume you're about to tell me another story from your childhood," she muttered. "Rest assured, Operative Aydrius, I have no romantic illusions about our homeworld."

"No, it's not that," Rajel whispered. After a few more seconds of angry pacing, he raised his voice and added, "I can live with what they did to me. I'm more afraid of what they'll do to you."

"And what, pray tell, is that?"

He came around the couch and sat down beside her with his hands on his thighs. "I don't know exactly what your captors did," he said, "But I assume that the purpose of their experiments was to push your telepathic talents to the limit."

"It was."

He turned his head slightly so that he had one ear toward her, no doubt listening for some indication of her mood. Perhaps a change in her breathing. "So, if the military put you in a cage to heighten your telepathic talents, what do you suppose they'll do if they ever get their hands on you again?"

Keli froze.

She hadn't considered that. Not that she trusted her people's military for a moment, but she had assumed that she would be under the protection of the Leyrians. After all, she *was* a part of their delegation. But a new thought occurred to her.

What if her people demanded her return as one of their terms? A few months ago, that wouldn't have bothered her. True, the Leyrians provided for her every need, but there were days when she felt as though she had traded one cage for another. An invisible cage with a soft bed and delicious food, but a cage nonetheless.

On Leyria, she was forbidden from using her talent to its full potential. For months, she had dreamed about going home, where she would not have to suffer such restrictions. She had even tried to persuade Tanaben to join her.

But what if the life of freedom that she had thought she would find on Antaur was a lie? Her people had thrown her into a cell once. Who was to say that they would not do so again? What if there was no freedom, only a choice between one cage and another?

A shiver went through her when she realized that she was starting to enjoy her life on Leyria. "So," Keli murmured. "Are you saying that I should be wary?"

Rajel's lips curled in the smallest smile she had ever seen, a smile that remained for only half a second before it vanished. "I'm saying that I have your back. I won't let them hurt you, Keli."

"How...gallant of you."

He grunted.

Resting her elbow on the back of the sofa, Keli pressed her cheek into the knuckles of her fist. "Do you still hate telepaths, Rajel?" she asked. "Have I changed your outlook, or is it only me that you tolerate?"

His head sank as he forced out a sigh, and those sunglasses of his seemed to slide down his nose. "I'm...working on that particular prejudice," he said. "It's not something a Justice Keeper should tolerate within himself."

"No, indeed."

"But you are different."

"Am I?"

Rajel stood up, exhaling slowly, and then offered a curt nod of respect. "You'll have to excuse me," he muttered. "I have some things to take care of. But I'll watch your back in case they try anything."

A moment later, he was gone.

Keli leaned back with her legs stretched out and her hands folded behind her head. She blew air through puckered lips. From the very beginning, she had known that this trip would be difficult, but she was only just starting to realize how much so. If her people did make a play to regain their wayward telepath, what exactly would she do?

The question lingered in her mind for hours.

Rajel wandered the corridors of the ship, lost in thought. He could sense the walls on either side of him. When he got close enough, he could pick up the slight protrusions of every doorframe, and the minor nicks and abrasions in the bulkhead, but after about thirty feet, they blurred into indistinct slabs of metal and duroplastic on either side of the hallway. He was told that spatial awareness was less acute at a distance than eyesight. At times, that irked him, but there were other ways to observe his environment.

He could pick up the scent of food – various meats and savory sauces – whenever he passed by any one of several restaurants and eateries on the ship. And there was the scent of sweat, perfume and alcoholic beverages when he got near the night club. Each deck had its own unique sound. The hum of the warp engines grew louder the closer he got to the outer hull.

A cloudy figure appeared on the periphery of his spatial awareness, one that Rajel recognized within seconds. Jack Hunter was striding toward him, clearly lost in his own private reverie.

With lips pursed, Rajel inclined his head to the other man. "Agent Hunter," he said in clipped tones.

"Hey, how's it going?"

A sudden warmth flooded Rajel's face, but he struggled to keep his face smooth and his tone even. "I…uh," he began. "I wanted to apologize for our sparring session the other day. I may have overreacted."

Jack stopped short right in front of him, and from the way he looked up to study Rajel, it was clear that the apology had surprised him. "Don't worry about it," he replied. "Sometimes I need a good ass-kicking."

"Well, you gave as good as you got."

"Fair."

Crossing his arms, Rajel leaned his shoulder against the corridor wall and felt his mouth twist in distaste. "I wanted to ask about this morning's briefing," he began. "Will you think me paranoid if I tell you that I'm uneasy?"

Jack stood in the middle of the hallway, nodding slowly as he phrased his response. "You mean the fact that we're supposed to be unarmed for the duration of this summit?" he asked. "It does have a real 'Meet me at the pier, and come alone,' vibe, doesn't it?"

Though he wasn't exactly well-versed in Earth's pop culture, Rajel had consumed enough Antauran and Leyrian fiction to get the gist. And Jack had it right. Last night, when the ship dropped out of warp to check in with Leyria, they had received an update from the Prime Council's office.

The Antaurans were now insisting that all Justice Keepers remain unarmed while performing their duties as protectors to the Earth and Leyrian delegations. To Rajel, that was a most unreasonable request, though he expected nothing less from his own people. You had to grow up on Antaur to truly comprehend the complexity of their stupidity.

Apparently, they justified this demand with the claim that the Justice Keepers were themselves living weapons. Anyone who thought *that* did not know the first thing about Justice Keepers – Rajel could feel his Nassai's firm agreement – but he would not expect his people to understand. "What do you suppose we should do?"

Jack's reply to that was a shrug. "I'm not sure there's anything we *can* do," he said. "Look, Rajel, this is gonna make me feel like a middle-aged dad who just bought his first mini-van, but: Now is not the time to be bucking the rules."

Half of that went over Rajel's head, but the significance was not lost on him. If Jack Hunter, of all people, was telling him to play this one by the book, well… Rajel felt his Nassai urging him toward caution.

With one finger, he pushed his sunglasses up his nose until they were flat against his face. "I suppose you're right," he said. "But I don't know. Something about this just feels off."

"You sure?"

"What do you mean?"

This close, he could sense the individual contours of Jack's face, could tell when the other man scowled. "You've got a bit of a hate on for your own people, Rajel," he said. "I can't help but wonder if maybe that's colouring your outlook."

"Do you know what it's like to feel the scorn of your own people?"

A smile curved Jack's lips, and he glanced down at the floor. "No," he admitted. "Only the scorn of my own family."

They started down the hallway together, sharing their concerns for the days ahead.

Pushing open the glass door to Larani's office, Melissa found the other woman seated behind her desk. The sound of her entrance made Larani look up, and the surprise on her face as her eyebrows climbed was priceless.

Melissa stood in front of her in the same clothing she had worn in the change room, silver hair waxed and pointed straight up. "What do you think?" she asked. "Is it enough to conceal my identity?"

Reclining in her chair with hands folded over her chest, Larani frowned, but at last, she nodded. "I believe so," she said. "But I am still reluctant to send a cadet on this kind of fact-finding mission. Such ventures are better left to the LIS."

"And do you think we can trust them?"

Larani got out of her chair and began pacing around the side of the desk, exhaling through her nose. "Is there some reason that we shouldn't?" she inquired. "The LIS has a long history of dutiful service."

Against her instincts, Melissa forced herself to step forward, to hold the woman's gaze without blinking. "The LIS operates under the direct authority of the Hall of Council. We, on the other hand, do not."

"Your point, Cadet?"

"How much do you trust the Hall of Council?"

From the way Larani flinched, it was clear that Melissa had hit on one of the other woman's fears. She had to suppress the urge to let out a whoop of joy. That would hardly come off as professional. If she let emotion get the better of her now, it would only serve to undermine her point. Containing her excitement and her anxiety, Melissa pressed her point.

"I'm sure you trust Sarona Vason," she said. "But we've all seen what Dusep has been saying on the news. Can you be sure that there aren't other councilors who feel the same way? And even if there aren't, what about the directors at the LIS?"

Backing away, Larani sat on the edge of her desk with her hands on her knees. She was slumped over, heaving out a sigh. "When did you become so incisive, Melissa?" she wondered aloud. "I see a talent for reading subtle political currents runs in your family. I wonder if I should be taking you to Council meetings instead of Agent Hunter."

When Larani looked up, her gaze was stern, and it took everything Melissa had not to shrink away under that stare. "Your point is well taken," Larani said. "I am willing to allow this investigation. *But* you will be working with a team."

"I understand."

"Well done, Cadet. Well done indeed."

Chapter 8

When the double doors parted, Harry found himself in a Slip-Gate chamber so very like every other one he had seen before. Just a big room with gray walls and a console that faced the gleaming metal diamond.

Several Keepers were taking their positions as guards for about half a dozen well-dressed diplomats, placing themselves in front of the Gate. A bubble formed around their group with a soft humming sound, and before Harry could count to five, it seemed to shrink to a point before vanishing, carrying its occupants with it.

At his side, Claire took his hand and looked up at him with a little bit of fear in her large, dark eyes. Harry could understand why. Kids usually picked up more than adults gave them credit for. Even without his prior warning that he might have to put himself in danger on this mission, Claire had to know Antaur's reputation.

"It's gonna be all right," Harry whispered.

In the corner, he saw Jack and Anna reminiscing with Aamani, and though they all had smiles on their faces, everything about their body language screamed tension. Harry led his daughter over to join them.

Aamani turned when she heard their approach, and her smile broadened at the sight of them. "My goodness, is this Claire?" she asked. "You've grown so much since the last time I saw you."

Claire looked up with a puzzled expression, her brows drawn together. "You used to work with my dad, right?"

"In a manner of speaking."

Anna stood at the edge of the group with arms folded, forcing a small smile when Claire noticed her. "Hi, sweetie," she said with a curt nod. "You excited to see Antaur for the first time?"

"A little," Claire answered. "What's it like?"

"I don't know," Anna replied. "I've never been before today."

At that declaration, Harry felt a profound urge to reach into his pocket and bond the N'Jal. There was no telling what he would find down there. The first group to descend was a team of Justice Keepers that had reported no hostility from the locals, but that didn't mean very much. If this *was* a trap, the Antaurans could be waiting for the entire delegation to arrive before they sprang it. Yes, technically, Harry was allowed a weapon – only Keepers had to suffer that prohibition – but everyone seemed to consider him one of the diplomats, and diplomats did not carry guns.

The N'Jal, on the other hand...

Squeezing his eyes shut, Harry stiffened as he drew in a breath. "Do we know how much longer it'll be?" he asked, surprised by the desperation in his voice. "I'm starting to feel a little warm in here."

His daughter gave him some serious side-eye. "Feels perfectly normal to me." Her words were soft-spoken as if she wasn't entirely confident in the declaration. Or maybe she was worried about her father's skittish behaviour. Harry was beginning to notice that the N'Jal became exponentially more tempting whenever he was on the verge of a fight or flight reaction.

Jack stood with his back to the Gate, shrugging his shoulders as he stared blankly at the wall. "A few more minutes, I guess," he said. "You and I are in the same group."

"Group Twelve!" the technician behind the console shouted.

"Speak of the devil," Jack muttered.

Anna stood on her toes to kiss him softly on the cheek and whispered, "Good luck." Harry didn't think he had been meant to hear that, but while she hid it well, he could tell that Anna was uneasy. That she hid it at all was an accomplishment; Anna was a heart on her sleeve kind of girl.

With a sigh, Harry took Claire's hand and led her to a spot right in front of the Gate, where they were joined by seven members of the Leyrian delegation. Men and women in high-collared shirts and jackets with embroidered patterns on the cuffs of each sleeve. At least half of them were well into middle age, but Harry couldn't say that he recognized a single one.

Jack and two Keepers that he didn't know came over to join the group. Jack took point, placing himself in front of the diplomats as if to shield them from any gunfire that might come their way on arrival. The other two each took a spot on the left and the right to cover them from all sides.

At that moment, Harry noticed Rajel and Keli standing by the entrance and talking softly with one another. Light glinted off the blue lenses of Rajel's glasses as he shook his head in obvious distress.

Leaning forward, Harry whispered in Jack's ear. "What's up with Rajel?" he asked. "I mean I know the guy had a rough childhood, but he has to feel *some* excitement about going home."

"Ha!" Jack scoffed. "If you knew the first thing about him, you'd know that going home is the last thing Rajel wants. The guy probably wishes he could Eternal Sunshine his entire childhood."

"Stand ready!" the technician shouted.

A bubble formed around them with a distinctive whir, blurring Harry's vision of anyone and anything on the other side. The technician and his console were just a smear of grayish black. A quick glance to the side revealed two hazy images that Harry thought were Anna and Aamani. His heart was pounding.

Before he even realized what he was doing, Harry reached into his pocket and felt the little ball of flesh uncurl, its fibers digging into his palm. The instant he was one with the N'Jal, a wave of relief washed over him. He was safe. Claire was safe. And that was all that mattered.

The bubble rushed forward, racing through an endless tunnel of blackness toward a point of light in the infinite distance. Though they travelled at a breakneck speed, they came no closer to it.

Suddenly, the tunnel came to an end on what appeared to be a large platform under a clear blue sky. The blurry images of people stood all around them, and Harry thought he saw skyscrapers in the distance.

The bubble popped.

Harry was instantly aware of a crisp, cool wind assaulting his face, causing him to shut his eyes and recoil. "God have mercy," he whispered, grabbing the front of his light jacket and holding it closed.

When he got his bearings, he looked around to see Antaurans surrounding them on all sides. Not soldiers. These were diplomats. People of all heights, all skin tones and a variety of ages. The only way to distinguish them from the Leyrians – or the Earthers, for that matter – was by their style of dress.

The Antauran men wore long jackets with no visible buttons or zippers on the front, jackets in shades of gold or bronze that fell almost to their knees. For the women, it was much the same, though their garments seemed to be decorated with ornate scroll-work patterns instead of a simple, flat colour.

A heavyset man with pink cheeks and wispy white hair on top of his head stepped forward to greet the new arrivals. "Welcome," he said in Leyrian, though his accent made it sound awkward. "Please join your fellows below."

And then their group was marching forward.

Carefully, Harry removed his hand from his pocket and let the N'Jal scan the air. He sensed nothing out of the ordinary. No electromagnetic spikes, no pheromones that might indicate hostile intentions. Harry realized that he should probably return the N'Jal to his pocket, but letting go was so hard. He felt so exposed without it! Finally, after a great deal of silent coaxing, he severed his connection to the Overseer device and returned it to its hiding place.

Harry trotted down a set of stone steps, wrinkling his nose at the thought of his own unjustified suspicions. *Think it through, Carlson,* he scolded himself. *Would they go to all this trouble just to kill a few diplomats and Keepers?*

Claire was taking the steps two at a time and grinning like a kid who had just found out that every present under the tree had her name on it. "It's gorgeous!" she said. "Look at those buildings!"

In the distance, glittering skyscrapers with sleek, curved edges caught the light of the afternoon sun. A shuttle came rushing out of the upper atmosphere and then dipped out of sight behind several highrises. Claire was right. It *was* beautiful.

Jack hit the bottom stair and then froze briefly, glancing this way and that, no doubt searching for any sign of trouble. When he saw none, he carried on across an open stone patio with potted ferns forming a perimeter around it.

The other Leyrian delegates were all there, standing in small clusters and talking in hushed voices. There were Keepers present as well. Even if they hadn't all been blessed with a youthful appearance, you could tell them apart by their posture. Each one reminded Harry of a cat that was ready to pounce, and several had hands hovering over their hips, fingers itching to grasp the sidearms they had been denied.

Harry chose a spot along the edge of the patio.

He stood behind Claire with his hands on her shoulders, remaining silent while she looked out on a field where elm and maple trees stood with leaves budding on their long branches. So, it was early spring on this part of Antaur. The climate was chilly, cooler than what he had grown used to in Denabria. It reminded him of home.

When the next group of delegates arrived, Aamani came down the stairs and rushed over to join the two of them. "This is better than what I had expected," she said, casting a furtive glance over her shoulder. "I thought there would have been some minor squabble by now."

A frown tightened Harry's mouth, but he nodded slowly without speaking. For the moment, he just wanted to enjoy the view. Things were bound to get tense sooner or later. No need to accelerate the process.

Aamani was at his side with her hands folded behind herself, her shoulders square like a sentry on watch. "Is it wrong that I expected something a little more alien?" she wondered aloud. "It looks so very like Earth."

"Any world capable of supporting human life would have to look a lot like Earth," Harry muttered. "And the Overseers brought a lot of our plants and animals to these new worlds." There were some small variations after over ten millennia of human agriculture. So far as he could tell, there were no blueberries on Leyria, but they had something called tartberries instead.

After the arrival of several more groups, the Antauran delegation descended the stairs, led by the pink-cheeked man who had greeted them earlier. This chap stood out from the rest by his distinctive red coat with gold trim along the fringes of its shoulder-pads. "We greet you on this auspicious day!" he said when he reached the final step. "For those of you who do not recognize me, I am President Adare Salmaro."

The Antauran head of state.

Harry swallowed.

Covertly, Aamani leaned in close to whisper in his ear. "Where are his guards? His Secret Service or whatever they call it here? I don't see any."

"If I had to guess," Harry replied, "I'd say that some of those diplomats we saw are not actually diplomats. You can hide a lot under that baggy clothing."

President Salmaro came forward with a great big grin on his face, nodding once to his assembled guests. "Our peoples have accepted an uneasy peace for far too long," he said. "I believe we can do better. I wish to officially begin negotiations toward a formal alliance between Earth, Leyria and Antaur."

People clapped softly at that.

Harry noticed small, disk-shaped cameras hovering above the crowd, each one of them oriented to get a good view of the president. So, the Antauran news networks were covering this event. It was good to know that some things were the same no matter where you went.

"These next few weeks will be difficult," Salmaro went on. "Our peoples have held divergent views on many issues for a very long time. We will have to find ways of getting around that. But I believe, with conviction, that is worth the effort. In a few minutes, the monorail will bring you to the Diplomatic Centre in Thrinavos. The opening ceremonies will commence in two days, at the Field of Kenkalazar, where the first union of nations that eventually became our planetary government was formed over five centuries ago."

"These Antaurans do love their pomp and circumstance," Aamani whispered.

Harry nodded.

"Well then," Salmaro concluded. "May this be the beginning of a new day for all of our peoples."

The ride on the mag-lev train was smooth, and Rajel found its soft, barely-audible hum to be soothing. He sat uneasily in an aisle seat, drumming his fingers on his knees. After all these years, he had finally come back here.

Some of the diplomats were talking behind him, but he paid little mind to what they said. The anxiety that squeezed his heart in a tight grip took up most of his attention. He was angry, and worried, and so many other emotions that he didn't really know how to make sense of it all.

Tilting his head back, Rajel breathed in through his nose. "Be calm," he whispered. "You're only here for a few weeks, and this will be your chance to show them that they were wrong about your limitations."

Antauran security officers in heavy vests were moving through the aisle between the seats, leaning over to speak briefly with each passenger. At this distance, Rajel could sense them as hazy figures in his mind. He knew what they were about, and he was eager to see what would happen when they reached him.

Leaning back in his seat with arms crossed, Rajel shook his head. *Nothing changes on Antaur,* he noted. *But then, this foolishness has been going on since the Overseers put us on this world. Did you really expect it to end in twelve short years?*

One of the security officers approached Rajel's chair, standing over him. Up close, Rajel could sense that the man had a square jaw and a prominent nose. "Sir," he began in heavily-accented Leyrian. "I need a genetic-"

Rajel thrust his hand out.

The security officer actually jumped back in surprise, but he recovered quickly and retrieved a small rectangular device from a pouch on his belt. He pressed it to the back of Rajel's hand.

The scanner was warm against his skin. A beep signified that its work was done. "Thank you, sir."

The other man grunted as he checked the readout. "Odd," he said. "This says you're of Antauran descent, but you've Bonded one of the Nassai. Why would you pollute your body with alien genetic material?"

Craning his neck, Rajel took off his sunglasses to reveal his glassy eyes. "You tell me," he said in a voice like ice.

The security officer flinched at the sight – typical; Antaurans often behaved as if disabilities were contagious – and then he moved on to the next seat with a muttered apology. Rajel let the interaction pass with no further comment, but he was so distracted by his irritation that he barely noticed Keli's silhouette approaching. It was the scent of her perfume that drew him out of his reverie.

She stood demurely before him with her hands clasped in front of herself, and Rajel could sense that she was smiling. "I thought I caught a whiff of frustration from you," she said. "May I join you?"

"Please."

He scooted over, taking the window seat, even though it would be of no use to him; spatial awareness did not penetrate solid objects even if those objects were transparent. He might be passing buildings with the most beautiful architecture imaginable, but all he could sense was a flat surface next to him.

Keli sat primly beside him, glancing over her shoulder and directing a fond smile his way. Fondness from a telepath? He would never have thought it possible. "This can't be easy for you, Rajel."

"No, it is not."

"Why did you come on this mission?"

Rajel hunched over, setting an elbow on his knee and covering his face with one hand. "I honestly don't know." His own voice rasped in his ears. "Maybe it was to show them that a blind man can achieve an honoured place among the Justice Keepers. Maybe it was because I thought we could somehow leverage Antaur into changing its ways."

Pursing her lips as she considered his response, Keli nodded. "Perhaps we can," she murmured. "It's hard to pick up specific thoughts, but there's a feeling of desperation. It radiates from the Antauran delegation."

"Can't you just scan their minds and figure out what this is all about?"

"Not without alerting them to my presence, and such an intrusion might result in a major diplomatic incident."

Rajel sat up and put on his sunglasses once again. Puckering his lips, he blew air through them. "So, I guess that means we'll just have to figure out what they want the old-fashioned way."

"So it would seem."

"Thank you," he said, "for checking in on me."

It was then that he noticed another figure moving through the aisle. This one was a man in what appeared to be flowing robes. It was hard to make out specific details at this distance, but Rajel knew trouble when it was right in front of him. On Antaur, there was only one group of people who wore such garments.

Telepaths.

He could sense Keli watching the man's approach with a tight frown on her face. It didn't take much thought to guess the source of her distress. Telepaths often worked with Antauran security units, which meant that this man was scanning the Leyrian passengers for any sign of hostility. And since Keli had spent most of her formative years having her mind routinely violated by intrusive scans…

"Are you going to be all right?" Rajel whispered.

"We shall see."

Sitting still with her hands on her knees and her gaze fixed upon the approaching telepath, Keli did everything in her power to keep her face smooth. She could already tell that he was brushing the minds of every person he passed with a gentle touch. One that would not offer much in the way of insight but would also go undetected.

The telepath was a tall and lanky man with a pale face and a brown goatee. He let his gaze linger on one of the Leyrian diplomats – an older woman with curly white hair – and then he continued through the aisle.

Rajel put a hand on her arm.

It startled her to realize that she wasn't repulsed by his touch. Odd, that. On multiple occasions, this man had expressed his dislike for telepaths, and now he was showing her sympathy? She wasn't sure what to make of it.

The Antauran telepath stopped next to her seat, frowned when he saw her and then raised a quizzical eyebrow. "I would not have expected the Leyrians to have one of our kind among them."

Cocking her head to one side, Keli favoured him with a sly little smile. "They got me out of a tight spot," she explained. "You might say that I owe them a debt I can never repay."

"Interesting. Will you submit to a scan?"

Closing her eyes, she let her head rest against the seat cushion and breathed slowly through her nose. "How can you be sure that I won't deceive you? Show you exactly what you want to see?"

The man had a puzzled expression as he considered her question. "You really think you could fool me?"

This time, her grin was cheeky, and she chuckled as she got up and stood toe to toe with him. "I've spent the better part of my life learning how to defend against telepathic attacks," she said. "You'd be surprised what I can accomplish."

She felt a pressure against her mind, and rather than fight this man's intrusion, Keli let him in. Olan. That was his name. The world seemed to change around them, and now, instead of a train car, she was face to face with Olan in the middle of a green meadow with wildflowers sprouting here and there from the grass and a blue sky overhead.

Olan's mouth dropped open as he looked up to blink at the heavens. "What is this place?" His gaze snapped down to her, and she could feel his anger radiating. "How are you doing this?"

"I told you," Keli replied. "I am a *very* skilled telepath."

The pressure built again.

She let it wash against her mind like surging water against a concrete dam. Try as he might, Olan could not breach her mental defenses. The meadow remained intact with some effort from Keli, but it never wavered.

Throwing her head back, Keli roared with laughter. "Honestly, this is getting sad," she mocked. "Hurl your strength against me if you want. You will see only what I wish you to see."

Clenching his teeth, Olan squinted at her. His face reddened from the strain. "What are you hiding from me?" He was panting like a man who had been forced to run a five-mile marathon after months of lethargy.

"My secrets are my own."

Finally, the vision faded, and they were back on the speeding train. Olan collapsed against the empty seats on the other side of the aisle. Sweat left a sheen on his forehead. "Keep your secrets then," he gasped.

Folding her arms, Keli frowned as she looked him up and down. After a moment, she sniffed disdainfully. "Is this the best that Antaur can offer?" she asked. "All of these long years wishing to see the fabled talents of my people and *this* is what you offer?"

"Keli," Rajel warned.

"Yes, of course."

She resumed her seat, crossing one leg over the other and flashing a devilish grin. "You must accept my apologies, Olan," she said. "I am easily disappointed."

They made it to the Diplomatic Complex without further in-cident.

Chapter 9

A cool breeze fluttered the curtains over the bedroom window, and sunlight came in to leave a bright square on the brown carpets. It was early morning, and the sun was just starting to peek over the tops of skyscrapers in the city's western quarter. A planet with retrograde motion. That would take some getting used to.

Harry stood at the window in blue jeans and a windbreaker over his t-shirt, glorying in the feeling of cool air on his skin. There were moments when he missed Ottawa and its crisp, clear spring days.

He caught the sound of the door opening and turned.

Claire burst into the room in a windbreaker of her own, her hair done up in twin braids that fell almost to the small of her back. "Ready to go, Dad?" she asked, flashing the screen of her small multi-tool so he would see the time.

"What's your hurry?"

She put herself in front of him with fists on her hips and replied with a glower that would make her mother proud. "This is like the *only* day that you're not gonna be busy," she said. "I want to see some of this planet."

Harry didn't bother arguing; the kid had a point. Instead, he took Claire by the hand and led her to the sitting room of the suite they shared. Being in here made him feel like he had been dropped into the middle of some movie about Victorian England. There were gilded chairs and sofas to match, all decked out in gold with ornate patterns on each one.

Small, wooden tables in each corner supported glass vases with some kind of red flowers that Harry didn't recognize. Something they had cultivated on Antaur, no doubt. But they filled the room with a pleasant scent.

On one wall, a screen – not SmartGlass but something similar to what they had on Earth – was playing a cartoon movie where the characters all spoke Raen. He assumed it was the kids' channel. At least, he *hoped* it was the kids' channel.

When he opened the door to their suite, he found two officers in blue uniforms and heavy black vests in the hallway outside. Both glanced his way. "Sir?" one said in a gruff voice. "Do you require assistance?"

"Just taking my daughter to the Alantu Zoo."

"We recommend against that, sir."

Harry leaned one shoulder against the door-frame, shaking his head in dismay, "Are you telling me that we're going to be cooped up in here for the duration of our stay?" He could already sense Claire's disappointment.

The guard on his left made a face, shared a quick glance with his partner and then returned his attention to Harry. "The Diplomatic Complex is safe, sir," he explained. "Not everyone in the general populace approves of these talks. Your Earther clothing is easy to spot and makes you a target."

"Yes, but are we forbidden from leaving?"

Turning his back on Harry, the guard tapped a comm-unit on his vest and spoke in Raen. Harry couldn't understand a word of it. He was beginning to feel a bit sheepish, but his desire to see at least *a little* of this planet was almost as strong as Claire's.

When the security officer turned back around, his eyes were as hard as diamonds. "No, sir, you are not prohibited from leaving," he answered. "But I would advise you to travel with at least one of your Justice Keepers."

"Noted."

The hallway was just as posh as Harry's suite: beige walls with gold trim in rectangular patterns and doors at even intervals. The blue carpets were so thick that his shoes almost seemed to sink into them, and the lights were shaped like candelabras that hung from the ceiling.

They found a bank of elevators with polished steel doors, but when Harry put his hand on the scanner, nothing happened. Well, not nothing. A harsh buzz filled his ears, and a computerized voice barked at him in a language he didn't understand.

Claire was at his side with hands in her jacket pockets, frowning anxiously at the elevator door. "Your ID card," she muttered. "Don't you remember what they told us on the train? You have to use it for everything here."

Harry shut his eyes, struggling to contain his irritation. That he would need an ID card just to ride the elevator… "Yeah," he said, nodding once. "You're right. I forgot about that annoying little rule."

He fished the card out of his wallet and then pressed it to the palm scanner. And to think, people had insisted that he would never need a wallet again when he left Earth. Ha! So much for that empty promise. Green LEDs flashed, and the elevator doors opened.

Once inside, he had to use the card again just to have the elevator take them to the main floor. Antauran citizens were given small biochip implants in their hands; that way, they would have their ID with them wherever they went. Harry, on the other hand, was a foreign dignitary who would not be staying. So they gave him a temporary card.

The main lobby was exactly what you might have expected after seeing the ritzy suites upstairs: polished tiles and marble pillars that supported a high ceiling. The front entrance stood between two large, rectangular windows.

To his left, a reception desk was staffed by holograms that remained present even when no one was availing themselves of their services. There were two of them: a young man with a mop of sandy hair and a young woman with dark curls. Beyond them, bright sunlight came through the main entrance, making his eyes smart.

Outside, they found Anna waiting on the curb of the u-shaped driveway that led to the gate. She had dark jeans and a jacket of her own, and the sunlight glinted off the black lenses of her sunglasses. "Hey, guys!"

Claire ran over and threw her arms around Anna. "Thanks for coming with us. This is the only fun I get to have on this trip."

"Aw, sweetie, I'm sure that's not true."

"Well, still…"

Stepping out of Claire's embrace, Anna came forward with lips pursed and nodded as if to say that he met with her approval. "Harry," she said. "I'm glad to see that you put on your business scowl today."

"It's these damn ID cards."

"Oh, don't get me started."

Harry turned his back on the complex, a light breeze ruffling his hair. "So, how do we get there?" he asked, stepping onto the road. "I'm told that they have a public transit system similar to the one in Denabria."

He felt Anna's hand on his shoulder, and when he glanced in her direction, she was wearing that impish smile that all but guaranteed she was up to no good. "You know how you're always telling me to be less impulsive?" she asked. "Well, today will be the perfect opportunity for you to be a little more so. Let's just head down to a bus monorail terminal and see what happens."

"Brilliant."

The sun was just shy of its peak as they walked along a wide stone pathway with smaller roads branching off here and there. One led to a domed structure that hosted an exhibit of bats and snakes and other such creatures.

Another went up a small hill to an enclosure for native gorillas. Or so Harry was told. He couldn't read Raen, so he had to get directions from the various holograms that served as tour guides, and then he had to piece it all together from memory.

Shielding his eyes from the sun with one hand, Harry squinted into the distance. "I think," he said, pointing, "that the big cat exhibit is in that direction. We should go. I'm told they have an offshoot breed of tigers we don't have on Earth."

Claire practically took off at a run.

Harry let his arm drop, threw his head back and stomped after her. "Claire, we've talked about this," he said. "You can't just rush off. If you get lost, you won't be able to ask the locals for help."

His daughter stopped in her tracks, then turned around slowly with her eyes on the ground. "Yeah," she muttered. "Sorry."

"It's fine."

A few minutes later, they were halfway to the jungle cat exhibit with Claire in the lead. She was about twenty feet in front of him, just far enough that she wouldn't hear it when Anna fell in at his side and whispered, "She's a kid, Harry. Let her have a little fun, why don't you?"

"It's not safe."

Anna was walking along with her arms swinging, smiling as she shook her head. "What's gonna happen to her?" she asked. "Our multi-tools can still contact one another even without the network, and the people here are just, well, people. They don't mean us any harm."

"That's a very Leyrian attitude."

"And what's wrong with that?"

Turning his face up to the sky, Harry blinked slowly as he searched for an answer that would not offend her. "You grew up on a world that was fairly peaceful and idyllic," he said. "You don't know what it's like to be afraid of strangers."

Anna's mouth became a thin line, but she stared directly forward, not bothering to so much as glance his way. "If you ask me," she murmured. "You've become a little *too* good at being afraid of strangers."

The jungle cat enclosure was surrounded by a tall concrete wall at the top of a hill. A sloping path ran down to join the main road, passing under a wooden archway, and Claire was already halfway up by the time Harry reached the bottom. She turned, waiting for him with a mischievous smile that was an almost perfect copy of Anna's.

Harry climbed the slope with his eyes closed, heaving out a sigh. "Heaven save me from impulsive young women." It had never occurred to him until now to wonder what kind of example his young Keeper friends were setting. Melissa had always been a little unsure of herself; he had never really worried about her picking up some of Anna's bad habits. On the contrary, she was more susceptible to Jack's unjustified mistrust in his own abilities.

But Claire...

Unlike her elder sister, Claire had some of that bullish excess of confidence. So, of course, Harry had made the perfectly sensible choice of dragging her across the galaxy to a potentially hostile world. He could just hear Della's admonishments. Hell, if she knew that her youngest was currently on Antaur, Della would probably fly out on the fastest ship just to regain custody of both daughters. How exactly *would* that work now that Harry and the girls were Leyrian citizens?

At the top of the hill, their path curved around the corner of the concrete wall and eventually came to a gentle slope that led up to a platform. From there, they could look into the enclosure.

Slanted glass panes at the top of the wall gave a view of what almost appeared to be a miniature jungle, complete with tall broad-leafed trees. There was a pond in the middle of the enclosure with two lionesses sitting by the edge. At least Harry thought they were lionesses. Their fur was a slightly darker shade of orange.

Bracing her hands on the top of the wall, Claire stood up on her toes and practically pressed her nose to the glass. "Cool," she said. "Think we can get their attention?"

"I don't think we want their attention."

"They can't hurt us, Dad."

Harry stood behind her with arms folded, glaring at the back of her head. "No, they can't," he agreed. "But teasing the animals is cruel, and it will probably get us kicked out of the park."

"Oh."

Anna seemed to take that as a cue to step up beside Claire and gently rest a hand on the girl's back. "It's okay, sweetie," she murmured. Whether Harry was supposed to hear that or not, he couldn't say.

"I didn't want to upset the lions," Claire said.

"I know."

They were interrupted by what seemed to be the rumbling of a door sliding open, and when Harry ventured a look into the enclosure, he saw something he would not have expected. A group of kids about Claire's age – maybe a dozen of them – were led by a zookeeper into the lion's habitat. The entire group stood on a small stone platform just under the concrete wall.

Sure enough two lions emerged from the forested area and came padding over to inspect the new arrivals. They came right up to the edge of the platform and then sat primly without moving an inch.

One of the youngest children walked up to them.

The lions just watched him.

"What?" Anna spluttered. "They let *kids* in there?"

A hologram appeared to answer her question, coalescing to form the image of a young, pale woman with short brown hair in a bob. "Low-level force-fields protect the children from harm," she said. "The lions will not be injured if they come into contact with them, but they have learned not to try."

Claire whirled around, leaning back against the wall with an enormous grin. "Can we go in there?" she asked. "Please! Please! Please!"

The hologram flickered, and when she reappeared, her expression had darkened just a little. "Access to the interior of the enclosure is limited to guests with Class X-2 status or higher."

Harry growled under his breath. Less than ten minutes after leaving the Diplomatic Complex, they had discovered the purpose of requiring ID cards to access even the most mundane areas and services. He had heard that the Antaurans embraced a social hierarchy based on one's proximity to the bloodlines that had produced the first generation of telepaths, but he had never really seen it up close.

There were five social classes, determined mainly by ancestry, with X-1 being the highest and X-5 the lowest. As foreigners, Harry, Claire and Anna were all designated as X-0. There was no way they were getting in there. Of course, that didn't stop Claire from asking. "Isn't there any way you can make an exception?"

"Of course," the hologram replied in a cheerful tone. "For a price of fifty tokens per person, you will be granted admittance to the enclosure."

"Wait," Anna said. "Tokens?"

The hologram flickered again. Harry liked to think that their propensity for asking questions that most Antaurans would consider to be common knowledge was overloading the damn thing's circuits. "Your ID cards will allow you to access your accounts."

"Yes," Anna replied in a tone that was growing more and more hostile with every syllable. "But how do we *get* tokens?"

"Tokens can be awarded by anyone from a higher class to anyone of a lower class."

Anna stepped forward so that she was right in front of the hologram. "Okay," she said. "So, how do members of the upper classes get tokens?"

"I don't understand."

"Where do the tokens come from?"

The hologram replied with a blank stare as if Anna had just asked why the sky was blue, and after a second, she said, "Tokens can be awarded by anyone from a higher class to anyone of a lower class."

"Forget it," Anna said. "Let's just go."

Chapter 10

Artificial gravity and uniform acceleration made their descent fairly smooth, and when the small transport shuttle touched down, it did so with only the softest jostle. A hatch in the starboard side opened to reveal a massive green field surrounded by a thick forest of skeletal trees.

Despite all the precautions to ensure a smooth ride, Jack stood with one hand on the overhead support bar. The diplomats in his group had taken all of the seats along the port and starboard walls. The Keepers stood.

Looking up at the ceiling, Jack exhaled through his nose. "All right," he barked at the others. "You all know your roles. Vranel, Taaz, Anderson, form a perimeter. Let's get this done quick and quiet."

The three agents he had named all leaped through the open hatch, though Veronica Anderson – a young woman from Saskatoon with a bob of short brown hair – gave him a nod of respect before she joined the others.

"Let's just pray nothing goes wrong."

Jack hopped out and landed in the soggy grass with his knees bent. He straightened cautiously and reached for a pistol that wasn't there. "Brilliant," he mumbled, recalling Rajel's complaints from the other day.

The first diplomat to emerge was an older woman in red who wore her gray hair up in a bun. Jack didn't know her, but she gave him a kind smile and took his hand to make the large step down.

Behind her, a dark-skinned man with a neatly trimmed beard stepped out without even sparing a glance for Jack. That was Brendan Taval, a man from Leyria's Threngali Province. And he seemed to be one of Dusep's sympathizers.

Next came an olive-skinned man in his mid-twenties with flecks of gray in his dark hair. He showed Jack a toothy grin before coming out. And it went on like that for several minutes, diplomats exiting the transport shuttle, forming a small cluster with a Keeper on each side. Jack watched his agents – they weren't really his, but he was the senior-most officer in this group – and he was pleased to see that they had their eyes on the trees that surrounded them. If anyone wanted to attack this summit, they'd do it from there.

When the diplomats had all clustered together, Jack's team ushered them along a red carpet that stretched from the shuttle to a round stone platform in the middle of the field. There were other lines of carpet, all expanding from that platform like spokes on a wheel, each one leading to a different shuttle where other diplomats disembarked. Their group set off at a quick pace.

Jack brought up the rear.

Pausing briefly on his long trek, he turned and looked over his shoulder toward the distant trees. There was nothing out there, of course. Just a quiet forest with the odd squirrel scampering through the dirt.

Closing his eyes, Jack dragged a knuckle across his forehead. "Don't go looking for trouble, Hunter," he whispered. "They've planned out every detail of this event. It's going to be a nice, quiet, uneventful day."

He ran to join the others.

The carpet went on for at least two hundred metres – give or take – before it ended at the edge of the stone platform. There were at least two hundred chairs spread out on it, all facing a podium at one end. There were dignitaries up there already. Jack could see the Antauran president reviewing notes for his speech on a tablet.

And there were guards.

Oh boy, were there guards! Antauran security officers in full tactical gear stood in between the many flagpoles that formed a ring around the stone platform. Another group of them were up by the podium, keeping eyes on their president. The sight of them made Jack uneasy, and Summer echoed his concern.

Antauran guards with assault rifles surrounding a few dozen unarmed Keepers. No, it wouldn't be a total curb-stomp – his people would put up a fight – but there was only so much that Bending could do against that.

Harry arrived with his own group and shot Jack a glance that conveyed his anxiety in a way words never could. It was the sort of thing very few people would have picked up on. You had to know a guy for years to read him like that.

Claire was with him in a maroon dress and a light jacket, and she smiled when she saw Jack. She offered a friendly little wave before taking one of the seats at the edge of the platform.

"Okay," Jack said into his earpiece. "I think we're good. Take position." He joined a group of Keepers about ten metres back from the platform. They were all dressed almost identically: jeans or cargo pants and windbreakers over light armoured vests. Nothing that would stop a rifle round, but some protection was better than none and body armour was not a Keeper's main line of defense anyway.

The weather was actually mild despite an overcast sky that threatened to drizzle at any moment. Though apparently, their brief shuttle ride had taken them a few hundred kilometres south of the Diplomatic Complex. Or whatever units the Antaurans used for measurement. Jack wasn't entirely sure of the geography.

President Salmaro stepped onto the podium, gripping the lectern in both hands and smiling for his audience. "We have finally made it here," he began. "It's taken us a long time – generations – but we are here.

"Today marks the beginning of a new alliance between Earth, Antaur and Leyria. We are all aware of ships from distant stars encroaching on our borders. Some claim it's the Ragnosians, others that these strange vessels represent a new threat. It doesn't matter. We will stand together, and we will stand strong!"

Anna trotted up beside him, gently nudging his arm and favouring him with a grin when he glanced in her direction. Her presence made him feel a little less uneasy. Those woods and the threats they might conceal were still weighing on his mind.

"Pompous windbag," Jack muttered. "Guy loves to hear himself talk."

"You say that about every politician."

"And I'm always right."

"The alliance," Salmaro said, adopting that stern stare every politician seemed to learn after two days in office, "will foster trade, will bring our worlds closer together and will keep us safe from foreign threats."

"Why are threats always foreign?" Jack whispered.

Anna gave him a playful elbow to the ribs, a gentle reminder that he was to be on his best behaviour. He took it in good humour. She was right, after all, but that did not make listening to the speech any less tedious.

It went on for several minutes longer, rehashing the same points in slightly different wording. Trade, culture and ixnay on those damn, dirty people from the other side of the galaxy. Or so Jack thought, at least. If he was honest, he had to admit that he really wasn't paying attention. But really, how many ways were there to say that they would all be the friendliest of friendly friends?

Politicians…

President Salmaro, Harry noted, certainly did love pomp and circumstance. That seemed to be a common trait among Antaurans. This five-minute speech was, well, fluff. But its central thesis was valid if a bit overstated. An alliance between their three worlds *would* protect them from the Ragnosian threat.

Harry sat with his hands on his knees listening attentively and sometimes nodding along. He could feel Claire fidgeting next to him – she was probably bored – but he paid it no mind until she let out an exasperated sigh.

A glance to the side revealed that his daughter was hunched over with her elbows on her thighs and her chin atop laced fingers. And that look on her face said that she was about ready to say something wildly inappropriate.

Harry arched an eyebrow.

Claire went red, then sat up straight and tried her darndest to look like she was enjoying every minute of this. Well, at least she tried. Melissa probably would have liked the ceremony, even if it was a little dull; it was a shame she couldn't be here.

Cautiously, Harry reached into his pants' pocket and closed his fist around the N'Jal. It unfolded as soon as he made contact, bonding with him, its fibers digging into the skin of his palm.

He raised his hand just high enough to let the N'Jal get a whiff of his surroundings without being conspicuous. Nothing out of the ordinary. No radio signals that he could not identify as Keepers or Antauran security talking on their comms; though he couldn't actually *hear* what they said, he could sense the signals zipping back and forth.

Harry shut his eyes and breathed out a sigh of relief, letting his hand drop to rest on his knee. *We're clear,* he thought. *Maybe we'll be able to get through today without some major incident.*

"And now," Salmaro went on, "I would like the assembled dignitaries gathered here to come forward for formal introductions."

"Everyone, get down!" one of the Keepers yelled.

Without even thinking, Harry grabbed the back of Claire's dress and pushed her down onto her knees. He joined her a moment later, panting. "Dad," Claire moaned. "What's going on?"

Squeezing his eyes shut, Harry drew in a breath. "I don't know," he whispered. "I think we might be under-"

He was cut off when force-fields sprang up at the edge of the platform, screens of white static that blocked a barrage of bullets. More of them popped up on all sides. They were being hit from every direction. He knew he had been a fool to believe that they were safe here!

Claire was whimpering.

With those force-fields popping up and vanishing on all sides – not to mention the commotion of frenzied bodies all around him – he couldn't get a good view of who was out there. Antaurans? Some dissident faction who opposed the peace talks. Or maybe Slade's people?

He looked to his right in time to see a small missile shoot out from the treeline, fly over the damp grass and then plant itself in the ground about five feet away from the edge of the platform.

It went off with a wave, like static electricity expanding through the air, and then sparks flashed around the platform as force-field generators exploded in the shockwave. Harry felt his hair stand on end.

Suddenly bullets were zipping through the open air. More than a few diplomats, Leyrians and Antaurans alike, tried to get up and run for cover. Some got hit before they even took two steps, falling to the ground with a spray of blood.

Claire was sobbing.

Harry threw his arms around her, wrapping his body protectively around hers. With one hand, he rolled up his suit-jacket sleeve and then tapped the screen of his multi-tool. Nothing. So, he was right. That missile had unleashed a massive electromagnetic pulse. Jack had told him once that the Antaurans had never developed EMP round technology. So, they had to use this more blunt approach.

They had never developed EMP round technology!

They didn't have it!

He raised his hand above his head and used the N'Jal to erect a dome-shaped force-field around himself and Claire. He made sure that its edge stopped a few inches off the ground so that air could get in. "It's okay, honey," Harry whispered. "We're safe now."

For now, at least.

Down on her belly, Anna wiggled like a worm in the grass as bullets rushed past above her. The EMP blast had left her hair a wild mess of flyaway strands. "We have to coordinate an offensive!" she cried out.

Jack was next to her, flat on his stomach and squinting at the distant treeline. "First we have to figure out *who* we're fighting!"

He was right. It was bloody pandemonium all around them. Bleakness take her!

The combatants who popped out from between two trees to fire a few shots at the platform wore the gray uniforms and black vests of Antauran security officers. But then so did the Antaurans who clustered around the platform, firing back at the trees. Their helmets lacked face masks, but all these men were strangers to Anna anyway. There was just no way to distinguish friend from foe, assuming, of course, that any of them could be considered friends.

Anna looked up with teeth clenched, a bead of sweat running down her forehead. "How did they even get this close?" she snarled. "They were supposed to have a security perimeter for miles around this place!"

Jack rose to a crouch and thrust his hand out to craft a Bending. The air before him seemed to pulse, deflecting the two rounds that the man who had decided to take a quick shot at them had unleashed. He let his arm drop, the Bending vanishing. "Fight now," he said. "Analyze later."

Anna nodded.

"We have to take the fight to them," she spat.

"All Keepers," Director Varno said in her earpiece. "We're going to make a retreat. Teams One, Three, Four and Seven will escort the diplomats to the transport shuttles. All other teams will enter the forest and engage the enemy."

"Who *is* the enemy?" Jack protested.

Anna growled.

That last order had her and Jack both headed into the woods. She suspected that was a tactical decision. Varno had sent teams whose members had distinguished combat records. Of course, they were going in without weapons, so…

Wincing, Anna gave her head a shake. "You ready for this?"

"I'm frantic," Jack said.

"So, load me up," she mumbled.

As one, they got up and started loping across the field like a pair of wolves chasing a rabbit, moving at a speed no ordinary human could match. One of their enemies poked his head out from behind a tree then raised his rifle and took aim.

In perfect sync, Jack and Anna raised their hands and crafted a Bending together. Sharing the load put less strain on each of them, for which Seth was very grateful. Anna corrected some of the geometric flaws in Jack's design, creating the same effect with less energy. He had less technical skill with Bendings, but his creative uses of Bent Gravity always left her speechless.

Bullets sped toward them, curved upward in a vertical loop and then flew back toward the man who had released them. They seemed to hit the tree instead. She heard the sound of wood splitting.

When they let their Bending drop, the way was clear.

So, they ran into the forest.

Under the protection of his force-field, Harry felt a bullet rico-chet off the surface of the dome. He also felt the strain of main-taining the barrier. This field wasn't projected by an emitter that relied on a rechargeable battery; the N'Jal was drawing energy from his body. And from something else, of course – vacuum energy, maybe? Harry wasn't exactly sure how the damn thing worked – but part of the load was his to bear.

Claire was watching him with large, dark eyes, her cheeks glistening from freshly-shed tears. But she wasn't crying any longer. In fact, she was eerily calm. "Is this what it's like for you?"

Shutting his eyes tight, Harry felt sweat oozing from his pores. He was trembling from the stress of holding the force-field in place. "Pretty much," he said through gritted teeth. "Ever since that day when you were six."

"When Anna came to Earth."

"Yeah."

Claire twisted on the spot, looking over her shoulder at the people scrambling all around them. Force-fields that had been generated by Overseer tech were a little different than the stan-dard variety. Instead of flickering static, this one looked like the shimmer rising off the ground on a hot summer day. "Dad, we have to help them."

"I have to protect you."

"You can't let them die!"

Harry felt his lips writhe, a growl rumbling in his throat. "They are not my family, Claire," he snapped. "*You* are."

"My life isn't any more important than any of theirs."

"Don't be stupid. Of course it is."

She slapped him.

His eleven-year-old daughter full-arm slapped him across the face, leaving a sting that almost shattered his concentration and caused him to drop the force-field. Harry was about to scold her, but the death-glare in Claire's eyes made the words die on the tip of his tongue. "My life," she said, "is *not* more important than any of theirs. Look around you. People are dying. You have the power to save them. Do something!"

Harry felt a sudden rush of shame. It was a sad day when a parent couldn't live up to their own child's moral standards. "Stay behind me," he said. "Keep low and tell me if you see anything."

Claire nodded.

With that, Harry dropped the force-field and stood up to face his enemies.

Chapter 11

"Split up!" Anna shouted when they crossed the treeline.

Jack didn't argue with her; he merely turned right down a winding path that snaked its way around twisted tree trunks. A moment later, he vanished behind a curtain of leaves from a drooping branch, leaving her to go her own way. This far south, it seemed that the trees were close to full bloom, which meant decreased visibility.

Anna went left, following the same path in the opposite direction. It wasn't long before the ground to her right began to slope downward with trees poking out at slanted angles. A carpet of dead leaves littered the hillside, leaves that would almost certainly squish or crunch underfoot, creating noise that would draw her enemies' attention. What was she doing? She had no weapon! Bloody Antaurans and their paranoia.

She noticed that none of them had entered the forest to provide support or cover fire for Justice Keepers who were supposed to be their allies. But that too was probably a tactical decision. With no way to distinguish friend from foe, it was far too likely that a Keeper would kill or hurt a friendly Antauran. Or that they would fail to react to a hostile and die from a split second's indecision.

Anna crept along the ridge at the top of the hill, moving with deliberate slowness, turning her head this way and that. To her left, the forest ended a mere ten paces away, and beyond that the Field of Kenkalazar was empty. There was still a commotion on the distant platform, but she couldn't think about that. Protecting the diplomats was not her assignment.

The slope on her right became a little less steep, and she noticed a clear path down the hillside just up ahead. She was toying with the idea of going deeper into the forest when the sound of footsteps made her heart skip a beat.

A man in an Antauran uniform was coming up that path.

Ducking behind a tree, Anna shut her eyes tight and drew in a shuddering breath. "You can do this," she assured herself. "A Justice Keeper does not need a weapon. She *is* the weapon."

Anna stepped out into the open.

The Antauran man was maybe twenty paces up the path, and he froze in mid-step when he saw her. As if he couldn't believe his eyes. Less than a second later, he regained his wits and began to raise his assault rifle.

Anna ran at him.

She dove, hitting the ground and somersaulting along the dirt path as bullets sped past above her. She grabbed a fallen stick and came up on one knee. With a growl, Anna threw it as hard as she could.

The man tried to adjust his aim.

Her stick went point-first into his thigh, causing him to shriek and lower his rifle. The gun went off several times as he compulsively pulled the trigger, bullets churning up clumps of dirt. But that gave her the moment she needed.

Anna got up and ran at full speed. She leaped, flying head-first toward him with her arms outstretched. The soldier looked up just in time for her to clamp both hands onto his rifle and force him down onto his back.

Wrenching the weapon from his grip, Anna flipped over to land crouched with her enemy just behind her. The very instant her feet touched the ground, she called upon Seth and threw up a Time Bubble.

The forest around her became a blurry haze of greens and browns with patches of cloudy sky shining through. Further up the path, another commando was in the process of turning around, swinging his weapon in a horizontal arc that would eventually bring it in line with Anna. She saw him as a blurry figure that rippled and pulsed. Still as a statue but distorted to her eyes.

Anna lifted the rifle she had stolen, lining up the shot as best she could and then squeezing the trigger. A line of bullets appeared just beyond the confines of her bubble, slowly inching their way to their target.

She let the bubble collapse.

The second soldier stumbled as bullets pierced his right leg just below the knee. He toppled over, falling face-down in the dirt, crying out as he hit the ground. His screams would almost certainly bring reinforcements.

Anna was already on her feet, running off through the trees, seeking cover. She had to lead them away from the diplomats; so, she went further down the hill. In the back of her mind, she couldn't help but wonder if Jack was all right, but she trusted him to take care of himself.

Jack had wandered for maybe five minutes without encountering any enemies. He followed the little trail as it traced the perimeter of the Field of Kenkalazar, periodically looking over his right shoulder to see what was happening on the platform.

It wasn't long before he heard the distant buzzing of gunfire. Antauran and Leyrian weapons – which used magnetically propelled ammunition – weren't as loud as Earth guns, but they still made noise. Cries of pain echoed through the forest. It seemed he was going the wrong way. The fighting was somewhere behind him.

Jack turned around.

Staying low, he followed the path back the way he had come. There were trees on either side of him, but on his right, the forest was considerably denser. A bad guy might pop up from behind one of those tall oaks at any moment.

Every now and then, he passed a narrow path that led deeper into the woods. Each time, he would hide behind the nearest tree and scan the trail for any sign of danger. He really hated feeling defenseless.

Wiping sweat off his brow, Jack frowned and shook his head. "Dad was right," he whispered. "This job *is* going to get me killed."

He was almost back to the place where he and Anna had parted ways when the soft sound of footsteps made him freeze. About fifty feet ahead of him, a man in gray stepped out from the brush and turned to face Jack, raising his assault rifle.

Spatial awareness let Jack estimate the trajectory of incoming fire. By instinct, he leaned to his right and felt a three-round burst rush past his left shoulder. The other man was adjusting his aim, but that wasn't the biggest problem.

A second commando came into the open behind Jack.

With a surge of Bent Gravity, Jack jumped and curled his legs, allowing this second adversary to rush past beneath him. He landed just behind the other man and quickly slid an arm around the guy's throat.

Holding his captive close, Jack used the man as a human shield. The other one hesitated briefly, not wanting to injure his comrade. The Antaurans' heavy armoured vests should stop anything short of a high-impact round, but there was always the chance of a stray shot hitting an arm or a leg.

Jack took the taser from his prisoner's belt.

Activating it, he pressed the sparking prongs into the other man's neck and felt a convulsion surge through the guy's body.

He dragged the unconscious man behind a tall tree and dropped to a crouch.

Bullets pounded the other side of the trunk. It was a massive oak, large enough to cover his whole body and thick enough to stop even a rifle round. Two or three, anyway. Those bullets would eventually punch through if that first guy put his weapon on full automatic.

Jack quickly drew the fallen man's sidearm.

More bullets hit the other side of the tree, landing like hard raindrops on a window. Chunks of wood flew this way and that into the forest. Jack couldn't stay here forever. It was time to move!

He threw himself sideways, rolling out into the open.

Coming up in a squat, he raised the pistol in both hands and let spatial awareness guide his aim. He fired. A bullet ripped through the soldier's shin, tripping him and knocking him down onto his knees.

Jack fired again.

This round grazed the other man's upper arm, causing him to drop his weapon and shout from the pain of it. It was a sound that saddened Jack. Sadness faded to bitterness when he contemplated the absurdity of feeling sympathy for a man who had just tried to murder him.

Striding forward with the gun in both hands, its barrel pointed down at the ground, Jack shook his head as he approached. "Stay down," he said. "Next shot is lethal."

He meant it.

The other man looked up at him with a gaping mouth. He squeaked, but there were no words. In fact, the guy fell flat on his face. Well, that was two enemies down, Maybe he could incapacitate these guys without having to kill them. Maybe.

Rajel moved like a ghost through the trees, following Tan Eldrana and Christopher Phillips deeper into the forest. The other two Keepers were shadowy figures in his mind, maneuvering around twisted tree trunks, making little sound that even his ears could pick up. The three of them had been together when their team was ordered into the forest.

Jerking his head toward a tree on his left, Rajel signalled the other two to follow him. He was behind the pair of them, but their spatial awareness would let them catch the motion. Silence was pivotal.

Pressing his back to the tree trunk, Rajel breathed in through his nose. "You should let me scout ahead," he whispered when Christopher stepped into view. "No matter how careful we are, one man is less noisy than three."

"Okay. But why you?"

Rajel felt a smile bloom along with a flush of heat in his face. Bragging about his talents always made him feel a little chagrin, but the other man had asked. "Because no one does silence like I do."

Tan emerged on the other side of the tree. A tall and slender man with very little hair to speak of, he scoffed at Rajel's suggestion. "You would be putting yourself in unnecessary danger."

Rajel shook his head.

"We should stay together," Tan insisted.

A thought occurred to Rajel, one that he could exploit. "Well, your title is Special Agent," he said. "Mine is Operative. So, you can officially consider that to be an order, Agent Eldrana,"

"As if that means anything to-"

Rajel gave the man a death glare. Coming from a blind man, it had a noticeable effect. Tan stepped back and then nodded his assent to Rajel's plan. Excellent. It pleased Rajel to know that he had properly imitated the gesture. Spatial awareness gave him a very good sense of other people's posture, but facial expressions required close proximity.

"You really wanna go alone and unarmed?" Christopher hissed.

"I'm not unarmed."

"But they said we couldn't bring guns!"

Rajel pulled up the sleeves of his windbreaker to reveal about three feet of thin, gold chain coiled around each forearm. Every link had tiny symbols etched upon it. Gold was not the strongest metal, but it would serve his purpose.

Tan narrowed his eyes as he studied the chain. "They just let you bring that into a diplomatic summit?" he asked, shaking his head. "Even when they went over us with all those scanners?"

"These are the ceremonial chains of the Horvati religion," Rajel said. "Similar to a Catholic Rosary." He had studied the religions of Leyria upon moving there, and, given that half of his new allies were from Earth, he had made it a point to familiarize himself with that world's cultures as well. Christopher, at least, appreciated the explanation and nodded to show his understanding. "Antaurans don't think of them as weapons."

"And what are you gonna do with those?" Tan protested.

"Just wait and see."

Moving with the utmost care, Rajel ducked low and began his slow trek deeper into the forest. It wasn't long before the trees around him grew taller and thicker. The sounds of animals scampering and wind sighing filled his ears. The scent of mud and rain hit his nose. He used spatial awareness to guide him and supplemented it with sound and smell and touch, each stirring of the air warning him of motion to his left or right, though none of it was caused by humans.

He uncoiled the chains from around his arms and fastened them together. Each end piece was actually a small clip. That would give him about six feet to work with. Not as much as he would like, but it would have to do. Now, he just had to decide where to-

Left and forward, a voice whispered in his mind.

Rajel stopped, looking up toward the heavens with pursed lips. "Keli?" he asked in a voice barely louder than a whisper. "Is that you?"

He felt a strong pressure on his mind and bid his Nassai to let Keli contact him. The images she sent him were jumbled and discordant, full of sensations he could not make sense of. Only after a great deal of effort was he able to calm himself and recognize the strange shapes as trees and logs and men. Was this what it was like to experience colour? What a horrid sensation! Why would anyone want it?

Rajel saw, in his mind, two uniformed men in a small clearing at the base of a ten-foot-high rock wall. They had their rifles hanging lazily, muzzles drooping toward the ground, and they seemed to be more interested in talking than in killing Keepers. Who were these men? What army would tolerate such a lapse? Forward and left. Less than two minutes away.

He maneuvered around a twisted tree and crept along the uneven ground, cresting a hill and then flowing down the other side. Soon, he came to a thicket, and when he slid his body through the narrow gap between two poplars – leaves rustled, but there was no helping it – he found himself on top of the rock wall.

At the edge, he found one of those mercenaries standing below with his back turned. Where was his companion? Well, no matter. Dispatching one would have to do.

Rajel flung the chain so that its jagged edge licked the back of the man's neck. That brought a yelp of pain, and the inattentive fool stumbled around to face the wall, gasping when he realized that he had been caught unaware.

The chain struck him right between the eyes, leaving a welt on his nose. He fell on his ass, moaning.

Rajel leaped from the wall.

He passed right over the other man and then dropped to land in a crouch, the chain held tightly in both hands. The young idiot was calling for help, but Rajel ignored him. Other sounds filled his ears. Panting. Footsteps in the mud. Before spatial awareness told him anything, he knew exactly which tree the other one was hiding behind.

Rajel spun to face it.

The second commando popped out into the open, snarling when he noticed Rajel standing over his fallen comrade. He clutched his rifle with both hands, lifting it with a throaty growl.

Rajel lashed out with the chain.

It took the other man across his naked cheek, leaving a fiery gash in the skin and knocking his aim askew. Bullets flew uselessly into the forest, some of them hitting trees and splitting the wood.

The chain's next target was the barrel of the other man's gun. It coiled around the rifle in a tight grip, and with one quick tug, Rajel yanked the weapon out of his enemy's hands. The fallen man was rising behind him.

The one that he had just disarmed stood there gaping at him for half a second. He quickly reached for his sidearm and drew that from its holster.

Rajel charged him.

He leaped into a flying side-kick that struck the man's chest before he could get his pistol up, pinning the man against the trunk of the tree he had been hiding behind. A high-pitched wheeze told Rajel that this enemy was defeated.

He landed with a grunt.

The other one was behind him, picking up the rifle he had lost when he fell to the ground, bringing it up to aim for Rajel's exposed back.

Turning quickly, Rajel lashed out with the chain, its end striking the other man's throat and leaving a shallow cut there. Shock made the poor fool stumble and lower his weapon.

Rajel struck out again, this time coiling the chain around his adversary's right leg. He gave a tug and threw the frightened soldier down onto his back. "Stop! Please!" the man called out in Raen. "What are you?"

" A demon," Rajel replied with a smile. "Flee."

Harry Carlson rose in wrath, his rumpled suit jacket hanging lopsided on his body, his dark hair a mess. He set his jaw and began a slow trek across the platform, stepping over dead bodies and fallen chairs. *Why did I ever think bringing Claire here was a good idea? I must be an idiot.*

He thrust his left hand out, fingers splayed, and waved it back and forth like a police dog searching for the scent of a perp. In truth, he was looking for heat signatures among the trees that surrounded the Field of Kenkalazar. At this distance, the N'Jal's ability to detect body heat was limited, but he could try.

There were Antauran officers here, men in gray uniforms who squatted over the bodies of wounded diplomats and reporters. They seemed to be treating everybody who needed it, not just their own people. God be praised for small miracles, as his grandfather used to say.

A tingling sensation in his hand as he waved it over a spot off to his right. Instantly, Harry spun to face that spot, thrust his palm out and raised a shimmering force-field that snapped into place just before a bullet struck the other side. "Claire! Behind me!"

She hopped to obey that order.

More bullets pounded the rippling curtain of electromagnetic energy. Harry grunted as he felt them land. It was too much to hope that he would be allowed to just see to the wounded without enemies trying to kill him. Hell, the only reason that he wasn't standing smack dab in the middle of a storm of gunfire was that the Keepers who had gone into the forest had most of those men occupied. But a few would slip past their nets and take pot shots at the survivors on the platform. The diplomats were the *real* target.

He let his force-field vanish when the gunfire stopped. His eyes saw a brief flash of gray moving between two of the distant trees. Then the man who had attacked them was gone. Bloody hell!

Harry felt his lips writhe, pulling back to show a rictus of clenched teeth, and then he growled. "You!" he spat, whirling around to face a uniformed man who was down on one knee in the middle of the platform. "Your sidearm! Now!"

The man looked over his shoulder to study Harry with a frown. A moment later, he shook his head and returned his attention to a young woman with bandages over her bare shoulder. Harry knew that his fluency in Raen was less than perfect, but he was sure that he had gotten the point across. "I said I need your gun," he insisted.

This time, when the other man looked at him, Harry produced another force-field that distorted his image. He could, however, see it when the security officer fell backward in shock and started scrambling away.

Letting his arm drop, the force-field winking out of existence, Harry kept his gaze fixed on the other man. "I don't have time for your fear or your superstition. If I'm going to protect-"

Something off to his left.

Dropping low, Harry extended his arm in that direction, and yet another force-field appeared just in time to stop a bullet that would have gone through his head. Claire hissed and ducked behind the cover it offered.

A quick glance at the security officer who was down on his backside revealed that he had gone deathly pale. "You... You need my gun." He had the weapon out of its holster in a flash, tossing it toward Harry. "The safety is unlocked by-"

Harry flicked a small switch just above the grip.

"Yeah," the guy said. "That."

Once again, Harry scanned his surroundings and noticed a team of Keepers running back to the platform, no doubt returning to escort the next batch of wounded to safety. In the distance behind them, a transport shuttle rose slowly above the treeline, and then it shot off into the sky.

With the pistol held tightly in both hands, Harry stood up and started making his way to the edge of the platform. "Wait here, Claire," he barked. "Stay low, and go with the Keepers when they take the next group to the shuttles."

"Yes, sir," she mumbled behind him.

Harry smiled.

That was the first time she had called him "sir."

He stepped onto the grass and began his inexorable journey to the treeline, scanning his surroundings all the while. Old instincts kicked in. Suddenly, Harry was back on the firing range.

The N'Jal was powerful at close range, but the force-fields it loosed would dissipate long before they reached the trees. Harry didn't think he could do that trick of making the ground shake either. Not with this much distance between him and his targets. Aside from protecting him with force-fields, the N'Jal could do little to help him in this fight.

But he didn't need it.

Harry Carlson was top of his class in marksmanship. For many years, the pistol he wore at his side had been his only line of defense, and it was all he truly needed. He let those long-buried instincts guide him.

In the trees to his left, he caught a glimpse of gray.

Harry pivoted, raising the pistol in both hands and fired twice, each round buzzing like an angry hornet. His shots hit the trunk of a tree before his enemy could jump out from behind it, splitting it wide open.

The one who had been planning to take a shot instead turned and ran deeper into the forest. One gone... for now. But there had to be others out there. A flash of motion off to his right.

Turning on his heel, Harry fired.

Once again, his shot grazed the trunk of a tree, tearing strips of bark off, and this time, the man hiding behind it poked his head around the other side. Harry's next bullet took him right between the eyes before he could even *think* about returning fire.

One dead.

Calm, cool and collected, Harry continued his slow march forward. He would not be able to keep this up for very long. Oh, he was good, but the forest surrounded the field on all sides, and sooner or later someone would shoot at his back. His eyes couldn't watch all directions at once. If only there was a way to sharpen his senses-

Harry nearly squeaked when the N'Jal detached from his palm and began to slide up his arm, ducking into the sleeve of his jacket. He felt it oozing over his skin, over his shoulder and up the side of his neck. There, it seemed to split in two, one half crawling into his left ear, the other into his right.

And just like that, his hearing changed.

Every sound became sharp, clear and distinct: the cries of wounded people on the platform, the squish of grass under his feet, the footsteps of Keepers escorting the next group to the shuttles. He knew, from her light footfalls, that Claire was with them. And there were sounds that he didn't recognize. A strange intermittent hum.

It took him a moment to realize that he was hearing the heat signatures he had been scanning for earlier. The N'Jal was telling him where his targets would be.

With his eyes closed, Harry swung the pistol in one hand, eventually settling on a spot almost ninety-degrees to his right. He fired.

When he turned in that direction, he saw that his shot had pierced the upper arm of a uniformed man, causing the guy to drop to his knees and clamp a hand over the wound. Harry continued his march.

Humming behind him,

Harry aimed the gun back over his right shoulder and fired without looking. There was a distant cry, and he spun around to find that his bullet had gone through the shin of a man who stood just inside the forest. That guy fell flat on his face.

A grin spread on Harry's face, and he shook his head slowly. "A man could get used to this."

Down the hill and around the trees, Anna moved with an almost inhuman grace, her light footfalls making barely any sound. She leaped over a big root and landed softly on the other side, perking up at a change in emotion from Seth.

Her route down the hill ran parallel to the open path now off to her left, and further down that path she sensed movement. Through the gaps between trees, she saw two men in gray near the base of the hill.

She ducked out of sight.

Pressing her back to the trunk of a thick oak tree with branches that stretched well above her head, Anna shut her eyes and soothed her nerves. *You have a weapon now,* she told herself. *This should be easy.*

Except that she wanted to do it without killing.

Anna aimed around the side of the tree, using the scope of her rifle to choose her target. At this oblique angle, she had to settle the cross-hairs on the side of one man's rib-cage if she wanted a shot that would do more than just graze him. His armour would stop the bullet but that suited her just fine.

She fired.

Her target stumbled backward and sideways, landing sprawled diagonally across the width of the path. The other man started swinging his rifle this way and that, looking for her. He seemed to spot Anna.

She took cover behind the tree.

Bullets grazed the side of its trunk, tearing chunks of wood off. Anna clicked her tongue in irritation. *Her* armour would *not* stop those shots, but heavy armour was more of a hindrance than help to a Keeper.

Keeping her back against the oak tree, Anna thrust her rifle out to her right so that its muzzle would be visible to her enemy. She then quickly retracted it and felt bullets zip through the space where her gun had been.

Anna spun to her left, aiming around the side of the tree, firing without using her eyes. Spatial awareness would have to do. A bullet hit the man centre of mass before he could adjust his aim, knocking him down on his backside.

The one she had already put down was rising.

Anna stepped out into the open with her rifle hoisted up, its scope lined up with her eye. "Stay down," she cried out in Raen. "Companion help me, you do anything that even *looks* aggressive, and I will end you."

She would. If she had to. Killing turned her stomach, but she had long since let go of the notion that she could defeat any enemy without using lethal force. A shot to the leg would leave each of these men incapacitated, but even *that* might be fatal if they lost too much blood. What's more, it would give them a chance to alert others to her position. These two were probably coming in response to a call from the others she had just taken down a few minutes ago.

Halfway to a standing position, the first man she had shot sank back to his knees with his hands raised defensively. She expected him to say something, but instead, he just looked up to the sky with an open mouth.

The other one did the same, sitting up with a hand over his bruised stomach and turning his attention skyward. There was nothing up there. Just clouds. But somehow, this felt ominous.

Anna lowered her rifle.

Pressing her lips together, she studied the pair of them, then shook her head. "Now what?" she muttered. "You Antaurans never run out of surprises, do you?"

She sensed Seth's alarm before spatial awareness alerted her to what had caused this strange behaviour. Only stepping out of the woods, onto the path, gave her a clear enough view.

Further up the hill, she sensed the misty silhouette of a robed figure coming down toward them. Glancing in that direction revealed that it was a tall and pale young man in blue robes with pointed shoulders and silver scrollwork on the sleeves.

Anna gave the man a spiteful glare, then jerked her head toward the entranced men. "You did this?" The venom in her tone was not intentional, but she knew a telepath when she saw one, and while that fact alone was not enough to make her distrust someone, she had no idea what this man's loyalties were.

"Have done with it, two-soul," the telepath replied in a voice as rich and smooth as the finest silk. "Kill them now."

"What? They're your own people."

The telepath moved awkwardly down the hill as if he feared that he might slip in the mud or dirty the hem of his robe. He grimaced, then took a few careful steps until he had closed the distance. "Any mercy that they might have expected from the courts was forfeit when they attacked the leaders of this world."

"Still, we can't question them if they're dead."

The telepath settled his green eyes upon her and waited a long moment as if he was not entirely sure how to respond. Finally, he said, "My people have already gathered the others that you have incapacitated. They will be questioned and the answers taken from their minds."

"You can't do that."

"This is Antaur. We can do as we please."

She said nothing.

With a sigh, the telepath stepped past her and extended a hand toward the pair of men with his fingers splayed. "If you will not do it quickly and efficiently, then I suppose it falls to me."

Both commandos folded up on themselves, each clutching the sides of his helmet and screaming. They were writhing, shrieking as if bees had flown into their skulls and started stinging their brains.

Anna whirled around, lifting her rifle and pointing it straight at the telepath's back. "Stop it!" she yelled. "Stop it, right now!"

The torture came to an abrupt halt, both men slumping over to lie passed out in the mud. Turning gracefully with a flourish of his robes, the telepath faced her with a raised eyebrow. "You would kill me? Your ally? To protect those who had tried to claim your life mere moments earlier? Two-souls are a curious breed. You do understand that I could stop you with a mere thought, yes?"

Anna kept the rifle trained upon her so-called ally, not moving so much as an inch. "You could try," she replied. "But my Nassai shields me from your influence. And I think I can pull this trigger before you can penetrate that shield. Shall we find out together?"

"As you wish, two-soul," the telepath murmured. "Gather them and bring them to the shuttle. We will learn the truth of this disgusting attack together."

He left her to do it alone, of course. Far be it for a prim and pampered telepath to get his own hands dirty. In the end, she had to disarm both men and carry them one by one up the hill to a spot where Keepers had gathered several other wounded combatants. Even with her enhanced strength, carrying two bodies at a time was awkward.

She was greatly relieved to find Jack tending some of the wounded in that group. Apparently, he was responsible for putting three of them there. What's more, according to the stories flying, two of those wounded men had been brought down by Harry Carlson wielding nothing but a pistol.

There were twenty-four captives in total, but from their best estimates over twice that number had attacked the ceremonies. Some of those men had died, others had fled. And they *were* all men. Anna wasn't sure what to make of that.

They had lost four Keepers in this skirmish and the Companion alone knew how many Antaurans. Not a very good start to what was supposed to be a lasting friendship between their two worlds.

After today, would peace even be possible?

Chapter 12

For a wonder, the clouds above Denabria had parted somewhat, leaving patches of blue sky in the ceiling of gray. The sunny weather brought with it a bitter chill. This far south, it only dropped below freezing for a few miserable days each winter, but this was one such.

It made Larani uneasy. The last waning days of autumn reminded her of the coming New Year and of the election that would follow. Anxiety had formed a lump in the pit of her stomach when she considered the possibility of Dusep's victory.

Larani sat in her office chair with legs crossed at the ankle, facing the large window behind her desk. "And what shall we do then, Jeral?" she murmured. "When you drag us back seven centuries?"

Her desk chirped with a priority message.

Larani swivelled her chair around.

A blinking red icon on the SmartGlass drew her attention. Pressing it conjured the hologram of a tall and pale young man in a high-collared shirt. "Director Larani Tal," the automated message began. "I am with the First Rinthalian Law Firm. We represent Jeral Dusep. Please see attached a summons to appear in court on the seventh day of Thronos. You have been served, madame."

The hologram winked away.

Spreading her hands along the surface of the desk, Larani enlarged an image of the court order and then flicked it onto the slanted screen in front of her chair. She felt her incredulity rising as she scanned the text. Dusep could not be serious. After a few minutes of deliberation, she concluded that there was only one way to deal with this before it got out of hand. It was time to do something she would never do under other circumstances.

It was time to make a scene.

Striding through the wide corridors of the Hall of Council with her arms swinging, Larani glared at anyone in her path. They all took one look at the fury in her eyes and stepped aside without comment.

She rounded a corner to find a set of double doors open. Inside, a room with beige walls was filled with dozens upon dozens of chairs as Jeral Dusep hosted another one of his many press conferences. The man stood behind a lectern at the front of the room, his thin glasses reflecting the bright lights as he read from a tablet. "It is time that we started putting Leyria first again," he said. "Sarona Vason's misguided policies have-"

"You have got to be kidding me!"

At least two dozen reporters twisted around in their seats to study Larani with anxious expressions. There were a few hushed murmurs – nothing her ears could pick up – and then the room was eerily silent.

Jeral Dusep looked up from his notes and stiffened when he noticed her. "Director Tal," he began. "I had expected that I would be hearing from you soon, but this is not the proper venue to share your grievance."

Lifting her chin, Larani held the man's gaze for a very long while. "You're suing Agent Hunter?" she asked, raising an eyebrow. "Is your ego really so fragile, Jeral, that you cannot endure even the mildest criticism?"

That triggered another round of frenzied whispers as reporters began tapping out notes on their tablets. Dusep's face reddened, but he took control of himself quickly enough. "At all times, the Justice Keepers will take a position of political neutrality," he intoned. "Special Agent Hunter violated that precept when he publicly disparaged me."

"A Justice Keeper's duty," Larani cut in, "is to defend this world from all threats, foreign and domestic. And your hateful rhetoric definitely qualifies."

This time, Dusep made no attempt to hide his anger. He trembled behind the lectern with a hateful sneer on his face. "I see." It was a raspy hiss, amplified by the microphone. "Perhaps I should include you in the suit."

Larani strode through the aisle between the chairs, laughing softly under her breath. "You see what he is?" she said with enough volume to be picked up by every recording device. "How easily he buckles at the first sign of resistance?"

Several people murmured their agreement.

"This," Dusep snapped, "is not the place for-"

"I am a Leyrian citizen with a distinguished history of service," Larani said. She didn't shout or yell, but her voice projected through the room. "A citizen that you hope to represent by taking the office of Prime Council. If you will not address my concerns as to your fitness to hold that station, then perhaps you should withdraw from the race."

For a wonder, Jeral Dusep didn't speak. He watched her with those hawk-like eyes, but he made no attempt to undermine her. The man had lost this round, and he knew it. "I think," he said at last. "That perhaps we should adjourn for the day."

Well, that much was settled at least. But Larani knew that this victory would be short-lived. Dusep would step up his attacks on the Keepers and on her personally. There was little she could do to prevent that.

She would just have to do what she could to discredit him while maintaining some veneer of impartiality. A difficult tight-rope to walk, but such was her fate. It startled her to realize that she wished Jack were here.

The boy had a talent for causing trouble.

The crowd had gathered in the Hub.

Almost every Leyrian city had one, and Denabria was no exception. A building at the centre of town where all the subway lines converged, home to city council – not to mention the largest SlipGate terminal – it was a bustling place at any time of day.

White carpets stretched across a room where five SlipGates – all triangular in shape – stood side by side. This port was for arrivals only. Technicians operated the Gates from control consoles off to the side.

Every now and then, the grooves on one triangle began to glow, followed by the emergence of a round bubble with over a dozen people inside. When the bubble popped, Melissa saw something that broke her heart.

Many of the new arrivals wore Earth fashions, jeans and hooded sweaters. These people were refugees who had fled perilous conditions in some of Earth's more unstable countries, and now she was going to have to do something utterly despicable.

A crowd of people, maybe a hundred in total, had formed off to the side, people who had all adopted a certain formality in their appearance. Some wore dress pants and sweaters over high-collared shirts. Others, both men and women alike, had chosen suit jackets cut in the Leyrian style. Clean-cut and formal: that was the way with fascists. Make yourself presentable, and people would give serious consideration to your hateful rhetoric. Many of these people shook their fists at the incoming refugees.

And they chanted.

"Terrans go home! Terrans go home!"

Melissa had put on black pants and a smart-looking blouse with sheer sleeves for this event. Her hair was still cut short and dyed silver at the tips. She felt strangely out of place, like a punk-rock girl in a fancy boarding school uniform.

Wincing at the thought of what she had to do, Melissa drew in a shuddering breath. "Terrans go home!" she shouted, striding forward to join the crowd. "Terrans go home!"

One of the young men on the periphery, a handsome fellow with olive skin, a bald head and dark stubble on his jawline, glanced in her direction and offered a curt nod of respect. "Terrans go home!" he echoed.

Some of the refugees looked at her.

It was like a knife in her heart.

The young man leaned in close to Melissa, sneering as he watched the next batch of arrivals. "Bleakness take me," he grumbled. "How many more do we have to take in?"

"No more," Melissa said a little too quickly.

That earned her a halfhearted chuckle.

Forcing those vile words through her lips broke her heart. Every time one of the refugees so much as looked at her, she wanted to run to them and declare that she didn't mean a word of what she said. This was an intelligence operation, a way to root out the fascist element of Leyrian society so that immigrants like them could be safe. She did no such thing, however. Instead, she maintained her facade and chanted along with the rest of the crowd.

"You're doing well, Melissa," Gabi whispered in her earpiece.

She didn't respond.

"I'm Bill," the young man at her side said.

"Sara," Melissa replied.

He stepped closer to her, but he never took his eyes off the SlipGates. "When did you decide that you had enough?" It was a simple question, and Melissa had practiced the answer several times, but she still felt nervous. Ilia sent calming emotions.

Setting her jaw with a grunt of displeasure, Melissa shook her head. "When all of my professors started talking about accommodating these bloody Terrans," she muttered. "Making room for them to practice their culture. If they want to do that, why don't they stay on their own damn world?"

"Because they're leeches," a voice said behind her.

Melissa didn't have to look to know that a slender woman with long hair had come forward to join their conversation, but if she relied too heavily on spatial awareness, her new friends might start to think that she had eyes in the back of her head. It wouldn't take long for them to suspect her true allegiances after that.

So, she gave a start at the sound of the newcomer's voice and turned around to find a beautiful young lady in her early twenties smiling at her. This woman was pale with a round face and long, golden hair. "Terrans," she said. "They have all but destroyed their own planet, and now they want to exploit ours."

"Yeah," Melissa grumbled.

The protest went on for the better part of two hours, and she was forced to watch as refugees from Earth joined a queue at the Customs and Immigration booth only to endure shouts from Melissa's new friends. And from Melissa herself. She felt like she had been covered in slime. A week's worth of showering wouldn't get her clean.

Finally, when it was clear that no more refugees would be coming through the Gate today, the protesters began to disperse. Half the crowd was already flowing up the stairs toward the Hub's main floor when Melissa decided that she could depart herself.

"I'm Tesa," the blonde woman said.

Melissa put herself in front of the woman, adopting the sternest expression that she could manage. "Sara Veranz," she said. "Good to meet you."

"You seemed pretty passionate today."

"Wouldn't you be?" Melissa countered. "These bloody Terrans aren't here for five minutes before they start imposing their culture on us."

For a moment, Tesa looked uneasy, but then she nodded slowly as if deciding that Melissa had passed some test. "I hear you," she said. "Look, some of us are grabbing a drink later. We can sit down and talk about it more."

"Sounds fun."

"Does that mean you're in?"

"Yeah," Melissa said. "Yeah, I'm in."

At this time of night, there was almost no one in the large gym in the basement of Justice Keepers HQ. The sparring ring in the middle of the floor was empty. The exercise equipment was put away, the treadmills silent. In fact, the only noise throughout the room came from the punishment that Melissa inflicted on a punching bag. After what she had been forced to do this afternoon, she needed it.

Melissa kicked the punching bag, knocking it back, then spun and delivered a fierce back-kick. This blow sent the bag swinging like a pendulum and nearly tearing it right off of its chain. Whirling around to face it, Melissa adopted a guarded stance.

She hit the bag with one fist then the other, leaving knuckle-shaped indentations in the fabric. A brutal series of punches through which she channelled all of her anger. The words she had spoken this afternoon made her sick.

Melissa bounced on the balls of her feet, her brow slick with sweat, her silver hair damp. "Why?" she screamed, pounding the bag again. Her punch sent it flying away until the chain was taut, and then it was coming back toward her.

Melissa jumped.

She spun in midair, kicking out behind herself, driving a foot into the bag with all her might. That last hit was finally enough to break the chain, and the punching bag fell to the floor,

Melissa landed with her back to it, bending over with her hands on her knees. "It's the same everywhere," she whispered, shaking her head. "Why is there no place in this galaxy where you can get away from it?"

"Get away from what?"

She hadn't noticed the man who now stood in the doorway that led to the corridor, and it took a moment to remember his face. He was tall and fit with Asian features and short, black hair. Melissa was sure they had met once before. "Novol," she said.

"That's me."

"You're Jack's friend."

The man braced one hand against the door-frame, shaking his head as he chuckled. "I certainly hope so!" he replied. "Given that I've committed treason for him."

Melissa stood up straight, breathing deeply through her nose. She should have been smiling – it was only polite – but she didn't much feel like smiling right then. "I'm sorry. I was a little distracted."

Novol's gaze settled onto the fallen punching bag, and he snorted. "So I gathered," he said. "Look, I didn't mean to bother you. They were kind enough to let me work out down here, but Jack's off doing…whatever."

"You can stay."

"I don't want to bother you."

Dropping to one knee, Melissa picked up the broken chain and inspected it. "It's no bother." She just knew that Operative Sarl Venson – the man who supervised cadets in their combat training – was going to write her up for this. "I'm sorry. This afternoon I had to do something I really didn't want to do, and I'm not very good company."

To her surprise, Novol stepped into the room with his arms crossed, his lips pressed into an anxious frown as he studied her. "Believe it or not," he said. "I've got more than a little experience in that area."

"Oh?"

"Kind of goes with the territory when you work for an imperialist military because it's the only way to pay your mother's medical bills." He snorted again, refusing to look at her. "Who am I kidding? A Leyrian girl like you isn't gonna understand money. Not like someone who's had to scrounge for it for most of his life."

"I grew up on Earth," Melissa corrected him. "Believe me when I say I understand money and how the lack of it can push you into choices you'd rather not make."

"Oh, aye?"

"Yes."

Novol took a few nervous steps forward, then knelt in front of her, examining the broken chain in her hands. "So, what did you have to do?" he asked. "That upset you so much, I mean."

The question twisted Melissa's insides in knots. Even knowing that she was only playing a role, acting as an undercover agent, she was still mortified by the prospect of telling someone that she had stood with a bunch of hateful bigots, repeating their vitriol and intimidating refugees who were just looking for a safe place to call home. "I had to…I signed up for this mission."

"What kind of mission?"

"I should probably keep that to myself."

When she looked up, Novol seemed concerned but not angry. "Classified," he said with a shrug of his shoulders. "I get that."

"Thank you."

A flush painted his face red, and he never took his eyes off the chain. "I don't think I can fix that," he said. "But maybe I can take your mind off your troubles. Join me for a cup of coffee?"

The invitation startled her, and she found herself searching for words. Ilia seemed to think that she should accept, but Nassai almost always preferred bonding to solitude. "Um…" Melissa stammered. "I just…How old are you?"

It was quite possibly the most tactless response she could have offered, but she was still flailing from everything she had been through with Aiden. Novol didn't seem to mind the question. "I'm twenty-one," he said without hesitation. "I joined the military almost four years ago."

A puzzled expression came over him, his brows drawn together. "I'm sorry. I hope I haven't said anything inappropriate," he went on. "They told me that Keepers always look younger than they really are, and I figured that if you were going on important missions, you had to have at least a few years of experience; so I thought you were maybe twenty-two or twenty-three. I mean if you're thirty-five, the offer still stands. I-I'm sorry. I didn't mean to offend you by-"

"No, it's fine," Melissa cut in when it became clear that his rambling explanation wasn't going to stop any time soon. "I'm eighteen, which is above the Age of Majority on both my world and Leyria. It's okay."

"Eighteen?" he mumbled.

"Yup."

"But you're…" His mouth worked soundlessly for a moment. "I mean they have you on a mission! How long *have* you been a Keeper?"

It was Melissa's turn to blush now. So much for effecting the veneer of a seasoned officer. Somewhere in the back of her mind, the part of Ilia that retained all of Jena's memories was laughing at her. "I'm not a Keeper," Melissa said reluctantly. "I'm a cadet."

Slowly, Novol stood up and backed away as if he had just learned that Melissa had a very nasty flu he didn't want to catch. "A pleasure to meet you, Cadet," he said. "Sorry to have disturbed your exercise."

He was out the door before she could say another word.

Melissa groaned.

Of course it would go this way. A hot guy displayed a tiny bit of interest in her, and she scared him off in less than five minutes. She could have *pretended* to be twenty-five or something. For a little while at least. After allowing herself a few minutes to sulk, she put the whole thing out of her mind.

She had more important things to worry about.

Chapter 13

When they returned to the Diplomatic Complex, all the Earthers and Leyrians had been herded into a large conference room and left to wait while their hosts decided how they wanted to proceed. It made Anna nervous, and Seth echoed her feelings.

Their surroundings were elegant but functional; the conference room was a large rectangle with peach-coloured walls and arch-shaped windows that looked out on a warm afternoon. Crystal vases with colourful plants were placed between the vases, and there was enough furniture for everyone to find a seat. Which was impressive in a room with over fifty occupants.

Every Keeper and diplomat who had not been injured in the attack was gathered here. Most were still in dirty pants and windbreakers or in the stained suits and dresses that they had worn to the opening ceremony.

It pleased Anna to see that her father was among those who had escaped unscathed. He was leaning against a wall on the other side of the room, his eyes closed as he tried to calm himself. She had seen him do that many times. Usually, after she had caused some mischief as a child.

They had exchanged a few quick words after coming in here, but Anna was worn out, and her mind was reeling. Why would Antaurans attack the peace summit? For that matter, were they really Antaurans? Anyone could put on a uniform. Those people could have been Ragnosian or Leyrian – or even Earthers. There was really no way to know, and she didn't think she would get the chance to conduct an investigation.

Anna sat on a couch with hands clasped in her lap, frowning thoughtfully as she considered the possibilities. *Why would they do this?* she asked. *Lure us here just to kill us? It would serve no tactical purpose in a war.*

Jack handed her a cup of hot tea.

He sat down beside her, and Anna gave him a loving smile, but when it was clear that she didn't want to talk, Jack just put his arm around her shoulders, pulled her close and kissed the top of her head. She loved him for that.

All noise in the room cut off when the door swung open to admit a dark-skinned telepath in flowing green robes. He was followed immediately by President Salmaro, while a second telepath – a woman in red this time – brought up the rear. She was petite with tilted eyes and long black hair that she wore in a braid.

Salmaro, still in his stained coat, stepped forward and nodded to them. "I cannot even begin to express my sorrow." He closed his eyes, his face reddening slightly. "This was supposed to be a day of peace."

Ambassador Drelina Jadoor, a tall, willowy woman in her middle years who wore her brown hair in a clip, sat on the arm of a couch. "You'll have to forgive us if we have a hard time believing that."

"Are we to be your prisoners?" one of the Keepers asked.

"Of course not!" Salmaro replied a little too hastily. He regathered his calm in an instant, standing with his shoulders square and his hands clasped behind himself. "If you wish, you may depart for Leyria today, but I hope that you will stay."

"And give you another chance to attack us?" Director Varno asked.

"With respect, sir," Jack said, rising from the couch. He took a few confident steps forward. Anna could only see his back, but she knew there wasn't a spec of anxiety within him, Which meant he was sure of what he had to say. "I don't believe they did attack us. I have some experience with these sorts of mishaps, and this has Grecken Slade all over it."

That got Salmaro's attention.

The Antauran president puffed up his cheeks and blew out a breath as he settled his gaze on Jack. "Grecken Slade," he said. "Forgive me; I have always had some difficulty with names, but wasn't that the former head of the Justice Keepers?"

"And a traitor," Jack added.

Anna sat back on the couch with her arms folded, shaking her head. *What are you doing, my love?* It was too soon to be sure of anything; Jack had nothing but a hunch, and she wasn't sure that tipping their hand to the Antaurans was wise in any event.

"Go on," the president urged.

Keepers and diplomats cleared the way, hugging the walls of the room so that Jack would have a clear, unobstructed view of the man. "Slade works for the Overseers," Jack went on. "Implementing some kind of plan of theirs. My task, this past year, has been to locate and neutralize moles that he left among the Justice Keepers."

The female telepath fixed him with a glare that should have cut him to pieces. "If this Grecken Slade serves the gods," she began, "then you are wrong to oppose him."

"That's a matter of opinion, ma'am."

Salmaro nodded in response to that. Clearly, his faith in the Overseers was not as strong as his servant's. "Slade may believe that he serves the gods," he said judiciously, "but that does not make it so. Tell me more."

Closing her eyes, Anna breathed in slowly. *Please don't tell him about the Key,* she thought at her boyfriend. *If he finds out that we're the reason the Ragnosians are poking around this side of the galaxy, it's all over.*

Maybe Jack heard her.

"There are some things that are best discussed in private, sir," Jack began, "But we have reason to believe that Slade's goals are to foster conflict between the major powers in this galaxy, particularly Leyria, Antaur and Ragnos."

Tren Varno, a tall and slim man with olive skin and short, black hair, leaned against the wall between two windows. His lip curled into a sneer of contempt. "And you are just telling us this *now*, Hunter?"

"Larani Tal ordered my team to keep this matter secret."

"And so you disobey that order?"

Jack spun to face the man with his arms crossed, and though she could only see the back of his head, Anna knew that he was losing patience. "To salvage these talks? You're damn right, I would. An order is only as good as the context that made it necessary, sir."

Before anyone else could speak, Jack rounded on the president and strode toward him at such a brisk pace that the telepaths actually moved to bar his path. That made him stop short. "Peace is valuable for its own sake," Jack went on. "But if the Overseers want us to fight each other, then that is the absolute last thing we should do."

"Jack," Harry said from the other side of the room. "I think you made your point."

The male telepath, in his bright green robes, stepped forward and looked Jack up and down. "There are those who would disagree with your assessment, Agent Hunter," he said. "These talks have been the source of much debate on our world. Many say that the gods brought us to different worlds for a reason. If, as you claim, their wish is that we should remain in conflict, then that is the *only* valid course."

"The Overseers aren't gods. They're just aliens."

The female telepath was hissing like a cat as she came forward to point a finger in Jack's face. "Blasphemy! I will not sit at a table with these two-soul dogs," she spat. "The will of the gods is made clear! We should be rid of them now!"

"Rothayne!" Salmaro barked. "Tiana! Restrain yourselves immediately! You serve at *my* pleasure, remember?"

Refusing to back down, Tiana turned back to the president and let her gaze linger on him for half a moment. "Your good standing with the Holy Order is tenuous at best," she said. "Lose our endorsement, and you will not have a second term."

"Which is irrelevant if I accomplish what I need to in the first." That left the room in silence for nearly half a minute. Finally, Salmaro let out a sigh and forced himself to go on. "We *will* have peace with Leyria."

"A president is not an emperor," Tiana countered.

Rothayne, the male telepath, nodded curtly in agreement with that last bit. "The gods have made their desires known," he said. "This alliance was ill-conceived from the beginning. We will go no further."

"Enough!"

Anna nearly jumped out of her seat. She would not have expected that kind of fire from the outwardly jolly and friendly Adare Salmaro, but the man's voice cracked like a whip, and for a wonder, both telepaths shut their mouths. "You serve as my bodyguards," he said coldly. "You don't set policy. My good standing is not the only one in question. Contradict me like that again, and I will end your tenure with the Office of the President. You can go back to your order in disgrace."

"We do not need the Leyrians-" Rothayne began.

"Yes," a voice called out from the back of the room. "We do."

Oh, boy... This should be interesting.

Men and women in tattered clothing parted to make way for Keli as she strode to the front of the conference room. She wore a simple white dress with a slit that rose to her knee and a necklace of gold.

Her face was grim – lips pursed, eyes focused on the president – and she nodded once as she approached. "Of all people," she said, "I am uniquely qualified to judge the character of the Leyrians."

Ambassadors and Justice Keepers looked at her, some mumbling that she might say something to further undermine this summit. Jack was standing between her and the president.

Adare Salmaro waited by the wall with hands folded over his large belly, watching her with avid curiosity. "I'm sorry," he said at last. "And you are-"

"A half-trained mongrel," Tiana broke in. Her eyes were like razors when they fell upon Keli. Oh yes, that one would be trouble. "One with no business here. Send her to us so that she may answer for the lives she has taken."

Keli let her head drop as she stepped past the other woman, laughing softly under her breath. "You know, it's funny," she began. "When I first started working with them, the Leyrians were quick to point out the arrogance I displayed in every conversation. I'm told that such a demeanour is common among telepaths."

Tilting her head back, Keli blinked several times as she chose her next words. "At long last, I begin to understand their plight." She rounded on the other woman, stepping forward so that Tiana was forced to retreat a few steps. "Keep your fool mouth shut, and do not speak on topics you cannot even begin to comprehend."

That left the room in silence for ten seconds.

Good.

"I am Keli Armana," she went on. "I was taken from my family when my talent was discovered, but rather than being delivered to the Holy Order, I was used as a lab rat in experiments conducted by *our* military. Experiments designed to heighten my abilities. Experiments that, I am proud to say, were quite successful. But I spent most of my life in a cell so small I could barely spread my arms."

Pointing a finger at Jack, she watched as he jumped back in shock. Most satisfying. He had displayed no such alarm when Tiana did the same thing just a few minutes earlier. "It was *these* people," Keli said, "who freed me from that cell. Who took me in when I had nothing to offer in return. Who gave me a home. Who forgave me even though I have betrayed their trust more than once."

Keli turned back to the president, and with a shy smile, she bowed to him. "Take it from one who knows," she concluded. "You would be fools to make enemies of Leyria and Earth. And you would be wise to accept their help in these dark days."

To her great surprise, that little speech earned her a round of applause from the ambassadors. Suddenly, feeling emboldened, Keli decided to add one more thing to her testimony. "The threats that Agent Hunter has articulated are real," she said. "I have seen them with my own eyes."

It pleased her to discover that a simple glance in Tiana's direction caused the other woman to back away. "If you believe that Overseers see you as anything more than a rat to use in their experiments, then you are an idiot. Designing your policies to align with their goals – whatever those goals may be – is putting your head in a hangman's noose."

The suite that he shared with Anna looked very much like the rest of the Diplomatic Complex: peach walls, arch-shaped windows. Their sitting room had gilded chairs and a sofa to match, potted plants in every corner. Everything you could want if you had grown up as a pampered Manhattan baby.

The door banged open to admit Tren Varno, who moved across the room in three quick strides. "Congratulations,

Hunter," he spat. "You nearly tanked this summit with your little stunt."

Jack was sitting at a small wooden table, his head lolling back so that he could stare open-mouthed at the ceiling. "I was wondering when you would show up," he said. "This the part where you lecture me on decorum."

"You should have never been made a Keeper."

"Great! Anti-Earth racism. That's-"

A flush put some colour in Varno's cheeks, and he shook his head vigorously as he approached the table. "No, not Earthers," he said. "Just you. You have been nothing but a disgrace since the day you joined this organization."

Biting his lip as he studied the man, Jack felt his eyebrows climb higher and higher. "Well, that's a new one," he said. "Look, Tren, you don't have to like me, but the fact of the matter is I've had a nose for Slade's schemes."

"And you think that's what this is?"

"I *know* that's what this is."

"How?"

Answers rose to the forefront of Jack's mind, explanations for how this attack on the summit would align perfectly with Slade's goals. Something about all this just *felt* slimy, but he knew that wouldn't satisfy the other man. More to the point, Varno's hostility made him wonder if he *should* be divulging any of this.

The junior director stood with his arms crossed, an incredulous smile growing on his face. "Of course," he said. "You have nothing. Just one of your hunches and a whole lot of bravado."

Anna was sitting primly on the sofa with one leg crossed over the other, her fingers laced over her knee, and her gaze never wavered for an instant. "Director, I would remind you," she began, "that Agent Hunter's 'hunches' have proved reliable before."

"Oh really?" Varno spat. "Well, this time, he gave the Antaurans the excuse they've been looking for to pull out of this deal." He returned his attention to Jack and thrust his hand out like a spear. "You just convinced them that their *gods* oppose this alliance! Can you even comprehend the damage you've done? What in Bleakness made you think that you were smart enough to play diplomat?"

Jack opened his mouth to speak, but Varno rode right over him.

The other man paced around his table until Jack felt very much like a suspect in an interrogation room. "So, *Agent* Hunter," he said. "I did a little reading when I heard you'd be on this mission. That formal reprimand that Larani placed in your file this past summer? The one with very little specification as to precisely *what* you had done."

For the first time since the start of this conversation, Jack felt a twinge of fear. He had never read the actual text of the reprimand; he didn't know precisely what it said. But it didn't matter. The reminder of his failures was enough to set him on edge. His failure to save Ben, and his attempt to exact bloody vengeance on Leo in the wake of that disgrace. Varno might have been able to piece the story together.

If he had, if the man knew the full extent of Jack's screw up, then Jack would take his punishment without complaint. It was no less than deserved.

"I'm going to make sure that you *remain* Agent Hunter," Varno went on. "When we get home, there will be a second reprimand on your record. You will never see another promotion for the remainder of your career with the Justice Keepers, which I pray to the Companion will be short."

"All right, Director," Anna said. "That's quite enough."

Varno turned slowly with shock on his face. Did the guy really think he was gonna mouth off to Anna Lenai's boyfriend without getting an earful? "Really, Operative Lenai," he began. "What business is this of yours?"

Anna strode across the room to plant herself in front of him. "If you think you're going to come into my sitting room," she said, "and speak that way to *my* partner, you're very much mistaken. I don't care if you outrank me; your conduct borders on abuse, and I will fight you on it."

"Now, I see where he gets-"

Pressing her lips together, Anna held the man's gaze and raised a thin red eyebrow, daring him to say more.

In response, Varno shuddered, turned away from her and walked back to the door. "From now on, Hunter," he said, "Keep your damn mouth shut unless you're directed to do otherwise."

He slammed the door on his way out.

"Thank you," Jack whispered.

Anna maneuvered carefully around his chair, then hopped onto the table so that he saw her in profile. "Don't thank me," she replied in a rasping voice. "He was out of line, but I'm pissed."

Shutting his eyes, Jack pinched the bridge of his nose and groaned into his own palm. "You too, huh?" The anxiety that had begun to fade as soon as Varno left the room came back in full force.

Anna sat with her arms crossed, glowering at the wall, not even looking at him. "He has a point, Jack," she said. "You jeopardized the success of these talks on a hunch. What in Bleakness were you thinking?"

"I was trying to *salvage* these talks."

"That's not your job!"

Jack slouched in his chair, his head sinking until his chin touched his chest. "I know that," he whispered. "But that attack this morning has Slade all over it, and I wasn't gonna let him win again!"

"And that's the problem!" Anna shouted. "I mean, do you even study the history of your own world? About seven hundred years ago, there was this guy called William of Ockham, and he was all, 'Check out this cool razor I invented.' "

In some ways, this was worse than when Varno berated him. Hell, it was worse than when the man had publicly called him out in front of all the ambassadors. Anna was the one person he trusted more than anyone else. If she wasn't on his side…

"Okay," Jack said. "Then how do you explain their ability to get inside the security perimeter? Slade spent years planting his cronies in key positions on Leyria and on Earth. It makes sense that he would do the same here."

"Maybe you're right!" Anna exclaimed. "I'm not saying that your ideas are entirely without merit. I'm saying that we need to have more than a vague hypothesis if we plan to present them to the assembled delegates. Right now, we have nothing. And if Slade really *is* involved, you might have just tipped our hand."

Jack looked up at her, his brow furrowing as he considered the possibilities. "And what if we're too late?" he asked. "What if the summit falls apart while we're looking for that evidence?"

Anna gripped the edge of the table with both hands, her eyes shut as she drew in a breath. "Then we've done all we can," she murmured. "Jack, I know you carry the weight of the world, but it's not your job to fix every problem."

"And if those problems end up killing people?"

Instead of answering, Anna jumped off the table and stood over him, shaking her head. "You wanna know what really pisses me off?" she asked. "It's not that you made a bad decision. It's that you didn't talk to me first."

She surprised him by sitting in his lap and gently running her fingers through his hair. "We're Jack Hunter and Anna Lenai," she went on. "We face everything together. I know a little more about Antauran culture than you do. If you had told me what you were planning, I could have warned you that they might react this way. And if, after talking it over, you still chose to go through with it, I would have your back one hundred percent."

Damn it, it had seemed like such a reasonable idea at the time. If he could convince everyone that they were being played, show them that there was a bigger enemy beyond each other, surely they would band together. Jack had always thought himself rather good at detecting political currents. Shows what he knew.

"You're right," he mumbled. "I'm sorry."

Anna touched her nose to his forehead, breathing in deeply. "It's okay," she said. "I will talk to Larani when we get back. You made a mistake, but Varno has no right to tank your career over it."

"Please don't," he whispered. "It's what I deserve."

"Don't even start with that," she said. "You're a good Keeper, Jack Hunter. And I'm not going to listen to any protests to the contrary."

Chapter 14

The sun was sinking toward the eastern horizon, casting golden rays through the windows of Harry's sitting room. They were segmented by the blinds over the windows, leaving bands of light on the floor.

Harry sat on the sofa with his arms around Claire, holding her close and breathing slowly. What an idiot he had been to think that he could bring his daughter on a mission like this. Why would he even agree to go? He was an utter failure as–

"Dad," Claire said, her voice muffled by his shirt. "Let go. I'm okay."

Blinking tears out of his eyes, Harry pulled away from her. "Okay?" he mumbled in a hoarse voice. "How can you possibly be okay after what you saw this morning? Jesus, why did I bring you–"

Claire looked up at him with a stern expression, her large, dark eyes surprisingly free of tears. God help him, his youngest daughter was handling this better than he was. "I was scared," she said. "But I'm not anymore."

"You're not scared?"

"If something bad happens," she said. "You'll protect me."

Harry doubled up on himself, setting his elbows on his knees and burying his face in his hands. He scrubbed those hands upward to run fingers through his thick, black hair. "Claire," he whispered. "I might not be able to protect you."

"I know that," his daughter replied. "But there are, like, three dozen Keepers here too. I'll be okay."

"You're in shock."

In a heartbeat, Harry was on his feet and pacing across the room, bracing his hands against the wall with his back to the couch. "Claire, I'm so sorry. I should never have let you come on this trip-"

"Dad, will you shut up and listen to me?"

He turned around to find her sitting primly with her hands in her lap. "I saw some of the bodies," Claire began. "Yeah, it's scary, and…And I'll probably have nightmares or something, but I don't feel like I'm in danger. I'm not afraid anymore."

"No kid should ever have to see what you saw."

Claire shrugged as she stared into her lap. A single tear rolled down her cheek. "No, they shouldn't," she agreed. "But I'm not stupid. Do you remember when I asked you if that Leo guy would come to my school?"

"Yes."

"Remember how scared I was?"

"Yes."

Claire rose from her seat and walked across the room at a slow, measured pace. She wrapped her arms around Harry's middle, resting her arms on his chest. "I don't feel that way anymore," she said. "I kinda get it now. Why Melissa wanted to be a Justice Keeper, I mean."

"I don't understand."

"Well, it's always been something," Claire explained. "First that Leo guy and then Slade taking over New York and then when we moved to Leyria, there was that woman who looks like Jena. At least Melissa can *do* something about it."

"And you think I'm just some dumb kid, but I'm not. I know that you didn't bring these things to Earth. They were gonna find us one way or another. It's not your fault. I know that."

Harry dropped to his knees before her, setting his hands on Claire's shoulders and gazing into her eyes. "Thank you," he said. "But that doesn't change the facts. When we get back to Leyria, I'm making an appointment with a councillor for both of us."

Claire looked upward, rolling her eyes and exhaling with obvious frustration. "If you think we have to," she said. "But I'll be okay."

"Maybe," Harry said. "But I'd feel better if I could scan you."

"Scan me? Dad, you're not a doctor."

"No, I'm not," Harry agreed. He reached into his pocket and let the N'Jal bond with him. Sensory information flooded his mind like water from a burst dam. It was almost too much to bear.

Lifting his hand so that Claire could see the Overseer device stretching from the centre of his palm to the tip of each finger, Harry said, "But with this, I'll know instantly if you're injured."

His daughter backed away from him, the colour draining out of her face. "Do you have to?" she whimpered. "I mean, wouldn't I know it if I were hurt? I feel fine! Really, I do!"

"No, you don't have to."

"But it'll make you feel better…"

Harry couldn't bring himself to say another word. He knew damn well that he had an overprotective streak. Maybe Claire was right. Maybe he was worried about nothing, but he couldn't stop blaming himself for letting this happen, for bringing his daughter to a place where people shot at her.

Claire seemed to sense his unease and came forward with resolve in her eyes. "All right," she said. "If it'll make you feel better."

"Are you sure?"

"Just do it before I chicken out."

Gently, Harry laid his hand upon her cheek and felt the N'Jal's fibers dig into her skin. Claire hissed at the sensation. It would have felt to her like a mild prickle, similar to what she might have felt if her leg were asleep.

She closed her eyes, drawing in a shuddering breath as she felt the N'Jal working. Harry focused, and within an instant, he was able to sense her entire body. His daughter was in perfect health. Her cortisol levels were a little high, but that was to be expected in light of the day she'd had.

Poor Claire.

It tore him up inside to think that she had been put into a situation where she had to fear for her life. If Harry had his way, his children would never have to endure that. He would protect Claire. Always.

Except…

No, that wasn't good enough. He couldn't be with her every second. Even *he* knew that much. Claire had to be strong in those moments when he couldn't save her. If Harry had his way, he wouldn't just protect her; he would give her the means to protect herself.

Claire's eyes flew open, a squeal of pain rushing from her lips. She trembled as the N'jal did…something. Harry couldn't say what, but he knew he dare not stop until the task was finished.

Neurons were firing in Claire's brain, synapses crackling with activity. What had he done? Panic welled up inside Harry. He had to force it down, had to focus on letting the N'jal do its work. The Overseer device seemed to respond to his wishes. If he wished too hard for it to stop, it would.

Finally, the N'Jals fibers retracted.

Claire slumped forward, falling into his arms. "Claire," Harry whispered as he held her. "Claire, it's all right. I'm here."

"Dad…"

"Yeah, sweetheart, I'm here."

Harry lifted his daughter and carried her to the couch. He set her down there with a pillow under her head. Within seconds, her eyes fluttered. Claire seemed to be drifting off to sleep. "Dad…" she mumbled drowsily. "Dad, I'm tired."

She was out like a light a moment later.

God have mercy on him; what had he done?

The gym in Diplomatic Complex was nothing like the one they had back at Justice Keeper HQ, but it would have to do. A large window looked out upon the garden, and the evening sunlight spilling through it fell upon the various pieces of exercise equipment that were spread out on the wooden floor.

Jack saw two people working out there – a man in his middle years using one of the pulley machines and an older woman running on a treadmill – but he didn't know either of them, and he was in no mood to be friendly.

At the back of the room, a large open space with blue gym mats on the floor and the walls was nearly empty. Maybe this was where they did yoga, or whatever the Antauran equivalent was, but at the moment, the only person who claimed the space was Rajel.

The man wore a pair of black sweat pants and a gray tank-top as he moved slowly through forms that reminded Jack of Tai Chi. He had removed his sunglasses, and his face glistened with a light sheen of sweat. "Can I help you, Agent Hunter?"

"Just came down to blow off some steam."

"I'm not surprised."

Jack paced a rectangle around the perimeter of the gym mats, blowing air through puckered lips. "Maybe you've heard," he said. "Maybe you haven't, but Varno stopped by my suite to give me hell."

Rajel continued his slow, graceful movements, revolving on the spot so that he was always facing Jack. "I hadn't heard," he said. "But I suspected that he would. Your speech today ruffled a few feathers."

"My girlfriend's among them."

"Not surprising."

Grinning as he marched across the room, Jack shook his head. "Well, it sure as hell surprised me!" he barked. "When I was up there this afternoon, I thought I was Captain Reasonable with a big shiny R on my chest. Turns out... Not so much."

"Anything I can do to help?"

"Yeah," Jack answered. "Think you'd be up for a little sparring?"

Rajel abandoned his complex forms, drawing himself up to full height – which was less than an inch taller than Jack – and breathing in through. "Gladly," he said, striding forward until they were within arm's reach of one another. "I could stand a little exercise myself."

"Sounds fun," Jack said. "So which of us starts-"

Rajel threw a punch.

Jack ducked, allowing the blow to pass over him. He drove a fist into Rajel's belly, then rose and used the same hand to slug the man's nose. That sent his opponent dancing backwards.

Rajel fell over, catching himself with one hand and twisting his body to bring one foot up in a wide arc. At the last second, Jack leaned back in time to watch a black shoe pass within a hair's breadth of him. That gave the other man the opportunity to get up and face him once again.

Rajel jumped and kicked high.

By instinct, Jack's hands came up to intercept his foot, and the very instant that he made contact, Jack applied a touch of Bent Gravity. His adversary went flying backward, right into the mats along the gym wall.

Rajel hit hard, then landed on his feet, hunched over with a hand over his chest. "Impressive," he wheezed. "You definitely have some pent up aggression."

"Damn straight."

Quick as a lightning bolt, Rajel was racing toward him on nimble feet. Jack braced himself, fists raised in a guarded stance, but just before they got within striking distance of each other, Rajel blurred into a streak of colour that flowed around him.

Frantically, Jack turned around.

A high roundhouse kick took him across the chin before he could react, fiery pain surging through his jaw. Tears blurred his vision, and he was forced to back away while Rajel pressed his attack.

The blind man offered a right cross.

Bending his knees, Jack reached up with one hand to grab the man's wrist. He used the other to jab Rajel's chest once, twice, three times, driving the wind from his lungs. A final punch to the face would settle this. He-

Rajel went limp in his grip, falling backwards. He planted one foot in Jack's chest, lifting him clear off the floor and sending him flying. The next thing Jack knew, he was flopping over to land on his back.

He winced on contact, groaning in pain. "Okay," he whimpered, sitting up. "I think I deserved that."

Rajel was standing over him.

The man began another roundhouse kick.

Reacting by instinct, Jack fell onto his side, lying stretched out on the mat. With a powerful scissor motion, he locked his ankles around the only leg that supported Rajel's weight and then twisted his body to bring the other man down.

Rajel hit the mat shoulder-first, grunting on impact. "Not bad," he wheezed, trying to get free of Jack's hold. Jack let him. Never try to hold onto someone with a symbiont unless it gives you a decent tactical advantage. Physical contact would allow for the use of Bent Gravity or other such abilities.

The man and woman who had been working out on the other side of the room were now standing at the edge of the mat and watching Jack and Rajel with gaping mouths. It was likely that they had never seen a pair of Justice Keepers sparring. Antauran soldiers might witness a Keeper's abilities first-hand, but unless these two had seen video footage, they would have to rely primarily on stories and rumours.

Jack felt a smidge of satisfaction when he considered how this little display would have elevated Rajel in their eyes. In all likelihood, they would never have believed that a blind man could fight as well as Rajel did.

"Thank you!" Jack said in Raen, startling the pair of onlookers. "We're here every Vranaday at seven. Tip your servers."

The pair of them wandered off, muttering under their breath, no doubt feeling more than a little frightened by what they had seen. To hear of the fabled power of the Justice Keepers was one thing. To see first-hand was something else entirely.

"You know," Rajel said, getting back up. He bent over, offering his hand. Jack took it, allowing the other man to pull him to his feet. "Instead of taking our frustrations out on each other, we *could* direct them at the people responsible."

Drenched in sweat, Jack shut his eyes and nodded. "We could," he agreed. "But it seems everyone is pissed at me for disrupting the talks. Not exactly looking to make that worse, you know?"

"You didn't."

"Didn't what?"

Rajel began to pace a circle around him. "Disrupt the talks," he said. "My people are idiots. You gave them a perfectly good reason to work with us, and they did what they always do."

Jack stood there with his arms hanging limp, his head drooping with the weight of his fatigue. "Maybe," he said. "But don't let appearances fool you. I make it look easy, but it takes a *lot* of effort to pull off this level of screw up."

"Then maybe you should screw up a little more."

"I'm not following."

184

Rajel twisted around to face him with arms crossed, a sly little smile betraying his amusement. It was quite possibly the first genuine smile that Jack had seen on the man. "If the subtext of our recent conversations hasn't been clear," Rajel said. "Let me spell it out for you: I'm of the opinion that my people's stupid beliefs need to be challenged."

"Yeah, that wasn't subtext," Jack countered. "That was text."

"So, why don't we do just that?"

The suggestion gave Jack pause. A few years ago, he would have pounced on the opportunity to follow Rajel's advice. Buck the system for the greater good and all that. Dear God, what was happening to him? He was becoming respectable. No, it was worse than that. He was becoming *Harry*.

Putting aside the urge to embrace his quarter-life crisis and prove that he was still the same charismatic rogue who made the Kessel Run in less than twelve parsecs, Jack chose his words carefully. "What exactly did you have in mind?"

"We do an investigation."

"What kind of investigation?"

"The kind where we prove that Slade ordered the attack on the opening ceremonies and then present the ambassadors with incontrovertible evidence of his involvement. We do that, and they'll *have* to listen to us."

Cynical laughter was Jack's first response to that. "See, now I feel like you weren't paying attention," he said. "Just a quick review for those of us who weren't in class this afternoon. Antaurans? Big with the stupid when it comes to evil aliens who like to pose as gods."

"So, let's challenge that stupidity."

A frown tugged at the corners of Jack's mouth. "Yeah," he snapped. "Because that worked *so* well throughout human history. 'Hello, angry mob. Your religion is stupid. Now, let's all put down our pitchforks.'"

"So, your answer is no."

"My answer is I'll think about it."

Jack did think about it. For many long hours. He went back to his suite and found that Anna was out. He wasn't entirely sure what to make of that; so, he chose instead to focus on Rajel's proposal.

He showered, ate a late dinner and considered the possibilities. If they conducted an investigation without authorization and found nothing, it would almost certainly mean the end of his career. Hell, it might mean the end of his career even if they *did* find evidence of Slade's involvement.

For the better part of two hours, he explored the Diplomatic Complex and mulled it over. Finally, he came to a decision. He knew what he had to do.

The long hike back to his room – which included the nuisance of using an ID card just to ride the frickin elevator – was not a pleasant one. Part of what had made him stay out so late was the fear that his fight with Anna would resume the instant that he walked through the door. But sooner or later, you had to face the inevitable. Step by laborious step, he made his way back to his suite.

When Jack entered the bedroom, he found it lit only by the glow of city lights through the windows. Anna was a lump under the covers, but she stirred, sitting up and holding the blankets to her chest.

Closing his eyes, Jack sighed and rubbed his forehead with the back of one hand. "Hey," he whispered, pacing across the room to the side of the bed. "Sorry, I got a little lost in thought."

He got undressed and crawled into bed with Anna.

The instant he was under the covers, she snuggled up, wrapping an arm around his tummy and resting her head on his chest. Jack was delighted to feel her soft warm skin against his. They had slept naked together almost every night since the first time they made love, but he had been worried that Anna was still angry.

She sat up, watching him for what felt like a very long while, and he saw the ghost of a smile on her face. "You worry too much," she said as if sensing his thoughts. "And I should apologize for being so hard on you."

"Don't you dare."

Anna froze.

Gently, he reached up to wrap his arms around her, pulling her close, and she was more than happy to accept his embrace. "You were right," Jack whispered. "About all of it. I shouldn't have acted on a hunch, and I should have talked to you."

Anna giggled, turning her head to nuzzle his chest. "Jack, I don't want you to feel like you have to run every decision by me," she said. "That's not the kind of relationship I want. Your independence matters to me."

She rolled off of him, flopping onto her back with arms folded and staring angrily at the ceiling. "I've spent the last two hours just lying here," she began, "trying to come up with a general rule for when you should talk to me first and when you should follow your instincts and..."

"No joy?"

"Oh, it's not just a lack of joy," she said. "After two hours, I was hip deep in some truly heinous anti-joy. I'm convinced this conversation is where fun goes to die."

Jack folded his hands behind his head, biting his lip as he tried to come up with an answer. "Maybe there shouldn't *be* a rule," he suggested. "Maybe it's the kind of thing we have to deal with case by case."

"Which would normally be fine."

"But?

With a groan, Anna cuddled up, slipping an arm around him again. "I don't want to be *that* person," she lamented. "You know the one who freaks out every time her partner does something she doesn't like."

"Sweetie," Jack whispered, "I think this is about more than me making a decision you didn't like. I thought about it a lot while I was puttering around, and something occurred to me. We haven't been professional partners in a long time. I'm used to working my own cases and following my own instincts, and that's what I did today.

"But on this mission, we *are* partners. I undermined you today by not including you in the decision-making process. And I think that's part of why it bothered you so much."

"I think you're right."

Jack rolled onto his side, facing Anna and running his fingers through her soft hair. "I'm really sorry," he whispered. Now that he had put his transgression into words, his old friend guilt was lurking in the back of his mind. and just begging for attention.

"You don't have to be sorry," Anna said. "I forgive you."

"Well, since we're partners," Jack murmured. "Rajel wants me to work with him to figure out who was behind the attack today."

"What did you tell him?"

"I haven't told him anything yet," Jack replied. "I want this to be a decision that we make together. If you think that it's best for us to just shut up and let the Antaurans handle this one on their own, then I'll support your play."

It surprised him when Anna laid a hand on his cheeks and kissed him on the lips. It wasn't just a tender kiss. There was passion in it, almost enough to make him forget this entire conversation.

When she finally broke contact, she smiled at him. "Actually," she said. "I think we would be stupid to trust the Antaurans without running our own investigation. And I think we had better figure out what's going on here. So... Partners?"

"Partners."

Jack offered his hand, but she slapped it away. Before he could say another word, she was pushing him onto his back and crawling over him with that dangerous glint in her eyes. "This isn't the kind of partnership we consummate with a handshake."

And then she was kissing him again.

Chapter 15

Harry didn't sleep a wink all night. He spent every agonizing second in a chair next to Claire's hospital bed. Convincing the staff at the Diplomatic Complex to let him leave had taken some doing. In the end, he had to call Anna's father and have him call the Antauran diplomats and have *them* pull some strings. And he had no idea what to tell any of them. "I experimented on my daughter with an Overseer device" was perhaps the most shameful thing a parent could say.

Harry would have endured that shame to get his daughter medical attention, but he feared the consequences of confessing the N'Jal's existence to his Antauran hosts. He had let some of the soldiers see him casting force-fields yesterday, but for all they knew, he had a tiny generator on his person, a piece of new Leyrian tech that was smaller and more efficient than the standard models.

If he told the Antaurans that he was wielding a device made by creatures that they considered gods, they might throw him in a cell. And who could say what they would do to Claire? So far as anyone knew, she had fainted.

The doctors had performed a number of medical scans, and they said that Claire's vitals were all normal. Harry didn't know if that was good or bad. Did it mean that she was all right? Or did it mean that the problem was subtle enough to elude detection by basic medical scans?

They had given Claire a standard hospital room, a cramped little space with green walls and a large window that looked out on the city. The only thing that Harry could see through it was the white-bricked skyscraper across the street.

He was slumped over in a chair with hands on his thighs, his head lolling as sleep threatened to claim him. *Just a few minutes rest,* he thought to himself. *There's nothing you can do for her anyway.*

But of course, sleep never made good on those threats.

Claire was under the covers with her eyes closed, her breathing slow and steady. If you didn't know anything that had happened in the last twenty-four hours, you might have said that she looked peaceful.

Harry sat with his elbow on his knee, rubbing tired eyes with the tips of his fingers. "Sweetie," he whispered. "I'm so sorry."

It startled him when Claire groaned and rolled over to face him. Her eyes fluttered open a moment later. "Hey, Dad," she said hoarsely. "Got any Frosted Flakes?"

"Frosted Flakes?"

"Yeah, I'm craving them."

Gaping at her, Harry blinked slowly. Was this actually happening? "Claire, we've lived on Leyria for almost a year," he said. "You haven't had Frosted Flakes in…in a very long time."

"Oh yeah. I forgot."

"You forgot."

She sat up and stretched her arms over her head, yawning as if she had just woken up from a good night's sleep. "This isn't our house on Leyria," she said. "It's not our suite in the Diplomatic Complex either. Where are we?"

A mix of emotions washed over Harry. Claire remembering their life on Leyria and that they had come to Antaur for the peace summit was a good sign. But relief mingled with fear and anger and shame that was strong enough to level mountains. "We're…We're in a hospital," he managed after a moment.

"Because you did something to me with that Overseer thing."

Harry forced his eyes shut, hot tears streaming over his face. "That's right," he said, nodding. "I…Oh, Claire, I am *so* sorry. I didn't mean to do it, but that thing has a mind of its own; I should have never…"

Claire wiggled her fingers and lifted her leg. For an instant, Harry felt panic flaring up inside him, but then he realized that his daughter seemed to be testing her motor skills. "Everything feels normal," she said. "I guess no harm done."

"I'm sorry."

"I know."

Was that supposed to be the end of it then? An apology and his daughter's assurance that she felt just fine? Somehow, it felt like he was getting off easy. *Della was right. I am a lousy parent.*

"That's not true," Claire said.

When Harry looked up, she was watching him. "Mom says a lot of dumb stuff," Claire went on. "I know Melissa sometimes used that to get what she wanted, but I never felt that way."

"You…You never felt what exactly?"

"Like you were a lousy parent." Claire scooched over, leaning over the bar of her hospital bed. Her bright smile was almost enough to make Harry forget that his terrible decisions had put her in that bed. "You always read me stories and tucked me in at night. You gave up being a cop so that we could be safe. You *always* put us first, Dad. But life is complicated. You think I don't get that, but I do."

Harry gripped the arms of his chair until his knuckles whitened. Cold sweat pasted his shirt to his back. Was there any chance that he had spoken his thoughts out loud? Any chance at all?

"Well, I heard you," Claire muttered. "So, you must have."

With a gasp, Harry leaped to his feet. He tried to back up, but the chair was behind him, and he tripped over it. Before he even realized it, he was sprawled out on the floor. "Dad!" Claire shouted. "What the hell?"

"Oh, god, what did I do?"

But of course, he already knew the answer. Harry remembered the thoughts that had tumbled through his mind as he scanned his daughter with the N'Jal. He would give her the means to protect herself. Well, he had done it.

It should have been impossible, of course – you couldn't just give a normal human being the ability to read minds – but the N'Jal was an Overseer device, and the Overseers had created the first telepaths. Which meant…

"That's ridiculous," Claire said. "Of course I'm not a-"

Her mouth dropped open, but she covered it with one hand. Her eyes grew larger and larger until even Harry could see that she believed it. "A telepath," she whispered. "I can read minds."

"Claire, I am so sor-"

"Cool!"

She stood up and started jumping on the bed, giggling with unrestrained joy. "I can read minds! Oh, that is *so* much cooler than being a Justice Keeper. Melissa is gonna be so jealous!"

"Absolutely not!"

Director Varno stood before a window in his suite. Behind him, the skyscrapers of Antaur's capital city sparkled in the sunlight, but the sight was ruined by the stormcloud that was Varno's face. "You will *not* be suggesting that we take over the investigation of yesterday's attack."

Anna sat in a gilded chair with a cup and saucer in her lap, choosing her words with care. Was Varno's reluctance to start an investigation simply a matter of skittishness – fear that they might offend the Antaurans – or was there something more sinister at play? Seth was on edge, but his mistrust might have been a reflection of her own thoughts.

Lifting her cup with one hand, Anna savoured the scent of peppermint tea. She took a sip. "Frankly, sir, I don't think we have any other options," she replied at last. "We need to know what the Antaurans aren't telling us."

"You're as bad as Hunter."

"I'll take that as a compliment."

Jack was on her right, in a gilded chair of his own, watching the other man with a guarded expression. "So will I," he said. "Do you recall what I said yesterday about how I've spent the last year looking for traitors among the Justice Keepers?"

Varno eased himself onto a couch in front of the window, spreading his arms out across the backrest. His smile belonged on a leopard that had just come across a wounded gazelle. "Let me guess," he said. "Your investigations implicated me."

"On the contrary!" Jack exclaimed. "You came out clean as a whistle."

"Then why are you bringing this up?"

"Because your psych profile pegged you as a patriot," Jack answered. "You're the kind of uptight windbag who used to drive me nuts. Mr. 'Look at me! I practice excellent decorum.' That's one reason Larani chose you for this mission. If I'd had any doubts about you, I would have told her, and you wouldn't even be here."

Jack sat forward with his hands gripping the chair arms, staring intently at the other man. "Grecken Slade is a blemish on our good name," he went on. "That fact gets under your skin more than you're willing to let on, doesn't it, Tren?"

Varno's smile never wavered, but it became somewhat less predatory, friendlier in a way that Anna couldn't describe. "I see it now," he said softly. "Why Larani chose you to ferret out the traitors among us. You are a thorn in the side of anyone with even a lick of authority, but you know how to push the right buttons."

Anna took another sip of delicious tea.

She leaned forward to set her saucer down on a small wooden table, then stood up. "Sir," she began, "I know you're worried about offending the Antaurans, but we have no idea who attacked us yesterday. Our delegation isn't safe until we can determine to what extent the Antaurans were involved."

"So, you would risk the talks?"

Folding her arms, Anna paced a line through the sitting room. Her mouth tightened as she shook her head. "What is there to risk?" she countered. "We have to acknowledge the possibility that the Antaurans staged the attacks yesterday, and if that's the case, these talks were a ruse."

Turning on her heel, Anna faced the man with a tight frown and nodded once. "We have every right to protect our delegates. If they're not willing to let us do that, then I say we should end this sham of a peace summit right now."

"And risk a war."

The question nagged at her. One reason she had been so nervous about taking this assignment, so fearful that she might say or do something to disrupt the talks, was the ever-present dread that she, Anna Lenai, might be responsible for an armed conflict that got thousands of people killed.

But some of Jena's lessons were bubbling to the surface of her mind. She could not control what other people did. Seeking nonviolent solutions was always preferable, but sometimes, people were determined to start a conflict, and when that happened, refusing to fight back wouldn't necessarily deter them.

Anna reclaimed her seat, crossing one leg over the other and speaking with as much serenity as she could muster. "If the Antaurans were behind the attack," she said. "If they lured our diplomats here just to kill them, then we're already at war. Refusing to admit it doesn't change the truth."

In the corner of her eye, she could see Jack smiling. She felt a sudden warmth and affection at the realization that he was proud of her. Seth echoed her sentiment and Jack's as well. "Director," Anna said, "We *must* learn the truth of what happened yesterday."

"You make a good point, Operative Lenai."

"Thank you, sir."

With a sigh, Varno stood up. He studied them both for a moment and then shook his head. "The situations we find ourselves in," he muttered. "Very well, I will speak to the diplomatic corps."

"With respect, sir," Anna said. "I think Jack should handle that."

"Oh, and why is that?"

"Because he seemed to make an impression on President Salmaro, yesterday," she answered. "And because I think the best way to gain the Antauran's cooperation would be to go through him. Maybe I'm wrong, but I get the impression that he was truly surprised by the attack. There may be factions within his government that want this treaty to fail, but I think Salmaro genuinely wants peace."

"Very well, Operative Lenai. I will leave this to you."

The double doors that led into President Salmaro's office had ornate handles that reflected the ceiling lights. Just looking at them made you think that they must have been polished every day. Antaurans and their love of spectacle.

Jack stood before those doors with his hands clasped behind himself, frowning as he worked up his courage. "You sure you want me to take the lead?" he asked. "After the show I put on yesterday…"

They had been waiting in this hallway for the better part of an hour, and that was after another *two* hours of calling diplomats and security officials just to gain permission to enter this building. He was worn out, his nerves frazzled and frayed. And though Jack would probably – as Tren Varno said – know how to "press the right buttons," his talent was in pissing people off, making them talk and sniffing bullshit from a mile away. He didn't have the soft, diplomatic touch.

Jack turned.

Anna sat in a chair with her knees together, smiling at the absurdity of his question. Well, *she* probably saw it as absurd, anyway. "The show you put on got through to him," she said. "That's what we need right now."

Rajel was a short way up the hallway, leaning against the wall with arms folded and grimacing like a man who had tasted brussels sprouts for the first time. "You can't sail an ocean without making waves."

"Huh?"

"A saying among my people."

"Making waves," Jack whispered. "Well, I've got a talent for that."

The double doors swung open to reveal a telepath in purple robes, a lovely young woman with fair skin and curly, blonde hair. "Three of you," she said. "As expected. Be warned that any aggressive action on your part will provoke an immediate response."

Any thought that it might have been an idle threat vanished the instant Jack stepped through the door. The president's office was large and imposing, not at all like the cozy, little study that Sarona Vason used.

Arch-shaped windows behind the desk looked out upon a garden, and there were screens on every wall, each displaying status reports and updates from the president's staff. But that was not what got his attention.

At least a dozen security officers in full tactical gear surrounded him on all sides, each one carrying a rifle in both hands, its muzzle pointed at the ceiling. And there were telepaths, an older man with Asian features who wore deep, black robes and a pink-cheeked, freckled young man with thick red hair.

Salmaro was behind his desk, watching their arrival with a frown that betrayed his unease. "Agent Hunter," he said curtly. "I thought I might be hearing from you again."

Jack entered the room, flanked by Anna and Rajel, but he closed less than half the distance before coming to an abrupt halt. There was no need to provoke any of these fine people, and getting too close to the desk would do just that. "Mr. President."

"I understand you have a proposal for me."

Licking his lips, Jack closed his eyes and nodded. "Yes, sir," he said, taking one more cautious step forward. "I believe that you should let the Justice Keepers participate in the investigation of yesterday's attack."

"By the gods!" One of the telepaths – the older man – came striding toward Jack, and Summer grew very tense. "Why would we do such a thing?"

"Vronal!" Salmaro shouted. His gaze settled on Jack a moment later, and there was suspicion in his eyes. "He makes a good point. The details of yesterday's attack have been classified from our own people. We would hardly share them with foreigners."

"Be that as it may, sir," Jack replied, "if my suspicions are correct and Slade is in some way involved, we have the tools and experience to deal with him."

"Can you prove his involvement?"

"Of course not."

"Then why would I allow your people to join the investigation?"

Jack tossed his hands up. "You got me!" he said, shaking his head. "I mean, it's not like the only way to prove Slade's involvement would be to examine the evidence. No, of course, your question isn't patently absurd. Hello, horse; I sure do hope you like following that cart around."

"Agent Hunter…" the president cut in.

But Jack wasn't finished.

Planting one fist on his hip, he stood before the other man's desk and shook his head. "Clearly, I should be able to just *divine* the motives behind yesterday's attack. The Scientific Method? Who needs that?"

When he finally ended his tirade, Salmaro turned his attention to Anna, and the flush in his cheeks made it clear that Jack had struck a nerve. "Is he always like this?"

The guards tensed up when Jack strode forward and took a chair across from the president, but thankfully no one had an itchy trigger finger today. It was a calculated risk but one that paid off. Sometimes, when a small dog was confronted with a bigger dog, the best thing he could do was growl.

"I have a very low tolerance for stupidity, sir," Jack said. "And after the last two days, I have reached my limit. You wanted cooperation between Antaur and Leyria. Well, here's your chance to put that into practice. If you're not going to live by the spirit of the deal that *you* proposed, why are we even sitting here?"

Claire stepped out of the washroom in green jeans and a white t-shirt, flicking a lock of wavy hair over her shoulder. She smiled when she noticed Harry watching her. "What?" she demanded.

Harry was bent forward with his elbows on the arms of his chair, his fingertips covering his mouth. "Just worried," he muttered. "Maybe we should ask the doctors to run some more tests. You might still be in danger."

"Because you gave me super powers?"

"This isn't a joke."

It startled him with Claire shut the washroom door and leaned against it with her arms folded. "You see me laughing?" she asked, raising an eyebrow. "I'm excited, yeah. But I'm also pretty scared."

With a groan, Harry stood up. His eyes dropped shut, exhaustion washing over him. "Well, at least there's that much," he said.

"Besides, I'm not sure how I could *convince* them to run more tests. And I don't think we'd like it if they found out you're a telepath."

Claire turned her head to stare out the door of her hospital room, into the hallway where nurses and doctors in lab coats scurried back and forth. "What happens when we get home?"

"I don't know."

"Won't you have to…register me?"

They were cut off when a nurse in a bright green uniform stepped into the room. He was tall, slim with tanned skin and brown eyes. "Ms. Carlson," he said in Raen. "So, how are we feeling today?"

Harry was about to answer for her – Claire only knew a few phrases of Raen – but he cut off when his daughter stepped forward with a warm smile and said, "Quite well, thank you very much."

Harry blinked.

The nurse was smiling down at her, clearly startled by her fluency in his language. "I'm surprised," he said. "I didn't think Earthers studied Raen. But I guess children pick these things up quickly."

"Something like that."

The young man turned his gaze on Harry, and just like that, he was the very image of square-jawed stoicism. "Her discharge papers are ready," he said. "We see no reason why she would have to remain another night."

"Thank you," Harry mumbled.

"We suspect that her collapse was the product of a mild electrolyte imbalance. So, make sure she eats three square meals today. And get a good night's sleep tonight. She'll be fine in a day or two."

"Well, Dad," Claire broke in, "I can tell you're pretty tired. So, how 'bout you go to bed, and I order some room service. They have to have room service at the Diplomatic-"

Her smile wavered.

Half a second later, Claire fell to her knees and then toppled over, lying stretched out on her side. She moaned, clapping both hands over her head, small fingers grabbing tufts of curly hair.

"Claire!" Harry shouted.

He rushed to his daughter, but the nurse was faster, kneeling down beside her and trying to roll her onto her back. Claire was trembling, her every limb shaking in the throes of a seizure.

The nurse grabbed a small communications device from his belt, pressed a button on the side and spoke into it. "Trauma team to room 451," he said. "Patient seizing."

Claire kicked her legs and flailed her arms.

Her screams ripped through Harry like the wails of a banshee. A part of him wanted to hold her in his arms, to calm her down, to do *something*. But cop training kicked in. He knew that the best thing you could do for a patient who was seizing was to position them on their side so that they wouldn't swallow their own vomit. Claire was already on her side. Harry pushed the chair back all the way to the wall so that she would have plenty of room, but that was all he could do for the moment.

Claire stilled, her trembles subsiding, and she began to gasp. Every breath was hoarse and raw. The nurse pressed two fingers to the side of her neck, counting slowly as he took her pulse.

He looked up at Harry with a gaping mouth, and the colour drained out of his face. "Her heart rate is over one hundred and ten beats per minute," he whispered. "We need to get her sedated and quickly."

A second later, two more nurses rushed into the room, followed by a doctor in blue. Short and plump with olive skin and long brown hair that fell to the small of her back, the doctor moved with the confidence of someone accustomed to authority. "Get her on the bed," she ordered.

Two of the nurses gently lifted Claire, and she groaned. They carried her to the bed and set her down. "Activate Scanners."

When the screen above Claire's bed lit up, Harry tried to read it. But though he had learned enough Raen to get by, reading the language was another matter. He recognized some characters, but it was hard to say exactly what they were measuring.

The one thing he *did* recognize, however, was the heart monitor. That seemed to be an almost universal fixture in any medical facility. By the sound it was making, Claire's heart must have been thundering.

"Twenty shenivals of Tresacline," the doctor ordered.

"Tresacline?" Harry shouted. "What's that?"

The doctor spared exactly five seconds to give him a withering glare. Then she was hovering over Claire again and gesturing to Harry with a thumb jerked over her shoulder. "Shut him up or get him out of here," she ordered her nurses.

The one who had been with them when this all started gave Harry a sympathetic look. But he did nothing more than that. Harry understood the rules. If he wanted to stay, he had to keep out from underfoot.

Beep-beep-beep-beep-beep-beep.

Harry was dry-washing his hands, backing up until his spine hit the wall and then grunting from the jolt of pain. This was his fault! This was his fault! How could he have done this to his own daughter?

The doctor and nurses had clustered around the bed, forming an impenetrable wall of bodies that Harry couldn't see through. What was happening? Were they giving Claire a sedative?

Beep-Beep-Beep.

"It's not working," one of the nurses said, checking the screen. "Her heart rate is still climbing. Her body temperature is now at forty-seven Kellans."

Kellans?

Harry didn't know the Antauran measurement system. Were they saying that Claire had a fever? Or was her body temperature too low? That was unlikely, given her rising heart rate, but Harry couldn't be sure of anything.

The doctor had her back turned as she checked something on a small tablet computer. "Synaptic scanners!" she ordered. "Quickly!"

The wall of bodies parted just enough to let Harry see one of the nurses putting two silvery disks on Claire's forehead. He had to resist the urge to speak, to demand an update on what was happening. His daughter twitched, arching her back, and then flopped back down on the bed.

"Gods above," the doctor whispered as she scrolled through images on her tablet. "I've never seen this pattern of neurological activity."

"Heart rate still climbing," one of the nurses said.

Harry bit his tongue. Every instinct told him to speak up, to insist that they tell him what was happening. But further outbursts on his part would only get him escorted out of the room. Claire was thrashing now, tossing and turning and screeching as if she were trapped in some horrible nightmare.

It was too much to watch.

Harry opened his mouth, but before he could speak, Claire settled down, lying still on her back with her eyes closed. For a second, Harry thought that was a good thing. But then he noted the sound of the heart monitor. Just one long tone that went on without interruption.

His child had flat-lined.

"Claire!"

The End of Part 1.

Interlude

The shuttle's hatch opened to reveal a large hangar bay populated by men in black tactical gear. Each one carried an assault rifle.

Slade chuckled as he emerged from the air-lock.

Dressed regally in a pair of gray pants and a dark-green coat that fell to mid-thigh, silver embroidery on the cuff of each sleeve, he smiled for the men who no doubt hoped to intimidate him with their show of military prowess. "The Inzari be praised," he said. "I am so rarely honoured with such a fine display of strength and discipline."

Two of the armoured men stepped forward, standing at the base of the ramp that led up to the airlock. They said nothing, of course; they only watched him, perhaps waiting for orders to escort him to the admiral.

Slade took one step toward them.

They both tensed up, pointing those rifles at him.

Spreading his hands, Slade bowed his head to the pair of them. "You need not fear me," he said. "I am only here to speak with the admiral."

"My men don't fear you, Grecken."

Standing at the top of the ramp, Slade was high enough to see over the heads of the assembled security officers. On the far side of the hangar bay, a door led to a hallway, and a woman in gray came striding through it.

As always, Admiral Telixa Ethran looked neat and professional. The red epaulettes on her shoulders seemed to be a little brighter today. A short bob of brown hair framed a face that was almost always set in an expression of disapproval. "You overestimate your importance if you think they will cower before you," Telixa went on.

"Indeed."

The crowd of men parted, creating an aisle for the admiral to walk through, and in less than ten seconds, she was standing before him with fists on her hips, sneering as if the sight of him made her sick. "Let's be done with this."

"As you say, Admiral."

Slade had visited this ship many times; he knew that Telixa Ethran would not bring him to her office, which was probably too close to the main bridge for her liking. No, she always seemed to prefer some out of the way room, far from any key systems.

This time, it was a short trek through wide corridors with gray walls and then a ride on an elevator. That brought them to the next level up, and from there, Telixa led them to a room that overlooked the hangar bay.

That troop of security officers was with him for every step of the journey, forming two lines, one on his left and one on his right. They marched in silence, never so much as glancing at him, but Slade knew that they were aware of his every move.

When he entered the room that Telixa had chosen for their meeting, two of those officers followed him in and took up positions on either side of the door. It was a simple setting: black floor tiles and gray walls.

A crescent-shaped desk was positioned in front of windows that looked out upon the shuttle bay. Perhaps this was some administrator's office. That didn't stop Telixa from taking the only chair, crossing one leg over the other and regarding him with the cool confidence of a queen on her throne. Slade put aside his irritation and focused on the task at hand. He had come here for information. "I wish to know what you've done in response to the Antauran peace summit," he said.

"That is not your concern."

"I beg to differ," Slade replied. "It was I who warned you about the summit, and now you will tell me what you've done in response."

Telixa reclined in her chair with an easy smile. Her soft laughter told Slade that – like her soldiers – she was not the least bit intimidated by him. He would have to change that. "Perhaps you've forgotten the rules, Grecken," she mocked. "On my ship, I give the orders, not you."

Slade crossed his arms as he stood before her, shaking his head slowly. "I have no patience for your bravado, Telixa," he said. "Your planet's response to the Leyrian threat was predicated on the assumption that Leyria and Antaur would remain bitter enemies. If that changes, it will undermine all of our plans."

"Thank you for explaining the perfectly obvious," Telixa replied. "Now, allow me to do the same. I don't like you, Grecken. I never have. In my opinion, even the cyborgs that you have provided do not justify the government's faith in you. You can rest assured that I will always prioritize the security of Ragnos and the Confederacy. Now, if there is nothing else, you can leave my ship before I have you thrown off."

Fury as hot as magma burned within Slade. He wanted to crush this woman for her insolence. He could have done it many times over, but he needed goodwill among the Ragnosians. Without their cooperation, the next stage of his plan would fail. The Inzari would not be pleased. He calmed himself.

"Come now, Admiral," he said. "I have been an ally to your people. I ask only that you communicate openly with me."

Telixa stood up in a hurry, the motion sending her chair wheeling backward until it hit the wall. "Enough," she said. "Do you really think that your genteel demeanour will persuade me? I know you for what you are, Grecken. Now, get off my ship."

"I had hoped that you would be reasonable," Slade muttered. Discreetly, he used his right hand to rip the button off his left sleeve. "I had hoped that you would listen." He did the same for the button on his right sleeve so that he had one in each hand. "But it seems I will have to teach you some humility."

The instant those words were out of his mouth, the two guards behind him stepped forward, each man raising his rifle to aim for Slade's back.

"Now, now," Slade began. "Perhaps I was a bit too hasty." He spread his arms wide in a gesture of surrender, a button clutched in each fist. "I spoke without thinking, and I humbly ask your forgiveness."

When his fingers uncurled, the buttons flew with the speed of low-calibre bullets, each propelled by Bent Gravity on a course that took it straight through the exposed neck of one of the guards. Some of their blood hit the back of Slade's coat.

He spun on the one to his left.

Slade kicked the rifle out of that man's grip before the fool lost his balance and fell to the floor. The weapon hit the wall, bounced off and then landed right in Slade's waiting hands. He whirled around to face the door.

On cue, a third guard appeared in the opening just in time to take a bullet through his visor. Blood spattered as the corpse fell backward onto the next man in line, and by the time that poor wretch was able to shove the dead body aside, Slade had a shot lined up.

He fired.

The next guard flinched as his visor shattered, and then he too was dropping to land atop the corpse of his fallen comrade. With the natural bottleneck the door offered, Slade was able to put down two more security officers, and now a pile of bodies blocked entry into the office.

In his mind's eye, he saw Telixa's silhouette behind him. The admiral was trying to discreetly draw her sidearm. Perhaps she thought that Slade would pay her no mind if she made no aggressive movements.

Twisting on the spot, Slade lifted the assault rifle in one hand and fired. His bullet pierced Telixa's right shoulder and then burst right through to shatter the window behind her. She screeched, dropping her weapon and collapsing against the wall.

The security team was no longer trying to get through the door. Slade could hear them muttering in the hallway, trying to come up with a plan. Poor bastards. They must have been at a loss for what to do. Even putting aside the dangers of using explosives in space, tossing a grenade into the room would only kill their commanding officer. "Relax, gentlemen!" Slade called out. "I'm not going to kill her."

He turned his back on the door but kept his rifle pointed out behind himself as he strode across the room. If one of those fools decided to poke his head around the corner, spatial awareness would alert Slade to the danger, and he would fire before the other man could get his weapon up.

Slade jumped onto the desk and then hopped off to land behind it. Telixa was squatting by the wall with her left hand on her right shoulder. Her face was red, and her cheeks glistened with tears.

One of the guards ventured a glance into the room.

Slade fired.

That man took a bullet through his visor and fell backward to land sprawled out on the hallway floor. Some of the others started shouting and cursing him, but none of them dared to approach the door.

Bending low, Slade grabbed Telixa's neck with his free hand. "No!" she croaked as he lifted her off the floor, but he gave her no time to protest. With a growl, he slammed her down onto the desk so that she was lying on her back.

He clamped a hand onto Telixa's face, his thumb and fingers pressed against her cheekbones, applying almost enough pressure to break them. "I have grown tired of your insolence, girl," he whispered. "I tolerated it, even when you refused to kill Jack Hunter, because I need your ships. But I do *not* need you."

"Security!" Telixa shouted, her voice muffled by Slade's palm. "Code X!"

Releasing her, Slade turned back to the door and took aim with his assault rifle. He fired when a blurry figure in black stepped into view, but his bullet curved upward as it passed through a patch of warped space-time.

Slade had only a second to duck before the bullet looped back and around and flew toward him. It sped over his head and through the shattered window, emitting a loud *ping* when it hit the hangar bay wall.

He stood up.

The Bending vanished to reveal an unarmed guard standing in the doorway, a guard who wore no gloves over his dark-skinned hands. It took Slade only a second to deduce what had happened. When the newcomer removed his helmet, Slade saw exactly what he expected to see.

Arin stood there with his teeth clenched, his face flushed and glistening with sweat. "You should have never come back here." His deep voice echoed off the hangar bay walls.

Tossing his rifle aside, Slade tittered as he shook his head. "So, she has made you into one of her lackeys," he said. "A fitting punishment, given the depth of your failure. I suggest you slink back to your cell."

"We've had many long talks," Telixa whispered, writhing on the desk. Blood from her wound had left a puddle under her body. "Arin hates you even more than I do."

"Does he now?" Slade asked, pacing around the desk, positioning himself in front of the other man. Arin stepped over the bodies of fallen soldiers as he entered the room. But he did not attack Slade directly.

Instead, he waited patiently, blocking the exit. "It's really quite amazing what you can learn," he began, "when someone pushes you to your limits. When every single day is a struggle for survival. I must thank the admiral for that."

"I have some sad news for you, Arin," Slade replied. "The fact that you're still alive means your captors weren't trying that hard."

"We'll see."

Slade answered the other man's bravado with a wolfish grin. "Yes, we will," he said softly. "But I can't help but note your insistence on stalling. Still afraid to face me, Arin? I suppose I can't blame you."

It seemed his words had an effect. Precisely the effect that he had been hoping for. Poke even the most cowardly kitten enough times and it would eventually swat at you. At long last, Arin came forward, his nostrils flaring with every breath.

His face was flushed, a sheen of sweat on his brow. "You betrayed me," he hissed. "You promised me that I would serve the Inzari, and then you betrayed me!"

Arin kicked high.

Slade ducked and felt a black shoe passing over his head. The other man brought his leg down and spun for a back-hand strike. As if that would do him any good.

In the blink of an eye, Slade rose and twisted to intercept the blow. He clamped one hand onto Arin's shoulder and the other onto Arin's wrist. With a quick shove, he sent his adversary face-first into the wall.

Arin's head rebounded when it struck the bulkhead.

The man turned around, snarling as blood leaked from his nostrils and dripped over his mouth. "You betrayed me!" he screamed. "You betrayed me!" He was charging across the room in an instant, drawing back his arm for a punch.

Once again, Slade ducked, ignoring the soft whoosh of air above him. He punched Arin's stomach, then popped up to offer a quick jab to the face, one that made his enemy's head jerk backward.

Seizing the other man's shirt with both hands, Slade pulled him close. He clenched his teeth and followed that up with a fierce headbutt, one that left Arin dazed. Why had he ever imagined that this pathetic wretch of a man deserved to be one of his lieutenants?

Power surged through every cell in Slade's body as he called upon his symbiont. He whirled around and threw Arin across the room with a touch of Bent Gravity. Just enough to make his point.

Arin went shoulder-first into the wall, then crumpled to the floor, sprawled out like so many of the guards that Slade had put down. The only difference between him and any of the dead men that littered the floor of this room was that he was still moaning.

Turning around, Slade found Telixa sitting on the desk with a hand on her bleeding shoulder. Her teeth were bared as she struggled to think through the pain. It was time to drive this point home.

The admiral looked up as Slade approached, her eyes widening at the sight of him. "No," she whimpered, shaking her head. "Please."

"Do you know who I am?"

"What kind of stupid question-"

"DO YOU KNOW WHO I AM?" Slade bellowed.

His shout made Telixa squeak in fright, but to her credit, she calmed herself within seconds and faced him with the same stubborn defiance that he had seen so many times. Tears or no tears, this woman had a core of steel. There would be no more pleading from her. The hatred in her eyes made that much clear.

Slade might kill her, but she would not give him the satisfaction of seeing her beg again. "Who are you?"

"I am Liu Bang," Slade answered. "The man who unified a nation, who broke a dynasty and raised another in its place. The peasant who became an emperor. I think that was why they chose me." Memories flashed within his mind. Memories of simpler days when he had actually believed it possible to change the world. Memories of days when he would have thought of himself as a good man.

With a quick shake of his head, Slade came out of his reverie. "To the Leyrians, I was Dravis Trovan. My armies subjugated the savages with the might of gunpowder. One by one their nations fell until the Tareli Empire stretched to every corner of the continent."

He leaned in close with a rictus smile, close enough to kiss the shuddering admiral. "Among your people," he went on, "I was known as Rajhi the Wise. But for my efforts, the miserable little country where you were born would never have existed."

"That's impossible," Telixa whispered.

"If only." It took a moment for him to realize that the bitter laughter he heard was his own. "I have lived for over two thousand years and died more times than I can count. I have worn a hundred faces, answered to a hundred names, guiding your pitiful species along the paths that the Inzari desire. And service brings with it many rewards."

He retrieved a mechanized syringe from his jacket pocket, flicking a switch to extend the needle. The horror on Telixa's face was almost satisfaction enough. He toyed with the idea of letting her go, letting this be an object lesson...But no. Left to her own devices, Telixa Ethran would find some way to frustrate his plans. It was time to bring her to heel.

Grabbing her arm, Slade rolled up her sleeve and plunged the needle into a vein. Telixa struggled, of course, thrashing about, trying to pull out of his grip, but a normal human being stood little chance against someone with a symbiont.

Slade injected the contents of his syringe into her bloodstream. "Nanobots," he said. "It's time we redefined our relationship."

At that moment, two more men in heavy tactical armour burst into the room, nearly tripping over the bodies that lay strewn about in front of the doorway. "Release her," one said as they pointed their guns at Slade's back.

His predatory smile returned as he turned slowly to face them. "Gone and found yourselves some reinforcements, hmm?" He strode forward, and though both men choked up on their rifles, neither one fired. They knew that trying to kill him would only result in their own deaths.

"We don't want to hurt you," the guard said. "You've made your point. Leave now, and there will be no further violence."

"But of course," Slade replied. "Far be it for me to remain where I am unwelcome."

"Your tests all come back negative."

Telixa sat on the edge of an examination bed, her head hanging as she fought off a wave of exhaustion. Her right arm was in a sling that she wore over a gray tank top. "Run them again."

The small examination room in her ship's medical centre was rather spartan in its decor. Unadorned gray walls surrounded her on all sides. There wasn't much in the way of furniture except for the bed, a chair and a rectangular control console that the doctor could use to display her scan results.

Dr. Toran Maderon, the chief medical officer who had joined her crew less than one month ago, replied with a smile. "We've run them five times," he said. "They all come back negative. There are no nanobots in your system."

Looking up just long enough to fix the man with a death glare, Telixa narrowed her eyes. "Run them again."

"Very well."

The doctor took his place behind the console, tapping away at the controls. "Far be it for me to challenge the will of hard-headed COs," he said. "But I would warn you that nanobots give off an electromagnetic signature that is not present in your body."

He turned his back on her, running his hand over the wall, causing a hatch to open. Inside, a plethora of medical supplies took up almost every inch of space on three shelves. Taking one of the syringes from the top shelf, he popped off the cap to expose the needle.

When he spun around to face her, he was smiling again. "And we have taken three samples of blood," he said, closing the distance in three quick strides. Without warning, he rolled up Telixa's left sleeve, stuck a needle in her arm and drew some blood.

She grunted from the pain.

Telixa hated needles.

It was over quickly enough, and then the doctor put a small bandage on her arm. She had three now, thin white strips across her upper arm. But as much as she despised needles, it was worth it to be sure.

Dr. Maderon went back to the console and pressed a few buttons that caused a tray to extend. He squirted a few drops of her blood onto that tray, and there was a whirring sound as the machine did its work.

Grinding her teeth, Telixa shook her head slowly. "Never underestimate Grecken Slade." It was a little late for that advice, but if nothing else, she could at least spare her crew from making her mistake.

Dr. Maderon looked up from the console with that stern expression so common to those in his profession. "There are no nanobots in your bloodstream," he said. "As far as we can tell, Slade injected you with a mild sedative."

"Are you absolutely certain?" Telixa grumbled. Nanobots could do any number of horrible things to a human body, and they could lie dormant for a very long time until they were triggered. "I will not resume command if there is any chance that I might be compromised."

"I see no reason for concern," the doctor assured her. "And after a few days' rest, I would say that you're fit for duty."

Telixa nodded.

Some people would feel slighted by her curt dismissal but it was the only thanks he could expect from her. She was not prone to sentiment. Thankfully, the good doctor had a thick skin.

The long walk back to her quarters was nerve-wracking. Gray-uniformed officers would pass her in the hallways, and though they all stopped to give a proper salute, she was very much aware of the sling. Telixa had never been comfortable with displays of weakness. Did her crew think less of her?

There had been a certain arrogance in her approach to the problem that was Grecken Slade. She was aware of the fabled Leyrian Justice Keepers and their incredible abilities, but surely Slade would never try anything foolish. Not when he was surrounded by an entire security team. And besides, she had Arin! The best way to fight a Keeper was with someone who possessed the same abilities.

Now, seven good men were dead, and Arin's skills had proved to be useless. The Admiralty Board would be wise to put her in review. If not for her many long years of distinguished service, she might lose her command. And there was still a good chance of that. Telixa was in no mood to talk to her subordinates.

Her quarters were dark when she entered, but the lights came on to reveal a large sitting room with a couch and coffee table that supported a vase of pink flowers. She did not bother to learn what kind.

Her desk along the wall to her right was neat and tidy without any stray tablets littering its surface. She prided herself on neatness. Perhaps she should sit down and start her report, but for now, she just wanted to rest.

Telixa sat down on the couch, hunched over and covering her face with her good hand. "Fool woman," she scolded herself. "You should have known better than to give him an opening."

"Hello, Telixa."

She jumped to her feet.

Though the room had been empty moments earlier, Grecken Slade now sat at her desk with his feet on its surface, a sly grin on his face. "My, you're looking unwell. I do regret having to resort to violence, but you refused to be reasonable."

Telixa scrambled across the room for the spare pistol that she kept in a drawer. It would do little good against someone who could curve bullets away from his body, but she would not die like a coward.

Suddenly, Slade was right in front of her, wearing that same mocking grin. "I would not do that if I were you," he said. "You'll only make a mess."

She turned around.

Another Slade was sitting at her desk, reclining in her chair with his hands folded over the back of her chair. "Yes," he said. "It's real. Calm yourself, Telixa. I assure you that you have not gone mad."

"What is this?" she whispered.

"Technically, you're hallucinating," the Slade who blocked her path replied. "But I am in control of everything you see." He stepped forward, cupping her chin in one hand, and Telixa gasped when she actually felt his touch. *Tactile* hallucinations. "I didn't inject you with nanobots. They would be too easy to detect."

A reddish glow emanated from the cavernous walls of a chamber deep in the heart of an Inzari ship. Those walls were not made of rock or steel but of flesh through which thin veins pulsed.

Up against the wall, Grecken Slade relaxed in a cocoon that covered him to his waist. His chest was bare, but tentacles thinner than the finest string wrapped around him, holding him in place. More emerged from the wall behind him, attaching themselves to various places on his scalp.

His eyes were glazed over as he stared blankly at nothing at all. "When it comes to mental conditioning," he went on. "I can do a little better than nanobots. You needn't be afraid, Telixa. If I wanted you to die, you would be dead."

Dropping back onto her couch with a soft whimper, Telixa grabbed two fistfuls of her short brown hair. "What did you do to me?" she panted. "What did you do?"

Grecken Slade stood before her in a fine red coat with gold trim on the sleeves, his long black hair hanging loose. His lips were parted in what might have been a smile. Or a sneer. She couldn't tell. "As I told you," he said, "The Inzari offer many, many rewards to those who serve them well."

"What rewards?"

"The use of their technology, of course," Slade replied. "The Inzari have evolved beyond the use of metal and circuitry. They sculpt flesh itself to serve their will. Their ships are living organisms, more powerful than anything you can imagine!"

"What did you do?" Telixa screamed. She didn't care if the members of her crew heard her through the wall. Even if this was all the product of an addled mind, the simple fact that she was hallucinating meant that she was no longer fit to command.

"I injected you with a benign virus," Slade answered. "One that lies dormant in neurons throughout your brain stem. When activated, it travels to the visual cortex, the auditory cortex, the language centres, allowing me to trick your brain into thinking that I am standing right in front of you."

With her mouth agape, Telixa shook her head. "Impossible," she whispered. "My people are the most technologically advanced civilization in this part of the galaxy, and we could not have developed this kind of germ warfare. There's no way that you or your little band of misfits could have done it."

In response, Slade threw his head back and laughed. "My dear Telixa..." He stood up, towering over her, and though she knew he wasn't really there, Telixa couldn't help but cringe. "The Inzari have re-engineered entire star systems. Developing a virus like this is the least of their accomplishments."

"Why?" she mumbled. "Why do this?"

"Because you belong to me now."

Hearing that put some fire in her belly, and Telixa stood up, facing him with her left fist clenched and her bottom lip quivering. "I belong to no one!" she spat. "If you think that you can undermine the Ragnosian Fleet by compromising me, you're sadly mistaken. I will resign my commission!"

"You'll do no such thing."

"Try and stop me."

She more than half expected some kind of outburst, but Slade just stood there, cool as an arctic glacier. Finally, he lifted one hand and made a fist.

Hot, stinging pain surged through every nerve in Telixa's body. It was as if someone had set her skin on fire. She fell to her knees, yelping in fright, lifting a trembling hand in a pitiful attempt to shield herself. "Stop!" she begged. "Please."

"Oh yes," Slade murmured. "I forgot to mention. The virus can activate the brain's pain centres as well. Perhaps another demonstration."

Suddenly, the pain changed.

The fiery sting vanished to be replaced with a wave of nausea that made her want to expel every meal she had ever eaten. It was all she could do not to throw up right there on her sitting room floor. "Please...Stop."

Squatting down in front of her, Slade answered her plea with a cruel smile. "You're going to tell no one about this virus, Telixa." His voice grated in her ears. "You're going to remain in command and carry out your duties as you normally would, but from now on, you will follow every order I give you to the letter. If you don't, I will leave the virus active, leave you writhing in pain until you're nothing but a screaming animal in a cage."

Just like that, the pain was gone.

Telixa looked up at him with tears on her cheeks, gulping air into her lungs. "Yes," she whispered. "I will do as you say."

Part 2

Chapter 16

The high-pitched squeal of the heart monitor filled Harry's ears. Claire was lying still on the hospital bed, her face ashen, her hair damp. The doctors crowded around her, but for one moment – no more than a second, but to Harry's mind it might as well have been an eternity – they were frozen, unsure of what to do next.

"Claire!" he shouted.

One of the nurses spun around to face him, stretching an arm out to bar his path. Harry tried to bulldoze his way through, but the other man was stronger than he looked. "Sir!" he said. "I'm going to have to ask you to give us some space."

Harry backed away with his mouth hanging open, tears streaming over his face. "No," he whispered, shaking his head. "You have to *do* something!"

"That's what we're trying to-"

Claire arched her back as she drew in a ragged gasp, then flopped back down onto the mattress. Suddenly, the heart monitor was emitting its standard *beep... beep... beep.* It was a miracle.

"She's stabilized," one nurse said.

The doctor was standing over Claire's bed with a tablet in hand, frantically checking the readout. "No," she muttered. "I'm still detecting abnormal synaptic activity. She can't maintain this level of-"

Something washed over Harry. Terror. Sharp, icy terror that punched through his chest like a spear. His daughter was going to die, and it was all his fault. His daughter was going to die! *Calm down,* he scolded himself. *Think.*

When he pushed his way through the fog of panic, he realized that the nurses were also trembling. Two of them were backing away from the bed. It was almost as if they felt the same fear he did. It took a second for him to put the pieces together.

They *did* feel it.

Because it wasn't his fear.

It was Claire's.

The doctor was bent forward with a hand over her forehead, groaning from the strain. "What is she…" In an instant, the woman took control of herself, gave her head a shake and checked the tablet. "Look at these readings."

She passed the tablet to the nurse who had been in the room when Claire collapsed, and the man wrinkled his nose as he scanned its contents. "This kind of neural activity is most consistent with-"

"She's a telepath," Harry said.

Everyone else in the room turned to him, and they all wore skeptical expressions. He could already imagine their objections. Claire was Earth-born. Antaur was the only planet in all the galaxy to produce telepaths.

Harry dropped into the empty chair, sobbing, pressing the heels of his hands to his eyes. "I did it," he whimpered. "I changed her."

"You changed her…" the doctor murmured.

Slipping his hand into his pocket, Harry allowed the N'Jal to bond with him. He raised that hand so the others could see it, and they all took a step back. "It's Overseer technology," he said. "I can control it. But I didn't…I didn't mean to change Claire."

Saying that out loud was like a blade in his gut. Well, now it was out in the open. Any hope that he could quietly sneak

Claire off this world before the Antaurans learned of her new abilities had just gone up in a puff of smoke.

He found the courage to look up and saw the doctor standing in front of him with her arms crossed. "Mr. Carlson," she began. "Whatever you did to your daughter, it's not stable. The neural architecture of a telepath's brain is different from that of a human who lacks the gift. You rewired her entire brain. Do you understand that?"

"Yes."

"I need to be clear about this," the doctor went on. "Mr. Carlson, *you* are not a brain surgeon, and even if you were, Antauran doctors have spent *centuries* trying to figure out how to change an ordinary human being into a telepath. Our best minds don't even know where to begin. Rewiring a human brain is beyond our skill. And it is beyond yours as well."

Harry shuddered.

"Even now," the doctor said. "Claire's brain scans are showing neural degradation throughout the cerebral cortex. And I suspect the damage goes even deeper. Her brain no longer knows how to control her body. If we can't find *some* way to stop the degradation, your daughter will suffer permanent, irreparable brain damage, and that's *if* she lives."

Harry let the words sink in, let the reality of what he had done wash over him until he could almost feel the fires of Hell waiting to swallow him whole. Finally, he found the will to speak. "Can you do anything for her?"

In answer to his question, the doctor rounded on her nurses. "Put out a call to Sarel Threos University," she said. "I want their best neurosurgeons here within the hour. And get some diagnostic bots in here. I want a full work-up on the girl. List every treatment option, no matter how experimental."

The nurse who had been with them when this all started gave Harry a sympathetic look. He turned his attention back to his superior. "How…How do you hope to procure such resources for a foreigner?"

"Tell them it's for a telepath," the doctor replied.

When the SlipGate bubble came to a stop, Jack felt a little uneasy. It was always hard to get a sense of exactly where you were when your vision of the outside world was so blurry that some objects merged together, but this time, they were in a place that was considerably dark. Not lacking in illumination – he could see the hazy figure of a guard just outside the bubble – but the walls were black.

A glance to his left made it clear that Keli wasn't feeling any better about this. She stood beside him in a short-sleeved blue dress, and that dangerous glint in her eye spoke volumes.

The bubble popped.

They were indeed in a black room, a room lit only by naked bulbs along the walls. As soon as they were clear, the guard stepped forward and glowered at the two of them. "Agent Hunter," he said. "Ms. Armana. Follow me."

With a quick about-face, the guard turned his back on them and led them out of the room. He guided them through long corridors with light-fixtures on the walls. They must have been underground; the air was stuffy.

"I'm concerned," Keli whispered.

"What's up?"

Her eyes got that distant look of someone in deep concentration. "There are other telepaths here," she muttered. "They are sharing thoughts with one another, and they do not seem to be the least bit concerned that someone might be eavesdropping."

Jack walked slowly with his hands in his coat pockets, shrugging his shoulders at that last bit. "If you go on safari," he said, "sooner or later, you're gonna see lions. But you don't have to go through with this if you don't feel safe."

"Concern for my well-being, Agent Hunter?"

"Of course."

It was a pleasant surprise when Keli patted his upper arm. Maybe he was wrong, but Jack was starting to think that she might actually like him, Anna and the rest of the team. "It is appreciated," she said. "But I will be fine."

The guard brought them to a large set of double doors that slid apart automatically when they drew near. Inside, they found a kind of prep room where men and women in black uniforms sat at computer stations, peering into monitors displaying camera footage of the various cells.

In the middle of the room, a round table with four chairs sat directly under a bulb that hung from the ceiling. That seemed as good a place as any to set up shop, but the instant he stepped forward, the leader of these people moved to intercept him.

This guy was tall with broad shoulders and a bit of a belly. His face was pale with a touch of pink in the cheeks, and his white hair was tucked neatly under a small black cap. "Agent Hunter," he said. "I'm Colonel Rath Lowen of the Presidential Security Staff."

"Nice to meet you, sir."

"We've been ordered to include you in the investigation."

Pursing his lips, Jack held the other man's gaze for a very long moment. He nodded once. "Well, let's get started then." It was the best he could come up with in light of the colonel's obvious reluctance to work with him. "I'd like to interview the prisoners."

"To what end?"

That question came from a woman in blue robes who stepped out of the shadows in the corner. She was just a few inches above the average height for a woman, slender with tanned skin and brown hair that she wore in a braid. "We have already extracted all of the relevant information from the prisoners. They are all members of an anti-Leyrian militia from the Ronoth colony."

"I see," Jack said. "And you are?"

"Tara Driath."

Sliding a chair out from under the table, Jack sat down and folded his hands in his lap. "Well then, Ms. Driath," he replied. "Maybe you can tell me what ship brought these people to Antaur."

The woman blinked as if he had just asked why the sky was blue. "What does that matter?" she asked. "The prisoners have been identified. We have confirmed their guilt through the use of telepathic scans. They will be convicted and sentenced."

Jack sat back with two fingers over his lips, watching her and choosing his words with care. "It matters," he began, "because a thorough understanding of how these men got here will tell us if they had outside support."

"I can simply take that information from their minds."

The thought of her poking around in some poor guy's brain left Jack feeling uneasy, and Summer was just as disturbed. Yes, his symbiont knew every thought in his head, but Jack had consented to that relationship. In their collective state, Nassai shared everything with each other, but that too was a willing exchange. Forcibly entering someone's mind without their permission? That was a violation. "Humour me," Jack said, and when Tara Driath got agitated, he pressed. "What ship brought them to Antaur?"

"I don't know."

Jack rolled his eyes. "Of course you don't." He stood up and paced over to one of the computer stations. The man sitting there – a handsome fellow with a scraggly beard of dark stubble – swivelled around at his approach. "Let's start at the beginning then. You say you've identified each of the prisoners."

"Yes, sir," the young technician replied.

"Bring up the passenger manifest for every ship to visit this world in the last ninety days," Jack said. "Cross reference that with the list of prisoners. Let's see if we find any matches."

A heavy sigh put him on edge, and when he turned around, he found Tara Driath striding toward him with a scowl that would make any man step back. "What is the point of this?" she demanded. "If you wish to know the name of the ship that badly, I will scan the prisoners' minds."

"Sure!" Jack exclaimed. "Let's violate due process. It's not as if these people have rights."

They were all staring at him, especially Colonel Lowen who, by the expression on his face, must have thought that Jack was speaking gibberish. Of course, he might as well have been. Jack wasn't well-versed on the finer points of Antauran law, but if telepaths were allowed to scan a suspect without that suspect's permission, it meant things were very different here.

"Sir?"

The young technician was sitting with his hands on his knees, frowning at Jack's back. "The computer has completed its search," he said. "None of the prisoners appear on any passenger manifest for any ship that entered the system in the last ninety days."

"Excellent!" Jack said. "What does that tell us?"

Several of the officers exchanged looks, and Ms. Driath exhaled roughly, turning her face up to the ceiling as if she were asking God why he had decided to subject her to this torment. "It tells us that this was a pointless exercise."

Keli waited by the door with her arms folded, and her sly smile suggested that she knew where Jack was going with this. Well, it was nice to know that *someone* was paying attention.

"All right, Keli," Jack said. "Enlighten us."

Keli glided across the room with the same haughty arrogance of her fellow telepath, but her wolfish grin put Tara's scowl to shame. "It tells us that the people who carried out yesterday's attack travelled to this world by illicit means," she replied. "There are several possibilities. Maybe they were brought here by a smuggler. Or maybe they falsified their travel documents. The exact specifics are less important than the implications."

"Which are?"

"Smuggling undocumented passengers past the sensor nets is no easy task. Neither is forging illegitimate travel documents. Yesterday, during the attack, I counted over fifty hostile minds. Some escaped; some died, and some were captured. Moving that many people without alerting the authorities takes resources. We cannot escape the conclusion that these people had support. Possibly support from *within* the Antauran government."

Clapping his hands with enough force to make several people flinch, Jack laughed. "Bingo Bango!" he shouted. "Got it in one! I think hanging out with us is rubbing off on you, Keli!"

She blushed.

"So," Jack said. "We have-"

"Excuse me," Keli broke in. "But there is another possibility we must consider. It is possible – albeit highly unlikely – that the prisoners did not travel here from the Ronoth Colony because they were never *on* the Ronoth Colony."

Turning his face upward, Jack frowned. He felt his eyebrows climbing. "Interesting theory," he said. "Okay, Keli, how would that work?"

"Yes," Tara agreed. "I would very much like to know how it is possible that these men are not from the Ronoth Colony when we saw images of that world in each of their minds. I myself scanned three."

Keli took a seat at the table, crossing one leg over the other and looking up at Tara with obvious disapproval. "It's quite simple," she replied. "What you saw in their minds could be false memories."

Covering his mouth with one hand, Jack narrowed his eyes. "False memories," he muttered into his own palm. Was that possible? With so many minds? Surely, there must have been *some* sign of telepathic intrusion.

Guessing his thoughts, Keli chimed in without prompting. "It would be incredibly difficult," she said. "But not impossible. I could do it. With enough time, I could implant a seamless narrative of false memories."

She flinched at the sound of Tara's laughter, and Jack had to admit that he shared her irritation. He wasn't sure what it was that made Tara so determined to be a roadblock, but he was running out of patience.

Exuding arrogance with every step, Tara paced a circle around Keli's table with each hand tucked into the opposite sleeve of her flowing blue robes. "Now, I know that your training was substandard," she said. "That kind of telepathic manipulation would be detectable to even the most inexperienced novitiate. True persuasion requires a subtle touch. You must work with what is already there."

"You underestimate my talent for subtlety," Keli replied.

"Okay, ladies," Jack cut in. "Could we just pretend we like each other for, say, five minutes and focus?" He turned to Colonel Lowen, who was now standing behind one of his officers and scanning the contents of a computer screen. "I think that Ms. Armana and I should interview the prisoners."

"Very well," the colonel muttered.

Tara muttered as she strode out of the room without so much as a glance in Jack's direction. Apparently, the woman thought that her services were no longer needed. If they weren't going to take her advice, then there was really no point in staying.

Jack went to the table and took the chair across from Keli, leaning back with his fingers laced behind his head. "Don't listen to her," he said. "I've seen what you can do, and it's nothing to scoff at."

"Perhaps," Keli muttered. "Perhaps not. I will be tested soon enough, and then we will-"

Her face crumpled with obvious pain, and then she put her hands over her eyes as if she were trying to shut out the light. "Gods above," she whimpered. "Such agony."

"What is it?"

Keli looked up at him with tears on her cheeks, and that was enough to put a lump of anxiety in the pit of Jack's stomach. Had he ever seen her cry before? Even once? "It's Claire," Keli whispered. "She's dying."

Chapter 17

The patter of rain on the window kept distracting Melissa, but whenever she looked through it, she saw only a blurred image of the street outside. Sheets of water cascading over the glass obscured her view of the small bakery and the arcade on the other side of the road.

The fash kids had rented a small room in a youth centre, a trendy space with white tiles on the floor, couches and chairs in a variety of neon colours and tables with game boards already set up. It was exactly the kind of place that adults would design for their teenage children: a safe space for good, wholesome fun. On some level, she wanted to roll her eyes at the whole thing, but another part couldn't help but wonder if growing up on Earth would have been easier with more places like this. Instead of house parties with alcohol that someone stole from their parents' liquor cabinet, you had game cafes where young people learned to drink responsibly.

And there were plenty of young people.

She wasn't keeping an exact head count, but there were at least twenty people here, all in their late teens or early twenties, and they had ditched the nearly-identical sweaters and high-collared shirts for a wide variety of clothing. Bill said the fash kids only did that when they wanted to make their presence known.

Melissa thought of them as "the fash kids" because she had no other name for them. This wasn't an organized group like the Sons of Savard. This was just — How did Bill put it? — "An informal gathering of like-minded friends."

Melissa sat on a neon green couch with her feet propped up on a round, white table, legs crossed at the ankle. "We gonna get this thing started?" she shouted. Her raised voice brought all the chatter in the room to a halt.

People were standing in little clusters of four or five, but they all tensed up, and a few turned around to glare at her. Melissa Carlson wanted to cringe under their scrutiny, but Sara Veranz was a boisterous loudmouth. Ilia was impressed by her self-control.

One young man, a handsome guy with dark, chocolate-brown skin and a goatee of stubble, stepped forward. "That eager, huh?" he asked. "Well, we like to get to know one another first."

Crossing her arms as she pressed her back into the seat cushions, Melissa lifted her chin and sniffed. "I'm here to discuss the alien problem," she said. "If I wanted to make friends, I could do that just fine on my own."

"Not likely."

That came from a skinny boy with freckles on his pale cheeks and messy red hair. He was waiting by the door as if he thought he might have to bolt at a moment's notice, which was not surprising. These kids had to know that their views on immigrants didn't fit well with Leyria's progressive culture.

"Not looking for your opinion, Brian," Melissa shot back.

The boy looked confused. He did a double take, shook his head and then said, "My name is-"

"Yeah, I don't care what your name is." Melissa stood up and ran her gaze over the crowd of young people. It pleased her when a few of them stepped back. "You look like one of those loser Terran kids."

The boy fumed, striding forward at a brisk pace and jostling several people out of the way. "I am not a Terran!" he snarled. "And you can-"

His mouth clicked shut when the ringleader of this little group – the handsome guy with the stubbly goatee – raised a hand for silence. Once he had control of the room, he let his dark gaze settle onto Melissa. "And you are?"

"Sara Veranz," she answered.

It surprised her when the young man replied to that with a warm smile. "A pleasure to meet you, Sara," he said with a nod of respect. "My name is Tarek Drath, and I prefer a cordial atmosphere at these meetings. I do hope you understand."

"If it'll get the Terrans off my planet, yeah."

Inwardly, Melissa chastised herself for coming off as too eager. She was desperate to get *something* incriminating – her multi-tool had been covertly recording audio since she arrived – but if she pushed too hard, they might start to suspect her motives.

With an almost fluid grace, Tarek spun to face the window and stood just a few feet away from the glass. He kept his back turned just long enough for the silence to become awkward. "It's a good point, isn't it?" he said at last. "This is our planet. Our ancestors built this great civilization."

Turning slowly, Tarek stood before them with the cocky smile of a man who knew he had an audience eating out of the palm of his hand. "They built this great society with blood and sweat and sacrifice. Every building in this city is a testament to their legacy, and yet that legacy is tarnished a little more with every passing day."

A few people murmured their approval.

"Our world is being invaded by foreigners," Tarek went on. "Foreigners with no connection to our history, with no appreciation for our culture. Foreigners who do not carry the blood of the men and women who forged us into a people who have stretched our hands across the stars."

Listening to this long-winded screed left Melissa feeling sick to her stomach. She had heard speeches like this one before; she knew where Tarek was going with this. Still, it was strange to hear such words from a black man, but then Leyrians did not have the same concept of race that had become so prevalent on Earth. "So, what are we going to do about it?" she asked, trying to sound impatient.

Tarek's self-assured smile returned. "What are we going to do?" he asked. "We are going to do the same thing we have been doing. The only thing we can do. We're going to protest; we're going to write letters, and we're going to campaign for candidates like Jeral Dusep. People who actually know what needs to be done."

Melissa was crestfallen.

None of that was illegal. She had been hoping for something, some clear violation of the law that she could use to start making arrests. A few taps at her multi-tool and a team of Keepers would descend on this place in a matter of minutes.

Protesting the arrival of foreign refugees skirted the edge of hate speech, but so long as these fash kids did not openly advocate violence, there was nothing the Keepers could do to silence them. This was going to be harder than she thought.

People had gathered around Tarek, and they were shaking his hand, exchanging smiles and pleasant words. His bravado seemed to resonate with these kids. Fascists had a tendency to gravitate to strongmen who radiated machismo, and-

The door swung open noisily.

When Melissa looked up, her heart leaped into her chest. The man standing in the entryway was one she knew all too well, a handsome man with a lean and fit built, dark hair and stubble along his jawline.

It was Novol.

"Excuse me," he said in perfect Leyrian. "A friend from school told me about this meeting. I was hoping that I could join."

Reclining in her chair with her eyes closed, Larani listened to the steady patter of rain on the window behind her desk. She was so tired. Her symbiont offered the gifts of strength and stamina, and still, she felt tired. Managing Justice Keepers was like herding cats at the best of times, and doing so while also trying to stop a fascist from gaining political power was nothing short of exhausting. She-

Her door flew open.

Before she even opened her eyes, Larani recognized the silhouette of the short and compact man who came striding into her office. A miserable little man with a square face and hair that he wore slicked back.

Dusep had come to pay her a visit.

Rising from her chair, Larani smiled for the man. "Councillor," she said. "How can I help you today?"

Dusep's mouth was a thin line as he scanned her office. "Spartan," he muttered as if speaking to himself. As if Larani wasn't standing right in front of him. "Not what I would have expected from you."

Tilting her head back, Larani felt creases lining her brow. "Surely, you're not here just to comment on my taste in decor." She paced around her desk, putting herself within arm's reach of the man. "Out with it."

A wave of crimson flooded Dusep's cheeks, but his gaze never wavered, not for a second. "I am tired of your meddling," he said. "It ends now."

"My meddling?"

"Don't be coy."

Larani sat down on top of her desk, gripping the edge with both hands. Her head hung as she exhaled. "This is about what I

said during your press conference," she said. "About how Keepers defend Leyria from all threats, foreign and domestic."

"Precisely."

"So, you've come to threaten me?"

In response to that, Dusep reached into the pocket of his blue suit jacket and pulled out a SmartGlass tablet just large enough to fit in his palm. He passed it to Larani, and when she ran a finger along its surface, she was confronted with a legal document.

"To present you with a court order," Dusep replied. "All copies of Agent Hunter's little performance are to be taken down, and you are forbidden from attending any of my press conferences from now on."

His face cracked with a grin that actually sent shivers down Larani's spine. "Justice Keepers are public servants," he intoned. "Your charter prohibits you from taking a direct stance in favour of or against any political party of candidates."

Larani held up the tablet, waving it back and forth in front of his face. The motion actually made Dusep retreat a step. "Very clever," she said. "But I could get this thrown out in less than twenty-four hours."

"You probably can," Dusep countered. "But I can find at least as many arbiters who are sympathetic to my position. You'll find that most hold a very strict interpretation of the mandate that compels you to adopt a stance of political neutrality."

Without invitation, he turned slowly and eased himself onto the couch, staring at the blank screen on the opposite wall. "Go ahead, Larani," he goaded. "Fight that court order. I'll tie you up in legal battle after legal battle until you're too busy fighting me to do your job, and when your performance inevitably suffers as a result, I'll invoke Article Thirty-Two."

Larani swallowed.

Article Thirty-Two of the Leyrian Accord gave the Hall of Council the authority to remove a chief of the Justice Keepers when there was sufficient grounds for a vote of no confidence.

Normally, leadership among the Justice Keepers was an internal matter, but Council could intervene under extreme circumstances.

"Of course," Dusep went on, "you could show up to the next press conference in defiance of that order. Justice Keepers are known for the willingness to disobey rules, It would be quite entertaining."

Dusep sat back with a lazy smile that he directed up toward the ceiling. "I'd love to see what happens when the security staff tries to escort you from the building," he said. "Will you go quietly and accept defeat? Or will you put down several of them and prove yourself to be the menace that I have always said you are?"

Larani said nothing.

"Well," Dusep said, getting to his feet. "I'll leave you to think on that. Think long and hard, Director Tal. We wouldn't want you to make any mistakes."

Harry paced.

One thing he had come to learn after seeing three different worlds was the strange reality that some things remained the same no matter where you went. The differences you expected. SmartGlass and holograms and houses that didn't cost a thing. Leyria was a different planet; why shouldn't things be different? But it was the similarities that really stuck with you, and this hospital was no exception.

Oh, some of the equipment was different. On Earth, they would need to put Claire inside an MRI machine. Here, they just put a couple of palm-sized scanners on her forehead. But for all the little differences, it was a hospital so very like the ones that Harry had seen back home.

They stuck him in a small, rectangular waiting room with light-green walls and no windows. Steel chairs with black cushions formed a box around him, and there was a wooden table in the middle of the floor.

Thankfully he was alone.

Harry paced with his hands in the pockets of his coat, shuddering as he approached the wall. He turned sharply on his heel and went back in the opposite direction, crossing the room in four quick strides.

The double doors slid apart to admit a doctor, a tall man with olive skin and thick, curly hair. "Mr. Carlson," he said, taking one step into the room, and the doors slid shut behind him. "I'm Doctor Chaz Thrayop, chief of neurosurgery at Seral Threos Medical Centre."

"What's the situation, doctor?"

The other man closed his eyes, and his sigh of resignation put Harry on edge. "We are trying to use nanobots to repair the neurological damage your daughter has suffered," he began. "But it's not going well."

Harry fell into a chair across from the man, gripping the arms. For a second, he thought he might throw up. "What do you mean?" He was surprised by his ability to form coherent sentences.

"Claire's neurons are burning out one by one," the doctor said. "There's extensive damage in every lobe of her brain. If we were somehow able to stop this condition from progressing, Claire would wake up, having lost about forty percent of her motor control. And her speech would be severely impaired. Not to mention various cognitive difficulties and a loss of memory."

"God…"

"Unfortunately, the condition is progressing. At this rate, we estimate that Claire will suffer complete brain death in less than seventy-two hours."

Gaping at the other man, Harry made no effort to stifle the tears that streamed over his face. "There has to be something you can do." He practically jumped out of his chair. "There *has* to be something you can do!"

The doctor regarded him with a stoic expression that made Harry want to punch him in the gob. "Mr. Carlson," he said. "I need you to hear me when I tell you that we are using cutting edge technology to save your daughter's life, and it's not working. You need to prepare yourself for the likelihood that Claire isn't going to make it."

Harry wanted to scream at the other man, wanted to shout and yell and call him incompetent, but something kept him silent. Maybe it was his guilt, the knowledge that he had done this to Claire. "What about Leyria?" he whispered. "Maybe their surgeons can save her."

"It's a five day trip to Leyria," the doctor replied. "By the time you arrived, Claire would be dead."

Harry started to pace again, only now, it was a furious march across the room. He strode right up to the wall and punched it hard enough to make his knuckles bleed. "Can't you...Can't you put her in stasis or something?"

Harry rounded on the other man, his upper lip curled in a sneer of contempt. "We're living in a goddamn *Star Trek* movie!" he bellowed. "Can't you use some of that fancy tech of yours to put her in stasis, keep her alive until we get there?"

He regretted his outburst when the doctor just stood there, staring at his shoes. "Mr. Carlson," he began at last. "I'm not sure what kind of technology you're imagining, but we do not possess the ability to halt the body's natural biological functions and keep the patient alive."

Harry couldn't find the words.

"I, um...I'll leave you to process," the doctor said. And then, he was walking out the door. Harry's first instinct was to ask him to stay if only to avoid being alone, but what good could that do? If the man was thinking about ways to help Claire, well...

The doors slid apart again, and this time, it was Jack who walked into the room. He turned abruptly to face Harry, but it was clear that he was struggling to figure out what he wanted to say. "Hey," Jack managed at last. "We heard."

"I... How?"

Keli announced herself by following Jack through the door and standing beside him with her hands on her hips. That look in her eyes... "I felt Claire's pain from deep beneath the Security Complex," she said. "There are several million people in this city, Harry. For me to hear her through all that noise..."

Harry winced as one hot tear slid down his cheek. "She's a telepath now." It came out as a croak. "I did it... With the N'Jal."

"Bleakness take me!"

Anna was the next person through that door, and before Harry could even put his thoughts together, she was striding toward him with her fists clenched and her cheeks flushed. "What did you do to that little girl?"

Harry's mouth opened and closed as he tried to find the words. Squeezing his eyes shut, he gave his head a shake. "I, I didn't mean to," he stammered. "I was trying to see if she was hurt."

"You were trying to see if she was hurt."

"Yeah."

Anna looked up at him with her lips pursed, and though she was much shorter, at that moment, she seemed a giant. "You want to know if someone is hurt," she said. "You take them to a doctor! You don't *expose* them to Overseer technology! Bleakness, Harry! You were with me when we rescued Kevin Harmon. You saw what that thing did to him."

"I know! I know!"

"Yeah, I bet you do."

"An," Jack cut in. "Let him be."

With a sharp hiss, Anna turned her back on Harry, but her righteous anger died, and her shoulders slumped.

"Yeah," she said. "You're right. This isn't helping."

Harry thought he was in for another lecture when Jack approached him, but the kid just spread his arms wide and pulled Harry into his embrace. "It's okay," he said softly. "We're here. We'll be with you through all of it."

The last of Harry's self-control withered, and he found himself sobbing. He could not remember the last time that he had cried like that. His little girl was dying, and it was all his fault.

"What the hell is your problem?" Melissa growled as she marched through the door to the small briefing room on the sixth floor of Justice Keepers HQ. Novol was in there, standing with his back to the door and looking out the windows on the other side of the long conference table.

He spun around to face her with his mouth open, then shook his head in confusion. "I don't understand," he said. "I was just trying to help."

Melissa stepped right up to him, her lips pressed into a tight frown, and held his gaze. Some of her alter-ego was bleeding through, and right then, she was willing to let "Sara Veranz" take over.

"You nearly compromised my op," she said.

Novol shut his eyes tight. "I didn't mean to." He backed up until his ass hit the edge of the table. "Your people have been so good to me. I did a little reading on the political situation here, and I thought I could help."

In the back of her mind, Melissa sensed it when the silhouettes of Cassi and Gabi came through the door behind her. They were close enough for her to make out their expressions, and by the look of things, they were just as angry. "Who is this man?" Gabi inquired.

"Novol Edan," he replied, sparing Melissa the effort of having to answer. "I helped free Agent Hunter from the Ragnosian ship."

Leaning against the door-frame with one hand over her belly, Cassi sighed. "It's true," she said. "He was there when we rescued Jack."

"Well, then I commend your bravery," Gabi murmured. "But I do not see why that qualifies you to be part of an intelligence operation."

"How did you find me anyway?" Melissa grumbled.

To that, Novol replied with a sly smile, his eyes practically twinkling with delight. "Did you think that shooting guns and throwing grenades is the only thing I learned as a Ragnosian security officer?" he asked. "I followed you, Melissa. And no offense, but, you're not very good at losing a tail."

Melissa felt heat in her face, but she did her best to keep her expression smooth. "I was in there for at least fifteen minutes before you showed up," she said. "What took you so long?"

"Well, I started by inspecting the building. Looking for alternate routes in and out. Emergency exits in the back. That sort of thing. It's always best to case the environment if you're going to be surrounded by dangerous people. After that, I stopped by the doctor's office across the street to ask if they were taking new patients. While his holographic assistant took my information, I watched the youth centre through the window to see who might be showing up. How many people went in and out? Were they armed?"

He turned his attention to Gabi, and that irritating smile of his widened. "I trust this answers your question as to whether or not I'm qualified to be a part of this operation."

Gabi sniffed.

"Look, I just wanna help," Novol said. "I've got experience with these kinds of things. Isn't there some way you can make me an official part of the investigation."

They all looked to Melissa as if the final decision on this matter should be hers. Which was irritating, to say the least. She was just a cadet. She was happy to be a part of the mission, but planning the whole thing was Gabi's department. She was the one with a background in intelligence. But apparently, Novol shared some of those skills. Melissa sighed. "Let's go talk to Larani," she mumbled.

Chapter 18

"All right, let's see it."

At first, white light shot up from holographic emitters on the black-tiled floor. Then colour bled into the image, shades of brown and green that painted the shape of rolling hills dotted with trees.

In the exact centre of the projected image, an almost circular blob of open field was surrounded by a thick forest on all sides. The Field of Kenkalazar. Looking down on this aerial did little to answer her many questions, and Anna was getting impatient.

Thoughts of Claire kept slipping into her mind. Try as she might, she just couldn't keep them out. That poor kid! She had cried in Jack's arms for almost half an hour this morning, and trying to focus on work just wasn't cutting it.

Anna stood over the hologram with hands on her hips, scowling and shaking her head. "Hundreds of acres of open land," she muttered. "Not a town in sight."

This large room several levels below ground was the Presidential Security Staff's equivalent of a crime lab. There wasn't much to look at. Just dark walls with light fixtures at even intervals and computer terminals on a raised floor, away from the projectors.

Those terminals were operated by men and women in dark uniforms. Colonel Rath Lowen was up there too, standing with his arms crossed and studying the hologram with an expression that she could only describe as "pinched."

Three steps led up to the raised floor, and Rajel sat on the top one, waiting patiently for her to end this exercise. Suddenly, Anna felt guilty. Rajel was a good investigator; that was why she had asked him to join her. But the hologram was nothing but sculpted light. It had no substance, and so Rajel would not be able to sense it with spatial awareness. Knowing him as she did, it wasn't hard to imagine that he was feeling a little perturbed by the fact that he couldn't contribute.

"You probably have a good sense of the geography already," Anna told him. "The Field of Kenkalazar is surrounded by miles and miles of forest on all sides. The attackers could have come from any direction."

"Are there any paths cutting through the woods?" Rajel asked. Cocking her head to one side, Anna raised an eyebrow. "That's a good question." She dropped to a crouch at the edge of the hologram, inspecting it for any visible breaks in the foliage.

She had fought several of the commandos on just such a path, but there had been no time to determine just how far it extended into the forest. According to Colonel Lowen, the planet-wide sensor net had detected no ships approaching the Field of Kenkalazar in the days leading up to the opening ceremonies, and you wouldn't generally expect to find SlipGates in the middle of a forest. With no obvious routes for land vehicles in sight, they could safely conclude that the commandos must have approached the field on foot. But that would mean days of travel over rugged terrain.

Her eyes noticed something almost due south of the field, at the very edge of the hologram. "Zoom out!" Anna ordered, standing up. The field grew smaller as the image expanded, and she saw what appeared to be a strip of open countryside in the middle of the forest. "What's that?"

Rajel stood to make way for Colonel Lowen who descended the steps with a loud harrumph. "The remnants of the old road," he answered. "Centuries ago, whenever our people held a ceremony at Kenkalazar, they traveled by automobile. When airship technology became more efficient, we destroyed the road to restore the land to its natural state. There are still gaps in the forest, however."

During the fight, Anna had been on the north side of the field. She had seen a few paths but nothing large enough to be called a road. This answered *some* of her questions. "Where does it lead?"

"The city of Halora is about one hundred kranaline south of the field."

"All right," Anna said. "Could they have come from there?"

"It's highly unlikely," Lowen replied. "We dug up the road, yes, but the remnants of it are still patrolled by Planetary Security Officers. Kenkalazar is a holy site."

Clasping her hands together behind herself, Anna tilted her head back until she was staring at the ceiling. She blew air through puckered lips. "Okay," she said. "Let's zoom out a little further."

Once again, the field shrunk until it was a dot of green no larger than the tip of her finger. To her dismay, there was very little to see. Just trees and hills and what appeared to be a river to the west. Well, that and Halora.

The tops of buildings were visible between streets that were laid out in an almost perfect grid. There was a road extending northward from the city, but it ended abruptly only after only a few kilometres. From there, it was nothing but forest.

Anna paced around the rectangular hologram, inspecting it from all sides. Halfway through her circuit, she noticed something north of the field. Another town, much smaller than Halora but a little closer. "What's that?"

"The town of Emil's Hope."

"Could they have come from there?"

On closer inspection, she saw roads extending from the town, cutting through the forest until they reached larger highways to the east. So, travel by auto was possible. At least as far as Emil's Hope.

Squatting down by the edge of the hologram, Anna pursed her lips as she ran a few scenarios in her head. "Does the town have a SlipGate?"

"It has *one* SlipGate," the Colonel answered.

"Pull up the records for the SlipGate," Anna said. "Let's see if the town received a sudden influx of travellers after the summit was announced."

The colonel exhaled roughly, and the hologram rippled as he strode right through it. "Do you really think we haven't tried that already?" he demanded. "We may not have the ability to Bend space-time, but we are not incompetent, Operative Lenai."

"All right," she said. "What did you learn?"

Colonel Lowen grunted as he paced around the opposite side of the hologram. He didn't so much as spare a glance for her. "There were no unusual visitors to Emil's Hope in the weeks leading up to the attack."

Slowly, Anna got up and brushed red bangs off her forehead with the back of one hand. "Well, then," she mumbled. "Maybe our next goal should be to visit the town itself and see what we can find."

Rajel was back on the top step, sitting with his hands on his knees and shaking his head. "You think that's gonna help?" he asked. "I don't see what we can hope to learn if the commandos didn't go through there."

"There are more ways to enter a town than a SlipGate," Anna said. "At this point, it couldn't hurt."

After nearly a week on the world that she had not seen since she was a toddler, Keli was finding herself less and less impressed with her people. She wasn't ready to declare her undying loyalty to Leyria, but any illusions about her people being wise and cultured had been shattered just by watching their pitiful attempts to conduct this investigation. Perhaps she wouldn't be so hard on them if she hadn't spent months watching the Justice Keepers in action.

This little hole in the ground that they used for an interrogation room was a stark contrast to the lavish suites they had given the visiting dignitaries. Nothing but four black walls with light fixtures on every one. Naked bulbs in wire-frame cages. It was probably supposed to look imposing, but it didn't work on Keli.

She sat in a metal chair with one leg crossed over the other, tapping a booted foot against the leg of a steel table. Yesterday, they had interviewed five of the prisoners, and she was fairly certain of what she would find in the sixth.

Jack was next to her, frowning at the door as they waited for the next prisoner to arrive. "You seem tired," he said. "You sure you're up for this?"

Shutting her eyes, Keli breathed slowly. "Our little trip to the hospital was taxing for me," she admitted. "So many minds. So much pain. I did not sleep well last night."

"We can take a break if you need."

"No, that will not be necessary."

Jack nodded.

Barely a second later, the door opened to admit a tall and lanky man who stumbled through, nudged by the rifle of a guard behind him. This prisoner was quite young, not pale but not dark either. His hollow-cheeked face was marked by a tiny mole on his chin, and his brown hair went straight up.

"Sit down!" the guard barked.

With an exasperated sigh, Jack stood up and shook his head. "There's no need for that." He meant it. Keli didn't need telepathy to know that Jack was disgusted by how the prisoners were treated. There was no evidence of physical torture, but every one of these men had been scanned without their consent. Keli knew first-hand just how painful that could be.

The young man sat down across from her with his back to the door, cringing as if he feared further violence from the guard. "What…" He licked his lips and then looked up at her. "What do you want?"

The door slammed shut, making Keli flinch.

Jack resumed his seat on her right, folding his hands on the table, and studying the prisoner with an unconvincing smile. "We just want to talk," he said gently. "Why don't we start with your name?"

The young man shuddered, turning his face away from both of them. "Paren," he said. "My name is Paren."

"Why did you attack the summit, Paren?"

"We can't have peace with Leyria."

"Why not?"

A shuddering breath rasped its way out of Paren's mouth, but he collected himself and sat up straight. "Because the Leyrians will subjugate us," he answered as if by rote. Keli had heard similar answers from the other prisoners. "Justice Keepers have attacked civilian ships. There have been raids on Antauran colonies…"

Jack sat back, pinching his chin with thumb and forefinger and raising an eyebrow. "Let's assume you're correct about that," he began. "Wouldn't a peace treaty put an end to such conflicts?"

Breathing hard, Paren hunched over, and spots of crimson appeared in his cheeks. "The Leyrians will subjugate us!" He was practically panting. Keli's first instinct was to touch his mind and find the source of his distress, but she restrained herself. She would not do to this man what her brothers and sisters had done.

"Why do you say that, Paren?"

"What do you mean?" the lad spat. "Just look around you!"

"Who organized the attack?" Jack asked. Keli already knew what the answer would be, but she waited patiently for the young man to respond. Conducting these interviews was an enlightening experience.

"Jayel Parathon led our cell."

"And he planned the attack?"

Paren closed his eyes and nodded, but he said nothing further. He seemed to slump in his chair, brought down by the weight of his own exhaustion. Keli almost hated to ask what she knew she had to ask.

She sat primly across from the young man, and though she forced herself to smile, she suspected that it was even less convincing than Jack's had been. "Paren," she said in the gentlest tones she could manage. "I'm a telepath."

Paren gave her the wild-eyed stare of a cornered animal. "And you're gonna poke around inside my head?" he growled. "Like the other one did?"

"Only with your permission."

"Why would I ever agree to that?"

Keli stood, trailing her fingertips along the table's surface as she paced around it. She faced the lad with her back against the wall, folding her arms. "We suspect that your thoughts might have been influenced by a telepath."

"You mean that woman in the blue robes?"

Stiffening at the memory of Tara Driath, Keli shook her head. "No," she said. "I mean before that, when you were still on Ronoth."

"We had no telepaths in our cell."

"That you know of," Jack cut in. "It would help us to know if a telepath has planted false memories in your mind."

Opening herself to the telepathic impressions all around her, Keli felt Paren's fear. She could not sense specific thoughts – that would require deliberate contact with his mind – but she could tell that the man was troubled by the notion that his thoughts might have been unduly influenced by someone other than himself.

He looked up at her with dark eyes, as if seeing her for the very first time, and then finally, he offered the barest hint of a nod. "All right," he whispered. "If you think you'll find something."

Keli gently laid a hand on his forehead. Physical contact made this easier for her. She stretched out with her mind and let her thoughts intermingle with Paren's. There was no resistance. That was good. Sometimes, even after giving verbal consent, a subject might instinctively try to wall-off his mind.

Memories filled Keli's vision, memories of what appeared to be the inside of a military supply depot. It was a large room with a ceiling at least two stories up and crates all over the place. Some of them were open, and she saw assault rifles and body armour inside.

In the middle of the floor, metal chairs were arranged in three notes rows, facing an open area where a man in civilian clothing paced back and forth. Aside from the armour that he wore over an old t-shirt, there was no sign that he had an affiliation with any military organization. These men were a private militia. They had to conduct their raids with whatever scraps they could scrounge or steal military bases or armoured convoys.

Keli recognized the man, though he looked slightly different here from the images she had seen in the minds of the other prisoners. No two people remembered the same event in exactly the same way. He was Jayel Parathon, a man of average height with copper skin and long brown hair to his shoulder-blades.

She recognized the people seated in the chairs as well, waiting for the speech to begin. Many of them were the same prisoners who now waited in cells for her and Jack to interrogate them, though they sat in different positions than they had during her last visit to this room. One man with a distinctive salt-and-pepper beard was now sitting in the front row. On her last visit, he had been standing in the back.

Jayel continued to pace a line in front of them, gesticulating as he spoke. "We can't allow this treaty!" he said emphatically. "If we do, we will lose what small gains we have made over the last ten years. The Leyrians will claim the Fringe."

There were murmurs of approval at that.

Keli stood in the back with her arms crossed, invisible to all of these men. She let out a sigh. "The news reports are saying that the borders will be locked in their current positions," she muttered under her breath.

An older man with thin gray hair stood up from his seat at the end of the third row. "The news reports are saying that the borders will be locked in their current positions," he said. "Maybe this won't be so bad."

Halting abruptly in mid-step, Jayel shook his head.

"Of course, they would say that," Keli muttered.

"Of course, they would say that!" Jayel echoed her. He turned to face his troops with one hand stretched out to his left and a mocking grin on his face. "You really think they would tell us their actual intentions?"

Stifling a yawn with her fist, Keli shut her eyes. "I think they would trade us all for peace with the Leyrians," she mumbled. "If this deal goes through, we'll probably end up in holding cells."

The instant her mouth closed, a skinny man with dark skin and a scraggly beard got out of his chair. "I think they would trade us all for peace with the Leyrians," he said. "If this deal goes through…"

Keli had heard it all five times already. People's recollections of conversations were never this exact; most people tended to remember the gist but not a word for word transcription. And yet every time she touched a prisoner's mind she saw this exchange play out word for word with no variation on what was said. That alone did not prove that the memories were false – constructing memories with this level of detail was no easy task – but it did suggest telepathic intrusion.

It was far more likely that the telepath in question had been subtly inflaming the passions of anyone watching this speech, reinforcing the emotional significance so that Jayel's words lingered in the minds of anyone who heard them.

"We have to disrupt those talks," Jayel said. "By any means necessary."

"How we gonna do that?" one man shouted. "They'll have security-"

Keli didn't bother listening to the rest. She moved forward through Paren's memory, and the world blurred around her. The supply depot became an indistinct haze of gray and then resolidified into a smaller room.

Only now, Jayel was blurry, and so was every other man who stood around a small rectangular table. He had holographic maps projected over that table, but Keli couldn't see them. Trying to make out the details felt like trying to recall the name of a song you hadn't heard in years.

The blurry Jayel gestured toward his men, and when he spoke, his voice sounded faint. Like a cry for help emanating from the depths of a cave. "We approach the field from the north...the north...the north..."

Keli struggled to hold onto the memory, but it slipped away like water through the cracks between her fingers. Every time she tried to get at the specifics, the images and sounds seemed to blend together into an indistinct cacophony. What was that phrase that Jack had used once? Sound and fury signifying nothing.

While memories of Jayel's speech had been heightened, Paren's recollection of the actual planning had been dulled. As had his memories of the trip from Ronoth to Antaur. She saw vague images of a dark and dirty cargo hold in a cramped, little ship, but it felt like a dream to her. For a second, she thought she could recall the ship's name. It was...It was...It was gone.

Keli severed contact.

Her eyes flicked open, and she found herself standing with her back pressed against the wall of the interrogation room, sweat beading on her forehead. "He is the same as the others," she said. "His memory has been tampered with."

"What?" Paren squealed.

Jack rose slowly, then made his way around the table. He sat down on the corner and gave the young man a sympathetic look. "We'll do whatever we can to help you," he said. "For now, I want you to *try* to remember everything you can. Anything you can tell us will make it easier to reverse the damage."

Fluffy white clouds filled the blue skies over Emil's Hope. A chilly breeze drifted down a street where small buildings with storefront windows lined each sidewalk. Anna passed a lawyer's office, a cafe, a therapist's clinic. She could read enough Raen to get the gist of every sign. But she didn't much care for the looks she got from some of the locals.

Anna stood on the sidewalk in gray pants, a white shirt and a thigh-length jacket, the wind teasing her hair. "It's pretty," she said. "You know, I grew up in a town not so different from this one."

Rajel was on her right, leaning his shoulder against the front wall of an automated tailor's shop, sunlight glinting off his dark lenses. "Must have been nice for you," he said. "For me, it was the big city."

"I take it you didn't enjoy that."

He turned to face her, pressing his back to the wall and breathing slowly through his nose. "This place looks quaint," he said. "That's how it's supposed to look. But let's see what happens when we go into one of those restaurants and ask for service."

Wrinkling her nose at the thought, Anna grunted. "No thanks." She ran her fingers over a curbside lamppost. "One day at the zoo was enough to drive *that* point home."

Remembering that trip made her think of Claire, and her heart sank. She had called Harry a few hours ago to check in – the poor guy hadn't left the hospital for almost two days – and he said that Claire was getting worse. It made her want to punch something, and thinking about Harry certainly didn't help.

Her feelings kept bouncing around where he was concerned. There were moments when she wanted to say something or do something to take his pain away, and there were moments when she just wanted to slap him. How could he have been so stupid? Seth was weeping in the back of her mind. "Let's see if we can find someone to talk to."

It wasn't long before they crossed paths with an elderly couple who were holding hands as they walked. The man, a distinguished fellow with thick gray hair and a dimple in his chin offered a curt nod of greeting.

"Excuse me, sir," Anna said. "Can we speak for a moment?"

"What about?"

Rolling up her coat sleeve produced gasps when the pair saw her multi-tool. Anna quickly tapped commands into the screen, ordering the tool to project a hologram on her badge with the text in Raen.

A two-dimensional image of Anna along with her rank and service number floated in the air above her forearm. "I'm Operative Lenai with the Justice Keepers," she said. "I assume you've heard of the attack on the summit two days ago."

The old woman was tall with curly gray hair, and she stepped back at the sight of the hologram. "You don't have any authority here," she said. "We don't have to answer your questions."

"Milli!" her husband admonished her.

Anna let her arm drop, and the hologram rippled several times before vanishing. "Actually, we've been granted special dispensation by the president," she replied. "We're investigating the attack, and we'd appreciate your help."

The old man blew out a breath, then lowered his eyes to stare at his shoes. "What can we do for you, Operative Lenai?" he asked. "I'm afraid we don't know much about whoever attacked your summit."

"Have you seen anyone you don't know passing through town?" Rajel asked. "Any unfamiliar faces in the last few weeks?"

"A few," Milli answered. "But whatever you may think of small towns, we're not a bunch of isolated country bumpkins. Strangers do pass through here every now and then. Most people don't even notice."

Anna's fingers danced over the screen on her multi-tool, and within seconds, the holographic projector was cycling through images of the prisoners that Jack and Keli were interrogating. There was a dark-skinned man with a beard of gray stubble, a youth with a round face and spiky black hair, a pale man in his late twenties who wore his red hair parted to the side. They were all male for some reason. She wasn't entirely sure what to make of that. "Do any of these look familiar?"

"That one!" Milli said.

The cycle stopped on the image of a young man with a large nose and curly brown hair. Milli frowned at the hologram. "I'm sure I saw him at the diner last week," she said. "At least, I think I did."

Rajel stood with his hands clasped behind himself, his gaze fixed straight ahead. "Let's assume that you really did see him," he said. "If he and his friends were here for more than one day, they'd need a place to sleep."

The old man gestured with his head toward a wide street on the other side of the road. "About a *krin* that way," he said. "There's a hotel."

"Thank you," Anna said. "We'll have a look."

As the couple left, she found herself thinking about Claire again. The part of her that refused to accept injustice kept insisting that there had to be *something* she could do. But Anna was no doctor. Some days, she hated accepting her limits.

The wind hit her face, and she forced her eyes shut. "Companion help me..." She leaned her shoulder against a nearby lamppost. "You ever have one of those days where your heart's just not in it?"

"Thinking about Harry's daughter?"

Anna nodded.

"I know it isn't easy," Rajel said, "but the best thing we can do is..." Anna stopped paying attention when spatial awareness alerted her to movement on the other side of the road. People were moving all the time; carry a symbiont long enough, and you learned to ignore most of it. But some actions were threatening by their very nature.

The silhouette of a tall and lean man came around the corner of a building. He was too far off for Anna to make out his facial features, but he crept toward the curb and lifted a pistol in his right hand.

"Get down!" Anna shrieked.

She tackled Rajel, and they both fell to the ground just before a bullet hit the front wall of an ice cream parlour with enough force to send chunks of gray bricks flying. In a heartbeat, Anna had one hand extended toward the road. A Bending snapped into place to shield her and Rajel from further attack. But she need not have bothered.

She got up and saw, through the shimmering curtain of warped space-time, a blurry figure in black ducking behind the blob of gray that could only be a building on the other side of the street.

Anna let the Bending die.

Her lips pulled away from clenched teeth, and she shook her head. "Oh, no, no, no," she growled. "You don't just shoot me and run away."

She loped across the street like a wolf on the hunt, crossing the road in less than three seconds, then leaped for the square building's rooftop. Bent Gravity propelled her upward. "Wait!" Rajel shouted behind her.

Anna shot up over the edge of the roof, somersaulted in midair and landed poised with her fists up. She scanned her surroundings. Nothing to see but flat concrete and the tops of buildings on neighbouring streets.

Quick as a blink, she was racing across the rooftop.

The shooter was down in the narrow alley behind the building, walking away from her with his back turned. He wore a black jacket and a ski mask that covered his entire head. He seemed not to notice her.

Anna stepped off the ledge and used Bent Gravity to ease her descent. Her skin was prickling now, but there was no avoiding it. Floating downward like a feather on a light breeze, she landed with barely a sound.

That didn't stop the shooter from turning around and hissing when he saw her. He had his gun up in an instant, its muzzle pointed straight at her chest, and he came striding toward her at a brisk pace.

Raising her left hand to protect herself, Anna crafted another Bending in the shape of a round shield. Bullets that should have gone through her instead curved upward and flew into the open sky. She marched forward, carrying the Bending with her. That added to the strain, and the prickling in her skin intensified. Within seconds, the man was right in front of her.

Anna released the Bending.

She tried to kick the gun out of his hand, but though her foot made contact with his closed fist, the shooter managed to hold onto his weapon. He retreated half a step and took aim once again.

Reacting by instinct, Anna fell backwards, catching herself with two hands on the ground. Bullets sped over her stomach, chest and face, whistling through the alley. She brought one foot up to strike the shooter's wrist.

That knocked his arm upward and sent the pistol flying from his grip. He blinked in surprise and backed away.

Anna snapped upright.

Charging in, she threw a hard punch, but the shooter's hand came up to grab her wrist. His other hand delivered a palm strike that filled Anna's vision with silver flecks. She was disoriented as she backed away.

The man rushed forward as if to tackle her.

Anna jumped, flipping over his head as he passed and turning upright to land right behind him. Without waiting, she threw herself forward, slammed her hands down on the ground and kicked out behind herself like an angry horse.

Her heel struck the man's chin as he rounded on her, forcing him backward. He spat a gob of blood onto the alley floor. "Stupid bitch," he muttered, wiping his mouth. That voice. It tickled Anna's memory.

Instead of trying to fight him, Anna got up and ran for the pistol that was lying on the ground about twenty feet away. She dropped to her knees as she drew near, sliding the last few inches and snatching up the gun.

Twisting around, she aimed for the man's chest.

He backed away from her with hands raised to shield himself, and suddenly the air began to ripple like heat rising off black pavement on a summer's day. The shooter was now a blurry figure who took cover behind a Bending of his own making.

"You have a symbiont," Anna whispered.

That explained *so* much. This guy was fast. Too fast. Had she not been busy trying to stay one step ahead of him, she would have noticed that sooner. It also explained how he was able to sense her arrival even though her descent from the roof had been silent. Warp space-time in close proximity to someone with a symbiont, and they felt it.

Whoever this man was, he did not seem to know the limits of his abilities. That ski mask would severely impair his spatial awareness. That was why he had not noticed her presence on the rooftop.

"Who are you?" Anna demanded.

Rather than answering her question, the man bent his knees and jumped, shooting straight up into the air. He landed on the same rooftop that Anna had jumped from just a few moments earlier.

She didn't bother with Bent Gravity. The tingle in her skin told her that she would have to use Seth's abilities sparingly if she wanted to survive this chase. Anna brought her hand down on her multi-tool. "Rajel," she said.

"Thank the gods," he replied through the speaker.

"The shooter is headed back in your direction," Anna said. Her mouth twisted, and she gave her head a shake to clear the fog. "Try to intercept."

"On it."

She ran around the building, through the narrow gap between this one and the next one over and back onto the street. Rajel was there, standing in the middle of the road with his fists up in a fighting stance, one ear turned toward the shooter.

That man stood on the curb with his back to Anna, and he spared a glance in her direction when she drew near. Her footsteps must have alerted him because he certainly didn't sense her with spatial awareness.

Abruptly, he took off down the sidewalk.

Glancing in his direction, Anna felt her eyebrows rising. "He's going for the Gate!" she said. "Come on!"

She and Rajel ran side by side in pursuit, moving at speeds that no ordinary human could match. Of course, their prey had a symbiont of his own, and he managed to stay a good twenty paces ahead of them.

As they passed a restaurant, several people stood to look out the storefront window with wide-eyed amazement. Milli had told her not to make assumptions about the people who lived in small towns, but just the same, it was likely that none of these folks had ever seen such a commotion. An idea blossomed in her mind.

She skidded to a stop.

Anna lifted the pistol in both hands, squinting as she aimed for the black-clad man's leg. He chose that moment to look back over his shoulder, and just before Anna squeezed the trigger, he blurred into a streak that curved around the side of a building. "Damn it!" she snarled, rushing after him.

Clenching her teeth, Anna felt sweat on her brow. "We're not letting him get away from us!" she barked. "If we take him in, we'll have proof that Slade's people are trying to sabotage these talks."

Rajel was on her left, his sunglasses bouncing up and down on his nose as he ran. "No argument from me," he panted. "But whoever this guy is, he's fast."

A figure in black rose out of the alley between two buildings, landing gracefully on a roof and continuing his mad dash toward the SlipGate in the middle of town. He ducked out of sight before Anna could get her gun up. Clever man. If he moved to the back side of every rooftop he traversed, Anna wouldn't be able to shoot him.

She had a fleeting glimpse of him leaping from one building to the next one over, but then he was gone again. Most of the rooftops in this part of town were flat, easy to run across.

"Maybe we should follow him?" Rajel suggested.

Closing her eyes, Anna shook her head forcefully. "I can't," she gasped. "He forced me to rely heavily on Bendings. If I push Seth too hard, I won't be able to continue with this pursuit."

Rajel's face was red, his hair slick with sweat. "Well, maybe if you hadn't run off on your own…"

"We'll argue about it later."

The street ended at a large plaza where several other roads converged in a star-shaped pattern. A wooden pavilion stood in the middle of a patch of grass, and beneath it, a triangular SlipGate was dormant, its grooves dark.

The black-clad man leaped from the final rooftop and used a brief surge of Bent Gravity to carry himself halfway to his destination. He landed on the circular road that surrounded the tiny field.

Anna raised her weapon.

Ski-mask or no ski-mask, the stranger seemed to guess her intentions because he stretched a hand out behind himself and erected a Bending that transformed him into a hazy shadow. He kept it in place until he ducked under the pavilion. If Anna tried to shoot, her bullets would curve away from their target. She saw no signs of anyone else in the plaza, but she wouldn't put it past the man to direct her shots toward the windows of nearby buildings. "He must be really desperate to push his symbiont that hard."

Rajel growled.

With an almost lupine ferocity, he leaped and used his own surge of Bent Gravity to fling himself toward the pavilion. He landed at the edge of the grass and then followed the other man beneath the overhanging roof.

Anna went after them.

She was fast – even exhausted, she was incredibly fast – but those last few seconds were a few too many.

When she got under the pavilion, the man in black was already standing in front of the SlipGate. Its grooves lit up, and a bubble formed around his body. Rajel was wise not to get too close. SlipGates had safety protocols that would prevent a bubble from forming if there was an obstruction in the way, but all the man in black had to do was pull Rajel close, and then they would both be whisked off to the Companion alone knew where.

The bubble collapsed to a point before vanishing.

Bracing one hand against a wooden pillar that supported the roof, Anna let her head hang. "All that, and he still gets away." A thought occurred to her. "But it wasn't a total waste. Now, we know Slade is involved."

Chapter 19

Four rectangular windows in one peach-coloured wall allowed morning sunlight to stream onto a wooden table where Antauran and Leyrian diplomats faced one another. From Anna's perspective, the Leyrians were on her left, a line of ten of them in colourful jackets and high-collared shirts. Men and women alike, all looking very serious indeed. Her father was about halfway down that line, watching her.

The Antaurans were on the opposite side of the table, and their fashions were a little more ostentatious. They also wore colorful coats – reds and blues and greens and blacks – but theirs were marked by embroidery in gold and silver thread. And the colours were a few shades brighter, which was one point in their favour.

All of that was nothing beside the telepath – a woman with a round face of tanned skin and brown hair that she wore in a braid – who stood on the far side of the room in an almost comical blue robe.

There were authors as well, men and women in suits and ties, all sitting at the far end of the table. Aamani Patel was actually in that group, and she gave Anna a nod of respect.

Closing her eyes, Anna blew out a breath. "Good morning," she said with a curt nod. "Thank you for meeting with me. I'd like to share with you our preliminary findings in the investigation."

A man with short black hair who sat on the Leyrian side of the table stifled a yawn by putting one hand over his mouth. "So, you said in your e-mails, Operative Lenai," he grumbled. "Let's get on with it."

Anna clicked her tongue.

Jack was on her left, and he stepped forward, approaching the end of the table with his hands folded behind himself. "For starters," he said. "Every one of the prisoners that we interviewed has had their memory tampered with."

That got more than a few people's attention.

Anna's father swivelled his chair and sat facing Jack with his elbow on the chair arm, one fist pressed against his cheek. "That is most distressing," he replied. "I assume that telepaths were the culprits."

Keli stepped forward on Anna's right, and she held Beran's gaze just long enough to make him avert his eyes. "You assume correctly," she said. "I have verified a telepathic intrusion in each of their minds."

Some of the diplomats started muttering anxiously. She saw a few Leyrians putting their heads together and speaking in hushed whispers. The Antaurans were also fidgeting and exchanging glances.

The black-haired man that Anna didn't know suddenly got to his feet. "Would that not indicate the involvement of the Antauran government? Who else would have access to telepaths?"

"I object to that!" one of the Antaurans shouted. It was a woman in red who wore her dark hair up in a silver clip. "You have no basis to assume-"

"We have every basis!"

"Hey!" Anna yelled over the din. It was the fierce cry of an angry teacher who had run out of patience, one that brought instant silence to the room. All eyes turned toward her. Quite satisfactory.

Anna leaned over the table, bracing her hands on its surface, and glanced back and forth between the two groups. "Before you start squabbling like children," she began. "I would remind you that Operative Aydrius encountered a man with a symbiont yesterday, and that almost certainly indicates Grecken Slade's involvement."

Not the most diplomatic response, but her patience for stupid, immature behaviour had run out. Somebody had to take these idiots by the scruff of the neck and *make* them see reason.

"I have another theory," one of the Antaurans cut in.

The speaker was a portly man with a round face of dark skin and thick eyebrows that showed more than a few flecks of gray. Otherwise, his head was bald. "You offer up no proof that these minions of Grecken Slade even exist. We *know* that Justice Keepers have been attacking our ships on the Fringe. Perhaps it is you that oppose these talks.

"Interesting theory," Anna said. "And you are?"

"Jarone," the man replied. "Ren Jarone."

"All right, Mr. Jarone," she said. "I invite you to compare the two theories. We've seen telepaths and people with the powers of a Justice Keeper trying to sabotage these talks." Despite her best efforts, Anna found herself thinking about the man in black. Who was he? She knew that she had heard his voice before, but where?

Jarone was watching her like a hawk and drumming his fingertips on the arm of his chair. Clearly, he was wondering where she was going with this. She gave him a second to put the factors together.

"So, what is more likely?" Anna went on. "That both the Leyrian and Antauran governments would try to undermine these talks while simultaneously sending diplomats to negotiate a treaty that they don't intend to honour? Or that a third party with access to both symbionts and telepaths is doing so?"

"I take your point, young lady."

Irritation made Anna want to snap at him. Young lady? Was this guy going out of his way to be a jerk? Forcing those feelings down into the pit of her stomach, she put on a warm smile. Well…Warm was what she was going for, but she doubted it came out that way. Idiot man.

"The question now," Aamani said, "is where we go next."

Biting his lower lip, Jack nodded as if the conversation had finally caught up with his train of thought. "As I said the other day," he began. "If Grecken Slade wants us to fight, it's in our best interest to make peace."

The telepath – Anna couldn't remember her name – leaned against the opposite wall with arms folded and studied Jack with eyes that might have set him on fire. "So you say, Agent Hunter," she chimed in. "But you also claim that Grecken Slade serves the gods."

"The Overseers aren't gods."

"Saying it does not make it so."

Keli strode forward with a sigh, shaking her head in disgust. "If you will not take his word for it," she growled. "then listen to one who has seen them first-hand. One who has touched them with her mind."

The other telepath gasped. "You would not dare."

It filled Anna with pride when Keli responded to that with a menacing smile and said, "You would be surprised what I would dare." Anna had to resist the urge to snort. Keli would dare quite a bit. "Their thoughts are strange, almost unrecognizable, but they do not know everything. This I can promise you."

The woman who had her hair up in a clip suddenly got out of her chair. "All of this is academic," she interjected. "An alliance between our two worlds might be preferable, but we have yet to agree on the *terms* of that alliance."

Beran had his elbows on the table, his chin resting on laced fingers, and he studied the woman with cold, gray eyes. "Perhaps you could reconsider the terms that we offered yesterday," he said. "The borders remained fixed as they are, and both governments agree to support each other in the event of an attack by the Ragnosians."

The woman sighed, shaking her head slowly. "Leyrian territory is significantly larger than Antauran territory," she said. "Such an agreement benefits you immensely."

"But you can still expand!" Beran shot back. "The Leyrian Alliance of Systems is trapped between your territory and Dead Space. Unless we expand toward the Core or the Rim, there is nowhere left for us to go!"

"That is not our concern!"

Anna winced, shaking her head as she listened to the petty bickering. "Enough!" she snapped. "You can hammer out the details another time! The point is we have enemies trying to drive us apart!"

That brought silence to the room.

"My daughter is right," Beran said. "Failing to unite could mean disaster for both our worlds." He took a moment to work up his courage, and then finally he added, "What would Antaur need as a gesture of good will?"

Anna opened her mouth to speak – it would be nice to finish her report before they resumed negotiations – but she paused when Jack put a hand on her shoulder and smiled. "Maybe we should just let them talk for a bit," he whispered.

Well, at least they *were* talking.

Claire was asleep.

Stretched out on the hospital bed with scanners on her forehead, she looked almost peaceful, utterly still except for the slow rising and falling of her chest. You would never suspect that she was dying. The doctors had her heavily sedated, and Harry was grateful for that. He couldn't imagine what it was like to live with a dying brain – consciousness slowly fading into a morass of confusion – but he wanted to spare his daughter from that. At the very least, they could do that much.

Harry couldn't cry. He wanted to cry, but it seemed that he had spent every last tear, and now he was just numb inside. Dead. Nothing to do but wait and helplessly watch as his child drifted away.

Harry was slumped over in a chair, his head lolling with exhaustion. It was a constant struggle to stay upright, and he no longer felt the desire to fight that fight. He had found a few hours sleep here and there, but nothing solid. The doctors urged him to go back to his suite, but he would not leave the hospital.

"Harry…" a voice called out behind him.

His eyes opened, and he sat up straight, a yawn stretching his mouth until his jaw hurt. "Hi, Jack," he said without looking. "You can come in."

A moment later, the kid was standing at Harry's side and watching Claire with the thousand-yard stare of a soldier who had seen too much death. "I still can't believe it," he said, shaking his head.

"Me neither."

Jack squeezed his eyes shut. "Sorry," he whispered. "That wasn't exactly the most sensitive thing I could say."

"It's okay."

Harry was startled by the flatness of his voice. He sounded like a goddamn robot, every last trace of humanity gone. No, no, that was too kind by far. The bloody robot in his house – the one that insisted on asking if Harry wanted breakfast no matter how many times he said no – had more inflection than he did right now.

"Is there nothing they can do?" Jack whispered.

Closing his eyes, Harry shed the tears he had been aching for just a few moments earlier. He shook his head. "No," he said. "They tried slowing the damage with nanobots, but it's not working."

"Do they know why?"

"The new telepathic abilities are putting too much strain on Claire's brain," Harry mumbled. "Her scans show heightened neurological activity for extended periods of time. Like driving a car at its top speed for hours and hours on end, never taking your foot off the gas."

"Eventually, there's just too much wear and tear on the engine," Jack said.

"Yeah."

For a little while, they kept a silent vigil over Claire, neither man speaking. Then a wave of guilt hit Harry like an avalanche. "It's my fault," he whimpered. "God help me; it's all my fault."

Jack didn't respond.

He just paced around the foot of Claire's bed and went to the window, pausing there with his back turned. Somehow, Harry could sense that the kid *wanted* to say something comforting, but he couldn't argue with Harry's sentiments.

"You have to give up the N'Jal," Jack said at last.

If not for the numbness, Harry might have felt alarmed by that simple declaration. A few weeks ago, he might have argued. He might have insisted that he could control the N'Jal, that having access to Overseer tech gave them an edge. Today, Harry could only bring himself to utter two words. "I know."

Jack turned slowly. In the dim light of the hospital room, he looked almost like a ghost. "I was expecting you to argue," he said. "I'm glad you didn't. When we get back home, we'll put the thing in storage. It'll never hurt anyone again."

Pressing a palm to his forehead, Harry shuddered. "I will never hurt anyone again," he corrected. "I did it. No one else."

"You didn't mean to do it."

"That doesn't make it better."

Jack leaned against the windowsill with his hands in his pants' pockets, frowning as he studied Harry. "Maybe not," he said softly. "But it makes *you* better."

Harry didn't say anything. What could he say to that? The awkward silence seemed to go on for several minutes – though, in reality, it was probably less than one – before Jack came over, patted Harry on the shoulder and said, "I have to get back. Call us if you need anything."

Harry nodded.

Then he was alone again, left to watch as his daughter faded. Claire...Melissa had been seven years old when Claire came into their lives. Harry still remembered the shock he had felt when Della told him she was pregnant again. They had not planned on having a second child, but it was a welcome surprise nonetheless.

By the time Claire was born, Harry had thought that he knew everything he needed to know about parenting. He had seen Melissa through the terrible twos, through her first day of school, through her first brush with a bully. He had been so sure that he knew what to expect. But Claire had defied his expectations from day one.

From the very start, she had been more strong-willed than her older sister. Melissa could be stubborn when you denied her something that she really wanted, but she had an almost soft-spoken nature. Claire? Claire told you what she was thinking without even a moment's hesitation. Oh, God. What had he done?

The N'jal.

It had been almost a year since the Overseer posing as Harry's grandfather had altered his brain, granting him the ability to control the N'Jal. He had lost track of how many times his friends had warned him that the N'Jal was dangerous. The truth was that Harry didn't want to let it go. He was surrounded by

Justice Keepers and telepaths and people who could crush him with very little effort. The N'Jal put him on equal footing.

Part of it was a desire to protect his family, but if Harry was honest with himself, he had to admit that there was more to it than that. Deep down inside, Harry wanted to be special too. It was a petty motivation, but Harry felt it nonetheless.

His friends had tried to warn him, but he selfishly clung to the one thing that made him special, and now that selfishness would claim his daughter's life. Jack was right. He had to give up the N'Jal.

The N'Jal...

Harry's eyes widened.

Looking down at his own creased palms, he shivered as possibilities took shape in his mind. The N'Jal had gotten Claire into this mess. The N'Jal could save her. In fact, it was the only thing that could.

Harry reached into his pocket and closed his hand around the ball of rolled up flesh, causing it to uncurl and bond to his skin. He felt a sudden rush of sensory information. It would have been intoxicating, but despair smothered any sense of empowerment that he might have otherwise experienced.

Harry slid his chair backward across the floor tiles, putting some distance between himself and his daughter. He was not foolish enough to make the same mistake twice. He lacked the knowledge to heal Claire's brain. Harry couldn't save his little girl, but the N'Jal could.

He lifted a trembling hand toward the window and focused on the sensations that set off a firestorm in his brain. The N'Jal was the Overseer equivalent of a multi-tool; it had many functions, including communication. He transmitted a signal into SlipSpace. The direction didn't matter. He knew it would be received.

Harry's mouth worked silently as he struggled to find the words. Taking control of himself, he shivered and spoke the first thing that came into his mind. "I know you can hear me," he began. "I have something of yours, and I know you want it back. Save my daughter, and you can name your price."

They had given Anna a cramped little room to work in: just four gray walls with a desk smack-dab in the middle. She had a computer console and screen that she could use to review data that she had collected, but there was no window and nothing to give the place any personality. She hated it.

Anna was hunched over the desk with a hand on either side of the keyboard, licking her lips as she stared into the screen. "All right," she said in Raen. "One last time. Please display the data from the SlipGate logs."

The door popped open.

Jack sauntered into the room with a playful smile on his face, shaking his head as he approached that desk. "I know that look," he said. "You're about ready to spit bullets at something."

Red-faced and fuming, Anna looked up at him. "Interested in being a target?" she shot back. "Sorry, it took them a day – a whole bloody *day* – to process my request for access to the Emil's Hope SlipGate logs, and now…"

She gestured to the computer.

Crossing his arms over his chest, Jack just stood there with that dumb, goofy grin. She wanted to kick him. "Ah, bureaucracy," he mumbled. "It truly brings out the best in people. Did you find anything?"

Anna dropped into her chair, covering her eyes with one hand, massaging away the beginnings of a headache. "Yes, I did," she said. "Now, if I can just get this thing to listen to me. Display the data via the holographic projectors!"

"Unknown command," the computer replied.

"Can't you just do it manually?"

"I've been trying," Anna lamented. "But I don't really know how to operate their user interface. It took me half an hour just to open the file. I've got it here-"

Jack maneuvered around the desk until he was standing behind her, placing a hand on the back of her chair and leaning forward to peer into the monitor. "This one here," he said. "That's him?"

His finger pointed to the top entry on a list of two. Not many people departed from the Emil's Hope Gate on an average day. There had only been two yesterday. First, the man in black, and then Anna and Rajel when they returned to the Diplomatic Complex.

"Yup."

"Do you know where he went?"

Plunking her elbow down on the desk, Anna rested her chin on one fist. "That's a very good question," she said. "This says that his destination was a Gate in Raderon City, but if I pull up a log from that Gate…"

Anna laid a hand on the screen and flung the window aside, allowing another one just like it to take its place. This list was *much* longer than the last one. Almost a hundred entries, each one an arrival through the Raderon City Gate.

"There's no corresponding arrival," Jack whispered.

"No, there is not." She flung the new window aside and enlarged a third one that displayed SlipGate diagnostics. It was difficult to make sense of the data, and not just because it was presented in Raen. The visual organization felt…odd to her. "If I'm reading this correctly, the Raderon Gate experienced an energy spike at the exact time when our friend in black should have been coming through."

Jack stood up straight, scratching his chin with three fingers as he stared off into space. His face took on that look of concentration he sometimes got when he was putting all the clues together. Anna didn't interrupt his train of thought. Would he reach the same conclusion she had? "The Raderon Gate forwarded him to another Gate in the network."

"My thoughts exactly," Anna replied.

"Which means he could be anywhere on this planet."

"Or on any of the ships in orbit," she said. "Or on any colony within a hundred and fifty lightyears…assuming the ship left orbit yesterday."

Jack turned around and sat down on the edge of her desk. He put his hands on his knees as he let out a breath. "Can we reconstruct his path?" he asked. "Follow the energy spikes from Gate to Gate?"

Anna stood up.

She looked down at herself with lips pursed, and locks of red hair covering her face. "We would need to get more data from the Antaurans," she said. "And they haven't exactly been forthcoming."

With two fingers, Jack touched the underside of her chin and turned her face up so that she was gazing into his eyes. "You'll figure it out," he whispered. "You always do."

"How's Harry?"

Asking that question brought the grief she had been ignoring back to the forefront of her mind. Whenever she let herself think about Claire, it became incredibly hard to focus on anything else.

True, she wasn't Claire's mother, but Anna had come to see herself as something of a cool aunt. Or maybe a fun cousin. It didn't really matter. After everything that they had been through together, Harry was family. His daughters were family too. Anna wanted to scream and cry and shout defiance at the Companion or the universe or whatever had inflicted this cruel fate. But there was no fate. No plan or divine will. There was just bad luck and poor decisions. She felt an echo of her own sadness, a pang from Seth.

Before Anna realized it, she was crying, and Jack hopped off the desk to snuggle her up in a hug. She let him hold her for a while, her tears leaving a wet spot on his shirt. "Harry's a wreck," Jack murmured. "He says he's gonna give up the N'Jal."

"Good. That thing is a menace."

"We'll get through this," Jack said weakly.

Anna backed away from him with tears on her face, sniffling and shaking her head. "We just keep losing people," she croaked. "Raynar, Jena, Ben…Now, we're gonna lose Claire too."

"Maybe not."

Wiping her cheek with the back of one hand, Anna brushed a tear away. "If Slade could see us now," she whimpered. "Or Isara…Or Leo. I bet they'd all have a good laugh at our expense."

Just like that, everything clicked in her mind. She suddenly had the answer to a question that had been nagging her for the last twenty-four hours. "Bleakness take me! It was Leo!"

"What do you mean?"

"The man in black!" she exclaimed. "His voice tickled my memory, but I couldn't place it." She had only crossed paths with Leo once before, in that old castle that he had been using as a base of operations. "It's him, Jack! I'm sure of it."

"Well," Jack said. "This little drama just got a whole lot more interesting."

Leo grunted when he hit the wall, his body dropping like a stone to the floor. He landed on all fours, but within seconds, he was trying to crawl away. The fool man had abandoned his ski-mask, and he looked up at her with blood dripping from his nostril, sweat matting blonde hair to his brow.

Isara flowed toward him in a black dress with a swooping neckline, her braided hair hanging in a tail that almost touched her shoulder blades. "Get up!" she growled. "Have some dignity and die on your feet!"

He did as he was bid, standing up in front of the brick wall and wiping dust off his fine, black clothing. His face became expressionless. That troubled her. After spending so much time as one of Slade's lieutenants, he was finally learning to restrain that feral rage. That made him dangerous.

"You might have ruined everything!" Isara spat.

A toothy grin was Leo's first response, and then, of all things, he bowed to her. "I do love to keep things interesting." He stood up straight again, and his smile vanished to be replaced with an arrogant stare.

Slamming a palm into his chest, Isara flattened him against the wall. She got up on tiptoes, brought her lips to his ear and whispered, "Let me explain something that seems to have eluded you."

"Go right ahead."

"Our plan's success hinges upon maintaining the secrecy of our involvement," she hissed. "Our telepaths spent weeks conditioning those fools into thinking that attacking the summit was their idea."

"It wouldn't have worked," Leo protested. "The Leyrians aren't stupid, and that tame telepath of theirs is with them. She would have told them everything."

Isara's full-armed slap took Leo across the cheek. His head whipped around, and he worked his jaw as if trying to discover if it had been unhinged. The red welt on his cheek did little to quell her anger.

Backing away from him with arms crossed, Isara felt her mouth twist in distaste. "That was the point, you blithering idiot!" Why had she been cursed with such worthless subordinates? "The Leyrians would discover telepathic intrusion in the minds of the Ronoth Militia. They would infer that only the Antauran government would have access to telepaths both strong and skilled enough to perform such a task, and the summit would fall apart."

She turned away from him, pacing across the floor of this small apartment, huffing in frustration. "Your orders were to wait in Emil's Hope and see if anyone managed to retrace the militia's footsteps. You were specifically told not to engage any member of Antauran law enforcement."

Leo's silhouette was there in her mind, standing with one hand braced against the wall. "I saw an opportunity to kill Anna Lenai," he said. "I took it!"

Oh, how she ached to be rid of him.

Isara was not immune to temptation. Under other circumstances, she would gladly take the opportunity to end Lenai's meddling once and for all, but not at the cost of her carefully-laid plans. She had tried to warn Slade, but of course, the man refused to listen to anything she said on principle.

Leo was a rabid dog. You set him loose when you wanted something savaged, but trusting him with anything that required subtlety was always a mistake. But what choice did she have? Slade had taken Arin from her, delivering him to that Ragnosian admiral for reasons that Isara couldn't begin to understand. And Valeth was on Earth, recruiting some miserable child who had claimed Flagg's symbiont. You worked with the tools you had.

Isara would have gone to Emil's Hope herself, but she had been busy coordinating her agents within the Antauran government, keeping tabs on the summit. If Leo could not be trusted with a simple surveillance mission, he certainly could not be trusted with *that.* It was time to remind him of where he stood.

Raising her left arm, Isara slid one finger across the screen of her multi-tool. She tapped an icon, enlarged a window and then activated the nanobots in Leo's belly.

He grunted, hunched over with a hand on his stomach, his face contorted in pain. "So, we're back to this, are we?" Isara felt a lump of fear in her chest when Leo stood up and put on a smile. "Funny thing about symbionts; they heal the body at an accelerated rate. I'm pretty sure mine has destroyed most of your nanobots."

Isara felt her jaw drop.

Squeezing her eyes shut, she gave her head a shake and hissed. "Very well then," she said. "Perhaps I will have to make this lesson more personal."

"You'll do no such thing."

Isara froze, a shiver running down her spine at the sound of a voice that she had hoped not to hear again for some time. When she turned, Grecken Slade stepped through the open door.

As usual, he wore a red coat with gold trim in the Antauran fashion. His straight black hair hung loose, and his gaunt-cheeked face was set in a rictus grin. "I need both of you fully functional," he said.

Lifting her chin, Isara studied him with lips pursed. What did his unexpected arrival mean for her plans? "I take it you are here to ensure that the summit fails. You need not have come. I have matters well in hand."

"No," Slade replied. "I trust you to complete your task without my supervision. I am here on a very special assignment. One of such importance, the Inzari actually took me away from my duties on Ragnos to see it done."

"And what assignment is that?"

"All in good time, Isara," Slade murmured. "All in good time."

Chapter 20

Anna should have been elated when she learned that the negotiations were going well. It seemed that representatives Antaur, Leyria and Earth had come to an agreement on major issues like borders and precisely what conditions would require member worlds to intercede on each other's behalf. The treaty would have to be delivered to the Hall of Council, the United Nations and the Antauran Assembly of Speakers for ratification, but it was a step in the right direction.

She should have been happy, but all she felt was a slight drop in her anxiety. Claire was still on her mind, as was Leo and what he might do next to disrupt the talks. She just wanted to go home.

Diplomats being diplomats, all three delegations had agreed that a celebration was in order, which meant guard duty for the Justice Keepers. Anna was at a loss for why she and Jack had been assigned that task – in her mind, the investigation was a higher priority – but Director Varno seemed to think that the best way to avoid an incident was to choose guards who knew what to expect from Slade's agents. And there was *some* logic in that. This time, at least, the Antaurans had agreed that the Keepers should be armed.

The banquet hall on the first floor of the Diplomatic Complex had beige walls and two lines of pillars running parallel to each other, one near the front of the room and one near the back. Long, rectangular windows with brown muntin looked out on a garden under the starry sky.

Round tables were spread evenly across the carpeted floor, each with a lily-white tablecloth and a vase of flowers in the middle. Roses and tulips and some breeds that were native to Antaur. Anna didn't recognize them.

Almost every seat was filled with a man or woman who wore the fashions of their homeworld. She saw Leyrians in high-collared shirts, Earthers in suits and ties or gowns, Antaurans in their ostentatious colours. It was quite the gala. And a perfect target for Leo. The man seemed to have a penchant for attacking parties. He had challenged Jack in the middle of a banquet full of Canadian diplomats. He had sent men to kill her and Jack at her sister's wedding.

Anna paced a circuit around the room with a hand on her holstered pistol, frowning as she took in the sight. "Nope," she said to herself. "Nothing out of the ordinary."

She passed one of the Antauran telepaths, a man in burgundy robes who offered a momentary glance in her direction. A sign of respect? Or was he just acknowledging her existence? It was hard to tell with telepaths. "Nice to see you too," Anna said, caus-ing the man to blink as if he were surprised by her ability to speak.

Jack stood with his back to a pillar, watching the crowd with consternation on his face. His eyes flicked toward her as she approached, but other than that, he didn't move a muscle. "Evening," he said.

"Let's hope it's a boring one."

Jack grunted.

Stepping up beside him with her arms folded, Anna pursed her lips and nodded. "I wouldn't have thought it possible," she muttered, "but we did it. We actually made peace with the An-taurans."

Grinning down at himself, Jack chuckled softly. "Typical Leyrian arrogance." He gave her a gentle nudge to make it clear that he was joking. "You guys have so little faith in other cultures."

"Well, we weren't the ones who came up with corduroy pants."

As she looked out on the sea of tables, she saw about three dozen people chatting amicably with one another. Her father was actually sitting with Aamani, and they were both smiling. She could tell that Beran was in the middle of a story by the way that he gesticulated. "Heh," Jack said when he noticed the pair of them. "I'm thinking there's a good chance you might have to start calling her 'Mom.'"

Anna elbowed him.

"If I could have your attention please."

Conversation died down when a bright spotlight hit the podium, and then one of the Antauran diplomats stepped up to speak into the mic. It was the tall woman in red, the one who wore her hair up in a clip. "Good evening," she said. "Tonight, we are here to celebrate a step forward for all our three worlds and all of their colonies."

Stifling a yawn with her fist, Anna shut her eyes tight. "It begins," she murmured. "Just what I need to make my night complete. More speeches."

Jack leaned back against the pillar, glancing up toward the skylight that stretched over most of the room. "Oh really?" he teased. "You know, I seem to recall you getting on my case for complaining about the speeches at the opening ceremonies."

"Even I have my limits."

The woman in red – Anna still didn't know her name – was smiling as she leaned over the lectern and spoke confidently into the microphone. "We will have the safety and security of a mutually beneficial alliance."

Her speech went on for several minutes. Anna tried to make herself pay attention – this was a historical moment, for the Companion's sake; she should *care* about what was said – but her mind kept wandering. The gist of it was pretty simple. Leyria, Antaur and Earth were going to have an alliance. That was a good thing.

About halfway through it, she patted Jack on the shoulder and started making her rounds again. She was cognizant of some people looking up when she passed their table; moving around during a speech could be distracting, but she was tired, and she knew that if she stayed still while listening to a long, droning sermon about the many benefits of cooperation, she would feel very sleepy indeed.

Worse yet, thoughts of Claire kept trying to force themselves into her mind, and every time one succeeded, she felt a pang of pain from Seth. Her symbiont was growing restless. Some people thought that Nassai took on the personality traits of their hosts to a limited degree. Anna wasn't so sure about that. Seth always seemed calm and even a little reserved while she was anything but. However, on this issue, they both felt like caged tigers, angered by their helplessness and ready to snap.

There had to be *something* she could do to help Claire.

Anna felt a tear on her cheek. It rolled all the way to her chin and then dripped onto her shirt. Putting those thoughts out of her mind took some effort, but she had a job to do right now. She-

Something caught her eye.

The skylight above the banquet hall was a series of rectangular panes held together by a metal frame, and a bright blue spark was tracing the outline of one of those panes, severing the glass from its mountings. In the flickering light, she saw what appeared to be a man in highly mechanized armour.

Anna looked up with a gaping mouth, then shook her head slowly. "I should have known," she growled. "Get everybody out of here!"

In seconds, the diplomats were rising from their chairs and flocking toward the exit in a mass of bodies. It was pandemonium. Noise and panic and fear. She had a glimpse of the woman in red heading for the door.

The pane fell inward.

It landed on a now vacant table, shattering into a thousand shards. A man in heavy black armour like the kind that Ben had used in the Battle of Queens dropped through the opening. Thrusters in his boots slowed his descent, and he landed in front of the stage.

Next came a woman in sleek white armour, and she landed only a few paces away from Anna, in an aisle between two sets of tables. She turned her head and light glinted off the blue visor of her helmet.

Bodies were clearing out of the room. In her mind's eye, Anna saw the silhouette of the telepath she had passed earlier. He stood on the other side of the banquet hall with a hand stretched upward toward the skylight.

The next man to appear in the opening didn't jump right away. Instead, he thrust a fist toward the telepath, and something shot out of his gauntlet. When it hit the carpeted floor, Anna heard a high-pitched whine. At this distance, the hypersonic pulse could not disorient her. But the telepath...

Anna whirled around to find him on his knees with his hands over his ears, crying out in pain. Her first instinct was to run to him, but before she took her first step, a bullet pierced the man's body, he fell over. Dead.

They're going for the telepaths first!

The armoured woman was a misty silhouette in Anna's mind, a silhouette that stood with her pistol trained upon the dying man. She quickly adjusted her aim to point the gun at Anna's back.

Bending her knees, Anna jumped and used Bent Gravity to propel herself backward through the air. She passed over the armoured woman's head, then dropped gracelessly to the floor.

Her enemy spun around.

Anna kicked the woman's stomach, forcing her to bend double. With one quick step forward, she delivered a punch that should have cracked that blue visor. Even a Keeper's fist did very little against that reinforced helmet, but it still bought her a few seconds.

Anna jumped and twirled in the air, her foot lashing out for a spinning hook-kick that clipped the other woman's chin. Her adversary stumbled drunkenly away, unable to aim her weapon. Good.

Landing hard on the carpet, Anna grunted.

In a heartbeat, she drew her own pistol, lifted it in both hands and screamed, "High Impact!" Just before she pulled the trigger, the other woman raised a gloved fist, and the speaker on her gauntlet unleashed a high-pitched whine.

It felt like being on a boat that was tossed about by violent waves. Anna nearly lost her balance as the hypersonic pulse agitated the fluid in her inner ear. She staggered, her arms flailing as she tried to remain upright.

Instead of pressing her attack, the armoured woman simply turned her back and walked away. It was as if Anna was just a distraction, relevant only so long as she was blocking the path to the woman's true target. Most likely one of the diplomats. Still, why not press the advantage? Anna got her answer when a pair of drones descended through the open skylight.

They were disk-shaped devices, each with a round aperture on its outer edge, and they reoriented themselves to point those guns right at her.

Anna put up a Time Bubble, one that expanded from her body and took the shape of a shimmering dome. The two drones were gray blobs hovering right above her, each one perfectly still. Now that she was no longer in time-sync with the rest of the world, the hypersonic pulse was no threat to her.

"EMP!" she growled.

The LEDs on her pistol changed from red to white, and then she took aim, targeting the one on her left. She fired, and a glowing, white bullet appeared just beyond the edge of the dome. With a quick pivot, Anna directed her next shot toward the drone on her right. She fired.

The armoured woman was frozen in mid-step about ten paces away from the edge of the dome. She had her back turned. Distasteful as it was, Anna could end this right now. And as much as she hated it, she knew that was exactly what she had to do.

"High impact."

A momentary lapse in concentration – the product of nausea and the growing strain of maintaining a Bending – caused the bubble to collapse. Her bullets hit the two drones, and sparks flashed over them. They fell to land at her feet.

The armoured woman paused when she heard the sound, turned and looked over her shoulder. Without hesitation, she unclipped a spherical grenade from her belt, popped the cap and hurled it at Anna.

Anna leaped for the ceiling.

Once again, she was forced to use Bent Gravity to fling herself upward. She "fell" toward the skylight with an acceleration curve almost twice that of her planet's standard gravitational pull.

As she passed through the opening, Anna reversed her Bending and brought herself down to the roof. She was about ten feet away from the skylight when the cacophony of an explosion below made her flinch. Worse yet, her skin was burning, a warning that she was pushing Seth too hard. She wasn't quite at her breaking point, but she would have to pace herself.

Hissing air through clenched teeth, Anna shook her head. "Damn that woman," she whispered. "She just won't quit. Multi-tool active! Nano-cameras!"

Nanobots the size of a grain of sand emerged from the metal disk that was strapped to her gauntlet. They crawled over her hand and down her leg, clustering together at her feet. Then, like a swarm of ants, they scurried through the skylight window and attached themselves to the banquet hall's ceiling.

Each one projected a hair-thin laser, mapping the room below.

The screen on her gauntlet lit up with an image composed entirely of pulsing, blue lines. But it was clear enough for her to make out individual objects. She saw tables and tall pillars and people scurrying about. Jack was fighting one of the armoured men, and her heart ached with a desire to run to him.

But of course, the woman she had been fighting was standing in the middle of the floor and pointing a gun up at the skylight, waiting for Anna to look through so she could receive a bullet to the head. "Sigh," Anna said. "Guess we'll have to go around the long way."

A stampede of people rushed toward the door, but Jack's attention was focused on the skylight. He saw a man in black armour drop through the opening and land in front of the stage. High-tech assassins. He had fought them before.

With his teeth bared in a snarl, Jack drew in a breath. "No Tony Stark wannabes at this party," he said. "We have a little thing called class." But how to get across the room with so many people in the way-

Of course.

Jack hopped onto the nearest table and loped across it. He leaped from that one to its neighbour, knocking over the vase of flowers when his feet landed on the tablecloth.

Now, he was confronted with an aisle that ran the length of the room, dividing the tables into two groups. Anna was already fighting a woman in white armour, but as much as he wanted to go to her, his first duty was to protect the diplomats.

Wincing so hard that he trembled, Jack turned away from his girlfriend. "She can take care of herself." It was true, and he bloody well knew it. But that didn't make leaving her any easier.

He leaped with all of his strength, flew across the aisle and landed atop the closest table on the side. A quick dash across that and the next one over brought him to the line of pillars near the front entrance.

People were crowding the door, trying to get through.

Jack spotted the man in black armour moving in to slaughter them. The guy was huge – though some of that might have been his mechanized suit – and the dark green visor only added to the intimidation factor.

Jack hopped in front of him with both hands raised defensively, approaching the man with a smile on his face. "I'm sorry, sir," he began. "But this event has a very strict dress code. I'm afraid you'll have to-"

The armoured assassin raised his left hand, and a wide force-field flickered into existence right in front of him, a wall of white static that crackled like a raging fire. Half a second later, it was racing toward Jack.

"Whoa! Okay!"

With a surge of Bent Gravity, Jack shot off the floor. He back-flipped as the force-field sped past beneath him, then uncurled to land on the plush blue carpet. "Did I say something wrong?" he asked. "I'm sensing some hostility."

A wooden chair was lying on its side between him and the other man, having been knocked over by the force-field. Maybe he could use it. Maybe he could... Any thought of complex strategy vanished when his enemy drew a pistol and raised it in one hand.

Jack leaned to his left, a bullet rushing past his right side. He kicked the chair, and it flew toward the armoured man, crashing into him and then shattering on impact. That stunned him for a brief moment.

Jack ran at full speed.

He jumped and spun in midair, turning his back on the other man and kicking out behind himself. His foot pounded that thick armour with enough force to crack bones. If not for the extra padding, his adversary would be gasping on the floor.

The assassin went stumbling backward, colliding with a nearby pillar. The gun fell out of his hand, and he groaned as he struggled to stay upright. In a heartbeat, Jack was moving in to finish this fight.

He was ready to kill if he had to, but the man looked up at him through that green visor. The assassin's hand came up, and a missile the size of Jack's little finger shot out of his gauntlet. It exploded in a puff of smoke and something that made Jack's eyes water. Something that made them burn.

Pepper spray.

Covering his face with both hands, Jack staggered. He lost his balance, fell hard on his backside and growled from the sting of it. Even the soft light of the banquet hall was too much for him now. And he couldn't stop coughing.

His opponent didn't bother retrieving his pistol. Instead, he thrust out his right hand, and a blade of nanobots extended from his gauntlets, each one joining with its neighbours to form a razor sharp edge. Jack saw it all through the hazy vision of spatial awareness. He didn't need his eyes.

The assassin came forward at a measured pace, raised his arm and made ready to plunge that blade through Jack's chest. His breathing was laboured. Wait…Just a second longer…Evading this required perfect timing.

The blade came down.

Jack rolled onto his side and heard the sharp, clear ring of nanobots striking the floor behind him. Curling his leg, he kicked the man's knee with all the strength that he could muster, but thanks to that armour, all he did was knock the guy off balance.

Jack was rolling away in an instant, forcing himself to get up and ignoring the pain in his eyes. Blurred vision made it hard to see, but spatial awareness made up for that. He would kiss Summer if she had a body. That made her blush.

The armoured man yanked his blade free of the carpet, and just as he turned toward Jack, an explosion went off in the aisle between the tables. Bits of shrapnel went flying their way. Some of it bounced off the other man's suit. Some of it flew right past him and landed in the wall. None of it hit Jack.

The black-clad hit-man raised a closed fist up in front of his face, light glinting off the edge of the blade that protruded from his gauntlet. With slow, careful steps, he closed in on Jack. This was not going to be fun. Jack could feel the wall looming behind him. If he wasn't careful, he would be pinned.

He pursed his lips and felt creases lining his brow. "I don't suppose you'd be willing to settle this with a friendly game of chess." Who was he kidding? Jack sucked at chess, and he knew it. "Yeah, that's what I figured."

The assassin slashed at him.

Jack hopped back and the tip of that blade almost grazed his shirt. With a hiss, the other man drew back his arm as if he meant to stab Jack through the chest.

Jack leaped, somersaulting over the guy's head and dropping to the floor behind him. Sweet Jesus, he wanted nothing more than to run to a sink and wash out his eyes. Thank God for a Keeper's enhanced stamina. That was the only thing that gave him the strength to turn around and continue the fight.

The assassin was coming at him again.

Jack spun and back-kicked, driving a foot into the man's chest, producing a wheeze of pain. His opponent went backward into the wall, and the whole room seemed to rattle when he slammed into it. But Jack wasn't done.

He jumped and snap-kicked, striking the green visor of that helmet. The assassin's head rebounded off the wall. That should have left the guy feeling dazed. At least a little. Even armour could only do so much.

Jack rushed in and punched the man's chest with one fist then the other. Screaming, he jumped and delivered a blow to the face that shoved his adversary's head into the wall. *That* had an effect.

The black-clad man slumped, sliding down until his ass hit the floor. Then he fell over, seemingly unconscious. Or worse. Jack nudged him with his foot a few times, and when the man was unresponsive, he decided to move on.

Scanning the room with spatial awareness – his eyes were still a mess – he located the trouble spots. There were still about half a dozen diplomats trying to push their way through the door.

One of the Leyrian ambassadors had taken a piece of shrapnel through the shoulder, and he was sitting on the floor with his back against the side of a table, one hand clamped over the wound.

Lareen Kai, a Keeper with long, honey-coloured hair was engaged in battle with a man whose armour seemed to be made out of mist. Jack hadn't seen it with his own eyes; so his mind didn't know what colour to apply. And there were telepaths coming in via the side entrance.

Their colourful robes were also mist in Jack's mind, which made for an odd image, but they moved with a purpose Three telepaths – two men and a woman – strode into the room with their hands extended toward a woman in white armour. The same woman that Anna had been fighting.

Where was Anna?

Suddenly, he remembered the explosion a few moments ago, but he drew strength from Summer and resisted the urge to imagine the worst case scenario. The woman in white clutched her helmet in response to a telepathic attack, but it did no good.

Puck-shaped drones flew across the room and converged on the telepaths, each one firing bullets from its aperture. The mind-readers shrieked as high-velocity rounds ripped through their bodies. Drones had no thoughts to influence.

Jack drew his pistol. "EMP."

Spinning on his heel, he swung his arm in a wide arc and fired once, twice, three times. Glowing bullets struck the drones before they could select new targets, and then they fell to the floor.

The woman turned her attention on him.

"Great."

Running barefoot down the stairs – she had abandoned her high heels two floors up – Keli panted as she rounded a landing and started down the next flight. The chaos below was a tempest in her mind.

She had volunteered to join the contingent of telepaths guarding the party, but of course, other telepaths saw her as a mongrel and they objected to her presence. And that idiot Varno. A typical Justice Keeper if ever she had met one. He was more interested in smoothing things over than in making sensible decisions.

Of course, a year ago, she would never have volunteered to guard anyone. Not of her own free will. Life among the Keepers was changing her – there was no denying that – but she liked to think that she was changing them as well.

Keli scrambled down the stairs.

On the next landing, she braced a hand against the wall, slumped over and tried to gulp air into her lungs. "Perhaps," she gasped. "If you are going to insist on sticking your fool neck out for these people, it would be wise to start exercising regularly."

She forced herself onward.

On the second floor landing, she found a door that led out to the roof. Kicking it open revealed a single-story wing extending from the main building. There were several skylights on that rooftop, each one looking into a different room, and Anna was perched next to the furthest one.

She looked up at the sound, then shook her head and gestured for Keli to go back inside. No doubt she didn't want to alert her enemies by shouting, but Keli ignored her. The rooftop was rough under her feet. She needed to acquire shoes that were appropriate for such adventures.

Baring her teeth with a growl, Anna shook her head. "What are you doing here?" she whispered. "Go back inside."

Keli sank to her knees, turning her serene face up to the stars. Her eyebrows began to climb. "I came to help." It was a soft murmur, barely audible, but she meant it. She did not give Anna the chance to protest.

She stretched out with her thoughts.

Really, she was powerful enough to have done this from the comfort of her room – she could have done it from orbit if not for the millions of minds in this city making it all but impossible to focus on a single individual – but telepathy at a distance was loud. She had learned the value of subtlety.

She saw through the eyes of a woman, through a visor that left a slight blue tint in her field of vision, and instantly, she knew the woman's name. Sharine. The banquet hall was a mess with tables upturned and pillars scarred by gunfire. There were holes in the walls as well.

Step by step, Sharine made her way toward the crumpled bodies of three telepaths who lay dying in pools of their own blood. Three disk-shaped drones hovered over them, and Keli knew that those robotic monstrosities had loosed the bullets that had killed her brothers and sister. She could do nothing about him.

Keli gasped as glowing bullets struck one drone and the next and the next, frying their circuitry. One by one, they fell to the floor. She forced Sharine to turn her head and saw Jack through the blue visor.

The man stood with a gun in one hand, its barrel alight with glowing white LEDs. His face was red and his eyes were scrunched shut. Tears slicked his cheeks. But it was good to know that he was alive.

Jack pointed the gun at her.

Instead of retaliating, Keli turned Sharine's back on him and aimed her weapon at an assassin in red armour who battled with a honey-haired Keeper that she did not know. She shot the man in the back. He flinched but his armour could stop ordinary bullets.

"Ooookay…" Jack said behind her.

The man in red spun in her, his golden visor reflecting the ceiling lights, but he did not fire. He looked toward the dying telepaths, assuming that one of them must have been responsible for Sharine's betrayal.

Of course, this gave the Keeper a chance to leap up behind him and kick him right between the shoulder blades. The man in red fell forward, landing on hands and knees. He looked up at her.

The Keeper jumped onto his back, snarling like a feral beast. "Stay down!" she ordered in Leyrian. Keli knew that the man would not understand the exact meaning of her words. But he would grasp the intent.

Sharine was struggling against her, trying to reclaim control of her body. And it *was* a struggle. The woman was remarkably strong-willed. Keli maintained a tight hold on Sharine's arms and legs.

She pointed her weapon at the man in red.

"It's me, Jack," Sharine said, her voice filtering through the speaker on this gods-forsaken helmet. The act of speaking felt strange. Words uttered by a tongue unused to mashing those particular syllables together.

"Keli?" he asked behind her.

"Yes."

Sharine struggled.

Keli forced the other woman down onto her knees, dropped the pistol and laced Sharine's fingers over the back of her helmet. "This one will give you no more trouble," she assured Jack.

"Well, then I guess it's over."

It was indeed. She saw in Sharine's mind that these three were a special operations unit that specialized in wetwork. They were sent by... By... The images became cloudy as her captive resisted. Her focus on sifting through Sharine's memory had allowed the woman to regain some small amount of control over her body. Just enough tap a few buttons on her gauntlet. "What's she doing?" Jack shouted.

Keli knew, but it was too late to stop the other woman. The sequence of commands activated a neural implant at the base of Sharine's brain stem. In seconds, she would be dead. Keli severed contact before it happened. She had absolutely no desire to experience *that* before her time.

"It's over," she told Anna. "For now."

The heart monitor kept time with a slow *beep... beep... beep.* Claire was lying on her back with her eyes shut, sedated. It had been almost twelve hours from the moment that Harry sent his desperate plea into the void. So far, no one had answered. And no one would. He knew it. The final embers of hope were starting to die.

Harry sat in the bedside chair with his elbow on the armrest, his forehead pressed into the palm of his hand. "I'm sorry," he whispered. Claire couldn't hear him, but he said it anyway. "I'm so sorry."

Della would hate him.

Melissa would despise him.

His head drooped until his chin touched his chest. How long had it been since he'd had more than a few fitful hours of sleep? Harry was losing track of time. The days were starting to blend together. Darkness through the window, followed by daylight and then darkness again. All the while, Claire was as still as a corpse. His fault.

The seconds felt like minutes, the minutes like hours. He was beginning to wonder if the agony of anticipation would be worse than the actual moment when he lost his baby girl forever. Would he be able to feel anything? Anything at all? Or would he be hollow inside? Wrung out by grief and guilt and fear? He supposed it didn't matter.

"Mr. Carlson?"

Harry sat bolt upright.

He knew that voice. So smooth and cool and arrogant. Jack had told him, but Harry wasn't sure if he really believed until this moment. Now, he knew.

He twisted in his chair to find a figure standing in the doorway, silhouetted by the light from the hallway outside. The shadow moved silently into Claire's room, and though Harry knew that he should protest, he couldn't find the will to raise his voice.

Grecken Slade did not wear the finely-tailored clothes that he loved so much. His garments were simple: tan pants, a brown coat and a cap with a brim about half as long as Harry's thumb. The man kept his eyes on the floor as he approached the bed. No doubt it was an attempt to hide his face from the nurses and doctors. You never knew who might recognize the infamous former head of the Justice Keepers.

Slade bent over Claire, gently laying a hand on her forehead. "I am so very sorry." That was real sympathy in his voice. Was it possible that he actually meant it? "How did it happen?"

"I did it," Harry whispered.

Glancing back over his shoulder, Slade studied him for a moment, At first, there was skepticism in that penetrating gaze, but then it finished. "Ah," he said. "The device you stole from the Inzari."

"It's called a N'Jal."

"In some languages."

Harry covered his mouth with both hands, shut his eyes and tried to breathe slowly. "Why are you here?" he managed at last. "If it's just to mock me, then you can leave now before I-"

"You know why I am here, Mr. Carlson," Slade replied. "You asked for this. And I suggest that we leave now because your daughter's time is short. If she passes before we bring her to the Inzari, even they will not be able to restore her."

Harry looked up at the man through slitted eyes. It took a moment for him to realize that the sound he heard was his own savage growl. "They brought *you* back, didn't they?" he snapped. "Why should it be any different with Claire?"

"Even the Inzari have limits."

That seemed to be all that Slade would say on the matter; so, Harry got out of his chair. His body ached, his head spun. Would he even be able to stay awake long enough to bring Claire wherever they had to go? "It will not be a long trip," Slade promised. Harry shivered. He didn't think that the other man could read his mind, but you could never be sure with Slade.

Slipping a hand into his pocket, he let the N'Jal bond to his palm. He wanted some insurance just in case Slade tried anything. Then he removed the scanning devices from Claire's forehead. He disconnected the heart monitor and lifted his daughter into his arms. The machine started screeching. There would be nurses on their way any moment now.

Together, he and Slade left the room and entered the painfully-bright hallway. A nurse in a green uniform came striding toward him. "Mr. Carlson!" she barked. "What do you think you're doing? You put Claire back to bed this instant!"

"It's all right," Harry mumbled.

The nurse stopped right in front of him with her fists on her hips, looking up at him with green eyes that promised pain if he didn't do what he was told. "I don't know what you're thinking," she began, "but any chance that girl has is right here in this building. You take her, and she's gone for sure."

Holding Claire tight with one arm, her head nestled under his chin, Harry reached out with the other to lay a hand on the nurse's cheek. He felt the N'Jal's fibers dig into her skin, and she gasped. "Sleep," Harry whispered.

A second later, the nurse collapsed, lying stretched out on the hallway floor, sound asleep. Harry stepped over her body and carried Claire to the stairwell at the very end of the corridor.

They went down three floors and out a door that led to a field of wet grass. There were tall buildings in the distance, all with tiny lights in the windows, all tickling a moonless night sky. Slade seemed to know where he was going.

He led Harry around the side of the hospital, and the instant that they rounded the corner, two men in security uniforms came trotting toward them. "Mr. Carlson," one said. "I'm going to have to ask that you return Claire to-"

Harry didn't have time for this.

He raised his hand, and a force-field snapped into existence, rippling and pulsing as it sped toward the security guards and knocked them down like a couple of bowling pins. "Mr. Carlson," Slade said, "I think I could grow to like you."

They continued their trek to a field behind the hospital. Wet grass squished under Harry's shoes. Claire was limp in his arms.

Breathing slowly through his nose, Harry closed his eyes and felt tears on his face. "It's gonna be okay, sweetheart," he whispered. "It's gonna be okay."

Slade pressed on through the grass, but there was nothing ahead but a big metal fence. Where were they going? Muffled voices in the distance told Harry that they were about to have company.

"Slade," he growled.

No sooner had he spoken than something rose out of the grass. Harry realized that there was a thick sheet of organic material lying flat on the ground, concealed by the darkness. It contorted, a lump rising and splitting apart to form the shape of a triangle. In seconds, the organic SlipGate began to hum.

Harry turned around to find several men and women in uniform rushing toward him. None of them carried firearms, but one had something that looked very much like a sparking stun baton.

The bubble formed before they got within fifty feet of him, and then they were just blurry figures on the other side of an impenetrable wall. They didn't even bother taking those last few steps.

Harry sighed.

The bubble raced forward through an endless dark tunnel, toward a distant light that never came any closer. The trip lasted maybe ten seconds, and when it ended, he was in a place almost as dark as the tunnel had been.

The bubble popped, and Harry felt the squish of something soft beneath his shoes. The air was warm and moist. It took a moment for his eyes to adjust, but he saw that he was in some kind of dome-like chamber. A chamber with walls of flesh. He had been in a place like this before. When he and the others fought to safeguard the Key from the man who now stood beside him.

Gaping at his surroundings, Harry turned his head. "My god," he mumbled. "Is this one of their ships?"

On his left, Slade was grinning and nodding slowly. "You might say that," he said. "Or perhaps it would be more accurate to say that you are inside a physical body shared by the minds of many Inzari."

"Where are we? The ship, I mean."

"In orbit of Antaur, of course." That made sense. SlipGates – even organic ones – had a very limited range. But something else occurred to him.

Harry shivered despite the warm air, cold sweat breaking out on his forehead. "But how can they be in orbit of Antaur without getting picked up by the sensor nets?" More thoughts popped into his mind. Did this mean that the Overseers had ships in orbit of every human world? Leyria...Earth?

Instead of answering, Slade just clapped a hand onto Harry's shoulder. "Come, Mr. Carlson," he said. "It's time to heal your daughter."

Chapter 21

This time, it was an outdoor protest.

A crowd of people, standing shoulder to shoulder, filled every inch of space on a road just outside downtown Pelor. The buildings on either side were only two or three stories high, each with storefront windows. Melissa saw a hair salon, a multi-tool repair station and a dentist's office with patients who looked nervously out at the malcontents that surrounded them.

Most of the protesters held up colourful signs printed on bioplastic that would disintegrate within a few days. And they shouted. "Terrans go home! Terrans go home! Terrans go home!"

The small white building on the corner had once been a tailor's shop, but soon it would be a community centre for the Earth refugees who had moved into the city. Even now, construction crews were expanding a nearby neighbourhood to make room for the Earthers. Leyrian robots could construct an entire house in a matter of hours. Power, water and data infrastructure had been laid out years ago in anticipation of the city's expansion. From what Melissa had been told, the algorithms designed by Ven before he flew off into deep space were remarkably accurate when it came to predicting patterns of human expansion. The neighbourhood would be completed before the year was out.

Many of the fashy kids who had gathered here today hated the thought of Leyrian resources being used to better the lives of Earth citizens, but that was only a small part of their grievance. The Pelor City Council had asked the tailor if he would be willing to move to a new location – and he had graciously agreed – but many of these protesters still saw it as an example of Leyrians being pushed aside to make room for foreigners.

Melissa stood near the front with a neon-orange sign in hand, her teeth bared as she chanted, "Terrans go home!" It was difficult to raise her voice. The thought that someone might hear made her cringe, and it didn't matter that she was surrounded by hundreds of young people chanting the same thing.

Squeezing her eyes shut, Melissa stiffened. *You can do this,* she told herself. *You're working to* end *the hate!*

Cassi stood on her left with a bright green sign of her own. She must have noticed Melissa's apprehension because she glanced over her shoulder with a raised eyebrow. "Is everything all right?"

"Yeah, I'm fine."

On her right, Novol shifted his weight from one foot to the other. He kept scanning the crowd like a hawk looking for a mouse to snatch up. Soldier instincts? Melissa was tempted to tell him to knock it off and blend in, but she wasn't doing such a good job of that herself. "Maybe we should back off," he muttered. "They're getting agitated."

"Watch out," Gabi said in her earpiece. "You have cops headed your way."

It wasn't hard to find the half dozen men and women in gray uniforms walking in the middle of the road. They seemed to be escorting a man who wore the Leyrian version of business attire – a black coat, over a white high-collared shirt – and the way that they clustered around him made Melissa suspect that he was important.

The well-dressed man was short with copper skin and flecks of silver in his dark goatee. He wore his graying hair cut short, and his wire-frame glasses gave him an almost studious appearance. Melissa recognized him.

Mr. Qualan, the tailor.

"This might get ugly," she muttered.

Cassi peered around her to get a good look at the newcomers. "Oh no…" she said, shaking her head. "These folks aren't gonna want to hear anything he has to say."

"Who is he?" Novol asked.

"The tailor who operated his business from this address," Melissa answered.

The cops guided Mr. Qualan to a spot right in front of his old shop's front entrance. He was separated from the crowd by a line of green bioplastic tape, but that did little to soothe his visible anxiety. He paused a moment before speaking.

Then he lifted his right forearm up in front of his mouth and spoke through the microphone on his multi-tool. "Please!" he said. "There is no need for this! My business is thriving at the new location!"

Novol squinted as if he wasn't entirely certain of what he was seeing. "A business without money," he muttered. "What's the point?"

Melissa had heard her father expressing similar opinions. She put the question out of her mind for the moment. They could debate the merits of Leyrian philosophy when they *weren't* surrounded by angry kids looking for a fight.

Mr. Qualan glanced to his left and then to his right before speaking through his multi-tool again. "The truth is I have been thinking about moving for almost a year now!" he went on. "Even with robots, the old shop had a lot of upkeep!"

"Terrans go home!" the crowd shouted over him. "Terrans go home!"

"Please!" Mr. Qualan persisted. "Listen to me! We should all welcome the Earthers into our community!" he said. "There is no need for this!"

"Boo!"

It was not one voice but hundreds all jeering in a chorus. It seemed the fashy kids didn't care all that much if the man they had come to support rejected their help. They just wanted an excuse to hate on Earthers. Ilia grew angry at the thought. Fascism as a concept was difficult for Nassai. Humans were humans to them, and the categories that humans liked to sort themselves into were all artificial.

Mr. Qualan stepped forward with a look of disgust on his face, shaking his head. "Stop this!" he bellowed with no need for the multi-tool to amplify his voice. "You claim to stand for Leyrian values! But Leyrians value compassion and acceptance of those who are different. You are a mockery of everything our ancestors stood for!"

"Booooo!"

The crowd was incensed now. Some of them crumpled up their bioplastic signs and threw them at the tailor who refused to be used as a justification for bigotry. Others swore or made obscene gestures.

Not ten feet away from Melissa, a young man ducked underneath the tape and ran for Mr. Qualan, heedless of the cops who surrounded the tailor. Hate-fuelled rage had a way of pushing people to do stupid things.

Those cops sprang into action.

Melissa was faster.

She jumped, curling her legs as she passed over the tape. A second later, her feet hit the ground, and she ran up behind the young man, grabbing the back of his shirt. With a growl, she threw him onto the sidewalk.

He landed on his back and stared open-mouthed at her, blinking in confusion. His face reddened, and it was clear that he was about to scream at her.

The cops had clustered around Mr. Qualan, insulating him from danger. Some stood with hands on their holstered pistols, watching Melissa with wary expressions. She had reacted without thinking, and now she had to justify it.

Melissa turned to the crowd, spreading her arms wide. "This is supposed to be a peaceful protest!" she yelled. "Let's not give them a reason to shut us down."

The shouts and jeers had faded to uncertain murmurs as people exchanged glances and shuffled their feet. She saw Tesa, the woman she had met at the last protest, standing just a short ways back from the green tape.

The young woman was snarling with teeth bared, her cheeks flushed as she tried to bore holes in Melissa's chest with her eyes. That might be trouble, later. But at least she had prevented a violent altercation.

Tarek approached the barricade with a sly smile, nodding to Melissa. "I think we've made our point," he said. "Everyone, let's disperse...for now."

Melissa pushed open the door to her house to find Michael standing in the front hallway. His blue eyes began to glow as soon as she stepped inside, and though his mouth was a circular speaker, she could swear it was curved slightly in a smile. Did he miss her? Was that why he was out here? "Hello, Melissa," he said. "It's good to see you."

Grinning, Melissa felt warmth in her cheeks as she nodded to the robot. "It's good to see you too, Michael." Sometimes, she was embarrassed by how easily she forgot that he *was* a robot.

"Can I get you anything?"

"No, thank you."

Melissa moved aside to allow a rain-drenched Cassi through the door, and the other woman was snarling. Her short, pink hair was soaked, and there were little drops on her forehead. "That was a bad idea."

Cassi kicked off her shoes and strode the hallway, barely even sparing a glance for Michael as she made her way to the kitchen at the back of the house. The robot turned his silver-blue head to watch her go.

With a heavy sigh, Melissa felt her shoulders slump. Her eyes were fixed upon the floor as she stopped after the other woman. "It was pure instinct," she said. "I didn't want Mr. Qualan to get hurt."

Her kitchen looked like the kind you might have seen on those cleaning product commercials back home. A white, wooden table was situated atop white floor tiles. White cupboards lined each wall at hip and shoulder level.

Cassi was already sitting in a chair with one leg crossed over the other, and the sour look she gave Melissa spoke volumes. "The guy was surrounded by cops," she said. "He didn't need your protection. Now you've blown your cover."

"I doubt that."

Melissa heard the sound of the front door opening, and when she ventured a quick glance down the long corridor – Michael was still standing there with his head tilted as he listened to their conversation – she saw Gabi coming in and closing up an umbrella that dripped onto the welcome mat.

Short, plump and gorgeous in a blue dress and dark stockings, Gabi was dry from head to toe. Her long, black hair hung loose almost to her waist, framing an olive-skinned face with a delicate nose and thin eyebrows. "My apologies for being late," she said. "Do bring me up to speed."

"Melissa blew her cover," Cassi chimed in.

"It's not that bad."

Gliding through the front hallway with surprising elegance, Gabi absently ran her fingers over the balusters of the staircase. She stopped in front of Michael, who turned around when he sensed her proximity.

Gabi studied the robot with her lips pursed, nodded once and then continued on her way. "I'm afraid it may be that bad," she said. "You broke character. Several hundred of your peers saw you leap to the defense of a man who denounced their movement. Would a young woman with fascist tendencies do such a thing?"

"I guess not. So, what happens now?"

Gabi entered the kitchen at a measured pace, went to the patio door and watched the raindrops pelting the glass. "Perhaps," she began, "it would be best to let the LIS take over from here. You've provided useful data."

Melissa leaned against the kitchen counter with her arms folded, grimacing as she shook her head. "I'm not sure I like that option," she said. "This is my mission. I want to see it through."

Cassi snorted.

A withering glare from Gabi did nothing to improve the woman's bad attitude. "It's too late for that, kid," Cassi said. "You go back in now, and you'll be putting yourself at considerable risk. Let the pros handle it."

Gabi stood with one hand on the pane, a look of solemn resignation on her face. "I am afraid I must agree with Special Agent Seyrus," she added. "But don't be too hard on yourself, Melissa. Many Justice Keepers have a hard time with undercover work. They struggle to restrain the instinct to save everyone."

"I guess you're right."

The whirring of mechanical joints announced Michael, who chose that moment to enter the kitchen and present himself to the three women. "May I offer any of you a drink or something to eat?"

"Doesn't that thing have an off switch?" Cassi muttered.

Closing her eyes, Melissa breathed in slowly. She was growing irritated with some of Cassi's comments, and she always felt protective of her robot. "Thank you, Michael," she said. "But we're fine for now."

She hopped onto the counter, turned her face up to the ceiling and blinked. "Okay," Melissa said. "I'll step away from this case."

"I think that would be wise," Gabi replied.

An awkward silence stretched on for several moments before Cassi stood up, gave Melissa a sad smile and said, "We should probably get going. You probably want to have dinner and relax."

A flush singed Melissa's cheeks as she stared into her lap. "You don't have to," she mumbled. "I was thinking we could get some dinner together."

It was a dumb suggestion, and she knew it as soon as the words were out of her mouth. Cassi was twenty-six and Gabi thirty-two. They weren't going to want to spend time with an eighteen-year-old cadet. They both exchanged glances, and then Gabi cleared her throat. "Perhaps another time."

Melissa saw them out – manners didn't go out the window just because you were feeling grumpy – and when she stomped back to the kitchen, Spock was waiting for her with that inquisitive stare cats sometimes got.

The fat orange tabby was staying with her while Jack and Anna were on Antaur, and truth be told, she was glad for the company. It had been over two weeks now. Just her in this big, empty house.

With an imperious strut, Spock padded across the floor. He jumped onto Cassi's chair and then onto the table, perching there and waiting for Melissa's attention. The look in his big green eyes said, "Feed me, human."

"You want your dinner?" Melissa asked.

She scratched him between his ears, and the kitty purred as he pressed his forehead into her hand. Before she knew it, she was scratching his chin, and that took the purring to a whole new level. "Okay," Melissa said. "I'll get you some-"

Knock, knock, knock.

Now, who could that be?

Michael turned to answer the door.

Before he got two steps, Melissa put a hand on his shoulder, and when the robot turned his blue-eyed gaze upon her, she said, "That's all right, I'll get it. Why don't you enter standby mode?" He set off for his charging alcove without a word of protest.

Melissa stood in the hallway with her arms hanging and her eyes fixed on the floor. "Now, who could that be?" Summoning the energy to walk took some effort. With a sigh, she went to the front door and pulled it open.

Novol stood on her porch with a cheeky grin and a bioplastic box in both hands. His dark hair was wet, and there were raindrops on his forehead. "So, I went on the Link to learn about Earth's culture," he said. "I thought you could use something to eat. I hope you don't mind."

Leaning against the door-frame with her arms crossed, Melissa smiled and shook her head. "I suppose that depends on what it is."

Novol opened the box, releasing one of the most delicious aromas imaginable. "Something called pizza."

Chapter 22

Gently, ever so gently, Harry set Claire down inside something that looked almost like a peapod. Except it was a dark brownish-red and large enough to swallow a grown man. The very instant he pulled his hands away, the pod began to seal itself, flaps of skin coming together with only a hair-thin line between them. It startled him when the seam shrank to a point and then vanished, leaving the entire pod as one solid piece of unbroken flesh.

Harry drew a breath through his gaping mouth, then forced his eyes shut and shuddered. "Won't she suffocate in there?" It was a very stupid question. If the Overseers wanted to kill his daughter, there were easier ways.

When he turned, Slade was standing in the middle of the massive dome, one fist on his hip as he smiled at Harry. "Claire will be fine, I assure you," he said. "Now, the time has come to discuss the price of our help."

Harry raised his left hand, palm-up, and ordered the N'Jal to detach itself from his skin. It curled up into a ball, and he tossed it once, catching it as he marched toward the other man. "Here you are."

Grinning, Slade shook his head. "No, no, no, no, no," he said. "I'm afraid it's not that simple. You see, the N'Jal…as you call it…is really just a trinket to the Inzari."

"Funny," Harry replied. "I seem to recall Isara trying mighty hard to get this thing back last year.

"That was because the device you carry was created by the Fallen Ones, the traitors who hid the Key from their brethren. As such, it almost certainly contained information on the Key's location. In fact, I do believe the trinket in your hand is how your little band of misfits located the first cipher. But now that the Key has served its function, the Inzari have no need of your N'Jal, Mr. Carlson. They can create thousands like it."

Harry stopped ten paces away from the other man, and his shoulders slumped. His head lolled as exhaustion hit him. "Then what exactly *do* they want?" The exasperation in his tone was probably ill-advised – these creatures had his daughter at their mercy – but Harry couldn't help himself.

Standing with his feet apart and his hands clasped in front of himself, Slade pressed his lips together and nodded. "Your devotion, of course," he replied. "You could do much to aid them in their endeavours."

"Like hell!"

Slade arched an eyebrow.

Harry turned slowly in a circle, craning his neck to stare up at the domed ceiling above him. "I don't know what it is you want!" he cried out. "But I will not help you kill innocent people!"

"Who said anything about killing?"

Would they stop dancing around the point and just tell him what was expected of him? "Then what do you want?" Harry demanded. "Please, just tell me, and I will do what I can."

He almost jumped when Slade came up behind him and laid a hand on his shoulder. "Be at ease, Mr. Carlson," the man said. "The Inzari do not blame you for your mistrust. Your mind was poisoned by liars like Jena Morane before you ever had a chance to know them. They are not what you think."

"Then what are they trying to accomplish?" Harry whispered. Raising his voice, he followed that last question with another.

"What is the purpose of the experiment? What data are you trying to collect?"

Cop instincts kicked in, and he felt Slade growing tense behind him. Harry couldn't say how, but he just knew that the other man was waiting on orders from his masters. And those orders might be to kill Harry where he stood. Until this very moment, he had felt no hostility from these creatures. But now, somehow, he knew that his life was in jeopardy. Harry had tipped his hand. He knew too much.

Not giving them an opportunity to issue those orders, Harry paced a line across the squishy floor, shaking his head violently. "Come on, don't act so surprised!" he said. "It's the only thing that makes sense! Dozens of worlds, all populated by humans. Except the lab rats aren't supposed to know they're being studied, are they? That's why you work through intermediaries like Grecken here."

With a heavy sigh, Harry pressed his hand to the wall and felt it pulsing beneath his fingertips. "Why us?" he asked. "What is it about humans that piques your interest? It's an enormous amount of effort, terraforming entire worlds. Humans must offer something that you can't get anywhere else. So, what is it?"

"Intelligence."

The voice that spoke did not belong to Slade. In fact, it was a voice that he did not think he would hear again any time soon. A voice that he was surprised to realize he missed. Not that he would ever say it out loud.

When he turned away from the wall, Della stood next to Slade in black pants and a purple blouse that she left untucked. Her blonde hair was loose, framing her pretty face. "You may go," she told Slade. "We will speak to him directly."

Harry tapped the side of his head with his index finger. "Telepathy?" he inquired, striding toward her. "Is that how you're doing this?"

His ex-wife replied with the smile that always melted his resolve whenever they were in the middle of a fight. "You impress us, Mr. Carlson," she said. "We are prepared to answer your questions."

The black walls that surrounded him were a bit imposing. There was nothing down here but a steel table and a chair for him to sit on. Three chairs, actually, which meant they would be interrogating him soon. That made him feel edgy. He briefly wondered if he might feel more secure with a "kill-switch." Not that he would ever consent to Telixa implanting one. The vile woman might decide to activate it herself.

In black pants and a matching sweater – the garments that he had worn under that fancy armour – Corovin sat uncomfortably on his chair. He was bent over and counting the spots on the floor. What else could he do to pass the time?

The door opened.

He sat bolt upright.

Fear clawed at him when he saw the young Justice Keeper who had knocked him senseless stepping into the room. A tall and slim man with pale skin, piercing blue eyes and messy brown hair, he took the chair across from Corovin.

Projecting calm as best he could, Corovin folded his arms and gave the man a flat stare that he hoped would conceal his anxiety. "How long do you intend to hold me?" Of course, the Justice Keeper didn't understand a word of it.

Gibberish came out of the man's mouth, but Corovin could tell by his tone that he was trying to soothe Corovin's fears. Even when they spoke slowly, people on this side of the galaxy mangled their words together.

A woman stepped into the room, came up behind the Justice Keeper and rested a hand on his shoulder. This one was tall and dark with a round face and barely any hair to speak of. She stared at Corovin as if her eyes could burn him to cinders.

He felt a strange pressure on his mind, but suddenly he could understand the other man.

"How many others are on your team?"

Corovin squeezed his eyes shut, then gave his head a shake. The woman must have been a telepath, though she didn't wear those ridiculous robes. Perhaps Telixa's intel on telepaths was not complete. "Why would I tell you that?" he asked. "If you're planning to torture me, I suggest you get on with it."

"Torture you?" the Keeper said. "What gave you that idea?"

Leaning forward, Corovin tapped a purple bruise on his cheek. He smiled for the other man. "It might have something to do with the fact that you beat me senseless a few hours ago," he said. "And maybe because we're enemies?"

"We don't have to be."

"My headache says otherwise."

The young man stood up, grinned impishly and then, of all things, thrust his hand across the table. "I'm Jack Hunter," he said. "And you are?"

"Unamused."

Jack Hunter sat back down, drumming his fingers on the table. His mouth was a thin line as he studied Corovin. "It's interesting," he began. "Your associates both had a neural implant that they used to kill themselves before we got them in here, but you don't have one."

"I'm freelance."

He probably shouldn't have said that.

"Hmm," Jack replied. "So, who hired you?"

Corovin stretched out, tilting his head back and stifling a yawn with his fist. "Are you planning to feed me anytime soon?" he asked. "Because it's been a while, and I have low blood sugar."

It startled him when Jack laughed. "I like you," he said. "So, you speak Vanasku, which means that you're from Ragnos or one of its colony worlds. Wanna tell us which Admiral wants to disrupt these talks?"

Corovin felt his mouth tighten, but he never took his gaze off the other man. "You seem to be very well-informed," he countered. "Why don't you tell me?"

"It was Telixa, wasn't it?"

Corovin froze.

That momentary reaction was all Jack needed. A grin blossomed on the man's face. "I had a feeling," he murmured. "I mean, it's not exactly confirmation, but this is the kind of needlessly aggressive plan she would try."

"What do you know of Telixa Ethran?"

Biting his lower lip, Jack looked up at the ceiling and blinked. "What do I know of Telixa Ethran?" he said. "Well, she held me captive for almost ten days, subjected me to all kinds of tests. She wanted to determine the limits of a Keeper's abilities."

Rubbing his smarting cheek, Corovin grunted at that last part. "Well, I can give her a first-hand account when I get home," he growled. "That is unless you plan on holding me indefinitely."

"It's not really up to me," Jack said.

"Oh no?"

"This is Antaur, my friend," Jack explained. "I have no real authority here except what the locals give me. They're about ready to lock you up in a deep, dark cell, but we might be able to change their minds."

"How?"

Jack stood up with a chuckle, shaking his head. "The treaty is a sure thing now," he said. "We know you're Ragnosian, and we know you're trying to prevent us from allying with one another. Funny how a common enemy brings people together."

Corovin looked up at the man, and he felt his eyebrows rising. It took an effort to keep his mouth shut, but he managed it. If information was the key to getting himself out of this mess, then he wouldn't share even the tiniest morsel of it without some guarantees from his captors.

"You would have been much luckier if the summit had been on Leyria," Jack went on. "The Leyrians are much kinder to their prisoners. Of course, we can ask that you be taken back to Leyria with us. But you would have to make it worth our while."

Corovin sighed.

Turning his back, Jack went to the door and banged on it a few times. It opened just a crack, and before he left the room, the Keeper shot one final glance over his shoulder. "Think about it," he said.

The telepath regarded Corovin with a disdainful glare. She sniffed, then followed her partner out the door. When they were gone, Corovin was forced to ask himself one uncomfortable question.

Just how loyal was he to Telixa Ethran?

"So, you need us for our intelligence."

Harry sat on the squishy floor with his legs curled up and his arms wrapped around them, and the look he gave his ex would make a hardened criminal take two steps back. It had no effect on her though. Possibly because she wasn't really here.

Della stood before him with a flat expression, not looking at him but rather at a spot on the wall behind him. "The capacity for abstract thought," she said. "It remains a rarity among life-forms."

"How rare?"

"We searched several galaxies before finding a species that met our needs." All the while, Della remained perfectly still. It was like watching a robot speak without even the tiniest fleck of emotions. "Intelligence is quite rare in this universe."

Looking up in shock, Harry blinked several times. "In this universe" he mumbled. "You say that like you've visited other universes."

"Correct."

Those two syllables, delivered in perfect monotone, left him feeling cold inside. It took a moment for him to process it. The Overseers had been to other universes? For the first time, he was beginning to understand Slade's awe. *Were* they just aliens, or were they something more?

Harry got up, turned away from Della and paced to the wall. He covered his mouth with one hand, breathing slowly. "You're…not from here, are you?" He realized that the question was vague. "Your species did not originate in this universe."

"We did not."

What kind of creatures could travel from one universe to another? No wonder they could engineer star systems to their liking! Clarke's Third Law started bouncing around in his head. Where exactly did you draw the line between a highly-advanced species and a pantheon of gods? It took a great deal of effort, but he forced himself to turn around and face Della once again. He would not cower before these creatures.

Drawing in a shuddering breath, Harry closed his eyes. "The place where you came from," he began. "Is it a parallel universe? Is there a version of me there?"

Instead of answering, Della cocked her head as if she were examining him. Maybe he had piqued the Overseer's curiosity. "No," she replied. "That is a human fiction. There are many universes, but they are not variants of what might have happened had your own gone down a different path. Many are governed by laws entirely different from those that govern this universe. Life as you know it could not exist within them."

"How many universes?"

"Unknown."

"And what created them?"

"Unknown."

So, the Overseers *did* have limits. That was comforting, though he was careful not to dwell on it. If they could project thoughts into his mind, they could probably read his thoughts as well. At least to some degree.

Harry composed himself, sifted through the evidence as he would when putting a case together and asked the most logical question. Perhaps the most pertinent question of all, given what he had discovered. "Why did you come to this universe?"

Della lifted her hand, and the chamber darkened. It seemed to Harry as if they were standing on nothing at all, smack-dab in the middle of an endless voice with millions of stars all around them. Blue stars and yellow and red as well. They formed constellations that he did not recognize.

It was just him and his ex-wife alone at some random spot in the enormous distance between solar systems. She turned her head, inspecting the galaxy she had created. "Our universe was dying."

Harry watched as the blue stars vanished and then the yellow. Finally, only the red stars remained, and even they were winking out one by one. It was a terrible thing to witness. Death on a galactic scale. "In time," Della went on, "There would have been no more light, no more energy."

"But these processes take billions of years," Harry mumbled. "Surely you had time to devise a solution."

"Many were proposed," Della answered. "Some of us believed that our civilization could make use of what you call white and red dwarf stars that would continue to provide energy at timescales that even our species would consider unfathomable. But this option did not provide a permanent solution."

Harry felt his jaw drop and then, after a long moment of tense silence, he shook his head. "A permanent solution?" he muttered. "There *is* no permanent solution! Everything dies! Even the universe."

"Others among us believed that the optimal solution was to find a universe similar enough to our own and enter that universe early in its life cycle. However, this solution was also impermanent."

"There is no permanent solution!"

Della's lips quirked into a small smile, and she nodded to him. "Yes," she said. "We have observed that many of your species believe that."

Harry approached her with his arms folded and his head down, breathing out a sigh of frustration. "Okay," he said. "So, how exactly does—whatever this experiment is—help you find a permanent solution?"

The galaxy faded around him, and once again, they were standing in a cavernous chamber with walls and floor made of tough, springy flesh. Della reached out to lay a hand on his cheek, and to his surprise, he *felt* it. "We have decided what we want of you."

Jack stood with one hand braced against the wall, trying to fight his way past his own fatigue. "The guy wants to talk," he said. "I can see it in him. We just gotta give him a little time to stew."

With spatial awareness, he saw a slightly blurry image of Keli standing just behind him with her arms folded, her lips compressed into a frown. "Perhaps," she said. "I *can* sense an eagerness to be free of this place."

"But?"

Sighing softly, Keli looked up at the ceiling. "My concern is that this man will say anything to free himself from captivity," she said. "It is a subject with which I have some passing familiarity. Perhaps you should let me scan him."

Jack spun around to face her, and the instant that he did, his mouth stretched into a yawn. He covered it with one hand. "No," he said, sleepily. "That might be easier, but we're not gonna violate this man's rights."

There was a loud *whoosh* as the double doors slid apart, and then Anna strode in, flanked by two of Colonel Lowen's armoured guards. The prep room was nearly empty at this time of night; only a few staff members operated the consoles spaced out along the walls. Unlucky saps who had been put on the night shift. The Presidential Security Team never slept.

Lowen sat alone at the round table, scanning a report on an Antauran tablet, but he looked up when Anna came in. "Operative Lenai," he said in that gruff voice. That was it. Just a simple acknowledgement of her presence before he went back to work.

Anna closed the distance in three quick strides, and before Jack could say a word, she was staring up at him with fire in those deep, blue eyes. "I just received a call from the hospital," she said. "Harry broke Claire out."

"Broke her out?"

"He knocked out a couple security guards with a force-field and took Claire to what they described as a SlipGate made out of skin. Before they could stop him, he and Claire were gone."

Closing his eyes, Jack scrubbed a hand over his face. He pushed dark bangs off his forehead. "This day never ends." His voice grated in spite of his best efforts. "Why would he take Claire away from the only people who can help her?"

"Well, we might have a clue," Anna replied. "It seems Harry had company on this little trip. The guards described a tall and slim man with tilted eyes and long, black hair. Which means..."

"Slade."

Claire woke up from what felt like a deep, peaceful sleep only to find that she was trapped in a tight cocoon of some kind. The air was hot and stuffy. She couldn't breathe! Panic welled up inside her, and she was about to scream when a crack of light appeared in the cocoon and the two halves split apart to reveal something worse.

She sat up, patting her shirt and her pants, expecting to find them covered in goo. Thankfully, they were dry. What was this place? The walls were dark with a soft reddish glow, and the air was only slightly cooler than inside the pod.

She stood up slowly.

It took a moment for her eyes to adjust, but when they did, she saw her mother and father facing each other in what appeared to be a giant cavern...A cavern with walls made out of skin. Gross! "You will keep the N'Jal," her mother said. "It will aid you in your purpose."

Harry stood there with his hands in his pockets, nodding along with the instructions like a kid who had just been told to clean his room. "I understand," he said. "I'll do it, but I don't have to like it."

"You do not," Della agreed.

"Mom?" Claire mumbled. "Dad?"

Harry jumped at the sound of her voice, and his jaw dropped when he glanced in her direction. "Sweetheart!" he exclaimed, rushing over to her. Gently, he took her hands in his. "Oh, thank God you're all right."

"What's going on?" Claire said. "Why is Mom here?"

She was dimly aware of a strange buzzing in her skull, a sound that had been there since the moment she woke up, but until now, she had dismissed it as just background noise. Everything else about this place was freaky. Why shouldn't there be weird noises? But when she really focused on it, she realized that it wasn't a buzz at all. It was voices. Dozens of voices, whispering all at once.

"Strange," Della said, coming up behind Harry. "She should not be able to perceive the mental projection we have placed in your mind."

"Mental projection," Claire whispered.

All the memories came flooding back to her: the attack on the opening ceremonies, Harry scanning her with that Overseer thing, waking up in the hospital. She remembered the doctors standing over her as her heart raced, her vision going blurry and the constant sound of the heart monitor.

Most of all, she remembered the thoughts that passed through their heads, the way they screamed without saying a word, every last one of those doctors making it perfectly clear that they expected her to die. "I'm a telepath," Claire whispered.

"Yes," her mother said, stepping forward. "We would never have believed that a human could master our technology even to this limited degree. What your father has accomplished is beyond-"

Claire turned a fierce-eyed gaze on her.

And just like that, her mother was gone. Those whispering voices all gasped in shock. How dare they! Claire couldn't remember the last time that she had felt this angry.

Her father turned around, looking for some sign of the woman who had been here just a few moments ago. But there had been no woman. Only an illusion that the aliens had forced into his mind. "Claire?" he said. "What did you do?"

Ignoring him, Claire strode into the middle of the cavern and turned her face up to the ceiling. "Don't you ever do that again!" she screamed. "Do you hear me? Don't you ever use my mother's face to tell your lies!"

The voices went silent.

Claire rounded on her father, her every breath a frantic gasp. "I was going to die," she said. "The doctors all knew it. They couldn't save me. What did you do, Dad? Why was I in that pod?"

Harry opened his mouth, but no sound came out. He shook his head so hard he must have made himself dizzy. "I brought you to thc Overseers," he said. "It was the only way to save you. So-"

"You made a deal."

"I couldn't just let you die."

Before she even realized it, Claire was marching toward him, and her face was on fire with the heat of her rage. "What did I tell you at the opening ceremonies, Dad?" she hissed. "My life isn't any more important than anyone else's!"

"It was the only way to-"

"And you made a deal with these... *things!*" She felt something from the minds that surrounded them. Not anger over her cruel words – no one liked to be called a thing – and not fear either. She had startled them, but the aliens weren't threatened by her power. No, they were curious. They couldn't understand why she would object to Harry saving her life. "Let's go," Claire rasped. "I don't want to stay here one minute longer."

Chapter 23

The SlipGate bubble rushed out of the endless black tunnel into a place almost as dark. They were somewhere outside. That was all Claire could say. She saw the blurry images of tall buildings under the night sky.

Harry was at her side, staring blankly at the edge of the bubble. "I'm sorry," he said for the fifteenth time. Right now, his was the only mind she could sense. She figured that was because they were cut off from the rest of the world.

"It's fine," Claire whispered.

The bubble popped, and she saw that they were in a park in the middle of the city. All around them, skyscrapers rose up to tickle the clouds. There were lights in some of the windows, but most were dark. It wasn't like Earth, where buildings kept their lights on all night long.

As soon as they were out, cold air made her teeth chatter. Her father had brought her to the alien ship without a jacket, and it was still early spring on this part of Antaur. Much too cold.

Claire hugged herself, rubbing her upper arms and shivering. "How far away is the Diplomatic Complex?" she whispered. "Can we take a bus or…"

She looked up to see two people standing side by side on a concrete path that cut through the grass, two people who made her feel very safe. Jack and Anna had come to meet them; Harry must have called them while she was still in the pod, must have told them to come here. She could feel guilt radiating off her father, but she didn't care about that right now.

"Anna!"

Claire ran to her, leaped and flung her arms around Anna's neck. Anna caught her and held her tight. "Sweetie," she whispered. "I'm so glad you're okay."

When Anna put her down, Claire brushed a tear off her cheek. "I thought I'd never see you again." Her voice squeaked, and she was crying for real now. On any other night, she might have tried to stop it, but not tonight.

"Hey, kiddo," Jack said.

Claire didn't bother calling him lame or sticking out her tongue or doing any of the things she normally did to hide the fact that she really did think Jack was awesome. She threw her arms around his waist, buried her face in his stomach and sobbed.

After a moment, she took control of herself, stepped back and brushed more tears away. "Can I stay with you guys tonight?" Claire hadn't planned on asking that question, but she realized she really didn't want to be around her dad. "I'll sleep on the couch."

"Claire," Harry said, coming up behind her.

Anna shot him a glare that made him freeze in his tracks, then dropped to one knee and put her hands on Claire's shoulders. Her smile made it seem like everything would be all right. "Of course you can, sweetie," she said.

"*I'll* sleep on the couch," Jack added. "I don't mind."

Gently, ever so gently, Anna shut the door to the bedroom. It had taken almost half an hour to get Claire settled down enough to sleep, and now it was well past midnight. Bleakness, the sun would be up in about four hours – seeing it rise in the west was still a bit disorienting – and she had an early-morning meeting with the diplomats.

In the sitting room, she found Jack on the couch with his hands folded in his lap, his lips pressed into an anxious frown. "I know what you were trying to do," he said. "But it was reckless and stupid."

Harry stood with his back to her, hunched over with his face buried in one hand. "I couldn't just let her die," he rasped. "What the hell else was I supposed to do?"

"Literally anything else!" Anna growled.

Harry spun around to face her. His face was red and glistening from freshly-shed tears; his hair was a mess, and he looked as though he hadn't slept in days. "I don't like her staying here," he said. "After everything we've been through, I don't want to let her out of my sight."

In the three strides it took to cross the distance between them, Anna managed to calm herself. But Seth's anger was still bubbling in the back of her mind. She could be calm. When she had to be.

Looking up to meet his gaze, Anna raised an eyebrow. "Oh really?" Her voice was dangerously quiet. "Because you scrambled that poor girl's brain, and then you let *aliens* experiment on her. As of right now, your parental authority is rescinded."

Harry closed his eyes, and new tears spilled over his cheeks. "So, what would you have done in my place?" he whispered. "Let her die?"

Anna stood in front of him with fists on her hips, gritting her teeth as she shook her head. "Has it occurred to you that Slade never does *anything* unless it benefits him?" she asked. "What if the Overseers did *more* than just heal Claire? Did you think about that?"

"Does it matter?" Harry protested. "Is anything they might have done to her worse than letting her die?"

"He's got a point," Jack muttered.

Casting a glance over her shoulder, Anna felt a searing heat in her face. "You want to get in on this?" She wasn't really mad at Jack, but a part of her wanted to snap at him for taking Harry's side. Which was irrational, of course, but there it was.

Jack raised both hands defensively and lowered his eyes to stare into his lap. "Hey, I don't agree with what Harry did either," he said. "But even if the Overseers did change Claire, I'm still glad she's alive."

"Me too," Anna whispered.

With a heavy sigh, Harry tried to go around her – on his way to the bedroom, no doubt – but Anna put an arm across his chest to bar his path. "I only want to look in on her before I go to bed," he said.

"She doesn't want to see you."

"I'm her father."

"Not tonight, you're not," Anna replied, making no attempt whatsoever to hide her anger. "Tonight, you're the guy who almost got her killed and then put her inside an alien pod. She's traumatized, Harry."

"Okay." Harry turned around, shuffling to the door. "You're probably right. I'll check in with you guys tomorrow."

When he was gone, Jack stood up and yawned. He slapped a hand over his gaping mouth. "You can have the couch," he mumbled. "I'll grab some extra blankets and sleep on the floor."

Before she could insist that she was quite happy sleeping on the floor, the bedroom door opened and Claire stepped out in pyjama bottoms and an old, blue t-shirt. She was standing in the hallway with one hand on the wall, her eyes fixed on her own bare feet. "Anna," she said without looking up. "Will you stay with me tonight?"

"Of course, sweetie."

It was a very long night, one in which she got very little sleep. For the most part, she just held Claire while the poor girl sobbed and trembled. Anna remembered when her own mother had done the same for her after she'd had a nightmare. Poor Claire had been living a nightmare for the last few days.

After about an hour or so, the girl fell asleep with her head on Anna's chest. Anna continued to stroke her hair until she too dozed off.

Jack watched as three armoured guards brought the prisoner – apparently, the guy's name was Corovin Dagmath – through the beige-walled hallway outside the conference room. The man's hands were cuffed, and he walked with his eyes fixed on the floor, like a condemned man on the way to the executioner.

His red hair was a mess, and when he looked up, Jack saw a scraggly red beard in severe need of a trim. Corovin opened his mouth to speak, but of course, he said nothing. No one would understand him without the aid of a telepath.

Speaking of which, Tara Driath came striding up behind him in purple robes with bronze trim. Today, the woman wore her brown hair loose, and when her dark eyes fell upon Jack, she sniffed.

They all filed through the door into the same room that Jack and the others had used to brief the diplomats not twenty-four hours earlier, the one with the long table in the middle. Already, there were Leyrians sitting on their side of the table. He saw Beran Lenai in a chair near the door.

Anna's father must have noticed him because he shot a glance in Jack's direction and smiled. Well, it was good to know that his girlfriend's father liked him. At least, he *thought* Beran liked him.

Jack kept it simple – basic black: pants and an open-collared shirt – and his bangs were a little messier today. "No time like the present," he muttered to himself. "Let's go get this over with."

Inside the room, he found Leyrians on one side of the table, Antaurans on the other and Earthers at the far end, every one of them looking up when he came in. Anna was at the head of the table – also dressed in black – and Keli stood next to her, casting furtive glances at the other telepaths.

There were three of those.

At the back of the room, Tara Driath was flanked by a broad-shouldered man with dark skin and buzzed hair – a guy who looked imposing even in those silly blue robes – and his polar opposite, a lanky kid with a lily-white complexion and barely enough fuzz on his upper lip to be called a mustache. That one wore green robes that seemed to hang off his body.

"Agent Hunter," Beran said. "You have news to report?"

Jack stepped up to the table, shut his eyes and then nodded once in confirmation. "I do," he said. "Meet my good friend Corovin. He's got an awful lot to say about how the Ragnosian admirals are trying to undermine these talks."

Aided by telepaths who translated his words, Corovin looked up, and there was steel in his gray eyes. "It may not have been the Admiralty Board," he began. "In fact, I would say that my mission was a rogue operation."

"Initiated by who?"

The question came from Lara Tinock, the tall Antauran ambassador who kept her brown hair up in a clip. She sat with her elbows on the table, fingers laced tightly, and her face had lost most of its colour.

"Several weeks ago," Corovin answered. "I was approached by Admiral Telixa Ethran. She hired me to disrupt the summit."

Lon Teryl, a brown-skinned man who sat on the Leyrian side of the table, swivelled his chair around to glower at the prisoner. "That is most distressing," he said. "What were your orders specifically."

Corovin stood there with his hands cuffed together, staring directly ahead at no one in particular. "To kill as many of you as possible," he said without hesitation. "Diplomats were the primary target, but we were instructed to eliminate Justice Keepers and telepaths if they got in our way."

At least half a dozen ambassadors shifted uncomfortably in response to his frank answer. Jack couldn't blame them. He would have felt much the same in their place, and he, at least, had the benefit of a Nassai.

"Will this...Admiral Ethran try again?" Beran asked.

"I doubt it," Corovin replied. "The plan's success hinged on making it seem as if one of your governments was trying to sabotage these talks. That's why we used Antauran weapons and armour."

Crossing his arms, Jack smiled down at himself. He shook his head slowly. "Which is exactly what we've been saying this whole time," he cut in. "There are plenty of people with a vested interest in keeping our three worlds apart."

Corovin looked at him and then nodded his agreement. "Agent Hunter's childish 'I told you so' notwithstanding," he said. "I'm afraid that I have to agree with that statement. The Admiralty Board and the Systems Parliament both see an alliance between Leyria and Antaur as a threat."

"And what about Earth?" one of the Ambassadors in the back asked.

"Our assessments of Earth's technological capabilities suggest that your planet is no threat to us."

That ruffled a few feathers, but Jack had very little concern over it. It was a simple reality that Earth didn't have warp drives and fusion reactors, due, in no small part, to the Leyrians' fear that sharing such technology would lead to its misuse. The real issue here was the Ragnosians and their meddling.

He knew a little bit about the Ragnosian Admiralty Board, mostly from what Novol had been able to share. And most of *that* was hearsay. Security guards on a battlecruiser really weren't privy to what was said in meetings between high-ranking officers, but no matter how tight a lid you tried to keep on things, people would talk.

Jack knew that Telixa Ethran had a reputation for favouring aggressive strategies, though he could have figured that out from the brief time he had spent in the woman's company. According to Novol, there were cooler heads on the Admiralty Board. The other man couldn't be certain of much, but apparently, Rob Ixalon and Jessi Vataro were known for preferring caution to aggression. Not that such knowledge would do him much good here and now.

"How did you acquire Antauran weaponry?" one of the Ambassadors inquired.

Heaving out a deep breath, Corovin slumped against the wall. He grimaced as if the question brought him pain. "That I can't answer," he said. "Telixa gave me the armoured suits along with two of her officers as backup. We entered Antauran Space via the Class-2 SlipGate in the Barnoth System."

Beran was sitting back with his hands folded over his stomach, a look of guarded skepticism on his face. "And why would you tell us all this, Corovin?" he asked. "Don't you have any qualms about betraying your own people?"

"It's my hope," Corovin said. "That in exchange for this information, I would be placed in a Leyrian prison."

Tara Driath sniffed at that, and her eyes blazed when they fell upon him. "So that you might have a life of luxury after murdering my brothers and sisters?" Jack wanted to protest; Leyrian prisons were by no means luxurious, but they weren't cruel either. There was a difference. A big one, in his estimation. But the last thing he wanted to do was get these people squabbling over minutiae.

"Let's focus on the big picture," Jack said. "We have enemies who are trying to keep us apart."

"Enemies who have failed," Ambassador Tinock broke in. "After last night's attack, we met in secret session."

"This should be good."

"We've agreed on a treaty."

Hearing that made Tara hiss like a cat, and she strode toward the table with a glare that could set a man's hair on fire. "You did what?" she demanded. "You know what he said! The gods themselves oppose this union!"

"Not everyone believes in your gods!" Ambassador Tinock shouted. The woman was on her feet in a heartbeat and matching Tara stare for stare. "We have the well-being of our people to consider. Not religious doctrine."

"How dare-"

"Copies of the treaty have been sent to Leyria and Earth for ratification," Tinock went on as if the other woman hadn't spoken. "I'm told that we should have final answers before the week is out."

Jack was so caught up in listening to the ambassadors congratulating one another that he barely noticed when Anna came up beside him and slipped her arm around his. "We did it," she said. "The summit was a success."

"Yeah…"

"So, why don't you look happy?"

His eyes dropped shut as the exhaustion he had been ignoring finally got the better of him. "Leo," he whispered in a hoarse voice. "He'll take this as a personal defeat, and he'll do something violent and stupid in retaliation."

Anna rested her head on his upper arm, sighing softly. "Yeah, he probably will," she agreed. "But we'll be ready."

A commotion in the hallway got Jack's attention. When he went to the door, he saw at least a dozen people hurrying past on their way to the main lobby. Some of them wore the white shirts and black vests that marked them as the staff of the Diplomatic Complex, but he saw a few diplomats in the crowd as well.

Jack stood in the doorway with a gaping mouth, blinking as he watched them rush past. "Now what?" he grumbled. "It never ends around here."

A young Keeper from Earth – you could tell by his gray jeans and leather jacket – paused at the sound of Jack's voice. "It's that retired cop who hangs out with you guys," he explained. "He's giving a press conference."

Harry?

Why in God's name would *Harry* be giving a press conference?

Not bothering to ask that question, Jack followed the group down the hallway, and Anna quickly fell in step beside him. The scowl on her face spoke volumes. She wasn't exactly Harry's biggest fan at the moment, and it looked like the old man was about to dig himself into an even deeper hole.

It turned out the crowd *wasn't* headed for the lobby but rather for a media room where chairs spaced out on a blue carpet faced a podium. Harry was at that podium with a hand raised into the air, a rippling force-field hovering over his head.

There were reporters with cameras and microphones covering the event, but no one spoke a word. They all seemed to be waiting to see what Harry would do next.

"I wield the power of the Overseers!" he said in a clear voice that reached every corner of the room. The force-field crackled as he intensified the power he poured into it. "You can rest assured that they bless this union."

Gaping at him, Jack shook his head. "No, no, no," he whispered. "Don't do this."

At his side, Anna had her eyes squeezed shut, and she was actually quivering with barely-restrained anger. "Every time I think he couldn't get any stupider," she hissed. "Do we stop him?"

"*Can* we stop him?"

The force-field vanished as Harry lowered his hand. He stepped up to the lectern with the confidence of a man who had given a thousand speeches and said, "It's time to put aside hatreds. It's time to chart a new course for your people."

The small metal disk on the floor – Leyrian technology – projected a hologram over the entirety of a brick wall. Isara was transfixed by the slightly-transparent footage that depicted Harry Carlson behind a lectern.

The man was standing with one hand upraised, having conjured a force-field with the device he had stolen from the Inzari. "I wield the power of the Overseers," he said. "You can rest assured that they bless this union."

Standing with his arms folded, Slade observed the hologram with pursed lips. "It seems Mr. Carlson has set us on an unexpected course," he said. "We will have to adjust our plans accordingly."

Leo was sitting on a nearby counter with his knees apart and his eyes downcast. "We should just kill him," he growled. "Him and Hunter and Lenai and the others. Let's get rid of them once and for all."

Isara held her tongue.

Waiting in the back with her face hidden under a bright scarlet hood, she felt her mouth tighten. What exactly *was* Harry Carlson up to? Slade seemed to know, but given their animosity, it was unlikely that he would share.

"Perhaps you are right, Leo," Slade murmured.

Isara looked up and felt deep furrows in her brow. "You must be joking," she spat. "Any attempt to sabotage the treaty will prove fruitless at this point." She cast a glance toward Leo, who flinched at the accusation in her stare. "Why waste resources?"

Slade whirled around to face her, and his icy smile would have made her shiver if not for decades spent learning emotional control. "You are correct," he said. "The treaty *will* be ratified. Harry Carlson saw to that."

"So, then why-"

"As I said," Slade murmured. "Mr. Carlson has set us on a different path. I suggest that we commit to it. If Antaur and Leyria are determined to be allies, then let us cement their union by offering a common adversary."

Isara felt her lips writhing, peeling away from clenched teeth, and she shook her head in contempt. "The three of us will not be a match for that many Justice Keepers and telepaths," she said. "This is futile."

"Not so."

As if on cue, the door to their little apartment opened to admit Valeth in a crimson dress. The olive-skinned woman wore a grin as she glided across the room, her brown hair left loose to spill over her shoulders. "You sent for us."

Us?

Behind her, a young man in beige pants and a denim jacket came stomping into the room. This one was tall, not slim but not exactly muscular either, with a dimpled chin and brown hair cut neat and short.

"Meet Flynn," Valeth said, gesturing to him.

Isara raised an eyebrow.

"He took Flagg's symbiont."

"Even with five, we are still outnumbered," Isara protested. "What do you hope to gain by this stupidity?"

There were times when Slade could be as volatile as Leo. Not as prone to violence for its own sake, but equally willing to toss aside all of their careful planning on a whim. "I want to put on a show," he said. "You know what the Inzari are planning. Those plans can be adapted, with a little effort, to incorporate this new alliance. So, instead of keeping them apart, let's drive them into each other's arms."

Leo was chuckling as he hopped off the counter and strode over to the other man. "You may want a show, Slade," he began, "But if you order me to leave Hunter and his friends untouched, we're going to have a problem. The first chance I get, I will kill Jack Hunter; I will gut Anna Lenai, and I will bathe in Harry Carlson's blood."

"I would expect nothing less," Slade replied.

Chapter 24

The light drizzle had stopped, but Melissa only noticed that by the silence. She had grown used to the sound of raindrops hitting the patio door. Gray light filled her kitchen through the window above the sink, making the normally-gleaming white tiles seem drab. It suited her mood.

The processing unit of her multi-tool – the little metal disk that was usually clipped to her gauntlet – sat in the middle of the white table, and it projected a hologram into the air. A lattice of thin transparent lines formed a globe. Like links in a chain, they all traced circles of latitude and longitude with tiny dots where they intersected.

The top hemisphere was mostly orange with only a few links dipping down toward the bottom pole. The bottom, however, was almost all blue. That was Melissa's territory, and she planned to expand it.

Leaning over the table, Melissa studied the hologram. "I think this will do it." With a hesitant hand, she touched an orange line on the top half of the sphere. It turned blue like an infection spreading from the equator to the top pole.

Novol smiled at her through the lattice. "That's not gonna work." With a swift wave of his hand, he spun the globe so that the line she had touched was now on his side. He touched one link deep in her territory, and the entire line from pole to pole turned orange.

"Damn it!" Melissa exclaimed.

"Hey, I'm just following the pattern."

Sinking into her chair, Melissa tossed her head back and exhaled. "I've been trying to figure out this stupid game for, like, a year now," she grumbled. "And you get the hang of it in *one* day?"

"It's not so hard."

He stood up to stretch his legs and frowned at the patio door behind her. "The real question is why you want to stay in here when there are *so* many interesting things to see and do in this city. And all of them free!"

Melissa closed her eyes, stiffening. "It's this," she said, pointing to her silver hair. "Six months ago, I got a lot of media attention as Melissa Carlson, the young cadet from Earth who stopped one of Slade's top lieutenants."

"Okay."

"Well, I'd be mortified if anyone thought that Melissa Carlson was hanging around with a bunch of fashy kids. Or if they thought I embraced those hateful ideas."

Standing across from her with his arms folded, Novol shook his head. "I don't think you have to worry about that," he said. "Besides, your assignment is over. Why not just dye your hair back to its natural colour?"

"Because I'm hoping it's *not* over…"

"Melissa…"

Scraping her chair backward across the floor tiles, Melissa stood up and grunted. "If you're going to remind me that I screwed up…" she barked. "You needn't bother. I am quite aware of that."

Novol spread his hands, and his gaze dropped to the table's surface. The globe was still hovering a few inches above it, revolving slowly. "You're not an intelligence officer," he said.

"Frankly, I don't think very many Keepers are suited for it. You all seem to have a problem with sneakiness."

Melissa sighed.

"I'm gonna get some supper," Novol added. "Wanna come with me?"

"No," Melissa said. "I think a quiet night is best."

She saw him to the door, gave him a friendly one-armed hug and then sent him on his way. It was only five or six degrees above freezing outside – Leyrian measurements of temperature were remarkably similar to those on Earth; both cultures seemed to have independently hit on the idea of defining water's freezing point as zero and its boiling point as one hundred – but Novol was dressed for it. She could honestly say that she was glad Denabria seldom saw snow. It might have been an affront to her Canadian heritage, but Melissa didn't like cold weather.

No sooner did she sit down on the living room couch than Spock came over to rest his head on her thigh. The kitty started purring, and Melissa absently scratched between his ears. That soothed him. She was-

Her multi-tool chirped.

The touchscreen was still strapped to her gauntlet – even though the processing unit was sitting atop the kitchen table – but a wireless connection between the two allowed them to communicate. Swiping her finger across the screen, she watched as Tesa's face appeared.

The young woman was flushed, her eyes puffy as if she had been crying, and her blonde hair was a mess. "Sara," she whispered. "I need you."

"What is it?"

Tesa looked over her shoulder as if checking to make sure that no one else was in earshot. "We both know what you are," she murmured. "I saw what you did at the protest the other day. Your name probably isn't Sara."

Melissa froze.

How exactly was she supposed to respond to this? Should she try to maintain her cover even though it was likely too late for that? Her silence must have confirmed Tesa's suspicions. "I'll take that as a concession," the other woman growled, keeping her voice low. "Look, I don't care who you are. I need your help."

"Assuming you're correct, why would I want to help you?"

"Because I'm LIS."

Melissa sat bolt upright, causing Spock to jump back. The big orange tabby gave her the feline equivalent of a withering glare and then imperiously dropped to the floor with a *thud*. Melissa ignored him. Her heart was pounding. "You're LIS," she breathed. "I didn't know they had an operative among the protesters."

"Well we do," Tessa hissed. "And my mission was going just fine until you decided to put on a show."

Guilt gnawed at Melissa. Outing herself as a Keeper was one thing, but she never imagined that she might be putting someone else in danger. Forcing herself to stay calm, she said, "Tell me what happened?"

Tessa glanced from side to side, and then she pulled her camera close until her face filled every inch of the screen. "Tarek got suspicious," she said. "He planted a bunch of anti-surveillance tech around the youth centre. They caught me recording this afternoon's meeting."

There had been a meeting this afternoon? The fact that Melissa had not received an invitation by text meant that they must have been suspicious of her too.

Tears welled up and streamed over Tesa's red cheeks. "Look I'm only twenty-one, okay?" she whimpered. "This is my first mission. They've had me locked up in a closet for the last three hours!"

"And they didn't take your multi-tool?"

"Oh they did," Tesa mumbled. "I snatched this screen from a girl's purse when she came in to check on me, reset it to default and linked it wirelessly to my tool. Look, they aren't very good at this. Bleakness take me, I don't think they know what to do now that they've got me."

Once again, Tesa looked over her shoulder, and when she turned her attention back to Melissa, she was even more frantic. "Tarek is talking about killing me," she squeaked. "He says it's the only way to not get caught, and I think he might actually do it!"

"Stay calm," Melissa said. "I'll have a team of Keepers there in ten minutes!"

"No!" Tesa squealed. "You do that, and I'm dead! They're watching the street. If they see strangers coming up to the building…"

Shutting her eyes, Melissa felt tears of her own. Now was not the time to be losing her composure, but she couldn't help but feel responsible for what had happened to this woman. "Then what can I do?"

"Come yourself," Tesa pleaded. "Just you. They're eager to get their hands on you, Sara. If they think that you don't know they're onto you, they'll let you in the building."

"And walk right into their trap?" Melissa protested.

Tesa sniffled. "There are only four of them," she whispered. "We both know that four dumb kids are no match for a Justice Keeper."

Melissa folded up on herself, pressing a palm to her forehead. Her breath rasped as she exhaled. "Okay," she said. "Try to keep them from doing anything stupid. I'll be there as soon as I can."

Running up the steps from the subway station, Melissa found herself standing on a rain-slicked street with small buildings on either side. She was on a road that ran parallel to one of the spoke streets that went all the way to the centre of town, and in the distance, she could see taller skyscrapers.

Hunching up her shoulders against the cold, Melissa walked with her head down. At least it wasn't raining. After a year here, she was getting used to roads that were all but silent, devoid of traffic. People rarely used individual cars on Leyria. Here, public transit was king.

The youth centre was a square building on her right, two stories high with metallic, photo-voltaic paint on its front side. Large windows looked in on a lobby, and she could see shadowy figures inside.

Melissa approached the door.

Before she got within arm's reach, it swung outward to reveal Tarek standing in the opening. He froze up as if the sight of her made him very uncomfortable. Time to put on a show.

"Heard you had a meeting today."

"We did."

Melissa crossed her arms with a sigh, then shook her head slowly. "And you didn't invite me," she said. "You know, a girl might take that personally."

She didn't give him a chance to respond; she just pushed past him into a lobby with potted plants and chairs in crazy neon colours spread out in little clusters. A round fountain in the middle of the room sprayed water almost halfway to the high ceiling. So far as she could see, they were alone...

Wait...

No.

There was someone on the other side of the fountain, a woman with long blonde hair who stood in the corner with her back turned. That had to be Tesa, but what was she doing out here? Shouldn't she be in a closet?

Melissa took off her coat, threw it on a nearby chair and then turned around to face Tarek. "Bleakness take you, why didn't you invite me to the meeting?" she demanded. "I haven't proven myself by now?"

"It's not-"

Staying in character – Sara Veranz was hot-headed and impulsive – Melissa did her best Anna Lenai impression as she made her way around the fountain. Tesa looked like a toddler who had been scolded. "You came," she said. "I knew you would."

Melissa strode across the room at a brisk pace, hissing air through her teeth. "What the hell is going on here, Tesa?" There was no point in trying to maintain her cover, not after the other woman had just revealed everything.

When she got within a few feet of the other woman, Tesa spun around to reveal a pistol in her right hand. The LEDs on its barrel were blue. Set for stun then. "We'd like some answers," Tesa said.

"I should have known."

"Yes, you should have."

Tilting her head back, Melissa felt her eyebrows climbing. "Threatening an officer of the law," she said. "You realize that's a pretty serious crime, right?"

A cruel grin split the other woman's face. If Tesa was afraid, she did a good job of not showing it. "It's really simple," she muttered. "We just want to know what you told your superiors about us."

"And if I refuse?"

Tesa pointed the gun at her.

Twisting on the spot, Melissa turned her body sideways and saw the bullet fly past in front of her chest. She kicked out to the side and slammed a foot into Tesa's stomach, driving the other woman back into the wall.

Melissa faced her again with fists up, sweat beading on her forehead. "Why?" she asked. "You know you're gonna-"

Footsteps behind her.

Bending her knees, Melissa jumped and back-flipped over Tarek's head, uncurling to land just behind him. The man skidded to a stop, then whirled around to face her with his teeth bared in a snarl.

Melissa jumped, rising almost gracefully with her arms spread wide, and kicked his face with the toe of her shoe. The blow sent him sprawling backward right into Tesa. The poor woman was sandwiched between him and the wall.

"I've always wanted to do that," Melissa said as her feet hit the floor. Sadly, this fight wasn't over. Tesa shoved Tarek off of her and regained her balance. Her face was red, and she was seething with every breath.

She looked down at her own empty hand – the gun was now lying in the corner – and when she lifted her gaze to Melissa again, strands of hair fell over her face. There was murder in her eyes.

The door banged open.

More enemies came flooding into the lobby from the room where they usually had their meetings. There were three of them. Misty silhouettes who ran around the fountain and tried to converge on Melissa. One was just a few steps ahead of the other two. Best to let them think they had gotten the drop on her. One…two…three and go!

Melissa jumped, twirling around to face the man and kick him across the chin. He went down with a *thump*, and then the other two were both stepping awkwardly over his body. One got tripped up, the other came at her.

Melissa landed.

Guy Number Two led with a brass-knuckled punch.

Leaning back, she caught his wrist in one hand and clamped the other firmly onto his elbow. A quick twist of his arm was all it took to make him double over and cry out in pain, and then she was spinning him around.

Using his own momentum against him, she sent the man running head-first toward Tesa who yelped when she saw him coming. They both collided and fell to the floor with the big guy on top. Tesa groaned.

Tarek was hissing. He glanced at the gun.

The man she had kicked was rising, blood leaking from the corner of his mouth. He was a handsome enough guy with coppery skin, black hair and a mole just above his left eyebrow.

Number-3, however – the man who had not yet engaged Melissa – was hanging back for some reason. That one was tall, a little slimmer than the others, and completely bald. He seemed to be waiting for the other guy to get back in the game.

Clenching her teeth, Melissa shook her head. "Are we really going to do this?" she asked. "Assaulting an officer of the law! Conspiracy to obstruct justice! You guys are looking at some serious charges."

Sure enough, both men attacked together.

Tarek went for the gun.

Mr. Mole and Number-3 both lunged for her, but a light application of Bent Gravity lifted Melissa high into the air. Curling up into a ball, she somersaulted over the fountain – water sprayed her back – and then landed on the other side.

There was nothing between her and the door, but of course, if Melissa left now, she would have to put this incident in a report, and that would mean another lecture on being careless. She could already see the disappointment in Larani's eyes. But, if she took these jokers into custody, maybe she could save face.

Ilia was skeptical of this plan, but Melissa reassured the Nassai. *I've got this,* she thought. *They're all amateurs, making it up as they go along.*

Melissa spun to face her enemies and found them coming around the fountain from both directions. Mr. Mole was going clockwise while Tesa and Number-3 came at her from the other side.

Thrusting her hand into the rising water, Melissa twisted gravity and sent a jet of it toward Mr. Mole, spraying him right in the face. He stumbled, raising both hands up to shield himself, and then fell on his ass.

With a quick pivot, she turned her attention to the other two.

Red-cheeked and snarling, Number-3 sprinted across the floor tiles. Tesa was right behind him. *Two birds with one stone, Melissa,* she told herself. *Let's do it!*

Melissa ran for the bald man.

She was on course to rush right past him, but Number-3 thrust his arm out to the side to bar her path. Just as she wanted. Melissa charged right into his arm, wrapping one of hers around his neck.

Using his body as an anchor, Melissa lifted her feet off the floor and brought them up to kick Tesa's chest. The tiny woman was thrown backward, gasping as she tripped over a neon-green chair.

Melissa slammed her feet down the floor and, with her arm still coiled around his neck, she threw Number-3 hard onto his backside. He was staring up at her in shock and blinking slowly.

Standing up straight, Melissa wiped her mouth with the back of one hand. Her hair was damp, and her shirt clung to her back. "Oh," she said. "Did I mention that you're all under arrest? Just thought I should-"

Motion in her mind's eye.

A blurry silhouette painted by spatial awareness. She focused on it and found Tarek standing in the corner with Tesa's pistol in his hand, its barrel pointed right at her. She had been ignoring him, dealing with the others. It was a tactical error that she understood in the split second before Tarek pulled the trigger.

Melissa whirled around to face him, her hands coming up to shield herself, but the Bending did not form in time. Tarek's shot took her just below her right shoulder.

She felt the tiny prongs on the end of the bullet piercing her shirt and digging into her skin. The bullet bounced off as a surge went through Melissa's body, turning every muscle to jelly. Everything went dark as she fell to the floor.

Her eyes opened a little while later, blurry vision coming into focus, and she saw Tesa kneeling over her. The other woman was peering down at Melissa with concern on her face. "Now, just relax," she said.

Melissa knew, somehow, that even though it had only been an instant for her, in reality, several minutes had passed. The only reason she had regained consciousness so soon was her body's accelerated healing. And she still couldn't move. She felt as though she should be able to move, but her limbs would not respond.

Tesa lifted Melissa's arm and rolled back her sleeve to expose the soft skin of her wrist. Melissa could only watch as the other woman poked her with a syringe and filled her veins with a dark-green liquid. "This will help you sleep," Tesa murmured. Her voice seemed to be coming from some unimaginable distance. "Soon, you'll be safe and sound, right where you belong."

Everything went dark again.

"Right where you belong…"

Chapter 25

Rapping on the bedroom door with the knuckles of her closed fist, Anna waited for the muffled "Come in," from the other side. Three days had passed since the ambassadors had announced the completion of their negotiations. Copies of the treaty had been sent to Earth and Leyria via the SlipGate network, and apparently, both worlds were more than happy to sign on. In an hour, they would be going downstairs for the closing ceremonies.

When she poked her head through the door, she saw Claire sitting at a vanity across from the foot of the bed. The girl had her back turned as she stared intently into the large mirror, and she seemed pleased by what she saw.

Anna stepped into the room with her hands in her pockets, smiling sheepishly at the floor under her feet. "How's it going in here?" For the last few days, she had been playing the role of big sister, and she wasn't sure that she was doing it right.

Claire twisted around on the stool, sat forward with her hands on her knees and grinned. "Just fixing my makeup." It was good to see her so happy. Almost like she was back to her old self. "I figured I should look nice for the party."

"Aren't you a little young for makeup?"

"I'm eleven!"

"Okay, fair point."

The smile on Claire's face faded as she looked over her shoulder to check herself in the mirror. Her head sank, and Anna had to resist the urge to rush over and hug the poor girl. She had been trying not to smother Claire with too much affection, trying to act as if things were normal for the most part. "Melissa usually helps me," Claire mumbled.

Sitting on the foot of the bed with hands folded in her lap, Anna nodded slowly. "I guess that makes it my job today," she said. "Sorry, but I don't think I can give you much advice. I never wore makeup."

Claire studied her with that look that Harry got sometimes, the one that said he was putting all the pieces together. "Why not?" she asked. "Is it because you were a tomboy growing up?"

Anna smiled, a sudden warmth in her face, and lowered her eyes to stare into her lap. "No, it's not that," she said. "The gender roles that you know on Earth aren't really a thing on Leyria."

"Then why?"

"Rebellion, I guess." The question reminded Anna of the many fights that she'd had with her mother on this very issue. Sierin Elana had tried to teach both of her daughters an appreciation for fancy clothes, pretty hairdos and anything else along those lines. Alia had been an eager student. Anna, not so much. "When you're a diplomat's daughter, they expect you to look and act a certain way. I've never really been good at doing what was expected of me. When other kids went through their primping in front of a mirror phase, I was all 'Hey, let's go check out that art exhibit.'"

"But makeup *is* an art form," Claire insisted. She hopped off the stool and giggled as she cocked her head, inspecting Anna like a sparrow that had just found its next meal. "Let's do yours!"

"Oh no!"

"Come on! It'll be fun!"

"For you, maybe!" Anna protested. The flush she had felt a few moments ago was nothing compared to the raging bonfire that must have turned her beet-red. After years of insisting that she would never wear makeup, she couldn't just put on some eye-liner and act like it was nothing.

Claire grabbed a couple things from the vanity, and when she turned around again, she had a brush in one hand and a jar of something that looked like blush in the other. Her smile made it hard to say no. "I could tell you that it's your job as my surrogate sister."

"Oh, okay."

Shutting her eyes, Anna endured it as the girl applied a light coat of powder to her cheeks. It tickled a little, but she forced herself to hold still. "So, am I gonna look like a clown when this is over?"

"Hush," Claire said.

Next came lipstick, which Claire applied with a delicate touch. "Ruby red, I think," she said as if speaking to herself. "You're paler than I am; so we'll have to choose a shade that works." The stuff was waxy. Anna had to resist the urge to wipe her mouth.

Even with her eyes closed, she could sense Claire's silhouette in her mind, and of course, the girl was grinning. Was this really how Earth women bonded? "Okay," Claire said. "What do you think?"

Anna looked into the mirror and saw that she looked pretty much the same as she always did. It took a moment for her to notice the difference. Maybe that was the point. She could say this much: Claire had a subtle touch.

Pursing her lips, Anna narrowed her eyes. "My mouth feels weird," she mumbled. "It's really hard not to wipe it off."

"Well, don't!" Claire replied, standing over her with hands on her hips. The girl was shaking her head slowly, and there was something ominous in her tone. "You look good. Show Jack."

"He won't even notice."

"I bet he will."

Anna winced, bowing her head and scrubbing a hand across her brow. It was the only way to keep that hand from wiping the gunk off her mouth. "That's what I'm afraid of," she said. "What if he likes it?"

Claire sat down on the stool, and this time, when she shook her head, it was with a burst of soft laughter. "Would that be so bad?" she asked. "You're not any less of a bad-ass just because you sometimes do girly things."

"When did you get so smart?"

"I've always been smart," Claire teased. "I'm just a brilliant young woman who is painfully underappreciated by her family and friends. Mine is a sad story. Doomed to a life of obscurity. History will look back and say, 'There was a woman who was ahead of her time.' "

"Yeah, yeah," Anna teased. "Take it down a notch, smarty-pants."

A grimace twisted Claire's face, and then she bent over, touching two fingers to her forehead. "Oh no," she muttered. "Why can't he just leave me alone?"

"Claire? What are you talking about."

"You'll see. Three…two…one…"

Anna nearly jumped when someone knocked on the door. It wasn't a knock on the bedroom door but on the main entrance to the suite she shared with Jack. Given Claire's reaction, she was fairly certain of who she would find.

Getting to her feet with a sigh, Anna turned and walked out of the room. Outside, a short hallway led to the sitting room where Jack's blanket and pillow were still spread out on the gilded couch. Afternoon sunlight was streaming in through the window.

She went to the door and pulled it open.

Harry stood in the hallway, dressed in a gray suit with a blue shirt and tie, and his eyes were downcast as if he were too ashamed to look at her. Good. "I was thinking that Claire should stay with me during the closing ceremonies."

Gaping at him, Anna blinked several times. She forced her eyes shut and then gave her head a shake. "You've really got some nerve," she growled. "How many times do we have to tell you no?"

"She's my daughter, in case you've forgotten."

Anna backed away with her arms folded, hissing as she stared down at the floor. "Oh no," she said. "No, any right you had to play that card vanished after that stunt you pulled the other day."

She spun around, turning her back on him, and paced over to the couch under the large rectangular window. Outside, the distant skyscrapers were glittering in the sunlight. "What in Bleakness were you thinking?"

Harry stood in the doorway with one hand on the frame, breathing out a heavy sigh of frustration. "It was necessary," he said. "You must have heard what the telepaths were saying about the Overseers. Without the Holy Order's support, Antaur would have never ratified the treaty."

"So, what? You speak for the Overseers now?"

"I don't think they'll care one way or the other."

Turning around with a grumble, Anna sat down on the couch and crossed one leg over the other. "That doesn't make it any better," she snapped. "Bleakness take you, Harry; you're using these people's religious beliefs for your political goals."

He flinched.

"Can't you see how not-okay that is?"

"It's not that simple."

"Then make it simple," Anna said. "Throw that damn thing away. Because as far as I'm concerned, so long as you keep the N'Jal, it's not safe for Claire to be anywhere near you. Or Melissa, for that matter."

The short hallway that led to the bedroom was just askew enough that she didn't sense Claire's approach. The girl stepped into the living room with a sour expression. "I'll stay with my dad this evening."

"Claire, you don't have to-"

"No, he's right," Claire said. "I can't avoid him forever." In three quick strides, the girl was standing in front of her father and craning her neck to stare up at him. "Maybe, instead of going to the party, we should talk?"

"I think we should."

Anna felt no small amount of hesitation as she watched Harry lead his daughter out of the room. It wasn't that she didn't want them to make up – she would be delighted to know that things between Harry and the girls were back to normal – but she didn't trust what the N'Jal was doing to him. He wasn't the same Harry anymore.

But Anna didn't think that Claire was in any immediate danger. She wouldn't have let the girl walk out the door otherwise. Maybe it would be good for them to talk it out.

So, she busied herself with getting ready for the closing ceremonies. She and Jack were on guard duty again; so, that meant black pants and a matching three-quarter top with a round neck. Mobility was key when you had to kick some ass.

She returned to the sitting room to find that Jack had returned from his walk. He was already dressed for the party – gray pants and a black shirt under his brown coat – and she had to admit that he looked good. "I saw Harry walking with Claire," he said. "I guess it's good that they're talking."

"I guess so."

"You wanna head downstairs? Check out the security arrangements?"

Outside their room was a beige-walled hallway with green carpets that led to a bank of elevators. Another hallway extended from there to the suites on the other side of the building, and she could see Harry's security team outside his door. Keepers didn't need a security detail; they *were* the security detail.

Anna felt her mouth tighten, then wrinkled her nose and shook her head. "I can't believe he's still using that thing," she muttered. "How much damage does he have to do before he realizes that it's dangerous?"

Jack walked at her side with his eyes closed, breathing deeply through his nose. "I don't know why Harry did what he did the other day," he began. "But I've known the guy long enough to say that he never does anything without a reason."

"What's that supposed to mean?"

Jack turned to her, placing his hands on her shoulders, drawing her in close. "You always had a very clear idea of what you believed," he said. "Right is right, and wrong is wrong. It's what I love about you."

"But?"

"But you were pretty hard on Ben too after you found out he armed the colonists, and...Maybe he had a point. Maybe if we had let him have access to the weapons that *he* developed himself, Leo wouldn't have been able to..."

Tears welled up as Jack squeezed his eyes shut, and he sniffled. "Maybe if we had been a little less rigid," he said, "Ben would still be here. The galaxy seems to be full of dangerous things. Why should Keepers have a monopoly on super powers?"

Anna couldn't help herself; she threw her arms around him and pressed her cheek into his chest. The gentle caress of Jack running his fingers through her hair made her sigh. "Maybe you're right," she said. "But the thought of Harry throwing force-fields around isn't what scares me."

"It's the source of his power."

"Yeah."

Jack held her a little tighter. "It scares me too," he whispered. "And for what it's worth, I agree with you. The sooner Harry gets rid of the N'Jal, the better. But maybe we could come up with something else for him?"

Anna nodded.

When they reached the bank of elevators, Jack waved his ID card over the scanner and received a *beep* for his trouble. It took almost a minute for the elevator to show up, and when the metal doors finally slid apart, they stepped into a cramped little space with white lights in all four corners of the ceiling.

The ride down was slow and quiet, but halfway through it, the elevator car came to a complete stop and the lights in the ceiling changed from white to red. Alarms blared over the speaker.

Anna shut her eyes tight, stiffening at the thought of what might have caused this commotion. "The ceremony doesn't start for two hours," she whispered. "Why attack the complex now?"

"Because they know we're still prepping," Jack muttered.

Lifting her forearm, Anna tapped deftly at the screen of her multi-tool. In seconds, she was on a call to the building's security office, a call that was answered by a pale man in his early twenties who stared wide-eyed into the camera. "Ma'am? Can I help you?"

"What's going on?"

"The building's surrounded, ma'am," he answered. "Maybe a hundred men firing at us. So far, force-fields are holding them back. The elevators are shut down until we can assess the situation."

"I'm a Keeper," Anna said. "I'm supposed to meet my superiors in the lobby. Can you get me there?"

The young man glanced down at his console and then back up at the camera. He blinked once. "I think so, ma'am," he said. "Let me just verify your security credentials…I have it!"

The elevator started to move again.

"Thank you," Anna said.

Claire was sitting in one of those stupid, fancy chairs with her arms folded, trying to work through her disappointment. She would much rather be going to the party, but her dad was upset;

she could feel that with her new talent. Maybe it was best if they took some time to talk it out.

She felt Harry's presence before he came up behind her with one hand on the back of her chair. "You know I'd never hurt you, right?"

"I know you'd never *intentionally* hurt me."

The spike of pain her father felt at that was so sharp it made Claire want to cry. Not fair! Arguing with your parents was ten times harder when you could feel their emotions. She was still learning how to tune it out. It was hard to explain. Telepathy seemed to have a kind of volume button. You could turn it down to the point where it was so quiet you could never make out anything specific, but you couldn't shut it off completely.

One tear slid over her cheek, and she wiped it away with the knuckle of her hand. "Dad," she said. "It's not that I'm afraid of you. I told you a little while ago that you could use that Overseer thing to keep us safe – and I still think that – but I also wonder what it might be doing to-"

The sound of an alarm made her jump out of her chair. Claire had turned down the volume of her telepathy to the point that she wouldn't be able to sense the initial spike of fear that preceded whatever had triggered the sirens.

She looked up through the window with her brows drawn together and focused. "We have to find out what happened."

"We?" Harry exclaimed. "You're not going anywhere near whatever it is."

Ignoring him, Claire turned up the volume – she couldn't say *how* she did it any more than she could tell you how she wiggled her fingers – and was suddenly confronted by hundreds of minds. It was like being in a crowd where everyone was jabbering at the same time, hard to focus on any one voice. Some were afraid; some were angry, and some were filled with such hateful thoughts she couldn't bear to listen.

It reminded her of those first few moments before she collapsed in the hospital, the overload of too much information at once. Only then, she hadn't been able to tune it out. Maybe that was where Harry went wrong, giving her telepathic powers without a volume switch. She shut out the mental noise enough to hear her father saying, "Whatever's going on out there, it's no place for a kid."

"The building is under attack."

Claire went to the couch, kneeling on the cushions and leaning forward to press her hands to the windows. "And I don't have to go anywhere near it," she added. "I can help from up here. I'd like to see Melissa top *that*."

She went to work.

When they reached the second floor, the elevator doors opened, and Anna heard the noise of at least three dozen panicked voices. She stepped out onto a balcony with thick red carpeting that stretched to a curved railing.

Anna sprinted to that railing, grabbing it with both hands as she peered down at the chaos below. "Bleakness take me," she whispered. "They're going to war."

On the main floor of the lobby, two lines of men and women in heavy tactical gear marched toward the main entrance. The windows on either side of the door flashed as force-fields lit up to intercept bullets.

There were Keepers as well: at least twenty of them, all standing in little groups and waiting for instructions or some sign of what they should do next. She saw Director Varno watching the scene play out with a tight frown.

Swatting Jack on the arm – an indication that he should follow – she turned and ran across the balcony to the curved staircase. Taking the steps two by two, she descended to the main floor and found Keli and Rajel waiting there.

The stairs ended near the mouth of a long hallway that branched off from the lobby. Anna motioned the others to move off to the side, out of the line of fire. Force-fields and bullet-proof glass stood between them and any incoming fire, but it was never smart to tempt fate. "Status report," she ordered.

Rajel looked odd in an ostentatious blue shirt with short sleeves and gold trim on the collar, cuffs and hem. Completing the ensemble, he wore a length of gold chain on each forearm. "As near as we can tell," he said, "a bunch of unmarked vans dropped off some heavily-armed men about five minutes ago. They've been shooting at the building since they arrived."

Keli, in her pristine white dress, glanced over her shoulder toward the ranks of armed guards. "They won't let me join the other telepaths," she added. "They just keep insisting that they have the situation well in hand."

"Okay," Anna said. "We should-"

"Do nothing!"

That came from Director Varno, who was striding toward their group and shaking his head in dismay. "The Antaurans have asked us to keep out from underfoot, and that's exactly what we're going to do."

"So, we just…hang out in the lobby?" Jack muttered.

Varno replied to that with a sizzling glare, then grunted as he turned his attention back to Anna. "I'm assigning teams of Keepers to patrol each floor," he explained. "Most of our diplomats are in meeting rooms on the fourth and fifth floors, but some are still in their suites on the ninth and tenth. If you wish, I can assign you to one of those teams."

Puckering his lips, Jack shut his eyes and blew out a breath. "This doesn't make any sense," he said. "This building is heavily fortified. They're not gonna get in with a frontal assault. A surgical strike like what we saw the other night, maybe, but a full assault on the Complex? It's suicide."

"What are you saying?" Varno asked.

"I'm saying it's a distract-"

Every bulb in the lobby went dark, leaving only the daylight that came in through the windows. The holographic assistants winked away, and force-fields no longer popped up to shield the entrance. Instead, bullets hit the reinforced glass with a *rat-a-tat-tat.*

"Main power's out," Anna said.

The emergency lights came on as she finished speaking, but they provided far less illumination. Some of the other Keepers were speaking in hushed voices and exchanging glances with one another.

"How did he do it?" Varno growled.

"Isn't it obvious?" Jack countered. "It's a classic Slade maneuver. Put someone on the inside, and have them sabotage the defenses at a critical moment."

Nudging the security officer aside – he fell out of his chair and hit the floor with an unceremonious *thump* – Tara Driath bent over the console and powered down the last of the security systems. The cramped little office where these men monitored the building's systems was barely large enough to fit three people. Almost every inch of floor space was covered by the body of a man in a black uniform and an armoured vest. She would have to step carefully on her way out.

The three guards had gone down easily. It wasn't hard to overwhelm a man with his worst fears until he passed out from the strain of it. She had taken the access codes from their minds. Really, they weren't supposed to let her in here – no one except authorized personnel were to have access – but so few people could say no to a telepath. She didn't even have to use her talent to gain entry! They were just so eager to please.

She felt something.

Hostile minds approaching.

Not just any minds, either. She was about to be confronted by two telepaths who did not share her devotion to the gods. Tara clicked her tongue in annoyance. She could not like what she had to do, but there was no way around it.

Moving gracefully in scarlet robes with gold embroidery, Tara squatted next to the body of a fallen guard and took his sidearm from its holster. It took some effort to shield her mind, but she couldn't risk any of her thoughts or intentions from leaking.

Tara stood and faced the door.

A moment later, it burst open to reveal a man in yellow robes and a woman in green standing side by side in the opening. Drez Niton and Teela Sakur. Both capable telepaths in their own way."What is going on here?" Drez demanded.

"Our security has been compromised," Tara said.

"We felt terror emanating from this place," Teela said. "Who could have put down three officers so-"

The tiny woman cut off when a bullet hole appeared in her forehead. Her body fell to the floor. Gasping, Drez turned his gaze upon Tara and lashed out with the full force of his talent. It was all she could do to shield herself from the mental assault. It was all she had to do.

So focused was he on putting her down swiftly that he barely noticed when Tara pointed the gun at him. Drez reacted too late, raising both hands to protect his face, and stumbled when her bullet ripped through his chest.

Leaving the room, Tara ignores the brains on the wall and the puddle of blood that was soaking into the gray carpet. Such a dreadful sight. A woman of her breeding should never have had to look upon it.

She retrieved a small, circular screen from her inside pocket and powered it up to find Grecken Slade glowering at her. "Report," he barked.

"You may begin the second phase."

"And the assassin?"

"You will find him on the sixth floor," Tara answered. "With the president."

Chapter 26

The lobby was dim except for daylight coming in through windows on either side of the door and the hard glow of emergency lights. Security officers in black tactical gear pressed their bodies up against the walls to stay out of the line of fire.

Every time a shot hit one of those windows, it bounced off with a loud *thunk*. Anna ventured a glance around the corner and saw that each pane now had at least half a dozen small, circular marks from the impact of multiple bullets. Even ballistic glass would give way eventually. She was just glad that the attackers didn't have high-impact rounds. That must have been the case, or they would have used them by now.

Armoured security officers had pressed themselves up against the walls on either side of the lobby, and each one of them had an assault rifle pointed at the door. If the attackers tried to storm the building, they would find a nasty surprise waiting.

She turned back to Varno.

"Your orders, sir?"

The director was frowning across the lobby at the small clusters of Keepers who were taking cover on the other side. "I have to get in touch with the others," he said. "If Hunter is right, and this is a distraction…"

He rolled up his sleeve to uncover his multi-tool and began tapping at the screen. His sudden curse made Anna very uneasy. "Comms are jammed!" Varno exclaimed. "I can't get through!"

"I'm blocked too," Jack growled.

Rajel held the small disk-shaped processing unit up to his left ear and hissed at the sound of static. "I as well," he said. "It seems they've done a masterful job of cutting us off from reinforcements."

Varno closed his eyes, breathing deeply to calm himself, and then nodded once. "I have to get upstairs," he said. "Someone has to coordinate the teams who are protecting our people. Lenai, you have command of this floor."

Anna nodded.

Without another word, Varno ducked around the corner, back into the lobby, and started up the curved staircase that led to the balcony. No doubt there was a stairwell up there that he could use to access the higher floors. Anna just hoped the ID card scanners were still operating when the building was on emergency power.

She turned and peered across the lobby to another hallway on the other side. There were about eight or nine Keepers standing there, milling about, staying out of the line of fire just in case the ballistic glass failed.

"Everyone okay?" Anna shouted.

The nearest of them – a pale man with dirty-blonde hair and a matching goatee – turned to her and smiled. "Yes, ma'am!" he called back. By his accent, she could tell that he was from Earth, from the Southern United States unless she missed her guess. "We're just waiting on orders."

The Antauran security officers were still in position on either side of the lobby, ready to gun down anyone who tried to force their way through that door. Someone was barking orders in Raen, but it seemed that they too had been cut off from their superiors. "Hey!" Anna called out.

Guards on the opposite wall turned their heads to look at her through the visors of their helmets. "Who's in charge among you?" Anna inquired.

An older man with his visor pulled up stepped into view and frowned at her. "That would be me," he said in a gruff voice. "Captain Taros Vanoor at your service."

Anna touched her hip and realized that she had not yet armed herself with a pistol. Those were supposed to be handed out after the briefing. Antaurans didn't much like the thought of off-duty Keepers walking around the Diplomatic Complex with guns, and she really couldn't blame them. "You all have procedures for the defense of this building," Anna said. "Which means we're going to support you. Tell us where you need us, and we will be there."

The captain smiled and nodded once in appreciation. "Much obliged, madame," he said. "We'll be sure to-"

A loud crash behind her made everyone tense up. It sounded like glass shattering. "The banquet hall!" Jack shouted. "The skylight!"

Mopping a hand over her face, Anna pushed her bangs back from her forehead. "Why can't I ever get an easy assignment?" Her words were so soft that no one but Jack would have heard. Raising her voice, she added, "Keli, get somewhere safe and do anything you can to slow down those people outside. Jack, Rajel, you're with me. The rest of you will support Captain Vanoor."

"Yes, ma'am!" the young Keeper shouted from the other side of the lobby.

Running side by side, Anna, Jack and Rajel hurried down the long hallway that led through the north wing of the Complex. Doors to conference rooms and the media centre where Harry had given his press conference stood open, but there was no one in sight.

The banquet hall, the same one where they had fended off Corovin Dagmath's team just a few nights ago, was at the very end of the corridor. She heard a noise coming from inside, a familiar hum…like that of a SlipGate.

Sure enough, when she stepped through the door, she saw that a large mass of flesh had crashed through the skylight and landed in the wide aisle that ran through the middle of the room. It had taken the shape of a triangle, a triangle composed of veiny skin that gave off a faint blue glow.

Anna ran past the pillars and through the narrow gaps between round tables. Jack was right behind her with Rajel bringing up the rear. Seconds later, they all skidded to a stop in the aisle.

The SlipGate's hum grew louder.

A bubble expanded from a point, growing to full size in less than one second, and within it, three blurry figures stood side by side. Anna couldn't see their faces clearly. Not through the refracted light. "There are three," she told Rajel. He wouldn't even know that much. Spatial awareness would only give him the dimensions of the bubble. Anything inside of it would be inaccessible to him.

The bubble popped, and the SlipGate collapsed into a puddle of skin.

A small woman with olive skin and long dark hair stood in between two men. One was Leo – sneering like a jackal about to pounce – but the other might as well have been his little brother.

Except for a pale complexion, the new guy looked nothing like Leo. He was quite tall and a bit lanky where Leo was all hard muscle. His cheeks were gaunt, his eyes and hair dark, but there was sadism in his stare. When he looked at you, you *knew* that he was thinking about carving you up into itty, bitty pieces.

"Hunter is mine!" Leo spat.

The woman turned her gaze upon the new guy and jerked her head toward Anna. "You've been eager to prove yourself, Flynn," she said. "Kill Anna Lenai, and Slade will reward you handsomely. I'll deal with the blind one."

Leo threw his head back and roared with laughter. "Your cowardice truly knows no limits, Valeth." His comment earned him a glare from the woman, but he didn't seem to notice. "Send the pup after Lenai, and choose an opponent who can't fight back."

Rajel stiffened at that.

Anna tensed up as well, but for different reasons. Valeth. Jena had told her about Slade's most elusive lieutenant, and Melissa had confirmed much of what she had heard. It seemed that Valeth was a coward, eager to avoid a fight whenever possible and to flee if things weren't going her way.

Anna's first instinct was to demand that the other woman fight her instead of Rajel. Mainly because she wasn't interested in fighting some half-trained pup. But there was a certain poetic justice in letting Valeth find out that her blind opponent was by no means helpless. "Let's do this," she said.

Jack watched all three of Slade's lieutenants standing in front of the blob of folded up flesh that had spread over the carpet. Leo still wore that mocking grin, and his gaze never wavered, fixed on Jack like a laser.

All three of them came forward at the same time, Flynn and Valeth breaking off to engage their respective opponents. Leo was charging straight for Jack, snarling like a dog who wanted to sink his teeth into his prey.

He opened with a fast right-hook.

Jack ducked, allowing the man's fist to pass over him. With one hand, he jabbed Leo's belly once, twice, three times and four, driving the wind from his lungs. He popped up and threw a hard punch to the face.

Leo's head snapped backward, and he stumbled as he tried to regain his balance. With one hand outstretched, he retreated through the aisle between the tables. "That's the spirit, Hunter! Make me pay for everything I've done!"

Jack strode forward to meet his enemy.

All around him, his friends were busy with their respective opponents. Anna was off to his right, battling with the newbie, and Rajel was leading Valeth through the maze of tables.

Baring his teeth, Jack felt a sudden heat in his face. "You never learn, do you?" he growled. "No matter how many times we smack you down, you keep on coming back for more. Well, this will be the last time."

Leo kept retreating until his shoes brushed the puddle of flesh that had once been a SlipGate. When he looked up, the mocking smile had returned. "I couldn't agree more," he said. "It's 'bout time we ended this."

"Past time."

Jack ran the last few steps, but the instant he got within arm's reach of his enemy, the puddle of flesh contorted, reforming into a triangle that stood over seven-feet tall. A triangle that began to glow with faint blue light.

Whirling around, Jack tried to flee – he had seen this trick before – but Leo grabbed the back of his collar and pulled him close. He threw both arms around Jack, restraining him. "No, no, no! You can't leave yet! Not after I've gone to all this trouble to arrange a little privacy!"

A bubble formed around them, cutting them both off from the rest of the world. The banquet hall was now just a haze of red and gold. White tables seemed to merge into one another so that it was hard to tell where one ended and the next began. If Jack strained his eyes, he could just make out Anna as she deflected blows from Slade's newest flunky.

Leo giggled behind him.

An instant later, they were racing through an endless dark tunnel with a light in the distance. A light that never came any closer. Jack felt no sensation of motion. They might as well have been sitting still for all he could tell.

Folding his hands over one of Leo's arms, Jack lifted his foot off the floor and then brought it down on the other man's shoe. That produced a high-pitched squeal, and Leo loosened his grip.

Twisting in the other man's arms, Jack drove his elbow into Leo's chest. The blow landed with enough force to throw Leo back against the inner surface of the bubble.

Despite himself, Jack held his breath.

The bubble looked like it might pop at the slightest touch, but it may as well have been made of stone for all the damage Leo did when he rebounded off it. Really, it was a force-field – a sudden flicker of white – that prevented him from passing through the thin shell and having his molecules scattered across SlipSpace. The Overseers had designed the Gates with any number of safety features.

Leo took one shaky step forward, then drew himself up to full height. His face was flushed, his blonde hair damp. "I'm going to make you suffer for-"

He cut off when the tunnel ended on what appeared to be a city street under a dark, twilight-blue sky. Of course, it was impossible to make out anything specific, but Jack could see the blurry image of another SlipGate behind Leo.

The bubble popped.

Wasting no time, Leo jumped, using Bent Gravity to hurl himself over Jack's head, and ran across a cobblestone street toward a white-washed building with black tiles on its gabled roof. Where the bloody hell was this?

Leo flew gracefully up to crouch on the peak of the rooftop. Then he was running down one sloping side and leaping onto the next building over. A chase? So, he wanted Jack to follow him?

Screw that!

Jack turned around to find a metal SlipGate on a street corner, the last light fading from its sinuous grooves. Aside from that, he saw no other signs of advanced technology. This little village looked like it had come right out of the Middle Ages.

White-washed houses lined both sides of a street that curved slightly as it ran up a hillside. The sky above was just dark enough that the first stars were starting to twinkle. It looked like dawn to Jack's eyes, but given that the sun rose in the west here, it must have been dusk. They had to be on Antaur. Slip-Gates couldn't send you to other planets. He-

Motion behind him.

With a quick about-face, Jack extended his hand to erect a rippling Bending with his outstretched fingers. Bullets that would have pierced his body instead curved away and buried themselves in the cobblestones.

Jack ducked around the corner, pressing his back to the wall of a house, and let the Bending collapse. He was breathing hard, sweat prickling on his brow. "So, you want me to follow you, eh?"

He had no intention of walking right into the other man's trap. He had already been stupid enough to let himself get near the SlipGate, and the sting that brought to his pride was bad enough. The smart thing to do was to get back to the others.

Rolling up his sleeve, Jack swiped a finger across the screen of his multi-tool. He tapped one of several icons and brought up the app for interfacing with SlipGates. Then he ordered it to scan.

A circle expanded from the centre of his screen to the very edge, and after it did that several times, the words "no Gates within range" appeared in bright red letters. No Gates within range. He performed the scan again and got the same result. But he was less than five feet away from one!

"Damn it," he whispered. "Okay, Leo, I'll give you this one." The other man must have programmed this Gate to shut down after it received incoming travellers. So, there would be no getting back that way.

He returned to the multi-tool's home screen and opened the communications app. With a few quick taps, he sent out a broadband distress call. "This is Special Agent Jack Hunter of the Justice Keepers. I've been transported to an unknown location, and I need immediate assistance."

Static came through the speaker.

"This is Special Agent Jack Hunter…"

Once again, no one answered. So, his transmission had been blocked, which meant he couldn't call for help. And the SlipGate wasn't functioning. That left him with only one option. He had to go after Leo.

When Jack Hunter finally left in pursuit of Leo, Isara stepped out from the narrow alley between two houses. The young Keeper was gone, thank the Inzari. She had been forced to rely on auditory cues, and there was always the possibility that she might have misread the sound of retreating footsteps. If Jack had been on a line of sight with her when she emerged from her hiding place, he would have sensed her presence with spatial awareness.

Slade would be enraged when he learned that she had not joined the others in the attack on the Diplomatic Complex, but she had much more important business. It would not take Jack long to find the arena that Leo had chosen for their contest, and then things would go one of two ways. Either Jack would incapacitate Leo with the intention of bringing him back to his superiors for questioning – in which case, Isara would have to kill both of them – or Leo would succeed in killing Jack. If she had to bet, she would bet on the former, but even if he won, the fight would push Leo to the limits of his endurance. And then she could finish him off with ease. One way or another, both men would die here tonight.

Anna kicked Flynn in the stomach, throwing him backward onto the surface of a round table. He slid across it, pulling the tablecloth with him, and then fell to the floor on the other side.

The hum of a SlipGate made her look around to find that the Overseer device had become a triangle again, and it had Jack and Leo trapped inside a bubble. They were too blurry for Anna to make out any details, but the fact that she could no longer sense either man with spatial awareness meant that it had to be them.

The bubble shrank to a point.

"Jack!" she screamed.

On the other side of the aisle, Rajel danced backwards from one of Valeth's kicks, but the tiny woman rounded on him and smiled. "Leo has done his part," she said. "Now, let us move on to our real target."

Without warning, Valeth shot upward through the broken skylight and landed on the roof. She ducked out of sight a moment later.

Flynn popped up on the other side of the table, grinning maliciously and shaking his head. "You Keepers," he said in a rough, rasping voice. "So naive. Did you honestly think we came here to fight *you?*"

He bent his knees and leaped, using Bent Gravity to propel himself upward in pursuit of Valeth. Then he too was gone with only the sound of his footsteps on the roof as an indication of where he might be headed.

Rajel stood in between two tables with a hand on his chest, gasping as he tried to catch his breath. His sunglasses were slightly askew. "What are they doing?" he panted. "What could they possibly want on the roof?"

Tilting her head back, Anna squinted as she considered the possibilities. "There's a stairwell door up there!" she growled. "They're going for the diplomats!"

She was soaring through the shattered skylight less than half a second later, tucking her legs into her chest and back-flipping to land on the roof. When she spun around, the north wing of the Complex stretched on for maybe two hundred paces, and beyond that, the tower rose up to stab the blue sky.

Valeth and Flynn were halfway to their goal.

Anna took off in a mad dash; it barely even registered when Rajel flew up through the opening to land behind her. Seconds later, he was loping across the rooftop on long legs. "Valeth! We're not done yet!"

Valeth looked back over her shoulder. Skidding to a stop, she retrieved a gun from her belt holster and turned around to face them.

Anna and Rajel both raised a hand, and together, they crafted a Bending that made the air seem to ripple like heat rising off the pavement. Sharing the load made it easier. A bullet suddenly appeared in the patch of curved space-time, its motion slowed to the point where it could be seen with the naked eye.

It veered off to Anna's left and followed a tight loop that took it back the way it had come. When she and Rajel let the Bending drop, Valeth and Flynn were lying flat on their bellies, and the stairwell door had a hole in it.

They had gained a few seconds.

Flynn was closest to the door, and he quickly rolled over, getting back on his feet. He didn't even look back as he ran the last few paces and grabbed the handle. Anna felt a twisting sensation.

Valeth pushed herself up on extended arms, gritting her teeth as she stared at them. "Your meddling grows tiresome, Justice Keeper," she said. "Quite tiresome!"

With the security systems down, there were no force-fields to prevent Flynn from tampering with the door. He was ripping the lock apart on a molecular level, twisting the fabric of space and time.

If you made a Bending that encapsulated only *part* of a solid object, the two halves would be torn apart as one piece bent away from the other. Flynn was doing exactly that to the lock.

Releasing his hold on space-time, he stepped back and kicked the door hard enough to force it open. Then he ran into the darkness.

Anna went after him.

Rajel was only two steps behind her, but Valeth jumped on him like a pouncing cat and tackled him to the ground. "No, blind man," she said, holding him down. "We are not finished, you and I."

Anna hesitated. Should she do something? Try to help? No, Rajel was one of the most skilled Keepers she had ever met; he could handle this himself. Her first priority was to protect the diplomats, and she knew damn well that if their roles were reversed, Rajel would do his job and trust her to take care of herself.

Through the door and up the stairs, she ran. It took a moment for her eyes to adjust, but even without windows, she could see quite well. The emergency lights provided more than enough illumination for that. LEDs consumed very little power but they shone like the sun.

Even with the stamina of a Justice Keeper, her heart was pounding by the time she reached the sixth floor, and the echoes of Flynn's footsteps taunted her from above. There was something in the man's eyes when he looked at you. It wasn't quite the same as the raw hatred she had seen from Leo. No, it was more like a desire to test himself.

When she made it to the eighth floor, she realized that the only footsteps she heard were her own. Which could only mean one of two things. Either Flynn had reached his destination... or he was waiting for her.

Closing her eyes, Anna felt a shiver pass through her. "You want me to find you," she whispered. "This isn't about achieving the mission objective. What you're itching for is a chance to test yourself against a Keeper."

She slowed her pace considerably after that, trying to stay as quiet as a mouse. If Flynn was planning to sneak up on her, she could at least return the favour. On the ninth floor, she paused.

Pressing her lips together, Anna looked up and felt her eyebrows climbing. "Yeah," she muttered. "I know you're up there."

She carried on at a measured pace, and when she reached the landing between the ninth and tenth floors, spatial awareness told her that she was no longer alone. Rounding the corner to ascend the next flight, she froze.

Flynn stood at the head of the stairs with his back to a door that was marked with a big Antauran ten. His laughter echoed off the walls. "To hell with killing diplomats," he said. "I want some time alone with you."

"Earth slang," Anna replied. "And a Brooklyn accent?"

"Very good."

"Is Flynn your real name?"

He replied to that with a mocking smile, shaking his head slowly. "Actually, it's Nate." His casual shrug of indifference was surprising, to say the least. "But Slade is real big on placing his people in key positions. He says I'll answer to a hundred aliases over the course of one lifetime; so, I may as well get used to it."

Anna began her ascent with one hand on the railing, but the instant she did, Flynn stepped back and drew a knife from his belt. "We don't have to fight," she assured him.

"Oh, we *have* to fight," he countered. "And I kinda want to."

Flynn threw the knife.

Anna put up a Time Bubble, a sphere – the simplest and least energy-intensive of all shapes – and through it, she saw a distorted version of the stairwell. The knife hung in the air about an arm's length away, and a few steps up, Flynn stood on the tenth-floor landing with his arm extended. She took one step to the left and let the bubble collapse.

The knife rushed past her.

Bounding up the stairs in three quick strides, Anna leaped and kicked out. Her foot slammed into Flynn's chest, pushing him back, flattening him against the wall. A wheeze of pain was her reward.

Anna landed in front of him.

She threw a punch, but Flynn's hand snaked up to seize her wrist. His back-hand strike took her across the cheek, blurring her vision. Dizziness made her want to fall over, but she fought her way through it.

It startled Anna when Flynn grabbed a fistful of her shirt and shoved her away. Her feet struggled to stay planted on the floor, but it was no use. Before she even realized it, she was tumbling down the stairs.

Falling over backwards, Anna put her hands down on one step. She flipped upright with a grunt, raising her fists into a guarded stance.

A knife came flying at her.

Her hands went up by instinct, trapping the weapon between clapped palms. She had only half a second to process that before the next one came her way. Anna leaned to her left, but the jagged blade ripped her sleeve and sliced a thin gash across her right arm.

Flynn jumped from his perch at the top of the stairs, and she had just enough time to look up and see a gray running shoe filling her vision. The blow to the head dazed her, and once again, she was stumbling. Down the stairs, onto the landing below and right into the wall. Dimly, she was aware that she had lost the knife she had captured.

In her mind, she saw a misty silhouette in the shape of Flynn's body. The man was coming down to meet her, drawing back his arm for a vicious punch.

Anna ducked.

His knuckles hit the wall instead, leaving cracks in the bricks, and the echoes of his anguished shriek were almost haunting. Like a ghost, Anna slipped past him, then jumped and drove her elbow into the back of his skull.

His forehead rebounded off the wall, and then he was staggering with the heels of his hands pressed to his brow. "Damn it!" he snarled. "I can understand why Slade wants you dead, woman."

Backing away across the landing, Anna winced and shook her head. "I'll take that as a compliment," she said. "You know you can't win this, right? All I have to do is keep you busy until a security team finds us."

"You won't last that long."

"Cocky," she observed. "You've had your symbiont *how* long exactly?"

Flynn spun on her with teeth bared and an ugly red welt on his forehead. He strode forward like an oncoming storm. *Not much room to maneuver,* Anna noted. *Why oh why did I have to fight him here?*

He kicked high.

Dropping low with both hands on the floor, Anna swept her leg in a wide arc and tripped him. Flynn toppled over backward, slamming his hands down upon the tiles. He was upright again in an instant, but it was too late.

Anna was already on her feet and charging toward him. She jumped and kicked him square in the chest, pinning him against the wall again. As she fell, she punched his ugly, arrogant face.

Once again, Flynn caught her shirt in both hands and this time, he gave a shove that was augmented by Bent Gravity. She was thrown into the opposite wall, grunting when her body hit the bricks.

Anna dropped to the floor, hunched over with a hand on her chest. The pain was intense. If not for Seth mending fractures before they had a chance to form, a hit like that might have broken her back.

She had a glimpse of Flynn dropping to a crouch and picking up two of his fallen knives. He stood up with that menacing smile on his face. "Should have paid attention," he said. "Knives all over the floor."

She *had* noticed, but pausing to pick one up while her enemy was less than ten feet away would have left her exposed. "This is gonna be fun," Flynn murmured. "I'm gonna carve me up some Keeper steak."

"Ew! Gross!"

Claire pushed open the door to find that the hallway outside her suite was empty. The security team was gone. Maybe they had been assigned to some other task. Her dad wasn't a diplomat; guarding him wouldn't be a priority.

She stepped out into a hallway with green carpets and gold trim on its beige walls. It had that hotel smell too. Like someone had sprayed air-freshener all over the place. She saw no one else. Maybe the neighbouring suites were empty, maybe not. She couldn't say.

Oh, wait, she *could* say.

Claire shut her eyes and stretched out with her senses, cranking the volume. Most of the neighbouring rooms were empty, but there were a few diplomats on this floor. And they were scared.

Harry came out behind her.

She turned around to find that he was striding toward her with teeth bared, shaking his head in dismay. "Where do you think you're going?" he asked. "If you're determined to get involved, you can do it from our room."

Claire looked up at him with what she hoped was a calm expression and blinked once. "We have to help," she insisted. "And I might be able to do it better if I can see the men shooting at us."

"Are you insane?"

"They won't see me! Not all the way up here."

In a flurry of motion, she turned her back on him and paced up the hallway, passing door after door. Eventually, she came to a line of windows that looked out on skyscrapers that glittered in the afternoon sunlight.

Bracing her hands on the windowsill, Claire leaned forward, almost touching her nose to the glass. "They're out there," she muttered. "If I can just get a good look."

It was no use.

On the tenth floor, she was too high up to see anything in the immediate vicinity of the Complex. But maybe she could find another way.

Once again, Claire reached out with her senses and felt the minds of several dozen people surrounding the Complex. She focused on one, a man who used his assault rifle to fire at the bullet-proof windows on the second and third floor. But what could she do?

Suddenly, she was aware of something else.

At the end of this hallway, a door led into a stairwell, and just beyond that door, two people were fighting for their lives. One had a mind so full of hatred that she immediately pulled away from it. The other must have been a Keeper. Claire could sense only the dark cloud of a Nassai's mind. She didn't even try to get through.

Claire thought about helping the Justice Keeper but decided against it. She wouldn't be able to do all that much – people with symbionts had some protection from telepathy – and if the hate-filled man became aware of her presence…

Claire shivered.

Harry stepped up beside her, peering sadly through the window. "What now?" he asked. "Can you do more from here?"

"Just watch my back."

Rajel hit the concrete with a grunt.

Valeth was perched on top of him, clutching his shirt with one hand, and leaning in close. With only inches between them, spatial awareness painted every smooth contour of her face. The woman was snarling. "Now, you die."

Rajel got a hand underneath her, pressed up against her belly, and a surge of Bent Gravity sent the woman flying. She collided with the wall next to the stairwell door and then dropped to land on her feet. "Is that the best you can do, blind man?"

Curling his legs against his chest, Rajel somersaulted backwards and came up in a crouch. He rose slowly, frowning as he ran scenarios in his head. Other Keepers might be tempted to point out that Valeth's quips only betrayed her unease, but Rajel wasn't other Keepers. Best to be done with this as quickly and cleanly as possible.

Valeth came running toward him.

She spun for a hook-kick, and Rajel stepped back in time to watch her boot gliding past in a sweeping arc. The woman came around to face him. She threw a punch.

Rajel brought a hand up to bat her fist aside. He used the other for a quick jab to the nose, one that made Valeth stagger.

The small woman retreated with a hand over her mouth, her eyes flaring in surprise. When she was inches away from the door, she spared a glance for the opening, no doubt wondering if it might be wiser to flee. But Anna was up there somewhere. So she thought better of it. Seconds later, she was sprinting across the rooftop, trying to mow him down.

Dropping to his knees, Rajel felt a stirring of air as his enemy flew past overhead. He quickly uncoiled the chain from his left arm. Thin golden links dug into his palm. Not the strongest metal, but it would do.

Valeth was coming up behind him.

He twisted around, flinging the chain at her. The tiny woman leaned back just in time to avoid a lash to the face. That earned him a brief reprieve.

Rajel threw himself down on the rooftop, rolling across its surface to put a little distance between him and his opponent. He got back up on his feet, steeling his nerves, using spatial awareness to track Valeth as she moved in close.

Rajel swung the chain above his head like the propeller blade of one of those old hovering vehicles. Two short steps brought him close enough, and then he sent it flying toward Valeth.

She caught it in one deft hand.

Valeth tugged on the chain with incredible strength, forcing him to stumble, almost knocking him down. She tugged again, and this time, Rajel let go. The petite woman fell hard onto her backside, growling.

Using core strength, she sprang off the rooftop and landed on her feet. Even from several paces away, Rajel could still sense it when she bared her teeth. Valeth twirled like a dancer – elegant and graceful – and whipped the chain around in a tight vertical circle. The air whistled with every turn.

She attacked.

Rajel bent backwards, one golden link almost grazing his chin. He retreated step by step across the rooftop, almost to the ledge. But with every step, he unspooled the other chain from his right arm.

Valeth flowed toward him like a demon, swinging her weapon with wild abandon. Rajel lashed out with his own whip. The two chains met in the air, one coiling around the other.

Rajel turned his back on the woman, lifting his own chain high above his head and tugging as hard as he could. He managed to rip the other one out of Valeth's grip and send it windmilling over the edge.

He spun around just in time to witness Valeth flying toward him in another cat-like leap. The woman drew her arm back and punched him hard enough to make his head ring. Dizziness hit him hard, but he fought through it. Other Keepers might have become disoriented by the momentary loss of vision, but Rajel had never learned to rely primarily on his eyes. When Valeth's fist struck him, he simply fell over backward.

Pressing both palms to the rough surface of the rooftop, he rose into a handstand. He was on his feet again in an instant and backing away with the chain held taut in both hands. Valeth screeched as she launched herself at him.

Chapter 27

The narrow cobblestone street sloped downward, curving slightly to the left. On either side, empty houses with black windows stood silent under the night sky. It felt like standing in a ghost town.

Jack moved carefully down the hill, frowning as he listened for any signs of life. He blinked once. "Okay, Leo," he whispered. "If you wanted a hiding place, what would you choose?"

Nothing stood out to him.

Step by step, he continued his journey, inspecting every inch of his surroundings with his eyes and with spatial awareness. Every now and then, Jack thought he caught a hint of motion, but it was too far off to be certain.

He went around a corner.

Another curving street stretched on before him with empty houses on either side. The air was chilly now that the sun was down, and crickets chirped nearby. Under other circumstances, that might have been relaxing, but here, it was eerie.

Chewing his lower lip, Jack felt wrinkles lining his brow. "I know you're skulking somewhere in this dump." Actually, the town was quite nice, but he was pissed off at the moment. "You wouldn't go to all this trouble if you didn't plan on fighting me."

Once again, he scanned the rooftops and saw nothing out of the ordinary. Summer was uneasy; Jack did what he could to comfort her, but he was pretty tense as well. Leo might pop out from any one of the alleys he passed.

Turning another corner brought him to yet another street, and this time he paused. On his left, a squat little building that might have been a tavern had lights shining in its windows. The door was open, but he heard no sound.

Pressing his shoulder to the wall, Jack crept closer and closer until he was able to peer through the opening. His suspicions were correct; it was a tavern.

Lanterns hung up on the white walls illuminated a stone floor and wooden beams that ran across the ceiling. A dozen round tables were spread throughout the room in three neat, orderly rows.

Jack went in.

Of course, Leo was standing with his back to the door, perfectly relaxed with his hands folded behind himself. "Finally," he said without looking. "I was starting to think I would have to go out and find you."

Jack had one hand on the door-frame as he shook his head slowly. "No pistol?" he asked. "I would have thought you'd be eager to put a bullet in me."

With a quick about-face, Leo stood before him with feet apart and head held high. "How little you understand me," he scoffed. "I would never attack you with a weapon if you were unarmed."

"Because of your unshakable sense of fair play?"

Leo began a casual stroll around the room, wiping his fin-gertips across one table and then checking for dust. "Because it would prove nothing," he answered. "When I kill you – and I am *going* to kill you, Jack; don't kid yourself – it will be a fair match so that everyone will know I am stronger."

"Well, as long as your motives are pure."

Jack began his own circuit of the room, keeping the bulk of the tables between him and the other man. Three neat rows of four tables each. He wouldn't have expected such precision from an old-fashioned tavern. "What is this place?"

Turning on his heel, Leo faced him and smiled. "A village that the Antaurans have preserved for historical purposes," he answered. "I'm told it's quite the tourist attraction, but today, it's closed."

"I see."

"A good thing too," Leo went on. "I wanted privacy, and I was afraid that I might have to motivate the staff and visitors to vacate the premises."

Squeezing his eyes shut, Jack trembled when he imagined what that might entail. "So, you want everyone to know you beat me in a fair fight," he said. "But you went out of your way to make sure there were no witnesses."

Jack stood between two tables with his hands in his pockets, smiling sheepishly at the floor under his feet. "I don't mean to be a downer, bud," he added. "But I'm sensing a critical flaw in your plan."

In response to that, Leo gestured to a shelf in the corner, and Jack noticed the man's multi-tool sitting upon it. A tiny red light on the metal disk was blinking. "Smile, Jack," he said. "You're being recorded for posterity."

"Just so we're clear, you know you're nuts, right?"

Leo threw his head back and cackled. "I'm going to miss you, Jack." He marched forward into the space between the first two rows. "Have we had enough banter then?"

Jack paced across the room to meet the other man. Fear melted away into an icy calm that made everything crystal clear. However, somewhere beneath that ice, the heat of anger pulsed. It was time to end this.

"You know-" Leo began.

Jack punched him in the face with one fist then the other, a vicious *snap-snap* that should have knocked Leo senseless.

The man only replied with that slimy smile of his. Rage boiling within him, Jack drew back his arm.

He threw another punch.

Leo's hand came up, swatting his wrist, deflecting the blow. The man lashed out with an open palm that smashed into Jack's nose and knocked him off balance. Anyone who lacked a symbiont would be unconscious after a hit like that.

Thrown backward by the force of it, Jack tumbled over the surface of a round table. He flipped upright to land on the other side, then grabbed a wooden chair as he recovered his wits.

Leo jumped over the table.

With a growl, Jack swung the chair upward to strike the other man as he descended, shattering the whole thing on impact. The hit threw Leo off course so that he landed in an aisle between two rows of tables. Blood pounded in Jack's ears as he moved in to finish this fight.

Leo jumped and kicked high.

Jack raised both hands up in front of his face, blocking the man's foot before it did any damage. A quick upward push destroyed his enemy's balance. Leo was turned upside-down.

He landed in a handstand, then flipped upright with a big, mocking smile on his face. "Nice try." Leo threw a hard punch.

Crouching slightly, Jack brought one hand up to intercept the man's wrist. He used the other to jab Leo's chest again and again, driving the wind out of his lungs. One final punch to the face settled things nicely.

Leo staggered.

Grabbing the other man by his shirt, Jack threw him sideways. A disoriented Leo fell hard onto a table, rolled across its surface and dropped out of sight. He popped up on the other side – in the open space between the final row and the tavern's back wall – and twisted gravity around the table.

All of a sudden, the damn thing was barrelling across the stone floor toward Jack, threatening to run him over.

Jack jumped, landed briefly on top of the sliding table, then jumped again and flew through the air like a wild man. Adrenaline made the moment go on for what seemed like hours. Leo was smiling up at him.

The man blurred into a streak of black.

Instantly, Jack constructed a Time Bubble around himself, a thin, vertical tube that stretched from the top of his head to the floor. His feet hit hard. For half a second, he saw a second tube snaking around his own and a blurry Leo moving at normal speed through it. Then the other man's Bending collapsed.

Leo was standing just outside Jack's bubble, frozen in the act of throwing a fierce left-hook. His teeth were bared – even through refracted light, that much was clear – and his distorted face looked inhuman. Jack took a step back, forcing the wall of his bubble to expand. Summer groaned from the strain of it.

The bubble popped.

Leo's punch hit nothing but air, and now the man was over-extended. A swift kick to the stomach made him bend double, and Jack followed that with a second kick to the face. "I don't know if you realize this…"

Leo groaned.

In a heartbeat, the man was standing up straight with blood dripping from his nose, trails of it streaming over his mouth. He charged like a bull, thrusting one arm out to the side as if he meant to knock Jack down.

Twisting out of his path, Jack grabbed the man's extended arm with both hands. He forced Leo down onto his knees with his wrist bent at an awkward angle. "But right now, you're losing-"

They were both thrown upward by some invisible force. Bent Gravity. The shock of it made Jack instinctively let go. Of course, Leo wasn't going to let himself *stay* trapped in the hold.

Jack laced his fingers over the top of his head, grunting when he hit the ceiling. He fell and landed on shaky legs, taking a second to get his bearings. A second was too long.

He looked up in time to witness a black boot striking him right between the eyes. Silver stars filled his vision, and his head rang like a gong that had been pounded several times. Something hit his chest.

Jack went stumbling backward, wheezing from the pain. His butt hit the edge of a table, and he flopped over, lying sprawled out on top of it. When everything finally came back into focus, he saw the wooden beams that went across the ceiling.

Leo came running at him.

Curling up into a ball, Jack somersaulted backward across the table and landed on the other side. He kicked the underside of it with the mildest touch of Bent Gravity. That plus Keeper strength was enough to send the whole thing flying.

It crashed into Leo, who stumbled on impact, wiping his nose with the back of his hand. "You know what I'm gonna do when I kill you, Hunter?"

"Die horribly when Anna comes to avenge me?"

In the corner of his eye, Jack saw something. A wooden leg from the chair he had shattered lying just a few inches away from his foot. Dropping to a crouch, he snatched it up. "You know what I like about you, Leo?" he said. "You know your place."

Jack stood up.

Halfway through his advance, Leo froze and then cocked his head. It was clear the man was wondering exactly what Jack was getting at. "You're a brute!" Jack exclaimed. "Plain and simple."

"It won't work, Hunter."

With a lopsided grin, Jack shook his head. "Oh, come on, buddy," he mocked. "We both know it's true. And hey! There's absolutely nothing wrong with being cannon fodder. *Every* overlord needs cannon fodder."

"You know nothing."

"Cool! I always wanted to be Jon Snow." Jack paused to think about it. "Wait, does this mean we're gonna have hot sex in a cave? 'Cause I'd be down for that."

Leo's face reddened, his lips peeling back, his hair soaked with sweat. "You tried to manipulate me before, remember?" he said. "You told me that they would never give me a symbiont, and look!"

"Yeah, they really wasted that one on you."

Leo hesitated, noticing Jack's weapon for the first time, and he stiffened with rage he could barely contain. "The coward's way, is it?" He drew a knife from his belt, holding it with the blade pointed down. "Very well."

The white-hot anger was still there, but Leo moved slowly, closing the distance step by step. This guy had been in knife fights before. You could tell by the way that he held his weapon, the way it almost seemed like a part of him. It was good to re-member that even before he had a symbiont, this man was win-ning duels in the slums of Rathatla's dirtiest cities. Putting fear out of his mind, Jack tensed up as his enemy drew near.

Leo slashed at his throat.

Jack leaned back, the edge of that blade almost nicking his skin. Growling like a beast. Leo tried to stab him on the back-swing, but Jack brought the chair leg down upon his forearm.

The knife fell to the floor.

Jack bent low, swinging his wooden stick into the side of Leo's knee. That elicited a yelp of pain, and the other man stepped back, hissing from the sting. Drops of spittle flew from his mouth.

Jack swatted Leo's ear, pummelling him with enough force to break the tip off the chair leg. His opponent was dazed, but that would last for only a moment. And this had to end now.

Tossing his weapon up, Jack caught it so that its jagged end was pointed downward, and then he drove it like a stake right through Leo's heart. Stunned by this turn of events, Leo wobbled as he tried to stay on his feet. "You… You don't kill… "

Jack spun and back-kicked, pounding the stake with the sole of his shoe, driving it even deeper into Leo's chest. The other man fell backward, landing face-up on the floor as blood pooled beneath him. Already, his eyes had that glassy look.

Using her talent, Claire watched the battle unfold through the eyes of a commando who was firing his assault rifle at bullet-proof windows on the second and third floor of the complex. She had to do something, but what? She hated the thought of filling people's heads with nightmares. So… Maybe something cute would do the trick.

It took a little effort, but she conjured the illusion of a gigantic teddy bear, one that stood over two-stories tall and waddled towards the shooter with a big smile on its face. Of course, the commando lifted his rifle and fired at the illusion. So, she made it speak. "No!" the teddy shouted in a booming voice. "Bear want to live! Grrrrrrrrrrr!"

She fed the images into the minds of several people.

They retreated across the street, and-

All of a sudden, Claire was yanked out of the illusion and back into her body. She had her hands on the windowsill as she gazed out upon distant skyscrapers that reached for a blue sky with puffy clouds.

"Impressive."

When she turned away from the window, she saw her father standing between her and someone else. Harry had his hands raised defensively, and she could tell that he was ready to use the Overseer weapon.

Claire stepped past him to find a tall, regal woman in red robes in the middle of the hallway, a woman who wore her dark hair in a braid. "You have remarkable skill for one so young."

"Who are you?" Claire demanded.

The woman spread her hands and replied with a warm smile. It might have seemed friendly if not for the hostility that radiated from her. "Who are *you?*" she countered. "By your clothing, I would say you're an Earth girl. An Earth girl with the gift of telepathy. I didn't think such a thing was possible."

Claire stood with her fists clenched, refusing to look up at the woman. "Who I am doesn't matter," she said. "The Complex is under attack. You should help me."

"Oh, I think not."

Fear made Claire tense up, and only some of it was hers. Her father was terrified. She could feel it coming off him in waves. And she knew that she was the reason. Harry wasn't afraid to die, but the thought of *anything* harming his girls tied his guts in knots. For the first time ever, Claire understood what that felt like.

The woman glided through the hallway on high-heeled shoes, and her smile never wavered, not for an instant. "You see, it's not every day that you're confronted with an impossibility," she said. "An Earth girl with the gift of telepathy. I think we shall have to run a few experiments to determine how this happened."

Harry put himself in front of Claire and thrust his hand out toward the woman. The air crackled with static electricity. "Not one more step!" he barked. "You come anywhere near my child, and I'll-"

All of a sudden, Harry fell to his knees, screaming as he raised trembling hands up in front of his face. The telepath woman was grinning. "Do that?" she mocked. "Yes, I'm very frightened. Bravo."

Claire focused.

She could feel something from the woman. A kind of pressure that came in quick pulses, each one washing over Harry like a tidal wave. Or maybe it was more like radio waves. If she could just counter it somehow...

What was it that Sora had taught her about electromagnetic waves? Claire suddenly wished that she had paid more attention in class. When one wave met its opposite, they cancelled each other out.

She released a pulse of her own.

In the blink of an eye, Harry was back on his feet and extending a hand toward the woman. A rippling force-field appeared, covering every inch of the hallway from corner to corner, and then flew off at blinding speed.

The telepath woman screamed as the force-field mowed her down, and when it dissipated, she was lying flat on her back and groaning. Harry didn't waste a second. He strode to the woman and knelt beside her.

Placing a hand over her forehead, he closed his eyes and concentrated. It made Claire nervous. She really hoped that he wouldn't use the N'Jal to kill. Not after everything they had been through.

A moment later, Harry stood up and nodded. "She's asleep," he said. "She'll be out for at least an hour. So, let's go back to the room, and-"

"No," Claire insisted, turning back to the window. "I have work to do."

Flynn stood on the stairwell landing with a knife in each hand, the gleaming blades reflecting the light from nearby bulbs. His soft laughter was almost haunting. "You know they told me about you," he said, starting toward Anna. "They said you were one of the most dangerous opponents I'd ever meet. Gotta say, honey, I'm not impressed."

"Aw," Anna teased. "See, now you've gone and hurt my self-esteem."

Flynn slashed at her chest.

Anna hopped back and felt a whoosh of air as the knife passed. He drew back his other arm and tried to stab her.

Turning her shoulder toward him – stepping out of the way – Anna seized his arm with both hands. She twisted his wrist, forcing his fingers to uncurl, the knife clattering on the floor. A kick to the back of his knee knocked him over.

Flynn landed on his back.

She hoofed him in the short ribs and sent him rolling across the tiles, tumbling down the stairs like a log down a mountain-side. Groaning, he came to a stop on the ninth-floor landing.

Anna squatted near the top step, taking the knife he had lost. "You're vicious," she hissed. "A lot like Leo, actually. But your anger is a pale thing beside his."

Flynn was rising with one hand pressed to his side, his face scrunched up from the pain. "Leo…" he said. "Valeth says he's nothing but a rabid dog. Unfocused rage. I know how to direct mine, and when I kill you, I'll prove it."

"Well then, let's find out."

Anna took off down the stairs.

In a heartbeat, Flynn was running up to meet her, his teeth bared, his cheeks flushed to a deep red. The knife he still carried was clutched in a white-knuckled fist. Hatred and rage. The man could say what he wanted, but he was no less rabid than Leo.

Anna jumped up, planting one foot on the nearby railing, and then pushed off of it. She spun in the air, turning her back on Flynn and striking out with a devastating kick to the face.

Flynn staggered, nearly losing his balance as he retreated down the stairs. He hit the wall next to the door, then bounced off it and flailed about as he tried to regain his wits. It was time to finish this.

Anna joined him on the landing.

The man whirled around on her with a broken nose and blood staining his upper lip. His eyes were wild, frenzied. Giving into the rage, he charged.

Anna jumped, turning belly-up, spreading her legs apart and bringing them together to trap his head between her knees.

Shifting her weight, she forced Flynn down onto his back. Now she was perched on top of him.

She raised the knife, ready to plunge it down.

Her opponent slammed a palm into her chest, and a surge of Bent Gravity sent her flying backward. She hit the metal door, rebounded and fell to her knees. The sharp pain was something she could ignore.

Flynn was suddenly standing over her.

He tried to kick, but Anna raised her hands up in front of her face, catching his foot. A quick twist of his leg flipped the man over, and he landed on his stomach.

Anna stood up.

Her adversary rolled onto his side, and with a lightning-fast motion, he trapped Anna's leg between both of his. Flopping onto his back, he sent Anna lurching toward the stairs. She fell and caught herself with both hands on the fourth step.

Quickly, she got up.

The foggy silhouette of Flynn was rising behind her, brandishing that knife. *Have to move fast.*

Anna jumped, using Bent Gravity to lift herself, and backflipped over his head. She dropped to the floor right behind him. Just like that, the man became a blur, and when he solidified again, he was facing Anna with one hand on her shoulder and the other one thrust toward her belly.

The thought that she should put up a Time Bubble occurred to Anna an instant before she realized that she had a knife sticking out of her gut. Hot blood spilled over her pants. Hot pain made her want to scream. *Oh, Bleakness...*

Flynn's cruel smile returned. "One mistake," he whispered. "One moment when you aren't fast enough..."

He was going to kill her.

Anna knew it.

He was going to-

Flynn's hand tightened on the knife, but just before he pulled it free of her flesh, Anna lashed out with every last drop of strength that Seth had to offer. A typhoon of Bent Gravity hurled the man upward and away from her.

His head hit the underside of the staircase above him, and that seemed to knock him senseless. Flynn somersaulted awkwardly in mid-flight and crashed hard onto the landing between the ninth and tenth floors. Groaning, he tried to get up but dizziness brought him down again.

Anna sank to her knees, clutching the knife sticking out of her belly. The blade did not go too deep. She could tell that much. It was like a hot poker through her middle, but when she imagined it piercing her major organs – or the abdominal aorta – Seth replied with reassuring emotions. The Nassai knew every cell in her body from head to toe, and his calmness made it clear that she wasn't in any danger of bleeding out in the next few minutes. But that didn't mean she was safe.

She couldn't walk. Trying to rise, moving even just an inch, produced a sharp flare of pain, and she was afraid that the attempt had worsened her injuries. Pulling the knife out wasn't an option; that would speed up the bleeding.

So, Anna was stuck here… Stuck in a stairwell with all of her friends seven floors down. None of them knew where she was. The comms were still jammed. She couldn't call them on her multi-tool. Which meant the odds of anyone finding her were low. And sooner or later, she *would* lose too much blood.

With a moan, Flynn stood up and rubbed his aching head.

Oh no…

He groaned from the pain and pulled his hand away to find blood on his palm. "That was not nice," he said. Spinning around to face her, he descended the steps with that cold smile. "Not nice at all."

Shutting her eyes tight, Anna felt tears streaming over her cheeks. *Somebody, help me!* she pleaded in her own mind. *Help me!*

Claire gasped as she wove illusions around one of the men attacking the Complex. She could see through his eyes, feel the concrete beneath his feet, hear the sound of his companions crying out as Antauran soldiers returned fire from the lobby.

Into this man's mind, she projected the image of a giant teddy bear with a red bow tie who lumbered across the street with his arms spread wide for a hug. "It's all right," he said as bullets flew through him. "I still love you."

The man choked up on his assault rifle and fired.

But there was nothing really there.

Her focus was broken when she felt a scream in her mind. Painful anguish nearby. And she knew the source. "Anna!" she panted.

Breaking contact with the man below, Claire stumbled backward from the window with a hand raised to her head. "It's Anna!" she cried. "She's hurt, Dad! She needs us!"

Harry was next to her, staring impotently through the pane with a frown on his face. "Anna…" He glanced toward the stairwell door at the end of the hallway. "I think she can handle herself!"

"She needs us!" Claire screamed.

Before her overprotective father could protest, she was running for the end of the corridor. "Claire, wait!" Harry called out behind her. "The doors are sealed, remember? You couldn't get down there if you wanted to."

Claire rounded on him, her body trembling with frustration. "Then blast it!" she said. "Dad, if you really love me-"

"You don't have to convince me."

Harry strode past her with his hand thrust out toward the door, the N'Jal bonded to his skin. A rippling force-field appeared, rushed down the corridor at blinding speed and ripped the door clean off its hinges, crumpling the metal like a pop can. It was so loud that Claire squeaked in fright.

Flynn was halfway down the stairs – his rictus grin promising endless pain – when a deafening explosion on the floor above made him pause. A slab of smoking metal, red-hot in some places, fell onto the landing between the ninth and tenth floors.

Looking back over his shoulder, Flynn shuddered. "What the hell…" He spared a glance for Anna and then – recognizing that she was helpless – he turned his back on her and went up to face the greater threat.

Gulping air into her lungs, Anna looked up with wide eyes. "What…" She shook her head slowly.

Terror clawed at her; even if Flynn didn't finish her off, she would die eventually without medical attention, but somewhere deep inside, she felt the tiniest flicker of hope. Was it…Was it possible that someone had come to help?

Flynn was almost to the top of the stairs when Claire appeared on the landing. The girl took one look at him, and her face became a mask of hatred. "Get away from her, you bitch!" she screamed.

Flynn laughed. "A child?" He twisted around to sneer at Anna. "A child who quotes Sigourney Weaver? This is your final line of-"

Without warning, Flynn fell on his knees, clutching his head in both hands and howling at the top of his lungs. The flash of pain lasted only a moment, and then he was rising again. "I have a symbiont, girl," he said. "It protects me from your powers."

Claire watched him with strain on her face, trembling with the effort of subduing him. "That's true," she hissed. "But one, your symbiont is one of those broken creatures. It has no loyalty to you. Which means it's not gonna fight nearly as hard as

Anna's would. And two, I don't need to beat you. Just keep you busy! Dad!"

Harry stepped into view, coming down the stairs and placing his hand on Flynn's forehead. This time, Flynn's shriek was truly blood-curdling. He thrashed in Harry's grip, his arms flying this way and that as if he had lost control of his body.

Bit by bit and inch by inch, Harry forced Flynn down onto his knees, and when he finally let go, Flynn toppled over, unconscious. At least, Anna hoped he was unconscious. As grateful as she was for the rescue, she did not like the thought of Harry using the N'Jal to kill.

Harry wasted no time on the other man. He scrambled down the stairs with Claire at his heels and dropped to a crouch next to Anna. His face was stone as he examined her wounds. "We need to get you to a hospital."

"Can't call for help," Anna panted.

"You can't," Claire said. "But *I* can."

The girl shut her eyes, and after only a moment, she nodded curtly as if the matter were settled. "A trauma team is on its way up," she said. "There are a few in the building, dealing with the wounded. You'll be okay."

"We're still surrounded," Anna gasped. "Can't get out."

Once again, Claire shut her eyes, and this time, she exhaled. "The bad guys are leaving," she mumbled. "I think...I think we scared them off. It's gonna be okay, Anna. We're gonna get you help."

Anna forced herself to smile. Everything was going to be all right. They would get her to a hospital. Accelerated healing would see her back on her feet in only a few days. Everything was going to be just fine. Her moment of relief ended when Claire gasped. The girl stood up with wide eyes and shouted, "The president!"

The conference room they had been using to hear his testimony was now lit only by sunlight that came through the three rectangular windows along one wall. Each one left a band of light along the narrow table that was now occupied by several people.

One was the Antauran President, a portly, balding fellow with pink cheeks and a creased brow. He looked up every now and then, but the fear in his dark-brown eyes was unmistakable, and he seemed to know. That was why he kept staring into his lap.

Another seated man was a spindly little guy with thinning black hair and a thick pair of glasses. The president's chief of staff, or something along those lines. His actual title was irrelevant.

In addition to them, three ambassadors – one from Earth, one from Leyria and one from this benighted little planet – filled chairs and sat with their backs to the windows. Nervously, they exchanged glances.

Corovin stood in the corner with his wrists cuffed together, and like the president, he kept his eyes downcast. No one had asked him a question in at least fifteen minutes. Not since the sirens had started wailing.

They had brought him here to testify, to share everything he knew of the Admiralty Board's plans for this half of the galaxy. He had been in and out of rooms like this since the moment that they woke him at some ungodly hour and drove him over here. He had spoken to at least twenty ambassadors from three different worlds on a variety of topics. And now, the president himself had come to hear Corovin's testimony first hand.

Security officers in heavy armour – both men and women – stood against the wall between the two doors that led out to the hallway. Each one carried a rifle, and there were more guards outside, keeping watch in case the invaders made it to this floor. But they were only the first line of defense.

Two telepaths – one in blue robes, the other in white – stood behind the president's chair with stoic expressions. Whatever they were doing, it must have required a great deal of concentration.

Corovin shut his eyes, breathing deeply.

"Are your people behind this, Ragnosian?"

With extreme reluctance, Corovin looked up to lock eyes with the speaker. It was the president's chief of staff who had voiced that question, and the miserable little man looked like he wanted to climb over the table and strangle Corovin. "I wouldn't know," Corovin answered. "I wasn't briefed on this attack."

Swivelling in his chair, the president gave his aid a sympathetic look. "It's going to be all right," he assured the other man. "The Complex is heavily fortified. They won't get anywhere near us." He kept repeating that last bit like a catechism.

"Someone's coming!" one of the telepaths shouted.

There were sounds of struggle in the hallway outside: the thump of bodies hitting a wall, the buzz of Antauran weapons firing. Muffled voices barked orders at one another, but Corovin could not make out the words.

The white-robed telepath fell back against the wall with sweat drenching his face. "I can't pierce his defenses!" His words came out as a squeak. "May the gods above have mercy on us!"

More thumping, more buzzing, more shouts of terror.

The guards who had remained inside this room as a last line of defense leaped into action without having to be told what to do. The five of them split apart, three going out one door, two going out the other. Once they were gone, the shouts intensified. It went on for maybe a minute or so. Corovin couldn't say.

He frowned down at his own shoes and tried to ignore the sweat that had drenched his dark-red hair. "Maybe we should leave." No one in this room wanted to listen to his suggestions, but what did that matter? "If they get through…"

No sooner did he finish his thought than one of the doors banged open, admitting two men in black robes with silver embroidery. They were both telepaths, but aside from their identical clothing, they may as well have been night and day. One was tall, the other short. One was dark, the other pale.

And they turned their attention on the pair that were guarding the president. Those two cried out in pain, sinking to their knees.

The telepaths were followed by a man in a red coat that was almost as ostentatious as their robes. A tall man with long black hair and tilted eyes that seemed to pry into your very soul. "Release the assassin."

Corovin backed up against the wall.

His mouth dropped open, and he shook his head slowly. "Look, I don't want any part of whatever you're-"

The pale-skinned telepath came over and used a key that he must have retrieved from one of the armoured guards to remove Corovin's handcuffs. When they were gone, Corovin rubbed his wrists. Having restraints on for any length of time was always quite uncomfortable. He wanted nothing more than to find a way back to his side of the galaxy. Everyone on this side of the Core was insane.

"Do you know who I am, assassin?"

Corovin spun to face the stranger with arms folded and tried his very best to project confidence. "I don't care who you are," he spat. "This isn't my fight!"

He was about to add that he had no interest in the outcome when the president got out of his chair and sneered. "So, Agent Hunter was correct," he said. "I recognize you, Slade. If you think you're going to sabotage this treaty, you're sadly mistaken."

"Sabotage it?" Slade purred. "Mr. President, I'm counting on it."

"Listen," Corovin said. "I only want-"

Slade didn't let him finish that sentence. The man strode forward with a smile that never touched his eyes and tossed the pistol he had been carrying. Corovin caught it by instinct. "Kill Salmaro," Slade ordered.

"Who?"

"The president."

Corovin felt the blood draining out of his face. Drawing in a shuddering breath, he backed up until he was practically wedged into the corner. "This isn't my fight," he said. "I'm not killing anyone, least of all-"

"You have two choices," Slade cut in. "Kill Salmaro and come away with me to freedom, or you can die here and now." One look into the man's eyes left no doubt that he meant every word.

Corovin shivered.

What else could he do?

Striding out of the corner, Corovin lifted his pistol and pointed it directly at the president's head. The portly man backed away, nearly tripping over his chair. "Please," he whimpered. "Don't."

"Oh, and Corovin," Slade called out.

A quick glance in his direction revealed that the man was holding a metal disk in his upturned palm, a disk with a blinking red light. "Make it look good for the camera," Slade murmured. "We won't be able to do a second take."

Chapter 28

Leo was flat on his back, and his skin was turning gray. Glazed eyes stared up at the ceiling. The puddle of blood expanded beneath him. Jack wondered if he should be feeling guilty. There was a bit of it – and he was grateful for that much – but all he really felt was resignation.

Wincing at the thought of what he had done, Jack let out a shuddering breath. "For what it's worth," he whispered, squatting next to the other man. "I really didn't want to do this...But you were just gonna keep coming."

"Indeed he was."

Jack stood up and whirled around to face the front entrance, sweat matting dark bangs to his forehead. "I was wondering where you were," he said. "Come to finish me off now that he's softened me up?"

He was very much aware of the tingle in his skin, the very light throb behind his eyes. So far, he had managed to use his powers sparingly, but a fight with *two* of Slade's lieutenants...well, the odds weren't looking good for him.

A woman in a red dress stepped out of the shadows, her face hidden under a hood. "Do you really think so little of me?" she asked. "I am not without honour, Jack Hunter. I thought our last encounter would have proved as much to you."

"It...made me wonder."

The last time he had seen Isara, she had defied Slade by refusing to kill him. She said that she would not come to Jack under a flag of truce and then turn on him when he refused to ally himself with her.

Taking hold of the hood in gloved fingers, Isara pulled it back to reveal Jena's face. Except now her hair was longer and tied up in a simple ponytail. Her mouth tightened at the sight of Leo's body.

"Will they bring him back?"

The question startled her.

Sitting on the edge of a table with arms folded, Jack sighed as he stared into his lap. "The Overseers," he clarified. "Will they bring him back?"

A small smile – one that barely showed Isara's teeth – made a shiver run down his spine. "You're very clever, Jack," she murmured, gliding between the tables to stand over Leo's body. "No, you needn't fear his return."

"Why not?"

Isara looked at him.

Jack held her gaze for a very long while and arched one eyebrow to drive his point home. "They brought Slade back," he grated. "So, why not do the same for all their little minions?"

"The Inzari cannot restore anyone to life," Isara began. "They must be present at the moment of death to do that, and there are no Inzari here."

He looked around the empty tavern and saw nothing but wooden tables – some of which were lying on their sides – and a bar with liquor bottles on the shelves behind it. The old-timey lanterns on the ceiling gave off a soft orange light. "Would I even know it if one was here? I mean, they have a ship in orbit, and none of the sensor nets can detect it. They could be watching us right now."

"I suppose you will have to take my word for it."

"Swell."

Isara stood with fists on her hips, nudging the body with one foot. "You impressed me tonight," she said at last. "I didn't think you had it in you."

"Go to hell."

The woman turned her head to study him with dark, penetrating eyes, but she said nothing in response to that. Despite himself, Jack began to shift uncomfortably under her scrutiny. It was the exact same look that Jena gave you when you screwed up. "Let go of your guilt, Jack," she said. "What you did was necessary."

"I don't have to like it."

"Not just necessary," Isara went on as if he had not spoken. "It was smart. You may not believe this, but I opposed Slade when he brought Leo to Earth to terrorize your city. And I did so again when he opted to give Leo a symbiont. Such power does not belong in the hands of a rabid dog."

Closing his eyes as he drew in a breath, Jack nodded slowly. "On that much, we can agree." The exhaustion in his voice surprised him. It was a weariness that went bone-deep and claimed more than his body.

"We have more in common than you realize."

"Such as?"

"A hatred of Grecken Slade, for one thing."

Jack stood up with a grunt, shuffling over to the wall. He turned around and leaned against it. "The enemy of my enemy," he muttered. "That has to be the oldest negotiation tactic in the book."

"And the most effective," Isara countered. "As your newly-minted alliance with the Antaurans demonstrates."

"So you want me to join Team Overseer? Is that it?"

Isara lifted her skirts, stepping over a river of blood that extended from the puddle, and flowed toward him with an almost sensual grace. "I could remind you that the Inzari need a man of your talents," she said. "But such overtures have failed before. I have no illusions about swaying you over to my side, Jack. You have made your loyalties clear."

"So…"

"A truce," Isara said. "Nothing more and nothing less. One day, you and I will face each other in battle, but until then, we stay out of each other's way. And when the time is right, we kill Slade together."

Jack smiled, shaking his head. "Two small problems with that plan," he said. "One, the Overseers will just bring him back."

Standing just a few feet away, almost pinning him against the wall, Isara looked up at the ceiling and rolled her eyes. "As I have already explained," she huffed, "there are ways to prevent them from doing so. And your second objection?"

"Killing Slade would put you in charge."

Her musical laughter startled Jack. It was a sound completely incongruent with that face. With Jena, you would sometimes get a rich belly laugh, but not…this. "Compared to Slade," Isara said. "I am a benign despot."

In one fluid motion, she turned away from him and glided across the floor, passing between two tables that were still standing. "Think on it, Jack," she said, looking back over her shoulder. "I have reactivated the SlipGate. I think it's time that you returned to your friends."

Melissa woke up slowly, consciousness coming one drop at a time until she was aware enough to know that something wasn't right. The first thing she noticed was Ilia's fear. Her symbiont was almost frantic with terror, and that was why Melissa remained still, feigning unconsciousness.

Spatial awareness painted a colourless image of her surroundings. She was tied to a chair in a cramped little room with walls of polished duroplastic. A single open door led to a hallway, and she could make out the silhouettes of people there.

One was Tesa.

Melissa fingered the handcuff that linked her wrists. It was easy enough to caress the metal with one finger. All she had to do was craft a Bending, splitting one of the links down the middle. She was about to try when something got her attention.

At the end of the hallway, a door that seemed to lead outside swung open, and a wispy silhouette stepped into the building. Melissa wanted so badly to use her eyes. As it was, she could only tell that the newcomer was a tall man with broad shoulders.

Stepping in front of him, Tesa raised both hands in a forestalling gesture. "Please," just listen to me," she whispered. "We had to capture her. It was the only way to find out what she knows."

"And so, you risked our operations by bringing her here."

Tesa backed up through the hallway, stopping only a few feet away from the door to Melissa's room. "I thought he would want to know."

The man chuckled softly and then spoke in a rich, Denabrian accent. "*He* has much better things to do. Babysitting a gaggle of incompetent school children is not one of *his* priorities. If not for the potential fallout of this little debacle, *I* would not be here."

"Do...Do you want us to kill her?"

The man slapped Tesa hard enough to send her tumbling sideways into the corridor wall. "Idiot child," he spat. "*That* is Melissa Carlson. I trust you follow the news closely enough to recognize the name."

Tesa nodded.

"Melissa Carlson's sudden disappearance would provoke no small amount of media attention. The girl is quite popular among people who still believe in the Justice Keepers, and media attention is not something we need right now."

Tesa was rubbing her sore cheek and trembling as if she expected another blow. It almost made Melissa want to leap to her defense. Almost but not quite. "So," Tesa began. "What do we do with her?"

"That depends. How much does she know?"

"She knows that we're organized, that we meet twice a week," Tesa answered. "She knows that we attacked her and knocked her out."

The man hunched over, covering his face with one hand and sighing. "You really are quite useless." He looked up, and Tesa stepped back from the intensity of his glare. "What does she know about your connection to us?"

"Nothing!"

"You are certain?"

"She's been sedated since we brought her here."

Exhaling noisily, the man turned his back on Tesa and trailed his fingers along the wall as he paced to the front door. "In other words," he said, "She knows that a group of radicalized youth attacked a Justice Keeper. A minor crime, unworthy of scrutiny from any of the major intelligence agencies."

"I…I guess."

The man paused, turning slightly to look over his shoulder. "Keep her sedated," he said. "Deliver her anonymously to a local hospital and let them deal with her. Make *sure* that you have left town by the time she wakes up. I will arrange transport off-world."

"Off world?" Tesa stammered. "But…But…"

"Yes, off world," the stranger insisted. "Your little group of misfits assaulted a Justice Keeper. When Ms. Carlson reports back to her superiors, your faces will be on every screen in every public building. This planet is not safe for you anymore. I will not risk any of you ending up in an interrogation room."

"Where will we go?" Tesa whimpered.

That question elicited more quiet laughter from the man. "Alios, I think," he said. "Our idiot leaders have given away an enormous amount of territory to secure this new treaty with Antaur. The Colonists will be most displeased by that. Fertile ground for the movement, wouldn't you say?"

The man was gone a moment later, and Tesa was coming down the hallway toward Melissa's room. Frantically, Melissa tried to decide what to do. She could get free of the handcuffs with very little effort, but she still felt weak from the sedative. Even so, there was a decent chance that she could fight her way out of here.

But...

She had just learned that Tesa and the others had support from some very powerful people. There was no telling what she might find when she went out that door. And once they discovered that she had overheard the entire conversation, they would kill her.

On the other hand, if she let Tesa sedate her, there was no guarantee that the other woman would actually follow orders and deliver Melissa to a hospital. What would Gabi do? Melissa made her decision in a split second.

She kept still as Tesa took her arm and plunged another needle into it. Once again, the darkness came, and the last thing Melissa felt as consciousness drifted away was Ilia's concern.

Waking up was a little easier this time; her eyes opened to reveal a blurry image of beige and gray, an image that solidified into the ceiling of a hospital room. A fair-skinned woman with curly, black hair leaned over the bed and smiled. "She's awake." Her voice seemed to be coming from somewhere far away.

Melissa sat up, groaning as dizziness washed over her, and touched her fingertips to her forehead. "Where am I?" Goodness, her voice sounded awful. Like the low croak of a frog. "How long have I been out?"

It was pretty much what one would expect from a hospital room: walls of a gentle, pastel green, an open door that looked out on a hallway where doctors in white lab coats walked past, a wooden table in the corner that supported a vase of fresh flowers. Except, this was Leyria. Which meant that there were screens of SmartGlass on the wall and over her bed. Some of them depicted her vitals.

"Take it easy, honey," the nurse said.

Pressing a palm to her forehead, Melissa tried to massage the fog out of her brain. "I have to get to a comm unit," she whispered. "Call Larani Tal. I need to speak with her right away!"

The nurse backed away with both hands raised defensively, and her frown made it clear that Melissa wouldn't be going anywhere anytime soon. "Whoa, whoa!" she cut in. "We found you with enough Ladrazine in your system to put down a horse. If not for that symbiont of yours, you might be dead."

"Where am I?"

"Marcus Vriol Memorial Hospital."

Melissa looked out the window and saw not the skyscrapers of Denabria but rather snow-capped mountains under a deep blue sky. A forest of skeletal trees stood between her and those distant peaks, and some had snow on their branches. "What city?"

"You're in Silver Falls," the nurse said, gesturing to the window. "Just under four hundred kilometres north-east of Denabria."

"I have to talk to Larani."

The nurse let her arm drop, shut her eyes and shook her head. "We'll call her right now if you want to," she said. "It's clear you're not gonna get a moment's rest until you say what you need to say."

"My multi-tool?"

"You didn't have one on you when they dropped you off."

Squeezing her eyes shut, Melissa stiffened. "Of course not," she said. "They would not have let me keep it."

Five minutes later, the nurse brought her a tablet with Larani's face on the screen. The Chief Director of the Justice Keepers looked rather displeased as she peered into the camera. "Cadet Carlson," she said. "Where have you been."

Melissa told the entire story, all of it from start to finish, including everything that she had learned. The expression on Larani's face darkened with every detail that Melissa shared. "I see," the other woman said at last. "Remain in Silver Falls until the doctors discharge you. Then return to Denabria as soon as possible. We have a lot to discuss."

Melissa cringed.

She was not looking forward to *that* conversation.

Chapter 29

Jack read from a SmartGlass tablet.

"Drawing fletchings to cheek," he began, "Seth narrowed his eyes. The purple moon was high above the forest, shining bright with magic. He loosed. The arrow flew true over Gant's armies, struck the heart tree and exploded with a wave of purple magic that washed over the soldiers."

He lowered the tablet.

A few feet away, Anna was lying on her hospital bed, but now she had a smile on her beautiful face. "Don't stop now," she murmured. "You were just getting to the good parts."

"Oh, thank god!"

Jack got up, striding over to her bed and grabbing the metal bar that ran alongside it. He leaned over to kiss her softly on the forehead. "I was so worried," he breathed. "I'm sorry I wasn't here to help…"

Anna's hand came up to touch his cheek. Her smile made all his worries drift away. "You're always with me, Jack," she whispered. "Always."

She tried to sit up, but a sudden flash of pain made her scowl and fall back against the mattress. "Okay," she croaked. "Not a good idea. How long have I been out? Did they save the president?"

Jack felt the blood draining out of his face. His eyes dropped shut as he drew in a breath. "No," he whispered. "Slade was there, Anna. He…He freed Corovin, and Corovin killed the president."

"Bleakness take me."

They were interrupted when a doctor in blue came in to stand over Anna's bed, a tall man with dark brown skin and thick curly hair. He shook his head. "Well, Operative Lenai," he said. "I have to say I'm impressed. I've heard stories about Justice Keepers, but…You've healed as much in a day as most people do in a month!"

Grinning, Jack let his head drop and chuckled. "That's my Anna," he said. "When death crooks his bony finger, she sticks her tongue out. And then she punches him just to drive the point home."

Anna gave his hand a squeeze.

The doctor frowned thoughtfully, then nodded once as if the matter were settled. "Just the same," he began. "I'd recommend staying off your feet for a week."

Despite his best efforts, Jack felt another grin coming on, and he bent over to kiss her forehead. "Which means I get to take care of you," he whispered. "Read to you, make all your favourite dishes…Or, well…*bring* you your favourite dishes. I don't think they'll let me into the kitchen at the Complex or on the ship for-"

Pulling his hand to her lips, Anna kissed it, and when he looked at her, she smiled that impish smile of hers. "You'll be wonderful, sweetie."

The scuff of footsteps announced Beran Lenai, who strode into the room in a blue coat and high-collared shirt. His graying hair was parted in the middle. "She's awake," he exclaimed. "I've been worried sick."

"I'm okay, Dad."

"Thank the Companion," Beran mumbled. "I would like some time alone with my daughter, if that's all right."

Jack was more than happy to grant that request. He knew how he would feel if it were Lauren in a hospital bed. Or his mother. He decided that he would take a walk and visit the cafeteria, maybe grab a muffin or something.

The others left Anna alone with her father.

Beran stood at the foot of her bed with his hands folded over his stomach, frowning anxiously as he took in the sight of her. "You know," he said at last. "This was why your mother and I never wanted you to become a Justice Keeper."

Anna shut her eyes, falling back against the pillow, and tried to ignore the burning in her abdomen. "It's my life, Dad," she rasped. "If I die in the line of duty, hopefully, that means I will have saved someone else."

Her father turned away, standing with his arms folded and peering out the window. "Stubborn as ever," he muttered, but Anna didn't think she was supposed to hear that. His expression softened after a moment of contemplation. "Just the same, I am proud of what you have accomplished."

"Thank you."

"The treaty has been ratified."

Crossing her arms over her chest, Anna glowered at the ceiling. "Well, at least we have that much," she said. "Maybe it was all worth it."

Beran sat down in the chair at her bedside, sighing as he shook his head. "What was that delightful Earth idiom?" he asked. "Something about frying pans and fires. I fear we may have ended one conflict only to begin a larger one."

It took her a moment to put the pieces together. Corovin Dagmath had assassinated President Salmaro. A Ragnosian man had killed the Antauran head of state, and the fact that Jack knew about it meant that it was probably common knowledge. "They're already saber-rattling, aren't they?"

"It's on every news station," Beran grumbled. "Politicians debating whether this constitutes an act of war. And we're allies now. If Antaur goes to war with Ragnos…"

"We go too."

"Still glad you came to the summit?"

With a grin, Anna turned her head so that her cheek was pressed into the pillow. "More than ever," she said. "We have to at least *try* for peace."

"You should have been a diplomat."

"Well, I *did* learn from the best."

They chatted for a little while longer, mostly small-talk, and then Beran said that he would check in on her again in a few hours. He had to pack for the flight back to Leyria. She was only alone for about ten minutes before Jack came back with a muffin made with some type of berries that only grew here on Antaur.

She asked him what had happened after Leo took him through the SlipGate, and he told her everything: the fight with Leo, killing the other man, Isara's sudden appearance and her strange offer.

"Rough," Anna said. "So, what do you think?"

Jack was in the chair now, hunched over and smiling into his lap. "I think that we should put off that decision for the time being." He looked up at her with his sharp blue eyes. "And whatever we decide, we'll do it together."

The crimson sun was hanging above the western horizon, dipping behind the tallest buildings of Denabria. For once, the perpetual cloud cover that came with the onset of winter had relented, and Larani could not be more thankful for that. A cold wind came in off the ocean, but even with the chill, she chose to remain outside.

In a thick black coat with flowers on the lapels, Larani stood on the roof of Justice Keeper HQ, her long, black hair tied back.

The glass of sparkling water that she clutched in one hand made a pleasant fizzing sound.

She took a sip.

Spatial awareness painted the rooftop behind her as a foggy silhouette, but Larani could still make out every detail; so, it surprised her when the stairwell door popped open and Gabrina Valtez stepped out in a belted trench coat.

Pretty and plump, the other woman also wore her hair tied back in a long ponytail, and she stiffened when the cold wind hit her face. "Director Tal," she said formally. "Do you often come here for stress relief?"

"And solitude."

Some people might have been put off by that – Larani didn't precisely mean it as a curt dismissal, but she couldn't find it within herself to be warm and inviting either – but not Gabrina. Perhaps a background in intelligence had taught the woman persistence. "I have never much cared for cold weather," Gabi said.

She joined Larani at the railing, gripping the metal bar in both hands and gazing at the distant ocean. "Don't be too hard on Melissa," she added. "The girl has the heart of a Justice Keeper. When someone calls for help, she answers."

"I have no intention of reprimanding Melissa."

"Oh?"

Bringing the glass to her lips, Larani closed her eyes and took another sip of water. "If I reprimanded every Justice Keeper who made a stupid decision in the service of their moral code," she began, "there wouldn't be a single one of us without at least three. We're not a military, Ms. Valtez."

Larani turned around, leaning back against the railing, looking up at the darkening sky. "We have the trappings of one," she said. "Rank, formality. But I honestly believe that the Nassai choose hosts who are willing to disobey an order that they know is wrong and suffer the consequences."

"Noble," Gabi said. "Though it must make managing them difficult."

"Like herding cats."

Gabi folded her arms on the railing, nodding as she considered that. "A difficult job indeed," she said. "But you do it well."

"Thank you."

Several moments of silence passed before Gabi looked up and the wind blew one strand of her dark hair out of place. "I've noticed you hold yourself apart," she said. "You rarely spend time with your colleagues."

"As I said, I prefer solitude."

"Too much solitude can leave you cut off," Gabi countered. "With whom do you share your struggles, Larani Tal?"

Now, how was she supposed to answer *that* question? And why was this woman prying into her personal affairs... And why was she not irritated by the intrusion? "It's been years since I've pursued a relationship."

"And why is that?"

Larani downed the rest of her water in one gulp. "Few people want to date Justice Keepers," she answered. "The danger that we're constantly exposed to... Most people can't handle the fear that we might not come home. Some Keepers bond with each other, but that is no longer an option for me."

"Because you're in charge now."

"It would be a conflict of interest."

Gabi drummed her fingers on the railing, and her dark eyes had that vacant look that people sometimes got when they were thinking long and hard about something. "So, what about me?"

"You?"

It had been so long since Larani had let herself think about romance; she had never really considered it, but looking at this gorgeous woman standing beside her, she had to admit that she was tempted. "You're... interested in me."

"What can I say?" Gabrina mumbled. "I've always had a weak spot for sophisticated women who know what they want."

"I…I don't know if I can do a long-term relationship. As I said, my job puts me in any number of dangerous situations."

Gabrina's shy smile made her heart flutter. Damn it! Larani Tal was forty-two years old; she was supposed to be past the phase of her life where she fell to pieces every time a beautiful woman flirted with her. "I'm not asking for a long-term relationship," Gabi said. Gently, she put one hand on Larani's arm. "I'm asking if – today, right now – you would like to have one night where you can forget about your worries and just be happy."

"Yes," Larani whispered. "I think I would."

She practically melted when Gabrina stood on her toes and kissed her.

Keli lifted a cone-shaped glass filled with clear red liquid. *Thrinakora.* What little she recalled from her childhood on Antaur said that it was a very potent beverage. She paused for a moment to consider before drinking.

The dulcet tones of a *lorel* came over the speaker. Normally, that would be too quiet to hear, but the lounge on the second floor of the Diplomatic Complex was almost empty in the middle of the afternoon.

In beige pants and a sleeveless blue shirt, Keli sat at the bar with a drink in hand, waiting…pondering. Her father had liked *thrinakora.* She remembered that much. Did she want to try it herself? Could telepaths get drunk the way ordinary humans could? She had never learned during her years of captivity, and constant wariness of everyone around her had dulled the urge to experiment.

A hologram appeared behind the counter, flickering several times before resolving into a pale-skinned man with bushy eyebrows and thick dark hair. "Is something wrong with your drink, madam?"

"Nothing at all."

"You have not tried it."

Keli lifted the glass to her lips and took a sip. *Thrinakora* had a bite to it, one that set her tongue on fire and scorched her throat. An interesting experience. Though it was as far as she was willing to go today.

The hologram watched her impassively, flickering several more times before he finally vanished. Those damn things unnerved her. They looked real; they sounded real, but there was no presence…No spark of consciousness.

So very unlike the man who came up behind her.

"Hello, Rajel," she said.

"I thought it was Keepers who had eyes in the backs of their heads."

Drumming her fingers on the countertop, Keli sighed softly. "Did you know," she began, "that I could sense Anna's presence while she was in orbit of the moon where they held me prisoner? It astounds me that you Justice Keepers are so impressed by your so-called spatial awareness."

Rajel stepped up beside her with hands in the back pockets of his pants, nodding in response to that. "And yet," he countered. "You couldn't track her now."

"Not in a city of three million," Keli admitted. "But I would assume that she is still safe in her hospital room."

Without invitation – not that he needed one – Rajel sat down on the stool beside her and folded his hands on the bar. "So," he said after a moment. "A lot has changed."

"Indeed it has."

Earlier this morning, the terms of the treaty – officially dubbed the Earth-Leyria-Antaur Accord – had been announced to the public. The media was abuzz with talk. Keli had come here to get some relief from the many shifting thoughts and emotions that she felt everywhere she went. She had spent most of the day seeking out empty rooms and quiet places. And when that had done little good, she had considered finding relief in alcohol.

Over the course of a hundred years, the Leyrians had discovered three habitable worlds on what would eventually become the Fringe between their territory and Antauran Space: Alios, Belos and Palissa. Of the three, Belos was the least populated, and now the Leyrians had decided to relinquish their claim on the planet in exchange for mutual defense and peace along the border.

"What do you think of it all?" Rajel muttered.

Keli lifted her glass, pausing for a moment to admire the swirling red liquid, and then took another sip. No, a gulp. "There will be consequences," she replied at last. "The only question is whether these will be worse than the alternative."

Anger crackled in the air like lightning, so intense it astonished her that none of the others could feel it. Anger and guilt from the security staff who felt that they had failed in their duty. Anger and fear in politicians who visited the building.

The death of Antaur's president at the hands of a Ragnosian had started ripples that were spreading across the entire planet. You didn't have to be a telepath to know that many people were calling for war. There were discussion panels on every news network. And now that Earth and Leyria had agreed to support Antaur in any military conflict, there was every possibility that this side of the galaxy might erupt in a firestorm.

Just as Slade wanted...

The thought made her shiver.

Rajel was leaning over the counter with arms folded on it, sighing softly. "More of our people will be joining the Justice Keepers," he said. "We will have offices on every Antauran world now. I've considered requesting a transfer."

Keli arched an eyebrow.

His cheeks coloured, and then he pressed a closed fist to his mouth, clearing his throat. "These new cadets will need someone to train them," Rajel went on. "A blind man might be just the thing to disabuse them of their prejudice."

"If that is your intention, I wish you well in it."

"You... You could come with me."

Keli was taken aback. What would compel him to make such an offer? As always, the Nassai shrouded Rajel's thoughts in an impenetrable fog. She could push through it with a great deal of effort, but that would be painful for all three of them.

However, Keli was reasonably certain that she didn't need her talent to intuit Rajel's thought process. "There was a time when I considered coming back here," she said. "But seeing Antaur with my own eyes has demonstrated to me that this world is not my home any more than Leyria is."

Keli stood up, resting a hand on his shoulder. Rajel turned an ear toward her, which for him was the equivalent of staring directly into her eyes. "I have grown to care for you a great deal," she said. "But Rajel, I have no interest in sex or in romance or any of it."

"Because of what your captors did to you?"

"What?" Keli spluttered. "Of course not! This is not a consequence of trauma. It is simply a facet of who I am."

Rajel nodded.

Keli smiled sadly. "Be well," she said, squeezing his shoulder. And then she left him to sort through his feelings. It seemed to her that there were people lurking in every last corner of this building – people that she would rather avoid – but Rajel needed the privacy of an empty lounge more than she did.

In the beige-walled hallway outside, Harry Carlson's youngest daughter stood with her fists on her hips, blocking Keli's path. "Claire," the child said in a reedy voice. "You will go to the Dagobah System! There you will learn from Yoda, the Jedi Master who instructed me."

"What *are* you talking about, girl?"

"I need a teacher," Claire said. "Someone to show me the ways of the Force."

Keli blinked.

A moment later, the girl's meaning became clear. "You wish to learn how to master your talent," Keli said. "And you want me to teach you."

Claire's response was a cheeky grin that promised all sorts of mischief. "Well…Can you think of anyone better?" She took Keli's hand and practically dragged her through the hallway, toward the elevators. "Come on! My bags are packed, and we have a few hours before we have to board the starship. What an excellent time for a first lesson."

Lying flat on her belly with her face buried in folded arms, Larani sighed as Gabi's soft hands massaged her back. The soft mattress beneath her felt wonderful but not as wonderful as the other woman's caress. Maybe Gabrina was right. Just how long had it been since the last time she had been intimate with another human being? Since before she had taken over for Slade. Eighteen bloody months in which Larani had done nothing but try to undo the damage inflicted by her treacherous predecessor. She needed a break.

Gabrina trailed soft kisses over the length of Larani's spine. "So tense." She flung Larani's hair aside to continue all the way to the nape of her neck. "You keep carrying that weight, and eventually you're going to collapse."

"I don't get a lot of choice," Larani whispered.

"Nonsense."

The other woman's skilled fingers were kneading her shoulders, and Larani almost felt as though she could fall asleep right there. Her bedroom was warm and the lamps had been dimmed to a soft golden glow. "You know," Larani murmured. "Most people think I'm cold, aloof."

Gabrina flipped her onto her back, and before Larani could say one word, the other woman's lips were melding with her own. It was a passionate kiss, full of heat. Larani couldn't help herself. She grabbed a fistful of the other woman's hair.

Gabi moaned her approval.

And then Larani was kissing her neck. She lost herself in the moment, marvelling at the softness of Gabi's skin, the warmth of her body. The sleepiness she had felt just a few minutes earlier was gone, consumed in the fire of raw, physical need.

She threw Gabi onto her back, trailing a hand over the woman's soft, smooth belly. Thought was a distant thing. All the while, they never broke their kiss. Dimly, Larani was aware of her Nassai's contentment, a faint echo of her own happiness, but other than that, thought was a distant thing.

Which was why she barely noticed when her multi-tool started beeping.

Larani pulled back, strands of dark hair falling over her face. "Bleakness take me," she panted. "Not now."

"Leave it," Gabi whispered.

"I can't."

With a sigh, the other woman pulled the blankets over herself and rolled her eyes. "Very well," she said. "Attend to your emergency. Maybe if I go out of my mind with lust, it will be that much more satisfying when you finally come back."

Snatching the multi-tool off her nightstand, Larani answered the message, which activated the screen of SmartGlass across from the foot of her bed. A news anchor behind his desk was leaning forward and staring intently into the camera. "It's confirmed now," he said. "Challenger Jeral Dusep now has a five percentage point lead over incumbent Sarona Vason. The councillor's popularity has surged as news that Vason's administration has ceded the Belos colony to Antaur as a concession during treaty negotiations."

"Damn it," Larani whispered.

She was grateful when she felt Gabi massaging her shoulders and pressing tender kisses to her back. The other woman really *did* want her to relax. But all she could think about was the news.

"For the very first time since declaring his candidacy last spring," the anchorman continued, "Jeral Dusep is leading in the polls. The councillor's policy of putting Leyria first – a philosophy that once only found traction with various fringe groups – is now gaining popularity as many Leyrian citizens feel that their government is not prioritizing their concerns."

"Off!" Gabi shouted.

The broadcast winked out, leaving only a transparent screen of glass on the cream-coloured wall. "Why did you do that?" Larani demanded.

Gabrina touched her cheek and turned her face so that they gazed into one another's eyes. Then she leaned in to kiss Larani's lips. "Because," she purred. "Fretting about the election can wait until tomorrow."

She pushed Larani down onto her back and began nibbling her collarbone. "Right now," Gabi whispered. "You're going to finish what you started."

Chapter 30

Jack woke up when Anna squeezed him tight.

She was snuggled up with an arm around his belly, her head resting on his chest, nestled under his chin. It was still the dead of night, and their room aboard the Silver Star was lit only by simulated moonlight from a window that looked out on the garden. Still, he felt refreshed from a deep, restful sleep. "Sorry," Anna whispered, "I didn't mean to wake you."

Closing his eyes, Jack kissed her forehead. "You don't ever have to apologize for that." His fingertips glided over her back; her skin was so soft. "You can wake me up for cuddles any time you need to."

"I was feeling vulnerable."

Jack felt a lazy smile come on, one that he didn't even try to hide, and he chuckled. "Not an easy thing to deal with," he murmured. "Especially not for Anna Lenai, the most bad-ass Keeper of all time."

"Some bad-ass," she growled. "I got stabbed by a man who had carried a symbiont for less than a year!"

Inch by inch, Jack's hand slid up her back, and he revelled in each unique texture. "Do you remember what you told me a few weeks ago, when I was beating myself up for letting Arin get the best of me?"

"Everyone loses sometimes."

"It's good advice."

"Yeah," she agreed. "But now I understand why you were so hard on yourself."

Jack wrapped his arms around her in a tender embrace, holding her close. Gently, he ran his fingers through her hair. "Anna," he whispered. "You are the bravest, kindest and strongest person I have ever met. Not a single day goes by where I don't wish that I could be more like you."

Anna sniffled, and he felt the warmth of her tears on his chest. "That's funny," she whispered. "Because I'm always wishing that I could be more like you."

"Well, I didn't say you were the *smartest* person I've ever met."

"Shut up!" she squealed through a fit of giggles. Jack flinched as her deft fingers tickled his belly; this had become her favourite way to win an argument. Within seconds, she had him squirming. "Whether you realize it or not, you're wonderful."

A moment later, Anna was snuggling up again, wrapping her arm around him and nuzzling his chest. "I wish we could make love," she lamented. Jack knew exactly how she felt; there was a part of him that wanted nothing more than to grant that wish.

"In a few days," he promised. "When your tummy is feeling better."

"Okay."

Jack pulled the blankets up over her shoulders, tucking them both into a cozy little cocoon. Anna sighed contentedly. With spatial awareness, he could sense every contour of her sweet face, and he knew that she was smiling. "Is there anything that we have to do tomorrow?" she asked.

"Nope," he answered. "We can stay in bed all day if you want."

"Good," she said. "Because that's exactly what I want. I want to cuddle, and I want to talk and laugh... And I do not want to put on a stitch of clothing."

"Sounds perfect."

Melissa wandered the halls of Justice Keeper HQ, lost in a tangle of her own thoughts. Her father and sister had returned last night, and Claire was…a telepath now. The exact specifics of how that had happened were not something that she could pry out of Harry, and God have mercy, she had pushed. She had demanded. She had cajoled. She had come close to screaming at her father.

A year ago, she might have done just that, but Melissa wasn't that girl anymore. By the time she had thought to ask Claire, her little sister was already asleep, and she had exams to write this morning. Two of them, back to back, and she would have more next week. Her little adventure with the fashy kids had seriously cut into study time. It had been a week since she had been discharged from the hospital, and she had been scrambling every day since. Thankfully, she had a handle on basic forensic theory.

What was she going to do?

Something must have happened to Claire on Antaur. Ordinary people did not just develop the ability to read minds. There was something in the way Harry averted his eyes every time she pressed for more information.

She-

Without thinking, Melissa stepped into Larani Tal's office and froze. Larani had sent a message requesting her presence twenty minutes ago, and every moment since which hadn't been dedicated to puzzling out the source of her sister's new powers had instead been spent bracing herself for the dressing down she knew would come.

Melissa knew there would be consequences for her botched operation. Blowing her cover was one thing, but she had compounded the error by walking right into Tesa's trap. It wouldn't surprise her at all if Larani chose to deny her the opportunity to go on any more field missions until her training was complete. Melissa had expected an uncomfortable conversation, but she would never have imagined that Larani would call her up short in front of everyone she knew and loved.

The Chief Director of the Justice Keepers sat on the edge of her glass desk, smiling beatifically as Melissa entered the room. "About time, Cadet," she said. "Punctuality is a trait found in too few Keepers these days."

Jack was leaning against the wall with his arms folded, smiling sheepishly at the floor tiles. "She has a point, kid," he said. "You don't want to turn into me, do you?"

"She has a long way to go before that becomes an issue, sweetie."

"What's going on?"

Harry sat on the couch with stiff posture, but he looked up at the sound of Melissa's entrance, and the nod of respect that he gave her spoke volumes. Claire was next to him, and for once, she didn't look bored or insolent.

At the back of the room, Anna stood by the floor-to-ceiling window that looked out on the glittering skyline of Denabria. And glitter, it did. The clouds were blessedly absent today, allowing sunlight to glint off every window.

Melissa stopped short three steps into the room, running her gaze over everyone present. With every passing second, her eyebrows climbed higher and higher. "All right. So, I guess I'm not here to receive a reprimand?"

Larani hopped off the desk and strode toward her with such intensity that Melissa actually retreated. The woman's face was a storm cloud. "I would curb that insubordinate tone, Cadet," she barked. "Especially after the stunt you pulled."

"Larani, I'm sorry-"

"Did I ask for an apology?"

Backing away from the other woman, Melissa closed her eyes and shook her head so fast it almost made her dizzy. "No, of course not," she stammered. "It's just I thought that we could talk it out in private or-"

Larani bent forward with a hand over her chest, wheezing with laughter. "I'm sorry, girl," she said. "I meant to draw this out a little – to surprise you – but that look on your face is too much."

Melissa was about to request some answers when Larani produced from her pocket a simple black box, the kind that might be used to store a piece of jewellery. It was small, no larger than the palm of her hand, and almost flat. Ilia was beaming with pride so fierce it almost overwhelmed Melissa's anxiety. And then it all made sense. "I think you would prefer a traditional ceremony," Larani said. "Though we haven't done this with so much formality in over a hundred years. Still, you strike me as the sort of young woman who appreciates tradition. Kneel, Cadet Melissa Carlson."

Dropping to one knee, Melissa bowed her head. "I accept this duty with grace and humility." She was quoting, by rote, words that she had learned in classes on the history of the Justice Keepers.

Larani gave her the box.

When she opened it, Melissa found a badge inside, a four-pointed star in a circle of silver with her name and serial number engraved on the outer rim. Every Keeper had one; she had seen Jack's once, years ago, though knowing him, it was probably in a junk drawer somewhere in Manitoba.

When she looked up, Larani was smiling. The kind of smile a mother might have for her daughter. "And now," she said. "Rise, Agent Melissa Carlson."

Melissa did as she was told, standing tall in front of the other woman and nodding once out of respect. "Thank you, Chief Director," she said. "I won't let you down. But I *am* confused."

"Confused?"

Melissa felt heat in her face. It was impossible to hold Larani's gaze for one second longer. "Most cadets are in training for at least two years," she said. "After my screw up, I can't imagine why you would promote me."

"Your performance in the field has been nothing short of exemplary," Larani said. And then she winked. "With one notable exception."

She turned her back on Melissa, pacing quickly to the desk with a raised finger that she pointed at the ceiling. "And we will be discussing that *one* exception," Larani went on. "At length. But for the moment, there are more pressing concerns. Operative Lenai, is there room on your team for one more Keeper?"

Anna stood formally with hands clasped behind her back, but the smile she directed at Melissa could have lit up the night sky. "I think that can be arranged," she said. "*If* she promises not to run headlong into any more traps."

"I promise," Melissa replied, and then, after a second's hesitation, she spoke aloud the retort that she would normally quash in an effort to be polite. "After all, we can't have the new girl copying your signature move."

"Oh-ho!" Jack exclaimed. "Now it's official! She really *is* one of us."

"Just what I need," Harry grumbled. "*Two* lippy daughters."

Claire twisted on the couch to face him with a devilish grin. "Take that back," she said. "I've got twice as much sass as she does."

The next thing Melissa knew, they were hugging her. Her father and her sister, Jack and Anna: everyone got a turn. Even Larani gave her a friendly pat on the back. "You still have much to learn," she said. "But even with your recent mistake, I believe that you are ready to go into the field unsupervised. And a panel of three senior directors agrees with me. Don't let it go to your head now. I expect you to avail yourself of your colleagues' knowledge and experience."

"I will," Melissa promised.

"Excellent," Larani said. "Then celebrate. You've earned it."

"Are you going to tell me what happened?"

Melissa stood by the kitchen table with her arms crossed, and the fiery glare that she fixed upon Harry threatened to peel strips off his hide. It was strange, seeing her with short, silver-tipped hair. "Well?" she demanded. "Why is my little sister a telepath?"

Leaning against the counter and gripping its edge with both hands, Harry kept his eyes glued to the floor. "I did it with the N'Jal." The last thing he wanted was yet another argument about his parenting skills, but Melissa would push until she got the answers she was looking for.

"With the N'Jal."

"Yes."

"Why?"

Claire was sitting at the table and frowning at a plate of grilled chicken with thick green beans. "He wanted me to be able to protect myself," she muttered. "So, he turned me into a telepath, and then he made some kind of deal with the aliens to save me."

His youngest turned a dark-eyed gaze upon him, and Harry flinched. "I've tried to figure out exactly what the deal is," she went on. "But I can't read his thoughts. Maybe I don't know how yet."

"Or maybe the Overseers protected him," Melissa said.

Harry looked up at her and felt his face harden with resolve. "That's enough! Both of you!" he snapped. "Claire, you will not read anyone else's mind without permission. I don't care how powerful you think you are, I'm still your father. As for you, Melissa…"

She just stood there with her arms folded, arching one black eyebrow as if daring him to assert parental authority. The moment passed when Harry refused to be baited, but it was clear that "do as you're told" wasn't going to win this argument.

"I seem to remember," he began, "you telling me just a couple months ago that you wanted me to keep the N'Jal."

"I *do* want you to keep it," Melissa replied. "That doesn't mean I think you should use it to mess with Claire's brain. You could have killed her."

Claire had a piece of chicken skewered on the tines of her fork, and she seemed to be trying to decide if she wanted to eat it. "He almost did," she said absently. "The aliens fixed me."

"Brilliant," Melissa grumbled.

Pressing the heel of his hand to his forehead, Harry sighed softly. "What's done is done," he said. "Claire is fine. And I would get rid of the N'Jal if I could... but the more I look around, the more I realize that without it, I can't keep you girls safe."

He strode forward, laying his hands on Melissa's shoulders. The disapproval in her eyes tied his guts in knots. "I promise that I will never use the N'Jal on either one of you. Never again."

"I suppose that will have to do."

"Good," Harry said. "Now, I have to run a couple of errands. Why don't you two stay in? Watch a movie?"

"Yeah. That sounds like a good idea."

Five minutes later, Harry was walking down a street in a thick trench coat, a light wind ruffling his hair. There were houses with dome-shaped roofs on either side of him, each one separated from its neighbours by leafless trees and empty flowerbeds. Winter had truly come, and though it was only late afternoon by his estimate, the sky was a deep blue as the sun sank toward the western horizon. The *western* horizon. Harry could not be happier to be on a world that felt normal again, even if it did have a purple moon.

A speedy walk to the spoke street that ran all the way to Denabria's hub, and then he was taking a set of stairs down to the subway platform. Except for a pale young man who looked very much like a college student, Harry was alone there.

The mag-lev train made almost no noise as it settled to a stop. Doors opened, and Harry quickly ducked inside. In the first car, he found a young family – two parents who could not be much older than thirty, and their sons, both around preschool age. Still, he wanted some privacy.

The next car had a young woman with curly blonde hair, an older, grizzled-looking man with a stubbly beard and a well-dressed guy in a black jacket and high-collared shirt. He pressed on.

Harry was almost at the back of the train when he finally found an empty car. The walls of the subway tunnel rushed past in every window, but despite the darkness outside, the car felt homey and warm, its bulbs configured to match the frequencies of sunlight.

He took a seat and removed the N'Jal from his pocket. The tiny ball of folded up flesh was warm to the touch. At Harry's command, it unrolled into a thin sheet, but it did not bind to his hand.

Instead, it slithered under Harry's sleeve, up his arm, his shoulder and the side of his neck. It split apart, one piece crawling into his right ear and the other into his left, and there, it connected with his nervous system.

Harry couldn't say *how* he did what he did, but an instant later, the illusion of his ex-wife stood in the aisle between the seats, watching him with an impassive expression. "You have a question?" she asked.

Harry was on the very edge of his seat with elbows resting on his thighs, his chin propped up on laced fingers. How to phrase this delicately? "When one of you changed me so that I could use the N'Jal," he said, "he told me that it would not twist my thoughts as it did to others."

Della nodded.

"And yet," Harry went on. "My friends believe that the N'Jal is changing me, that it's making me into a different person. I have to know... Are they right?"

For a very long moment, Della only studied him, but then her lips twitched in the barest hint of a smile. "Our fallen brethren created neural networks in your brain," she said. "Networks that allow you to interface with our technology. You control the N'Jal; it does not control you."

"But the decisions I've made over the past year-"

"Have been yours and yours alone," Della said emphatically. "Your friends seek to rationalize the decisions they do not approve of, to absolve you of responsibility. Humans find it comforting to attribute aberrant behaviour in a loved one to some outside force. Your free will remains very much intact, Harry Carlson."

He shut his eyes, tears welling up and streaming over his cheeks. "But the things I've done," he whispered. "How could I...I would never have imagined torturing another human being for information or...or rewriting my daughter's neural architecture."

It surprised him when Della laid a comforting hand on his shoulder and shocked him when he felt as clearly as he would have if she were actually standing there. "The human mind is not insulated from outside influence," she said. "Power is seductive, Harry Carlson, and you may very well be the most powerful of your species."

Harry shut his eyes, slumping over with hands resting on the empty seat in front of him. "Yeah," he whispered. "That's what I was afraid you were going to say."

When he looked up, Della was gone.

The train came to a stop at a station on the north end of Denabria. About as far from his house as you could get and still be within the city limits. He had chosen this location deliberately. If he had to follow-through on this deal with the Overseers, he wanted to minimize the chances of Melissa or Jack or any of the others running into him.

And he would do it his way!

Harry knew that there was no chance of him stopping the Overseers from carrying out their grand plan, but he could inject a little compassion into it. A little humanity. With a thought, he ordered the N'Jal to detach itself from his ears.

It slid down his neck – reforming into one piece – under his shirt, along his arm and right into the palm of his left hand. There, it bonded with him once again. Harry focused and ordered the Overseer device to camouflage itself.

The N'Jal retracted its neural fibres, adopting the texture and pigment of his palm. Practically invisible to the naked eye except for a thin seam along the side of each finger. From now on, Harry would take it with him wherever he went.

He stepped out of the train when the doors opened.

It was time to go to work.

The End of the Ninth Book of the Justice Keepers Saga.

Dear reader,

We hope you enjoyed reading *Fragile Hope*. Please take a moment to leave a review, even if it's a short one. Your opinion is important to us.

Discover more books by R.S. Penney at
https://www.nextchapter.pub/authors/ontario-author-rs-penney

Want to know when one of our books is free or discounted? Join the newsletter at http://eepurl.com/bqqB3H

Best regards,

R.S. Penney and the Next Chapter Team

About the Author

Richard S. Penney is a science-fiction author and futurist from Southern Ontario. He graduated from McMaster University with a degree in mathematics and statistics. Rich knew that he wanted to be a writer ever since he was a child, when he would act out complex stories with his action figures.

He has worked in a number of different fields, including banking, teaching and software QA.

In 2014, Rich published his first novel, *Symbiosis,* the first volume of the Justice Keepers Saga. The story was one that he had been planning to write ever since he was a teenager. The Desa Kincaid novels grew out of a tandem story that Rich started on Theoryland.com, a Wheel of Time discussion site.

Rich has been an environmental activist since his early twenties, and he has given talks on sustainability in Greece and Australia.

Contact the Author

Follow me on Twitter @Rich_Penney

E-mail me at keeperssaga@gmail.com

You can check out my blog at rspenney.com

You can also visit the Justice Keepers Facebook page
https://www.facebook.com/keeperssaga
Questions, comments and theories are welcome.

Lightning Source UK Ltd.
Milton Keynes UK
UKHW021116021120
372650UK00005B/946